Lindian Odyssey

John Wilton

ISBN: 9798643751809

Copyright © 2020

All rights reserved, including the right to reproduce this book, or portions thereof in any form. No part of this text may be reproduced, transmitted, downloaded, decompiled, reverse engineered, or stored, in any form or introduced into any information storage and retrieval system, in any form or by any means, whether electronic or mechanical without the express written permission of the author.

This is a work of fiction. All names and characters are the product of the author's imagination and any resemblance to actual persons, living or dead, is entirely coincidental.

PublishNation

www.publishnation.co.uk

Acknowledgements:

Yet again I would like to say another huge thank you to all my very good friends in beautiful Lindos. My warm thanks go to my good friends Jack Koliais and Janis Woodward Bowles, both of whom encouraged me greatly to get on and write all my Lindos novels - Lindos Retribution, Lindos Aletheia, Lindian Summers, Lindos Affairs, as well as this one. Special thanks to Jack for giving me the idea for a novel based on Lindos stretching back to the Second World War. My thanks also go to everyone in Lindos and beyond, including the many regular Lindos visitors, as well as all those who have said and written such nice things about my previous novels. Finally, my endless gratitude goes yet again to Fiona Ensor for her tireless proof-reading efforts identifying my errors. Any that remain are, of course, entirely down to me.

Needless to say, overwhelmingly this story and the characters within it are fiction. The exceptions to that being the events of the 1943 Battle of Rhodes and the Greek Civil War. Nevertheless, without the magical village of Lindos and the people in it, it could never have been written. For that reason, as with my previous Lindos novels, I will always be eternally grateful to the people there, my friends in that magical paradise.

Author's website: www.johnwilton.yolasite.com

Previous novels by John:

The Hope (2014)

Lindos Retribution (2015)

Lindos Aletheia (2016)

Lindian Summers (2018)

Lindos Affairs (2019)

All available on Amazon and Kindle.

MAP OF LINDOS

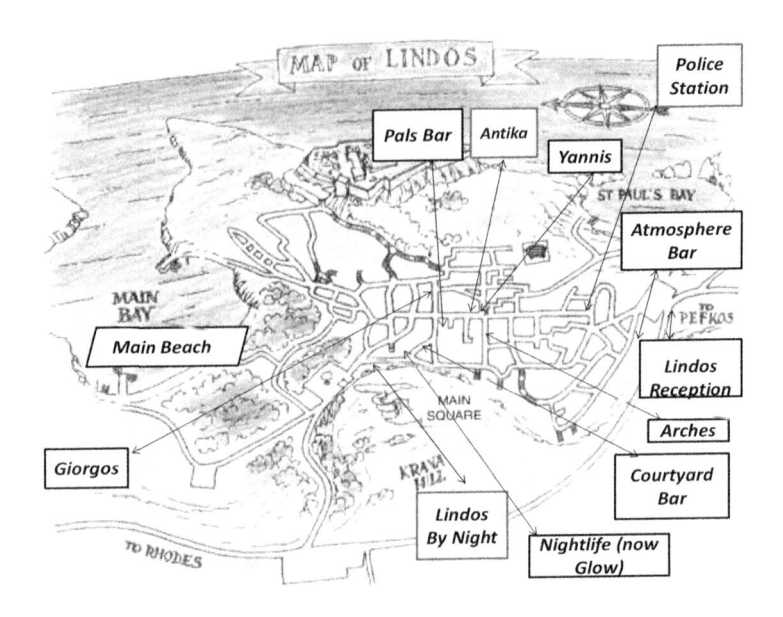

- Police Station
- Pals Bar
- Antika
- Yannis
- Atmosphere Bar
- Main Beach
- Lindos Reception
- Arches
- Giorgos
- Courtyard Bar
- Lindos By Night
- Nightlife (now Glow)

MAIN BAY · ST PAUL'S BAY · TO PEFKOS · MAIN SQUARE · KRANA HILL · TO RHODES

Part One: Enough

1

Kathleen O'Mara

This is a story about a woman's journey and experiences, an odyssey - a word derived from the Greek epic poem written by Homer. Her odyssey encompasses lies and truth, family and love, within a story of mothers and daughters, friends and lovers.

Kathleen O'Mara was an assassin, a clever, smooth, slick, well-trained assassin. Every kill she made was meticulously planned and executed, right down to the minutest detail. This one was no different. She carefully, silently, but purposefully, moved quickly through the crowd of commuters until she was positioned closely directly behind her completely unaware victim. Her victim was standing at the edge of the busy London underground Oxford Circus station Victoria line platform waiting for the next train towards Brixton. It was a woman she knew well and totally despised. She had carefully and discreetly followed her from outside her office in nearby Great Castle Street, just off Oxford Street. Then she waited for the information board on the platform to show the next train would arrive in one minute before making her way through the crowd to take up her position. She timed her move to perfection, such that she was directly behind her victim for only a few seconds before the train emerged from the tunnel. When it was five yards away from the two women, and was slowing down to come to a stop, she leaned gently forward with the slightest movement, placed her right hand unnoticed in the small of her victim's back and nudged her off the edge of the platform onto the track in front of the train. Just as she had planned, at that time of the late afternoon the platform was so crowded with bustling commuters striving to get the best position by the doors to get on to the arriving train that no one noticed her nudge her victim. She wore a baseball cap over her short dyed blonde hair and made sure that she kept her head down so that any CCTV cameras on the platform couldn't pick her out as the killer, should anyone think it was anything other than suicide. On those cameras, and to those commuters on the platform immediately around her, it appeared precisely that, a suicide. It was just as Kathleen and her handlers had planned.

Only a few short weeks before her victim, Sandra Weston, would have been much more aware, much more alert. That was what she had been trained to do in MI6, be aware of your surroundings at all times. Now though her mind was shot, blown. She'd verged on a nervous breakdown after what had happened to her professionally and personally, all thanks to Kathleen. At this time, therefore, she wasn't focused at all, not concentrating in any way on her immediate surroundings. She had no inkling or sense whatsoever of the danger that she was in from the baseball capped woman who had sneaked up behind her. A woman who until a few weeks previously she had believed was her best friend, and, like herself an MI6 operative.

Within a millisecond Sandra's shuddering high pitched scream was piercing the air and rebounding off the curved station walls. People gasped and screamed as Sandra's body lurched forward, plunged on to the tracks and then quickly disappeared beneath the wheels of the tube train. The panic and mayhem that followed gave Kathleen the anticipated perfect cover to leave the scene quickly. Just as had been planned she continued to keep her head down as she slipped back away from the platform's edge and through the shocked and panicking commuters to make her way towards the exit marked Central Line. She never hurried unduly. She knew not to. She was well aware that there were CCTV cameras all over the station. So, she remained calm, confident that the plan would work to perfection and that her mission had been completed. Within two more minutes she was boarding a westbound Central Line tube train to West Acton station. There she would be picked up outside the station by her London based handlers, complete with her overnight bag and false American passport, and then driven straight to Heathrow Airport Terminal 5 for her eight-thirty flight back to Boston that evening.

As she sat on the speeding tube train full of commuters heading home at the end of their working day and waited for it to negotiate the eleven stops to her destination she initially still felt excitement, fulfilment that her revenge was finally complete. However, that turned to an utter feeling of emptiness quite quickly. She was completely overwhelmed by it. She knew now that this was the time to end the hidden other life that she had lived for the past twenty years or so. It was time to change and she knew clearly what she needed and wanted to do.

For twenty years her greatest weapon in her professional life, her strength, was her silence. Listening, observing, being aware of all those around her, and everything around her, mostly while operating undercover. She'd allied that successfully to her cold, ruthless, dispassionate, minutely planned and detailed methods.

She'd been recruited to MI6 near the end of the first year of her media studies degree in 1997 at Bristol University by a student on the same course, Sandra Weston. Sandra only knew her then though under another of her false identities, Aileen Regan. Sandra had deliberately developed what she thought was a deep student friendship with her throughout that first year. She had been recruited herself into the British Secret Service a year before, having been identified by them while still in her private school sixth form as having the right attitudes and political beliefs for possible recruitment and training as an MI6 operative. In fact, it was one of the teachers at her school – a Secret Service contact and associate – who identified her and recommended her. She was already very active and prominent in the Young Conservatives group in the school, and the Conservative Association locally. She was very vocal in both those arenas in her support for Britain and British, particularly English, nationalism. She hated the Irish with venom that was unusual in a seventeen year old. That had its origins in her family British military background.

So, when Sandra was approached informally, and initially tentatively, by the same teacher about a possible future career working for a British government agency she was immediately curious. She didn't take much convincing at all and was quickly receptive to the idea. Her interest was only heightened when it was explained to her that MI6 was developing a programme of identification and recruitment of exceptional young people with what the teacher described as, "the right sense of patriotism". She was one of those young people. Their role and purpose was to infiltrate the student movement at various key universities, identify like-minded sympathetic students, and change the political climate and agenda within the student body. A Labour government under Tony Blair was looking more and more likely to be elected that year and the fightback against them was to begin by being pursued amongst the young people, particularly students. The attitudes and values propagated so successfully within sections of the UK student body during the years of the Thatcher government in the nineteen-eighties, and so evident in many of the thirty-something generation of the nineties, were being challenged by the middle of that decade. Sandra Weston, and some carefully selected young people like her with similar values, was to be one of the instruments MI6 employed to meet that challenge. She embraced it, as well as her role of unofficial 'recruiting officer' within the student body, eagerly and energetically.

Aileen Regan quickly became her prime target and she keenly cultivated their friendship during that first year. They became inseparable. Sandra pursued her aim carefully and slowly, just as she had been coached and advised to do by what was by then her MI6 handler. She occasionally made a few carefully placed right-wing politically loaded remarks throughout that first year, just to test the water. Aileen always appeared receptive and in agreement, even when Sandra was deliberately scathing about Irish nationalism. She was from Bantry Bay in West Cork, but never betrayed any indication to Sandra that she disagreed with anything derogatory that Sandra said on that subject.

Aileen's southern Irish origins made approaching her look a gamble. Because of that she didn't appear to be the most likely type ripe for recruiting to MI6. For some reason though, Sandra was convinced otherwise and was determined to go ahead. So, by late March 1997, after various consultations with her handler and numerous MI6 investigations and background checks, it was agreed that Sandra should take the plunge and put the suggestion of MI6 recruitment to Aileen. In effect, it turned out to be not at all difficult or awkward. She was very receptive, even though she feigned some surprise initially and then a little apprehension. What Sandra never realised at the time was that all along it was the aim of Kathleen - in the guise of Aileen - to allow, and even provoke Sandra to recruit her. Kathleen's true allegiances certainly never resided with the British State, let alone MI6. They lay elsewhere. In fact, her purpose and mission was to infiltrate that organisation as a 'sleeper' for her Irish nationalist heritage and the IRA, of which she had been a secret member since she was sixteen. In that aim she was successful, thanks to Sandra Weston.

Kathleen maintained that deceit for almost twenty years, including within her continuing supposed friendship with Sandra. Even when both women married they maintained the secret of their MI6 lives between them without sharing it with their husbands. In any case, that was a condition of the Official Secrets Act they had signed. Kathleen, as Aileen, subsequently divorced her husband, but Sandra remained married, even though her husband was a blatant womaniser. Neither woman had any kids. Far too complicated in their secret profession they agreed. Sandra had her own freelance fashion photography agency as cover for her other activities for MI6, while Aileen had various jobs as a P.A., as Kathleen O'Mara.

By 2016 both women were thirty-eight. Although approaching middle-age Kathleen was still an attractive woman. It was an attribute she had no hesitation in using to her advantage when required. She could use men easily to achieve her objectives professionally and personally, and had no qualms or remorse in doing so. She enjoyed it, revelled in it, and was undoubtedly very good at what she did, in every conceivable way. She was five foot six inches tall with a good, slim figure. Her high cheekbones were perfectly framed by her shoulder length dark black hair that was ever so slightly curled at the ends, emphasising her striking features and her dark brown eyes. In her secret professions though - both as an IRA operative and an MI6 agent - she wasn't averse to changing the colour and length of her hair, altering her appearance somewhat for disguise in the same way as she changed her name. In the middle of June 2016 it had been shoulder length and dark black, as it had been for some time. Soon after, from necessity, she changed it again to short dyed blonde for her mission to London to assassinate Sandra. Whatever the length and colour of her hair however, if features exposed character, then Kathleen's immediately exuded and prompted a wilful determination and strength. Most of all those characteristics were constantly exposed in her piercing deep brown eyes.

Sandra wasn't as slim as Kathleen, although by no means fat, and was about the same height. She had engaging blue eyes and natural dirty blonde short hair, cut in a bob that highlighted her slightly chubby cheeks. Both women could be ruthless in their own fashion. There was an often hidden hard edge to their characters. When necessary they were totally determined and focused on what they had to do, without any trace of remorse or hesitation. Those elements of their characters, and the unavoidable clash between them, were to be fully evident in the eventual final chapter of their supposed friendship in the mid-summer of 2016.

From just before Christmas 2015 Kathleen, as Aileen, embarked on a mission to secure the ultimate complete revenge for herself and the Bhoys - as she referred to them - on Sandra and MI6. It was an act of personal revenge for her that she had worked towards as an IRA infiltrator of MI6. The vehicle initially for that was her affair with Sandra's arrogant womaniser husband, Richard Weston. The overall aim was to destabilise Sandra psychologically by destroying her already fragile marriage, and then discredit her professional reputation with MI6. It was revenge for the Bhoys after all the problems and troubles Sandra had unleashed on them as an agent in the 'Irish Section' of MI6 over the years. That revenge was twenty years in the making, beginning with Kathleen befriending Sandra at university as Aileen, and eventually allowing her to recruit her to MI6. Finally, the plan required Aileen being eventually revealed as an IRA infiltrator after she had disappeared, one recruited by Sandra, which would ultimately in turn discredit Sandra professionally within MI6.

However, there was an even more pressing personal element to the plan for Kathleen. The assassination by MI6 in 2002 of the Irish man she knew as her father, coordinated by Sandra Weston, a fact that was revealed to Kathleen by the Bhoys a couple of years later. At that time Kathleen knew him as her father simply because he was married to her mother, although it stated on her birth certificate, 'Father unknown'. She had asked her mother about that a number of times before she died, but got no explanation. Kathleen was always their daughter, not just her mother's. It was that way in the Ireland of that time.

Kathleen was told by the Bhoys that their informant had told them that it was definitely Sandra who had set up the killing of the man she knew as her father. Because of Kathleen's false identity and name as Aileen Regan, Sandra had no idea that it was her father of course. There was a bombing, and Kathleen was convinced that although they had no clues or evidence as to who was responsible British Intelligence was determined to have a sacrificial lamb, even though there was clear evidence he was nowhere near the bombing. The evidence, and his alibi, was there plainly for them to see, but they hid it. Then they let loose one of their death squads on him, even though it was five years after the Good Friday Peace Agreement. Because of that it was all kept quiet under the Official Secrets Act. Even though Kathleen, as Aileen, was working for MI6 at the time, or at least they thought she was, it was all kept so tight security-wise that she never even got a sniff of it, and nor did many people at all, except for Sandra. She was right at the heart of it, coordinated it all, according to the Bhoys. Because of the sensitivity of it being well after the peace agreement Sandra kept it all to herself and her tight small MI6 team, which Aileen was not part of at that time. All she understood at the time was that the man she knew as her father had committed suicide. Such was her undercover identity that she could not even attend his funeral, for fear of that being discovered by MI6. The Bhoys made sure she kept away, as she was ordered to do.

What at the time she believed would be the beginning of the final chapter of Kathleen's revenge came to a head during a two week holiday she took as Aileen with Sandra in the picturesque tourist village of Lindos on the island of Rhodes in mid-June 2016. She'd planted the idea that the two friends should take a holiday together a few weeks before, taking advantage of the fact that at the time Sandra was telling her that she and her husband, Richard, were having difficulties in their marriage. Sandra told her she could do with a break, a holiday with just the two of them, her and Aileen. The choice and suggestion of Lindos was Sandra's, however. She said she had a friend who recommended it and went there regularly. Of course, Sandra's marital difficulties were related to the affair her husband had been having with Aileen, not that Sandra had any inkling of that at that time. It wasn't an unusual occurrence though where Richard Weston was concerned. He had a history, a predilection for them. Sandra had already caught him out at least once before and forgiven him. From the background briefing information she'd been supplied by the Bhoys Aileen knew there had been more than one or two marital slips, and affairs, by Richard. By the time of their holiday, however, Aileen had brought the affair to a halt, as was the plan, knowing that although Richard agreed they should stop at the time he wouldn't be able to leave her alone. He was that type of man. Never took no for an answer.

So, the plan involved conveniently, supposedly accidentally, allowing Sandra to discover some texts to Aileen from Richard. She had seemingly carelessly left her phone on a small table between the two women's sunbeds on the beach on the first day of their holiday, switched on while she went for a swim in the clear sea. Earlier that day she had purposefully texted Richard, knowing that he wouldn't be able to resist replying, and she was determined to ensure Sandra would see his text so that their affair would be revealed to her. Richard had initially wanted to go on holiday with the two women, worried over the very fact that Sandra would discover the affair if she went with Aileen alone. Besides some comments in the text Sandra saw from Richard about missing Aileen, it also included some revealing details about their affair, as well as that he was insistent about joining them for the second week of their holiday. So, that is what he did.

At that point things weren't quite going according to the plan as far as Aileen was concerned. It wasn't part of the plan that Richard Weston should turn up for the second week of their holiday. So, in order to initially avoid him, Aileen embarked on a sexual liaison with an English academic, Martin Cleverley, on the holiday. The two women met him on the flight to Rhodes and Aileen spent some time with him in the first week of the holiday before Richard arrived, including sleeping with him a couple of times, largely for her own pleasure. Eventually realising soon after Richard arrived that, as planned, Sandra now knew about her affair with Richard, Aileen decided that there was no point in hanging around in Lindos any longer. There was no need. So, within a couple of days of Richard's arrival Aileen persuaded Martin to leave with her abruptly and go back to England. Coldly and ruthlessly she used him as cover in Lindos, and then to leave the island. It was almost as though she used him as a side interest to amuse herself while she screwed over Sandra. After a few days back in the U.K. she left Martin suddenly, without warning. She disappeared without trace to resume her real identity as Kathleen back in her home in Boston, U.S.A.

By the end of June and early July 2016 therefore it seemed as though Kathleen's revenge was completely successful. She was informed by the Bhoys that Sandra's marriage was completely destroyed and that she'd almost had a nervous breakdown. Her professional reputation was also in tatters when it became obvious that Aileen was an IRA infiltrator into MI6 for almost twenty years, recruited and recommended by Sandra herself. However, that wasn't quite enough to satisfy the Bhoys thirst for revenge, or ultimately Kathleen's. Her IRA Boston handler, Michael, told her in a phone conversation in the car that picked her up from Boston airport on her return home after her Lindos episode, and then her disappearing act from Martin Cleverley back in the U.K., that the Bhoys had decided they wanted more, that Sandra Weston should be eliminated. Kathleen immediately volunteered to finish the job. Her handler told her that is what the Bhoys thought she would say, and that they had agreed she should do it.

Two days after she arrived back home in Boston Kathleen was informed in another carefully worded phone call from Michael that she was to be provided with yet another false passport and identity, and that the job would take place in London in a week or two. In fact, the way he put it, what he actually said to her, was that the necessary documents and name she needed would be delivered to her shortly and what she needed to do would take place in London in a week or two. She would fly into the U.K and be met by one of a team of two colleagues on one evening when she landed, do what was needed the next day, and then fly out again later that evening. The team would identify what she needed to know about where her friend was now living and working in London, then sort a scenario and place to make it look like they wanted it to look. Reading between the lines Kathleen fully understood what Michael meant by, "scenario" and "place", and that by, "make it look like they wanted it to look," he meant a suicide. The "friend" he referred to was obviously Sandra Weston. After her almost nervous breakdown the people at MI6 would be easily convinced that is what happened.

She got another call from Michael two days later telling her again in a carefully coded way that the job would happen in a week's time now that the London team had sourced a scenario and location, and had tracked her friend's daily movements. All the details would be delivered to her in the usual way. However, Kathleen had a surprise request for him to convey to his superiors.

"This is the last, Michael, the last one. Tell that to whoever needs to know. This will complete it for me, and I've had enough now. It's been nearly twenty years. My revenge will be complete and I want a life, a change, a new life. I've decided. I hope they'll let me do that, understand that. I think that I've done enough for them now."

"Okay, Kathleen. I'll tell them, of course I will, to be sure I will. Hopefully, they'll understand and agree. With your record you certainly deserve that, but you know they don't like to let the good ones go easily, and you're one of the best."

She couldn't resist a softly agreed, "I know, Michael." He couldn't see it of course, but she had a very small smirk of satisfaction across her lips as she finished telling him that. "But I'm done now, or I will be after this last job. They owe me that after twenty years. They do or else-"

He didn't let her go on. "Enough, Kathleen, don't say anymore. That really wouldn't be wise and I know you're cleverer than that. You surely wouldn't be so stupid as to say what I think you were about to say. I'll tell them and get back to you on that as soon as I hear back from them."

With that the line went dead.

2

The final job

A day after her second phone conversation with Michael a package containing all she needed was hand delivered to her Boston flat. She never knew the person who delivered it, and didn't want to know. They wore a crash helmet with a dark visor pulled down, so she couldn't see their face anyway. She assumed they had delivered the package on a motorbike, the reason for the crash helmet, along with the desired anonymity. They never spoke, except for her saying, "Hello", and the presumed motorcyclist merely replying with one word, "Delivery", after she answered the buzzer for her flat on the main entrance to her apartment block. As she opened her flat door the package was thrust into her hand and the helmeted motorcyclist turned and left immediately.

Five days on she was sitting comfortably relaxing in First Class on an early morning flight from Boston to London on her new passport – another American one –and yet another new name and identity, Sheila Riley.

Just over eight and a half hours later she was met at Heathrow airport and taken to a hotel, The Grosvenor in Grosvenor Square. It was only going to be for just one night, but she always insisted on nothing but the best. The two operatives thoroughly briefed her in her hotel room on the next day's scenario and place; the tube train at Oxford Circus station just after five o'clock when Sandra would finish work. They had located where she was working and had studiously tracked her regular movements after she finished work over five days. She was working as a temp in a photography agency off Oxford Street and living in a flat in Brixton in South London, at the end of the Victoria line. She was a creature of habit and regularly left her office spot on five o'clock to takes the Victoria line tube from Oxford Circus towards Brixton, they said. They added that the station and the platform would be busy in rush hour. So, it would be easy to come up behind her and nudge her in front of the tube train onto the tracks as it entered the station and a few seconds before it reached where she would be standing. They also told Kathleen that Sandra being an obvious creature of habit, as they put it, always stood right on the platform's edge at the front of the crowds of commuters waiting to board the train.

Finally, on that part of the operation, one of them told her, "Wear a cap pulled down and keep your head down because there is CCTV everywhere on the platform and throughout the station."

She was not best pleased with them thinking she had to actually be told that. She wasn't some amateur doing this sort of thing for the first time. She was a professional. She didn't know the two men, of course, but she thought they surely would have been informed of her experience and expertise. She pulled a face and decided to just simply comment somewhat sarcastically, "Oh, really?"

The two men exchanged a quick brief glance. Then one of them continued with the rest of the plan, telling her that as soon as she had dealt with Sandra she should go to the Central line platform and take the westbound train to West Acton. There they would be waiting with her overnight bag, pick her up, and take her back to Heathrow for her eight-thirty flight back to Boston. They would be at West Acton station from five-thirty, and they estimated that she should get there just after that, adding, "It's only twenty minutes from there to the terminal."

So, that's exactly how it went. A complete success and by nine-thirty that evening she was once again sat relaxing in First Class, this time on her way back to Boston and home. She should have been completely satisfied, contented that at last, finally, her revenge on Sandra Weston for her part in the assassination of the person whom she knew as her father was complete. But she couldn't shake off the feeling that had overwhelmed her on the tube to West Acton, one of total emptiness. She knew what she had to do. What she'd decided to do to rid herself of that feeling. What she had planned to do and told her handler, Michael, on the phone in Boston previously.

She wanted to give up the chaotic and dangerous life she had and find out a lot more about who she really was; about her family background and their history. She had spent years being someone else; Aileen Regan, now Sheila Riley, and before them a multitude of other fake identities and false personalities within them. Now she just wanted to be herself, find out where her roots where. She knew that she'd been born in Bantry, West Cork, or at least in a small village near there, Ahakista. She had fleetingly been back there for a couple of days a few years ago. It was a village by the sea, with a few houses, some farms, two pubs and a church, but that was it. Her mother, Mary O'Mara, came from there. She knew that much, but now she found herself increasingly wondering if the man her mother had married – Niall - and whom she grew up knowing as her father, was actually that, not least because of the 'Father unknown' entry on her birth certificate. Plus Kathleen's birth had been registered in her mother's maiden name, O'Mara. Her mother was now dead, but would never talk about it when she was alive, despite Kathleen asking her over and over. Her mother didn't share things easily, or her thoughts liberally. All Aileen managed to get from her occasionally was a small inkling for some reason that her birth father wasn't Irish, wasn't Niall. It was Niall whose assassination Sandra Weston had organised in MI6.

Her mother died two years before what Kathleen had decided would be her final job for the Bhoys. They were never really close. Maybe it was her lifestyle, her profession, but she was distant from her mother for over ten years, not just geographically, but emotionally. As she was clearing her house after she died she came across an old shoe box under her bed. Inside she found her mother's marriage certificate for her marriage to Niall. It was dated the 12th of April 1981, three years after Kathleen was born. There were also some letters, a notebook, and a few other small nondescript things. In amongst those she also found what appeared to be some sort of contract of employment as a Tour Representative with a company that specialised in holidays to the Greek islands, Olympic Holidays. It was dated May 24th 1976, two years before Kathleen was born. As she sifted through the contents of the shoe box she also came across three letters that were written in broken English and signed, "Love, Dimitris." In one of them was written, "I miss you very much, Mary. I wait you very long time in Lindos, to see you with our new arrival." When she read that it started her thinking that perhaps in fact her father was Dimitris, a Greek. It seemed a strong possibility given that she was born in 1978 and that particular letter was dated March of that year, plus what Dimitris had written about their "new arrival". Of course the real meaning could have been lost in his broken English, and he was simply referring to Kathleen's mother's "new arrival" back in Lindos, her return to the village. Whichever was the case, now she was more determined than ever to try and find out if her assumption was true and if this Dimitris really was her birth father, even though at that point she didn't even know his full name. None of his letters were signed that way, just simply "Your love, Dimitris."

In the box she also found a small black notebook. Inside it were some scribbled notes in her mother's handwriting. They were about Lindos, and various dates in the summer of 1976 and 1977. It looked to Kathleen like her mother had started some sort of diary of the time she worked there, intermixed with notes for her Tour Rep job, background on Lindos and Rhodes for her to inform the tourists. There were a couple of notes about the "beauty of unspoilt and undeveloped Lindos, as well as the charm of the place, including the donkeys and donkey rides." Under a heading of 'Nightlife' there was a note saying, "The tourists should sample the good, cheap food and wine in the various, though not a great many, quite basic tavernas in the village, plus the few equally basic and cheap bars." There was a further comment that the Lindos Beach restaurant, down on the Main beach, turned into the only disco in the village late in the evening, if the tourists wanted some late entertainment. Mary O'Mara had written that, "On some nights it appeared that almost half the local population of the village headed down there, although female tourists and our guests should be aware that it was also a favourite place for young male Greek locals to head for after midnight to try to meet the foreign female tourists." She had added, maybe as a reminder to herself as much as the tourists, what sounded like something out of a travel and tourism brochure. "It is a very romantic spot late at night, overlooking the main bay, with the

Rhodian moonlight glittering on the Aegean Sea underneath the Acropolis."

When Kathleen read that she commented softly, "Hmm ... maybe my mother had some personal experiences of the effect of that? Perhaps that's where I came from – a romantic encounter in the moonlight by the Aegean Sea under an Acropolis? Conceived under an ancient citadel of the Greek gods, with all their turbulent relationships and thunderbolts?"

She hesitated while she held the notebook in her left hand, stopped reading from it, and looked up from it for a long perplexing moment. Her mind was whirring with fleeting comparisons and conclusions. Eventually, there was a stuttering hesitation in her voice - betraying a self-revelation that she instantly disliked - as she once again softly murmured, "Hmm ... maybe that explains some of my character and the violence and turmoil in my life over the past twenty years?"

A deep frown of dissatisfaction spread across her forehead as she finished mumbling. Then as she cast her eyes further down the page of the notebook she saw something that turned that into a grin. Her mother had written, "Don't forget to inform the tourists that visitors to Lindos, and to Rhodes in general, could buy tax-free items such as alcohol and cigarettes." It made her smile because she remembered that her mother liked her fags, as well as her drink. Well, after all, she was Irish. So, the note was probably as much for her as for her customers, the tourists. It was 1976, five years before Greece joined the European Economic Community, fore runner of the European Union, so duty-free was still available to the visitors from the U.K.

That wasn't the only things that she found while clearing her mother's house though. At the back of the top shelf of an old shiny walnut wood double doored wardrobe, tucked behind some jumpers and a long black cardigan, she discovered a foolscap sized brown padded envelope. It was covered in a thin layer of dust, so she guessed it must have been there undisturbed by her mother for some time. It wasn't sealed. The flap was merely tucked inside. She took it down from the top of the wardrobe, pulled out the flap, and emptied the contents onto her mother's bed. Three medals with ribbons attached and what looked like some kind of identity card tumbled out onto the duvet. The identity card was in a foreign language which she thought was Greek, and the photo on it was of a very young woman who resembled her grandmother. She assumed that was who it was, although the name on it was in Greek so she had no idea what that said. Her grandmother had died when Kathleen was very young, just five, but from photographs of her grandmother that her mother had which she'd seen she was pretty certain that the woman on the identity card was her. She had no clue what the medals were for though. They were obviously some sort of military medals, but beyond that she had no idea. One of them had an inscription on the back in Gaelic. Speaking some of that herself she managed to make out her grandmother's name and that it was awarded to her for services to the State of Éire, the name adopted in the 1937 Constitution, Ireland in English. The inscription on one of the others was in what she thought was Greek, although she had no idea whatsoever what it said, except for the years of 1943 and 1946. The final one was in English and the inscription on the back read, "Bernadette O'Mara. For gallant and brave services. S.O.E. 1946." She decided she would investigate them, and the identity card, later, when she had more time, when she had finally finished with her double-life.

By coincidence, the initial part of what she'd decided would be her final job for the Bhoys – culminating in the assassination of Sandra Weston and the completion of her revenge – had actually included the holiday in Lindos with Sandra. Lindos was Sandra's choice though, so Kathleen, or Aileen as Sandra knew her, hadn't planned that. And the turmoil of the days and nights of that holiday, as long as it lasted, prevented her doing any investigating about her possible birth father. Besides which, she was engaged on a job, a mission, for the Bhoys, as well as her own satisfaction, and she didn't intend to get distracted or side-tracked over the issue of searching for her birth father. As it turned out though, she did get somewhat distracted on that holiday over her new and growing relationship with the academic she met on the plane, Martin Cleverley.

Now, however, she was free of all that intrigue and subterfuge, and she could start her new life, which she'd decided would be on the island of Rhodes, and specifically in Lindos itself. She would disappear to there and start exploring what she believed was part of her roots. Find out about herself and her family. Try and find out if the Greek man, Dimitris, who wrote those letters to her mother really was her birth father. She wasn't sure quite where to start in Lindos, although she had got to know a couple of people – Greek bar owners – during her brief holiday with Sandra there. So, she reckoned there would surely be some local people who could help her, people who had grown up in the village and lived there all their lives, and maybe remembered her mother from those years she spent there in the seventies.

3

To Lindos and a new life

Two weeks after her London job Kathleen was once again on a plane. This time she was bound for Athens from Boston on an overnight flight, and then another short flight to Rhodes and her final destination of Lindos. She'd had no reply from the Bhoys about her decision to end that part of her life, so she decided to just get on with her plans, go to Lindos, try and find her roots as far as her birth father was concerned, and start a new life.

She'd had enough of the double life and the secrets. Enough of the killing and the subterfuge. Now she wanted to stop all that and start a new life – a life anchored in reality, the reality of her family past, what it meant and where it came from. She was determined. Determination and fortitude were part of her character. In fact, they were what had kept her going throughout all the past twenty years of her double life. Now she wanted, desired, to put those traits to a more positive use, to search for her soul and her roots. So, that was precisely what she was doing, without even waiting for the all clear from the Bhoys. She was putting the old Kathleen O'Mara of the past twenty years behind her and investing in a new life on Rhodes, in Lindos, as Aileen Regan again – the name and passport she'd used and was known as when she visited there on holiday with Sandra Weston six weeks earlier. As well as reverting to the name of Aileen Regan she had reverted to the dark black hair colour shown in the photo in that passport, rather than the dyed blonde, just to avoid any unnecessary difficulties at the various passport controls and avoid any undue attention. Her hair was much shorter now, but she didn't think that would cause any problem.

She had rented an apartment right in the centre of Lindos for three months initially, from the beginning of August until the end of October. On the one hour Athens flight to Rhodes she found herself sat in the aisle seat next to a British couple that she guessed were in their mid-fifties. Although she never intended to strike up a conversation with them they were not as reticent. She had firmly decided that the least contact she had with people on her journey the better, just in case someone whom she preferred not to was trying to trace her movements and whereabouts. Soon after she took her seat alongside them however, the man readily said, "Hello," and almost immediately followed that by volunteering the information that they had spent three nights exploring the Greek capital for the first time and were now off to spend ten days on Rhodes.

Not wishing at all to give away any information about herself and her travels she simply offered a short, "Hi," followed by, "Sounds nice," hoping that would kill his attempted conversation.

But he wasn't taking the hint, and without any prompting on her part the guy's comments soon veered on to Brexit and the recent U.K. referendum.

"Bloody good thing if you ask me. We'll be out of there soon enough, the E.U., no problem," he announced.

At that point her reticence was quickly breached. She couldn't resist responding to what she clearly thought, knew, was a crazy, simplistic statement. Kathleen O'Mara, or Aileen Regan, as she was now calling herself, was by no means a stupid woman. Quite the contrary. She was a very intelligent, well read, knowledgeable individual, who could never resist getting into a discussion over what she considered ill-thought out statements, such as the one she'd just heard.

"Really? You think so, think it'll be that simple, straightforward?" she asked, without any hint whatsoever of condescension in her voice.

"Yep, easiest deal in history is what one of the British government Ministers said," he told her.

"I see," she half nodded in fake agreement as she said that, then hesitated for a few seconds and turned her face away from him slightly. She turned back to face him and ask, "But what do you think they'll do about the Irish border though, you know, the one between Ireland in the E.U. and Northern Ireland? With Northern Ireland being part of the U.K. it won't be in the E.U. once the U.K. leaves, so won't that be a problem?"

She guessed that had not even entered his head, and from what she'd seen and heard neither had it entered any of the heads of the U.K. government Ministers.

"Oh, yes, I suppose that would be of some concern to you," he responded, obviously detecting her southern Irish accent, but without even a thought about, or reference to, the point of her question.

"Well, yes it is really, and quite a few other people who live near the border, as well as companies and businesses that regularly trade between the two countries," she pointed out.

Now there was a clear, irritated edge in her voice, displaying her inherent intolerance at what she perceived as the chauvinistic arrogance of the English towards Ireland and the Irish people. An irritation that had built up within her over many years since she was a teenager. Over that period she had transferred and transmitted it into fighting the English at every opportunity and in any way she could, mostly in the service of the Bhoys, often undercover. It had left her scarred, brutalised and bitter. She trusted very few people, if anyone. All of that had above all left her exhausted, extremely weary with her life, which is why she had finally now decided to change it.

The evident irritation in her voice was lost on the man though, as was obviously her annoyance at his condescending dismissal of the concerns of her country and the Irish people. In fact, his patronising only got worse.

"Don't worry. They'll sort that out somehow." He dismissed her concerns, and those of millions of Irish people, in just a few words, just as the English had always dismissed the concerns of the Irish people over hundreds of years she told herself.

But she wasn't letting him off that easily. Her intention not to get embroiled in conversations and contacts on her travels had well and truly been abandoned as she added, "And the Good Friday Peace Agreement? What about that? How does that fit into Brexit do you think? That's quite important to us in Ireland and Northern Ireland, and it's a bit trickier trying to preserve that in any Brexit agreement between the U.K. and the E.U."

He wasn't biting though. Much to her spiralling annoyance he just replied, "Yes, you're right, there is that to consider, but I'm sure they'll work something out."

He almost got away with that, and she was telling herself to back off and calm down, rapidly remembering her pledge to herself to keep a low profile. That was until he added an even more condescending and patronising, "You shouldn't worry yourself about it all. You'll see, they'll work it all out quite quickly and it'll all be ok. They're clever like that. I'm sure you've got better things to worry about as a woman travelling on her own."

That definitely pushed over the edge, especially the "woman" bit. She didn't take being patronised by anyone at the best of times, and she certainly wasn't going to take it from this English idiot. She let him have it intellectually with both barrels. She rapidly rattled off a potted, succinct analysis of Brexit and the effect on the U.K. in the context of the world economic system.

"Right, so as a woman I shouldn't worry that besides Brexit in the next few years there'll be, let me see, a shock to global trade, especially if that pompous maniacal idiot Trump gets elected, financial instability in China, global monetary tightening with rising interest rates and the end of quantitative easing, rising private debt in the developed world, and of course, the unresolved ongoing Eurozone crisis. Financialisation of the British economy over the past thirty odd years, the deep structural change in how the British economy operates, with almost complete focus on finance and the City of London financial institutions, is going to leave the U.K. particularly vulnerable. So, from all that on top of Brexit, the U.K. will be well and truly stuffed by another recession towards the end of 2020 I reckon, just like after 2008. Seems to me that it'll only need some sort of unforeseen global plague or virus undermining and destroying the economy to really top it off and stuff it completely. I'd say that given all that, from my point of view, besides anything else we'll pretty soon be looking at a reunited Ireland at last. At least something good will come out of the shit of Brexit anyway then."

She stared straight ahead at the back of the seat in front of her as she rattled all that off. As she finished she turned her head towards him and tilted her head slightly, opening her eyes wide as she stared into his face as if to say, "What do you think of that then? Not bad for a woman."

Even his wife, who had been ignoring all their previous conversation while she studied closely her glossy 'Hello' magazine looked up and across at her.

"Err ... well, that sounds a lot to take in. Perhaps, you're right, it is all a bit more complicated than you'd think," was all he could say in response.

He was saved from his awkward moment, and Aileen from her now on the verge of erupting irritation and anger, by the stewardess asking if they wanted any drinks. By the time they had been served Aileen had regained her composure and her determined intention not to engage in conversation with people on her travels had returned.

Part Two: Lindos

4

August heat

Just over an hour and a quarter after engaging in the exasperation of her Brexit conversation on her flight from Athens Aileen emerged from her taxi from Rhodes airport into the bright, extremely hot, midday Lindos August sunshine and the village Main Square. It was a heat that hit her full in the face, like the opening of a furnace door, as she wriggled across the back seat of the taxi towards the open door to leave its cooling air conditioning.

"Phew! That's hot," she exclaimed.

"Over forty degrees now, it's always like this, it's August," the taxi driver informed her with a shrug as he opened the boot of the taxi and removed her suitcase while she searched in her bag for the euros to pay him,

The square was buzzing and humming with a mixture of crowds of daytime tourists from Rhodes Town and an endless stream of vehicles of all shapes, colours and sizes weaving their way in a long line down the hill, into the main square, around the large tree and low white stone wall surrounding it in the centre, and then trying to head off down the adjacent quite narrow road to the car park. It had been busy there when she arrived with Sandra Weston in June, but this was a whole different scale of busy and accompanying chaos, plus it was a lot hotter, sweaty and bordering on uncomfortable. The heat obviously wasn't assisting the patience of drivers or pedestrians alike. Towards one side of the square, near to where Aileen's taxi had stopped, waited the shuttle bus which ferried people back and forth up the hill from the square to Krana at the top, where various self-catering complexes were located. The whole scene was one of unstructured chaos, valiantly trying to be regulated by a Traffic Marshall, come policeman, in the midst of it all. He wasn't having a great deal of success as the traffic became gridlocked, with vehicles desperately attempting to edge forward in the queue while tourists squeezed between them.

The little village of Lindos was a maze of narrow, very similar looking alleyways between white-washed houses and apartments. It was easy to lose your way, and yet eventually never be lost. It is said that historically the similarity of the alleys was deliberate, so that invading pirates would get lost. Many of the larger houses had belonged in the past to Sea Captains. During the seventeenth century the Ships' Captains became very wealthy and built themselves magnificent homes that were much larger than the traditional village homes. One was now a bar called the Captain's House. Originally many of the houses in the village were built with volcanic rock and stone, but were then painted white to reflect the heat of the sun and keep them cool inside.

In the very centre of the village the alleys were lined with shops, many open fronted, and all appearing completely overstocked with souvenir t-shirts, bags, linen and the obligatory soft toy donkeys. Lindos was famous for its donkeys, or Lindos taxis, as many of the donkey owners referred to them. There was lots of the donkey Lindos taxis. At times they gave some of the alleys a very distinctive smell as they left their deposits. An endless stream of donkeys, and their owners, did a good trade ferrying the tourists from the Main Square down to the small scenic Pallas Beach or up to the ancient Acropolis above the village. Equally, the guy who had the hardly envious job of sweeping up the donkey deposits as he followed them from the village square to Pallas beach or to the Acropolis was also seemingly constantly employed dealing with the endless stream of Lindos taxis. The village itself was off limits to cars or any other vehicles, except the small trucks that squeezed through the narrow alleyways in order to make deliveries to the bars, cafes and supermarkets, often scraping the walls each side. Some of the residents often joked that you could always tell if you'd had too much to drink the night before if you woke up with whitewash dust on your arms from bouncing off of some of the walls of the narrower alleyways.

Along with the shops, houses, and apartments there were a myriad of restaurants and bars in the village. Each of them had its own particular characteristic and its own characters that frequented, worked in, or owned them. Most of them relied on summer season workers for staff. Peculiarly, as well as young Brits and Greeks, a good many of those were Albanian. All of the staff in the restaurants and bars had the Greek way of friendly service. Instantly you felt you were their friend. No doubt because of that, and the charm of the picturesque village itself, people returned year after year for their holiday.

The wife of the Greek couple who owned the apartment she'd rented had emailed her directions to it, along with her mobile number, telling her to call when she arrived at the square to arrange for them to meet at the apartment to give Aileen the key and show her what was necessary to know about in the flat, such as the operation of the water heater and the air conditioning. As soon as she'd collected her suitcase from the taxi driver and paid him the fare she called, and although the woman only spoke broken English somehow she understood. Aileen set off across the square wheeling her suitcase, weaving between the queuing vehicles and the tourists. Fortunately the apartment was only a short walk from the square, and although some of the alleyways were equally as crowded, at least there were no vehicles to manoeuvre around with her case, just the occasional awkward cobbles trying desperately to move its wheels off course. The apartment was right in the centre of the village, just a couple of minutes from the square. As she turned right and up the slight slope of the alleyway opposite Yannis Bar as per the directions she'd been sent she recognised the sign for Arches nightclub on the left, where she had spent some very late evenings during her June visit. Twenty yards further on the figure of a small, quite elderly woman, dressed all in black, was waiting in front of the door on the right to the courtyard in which Aileen's flat was located.

"Hello, Aileen?" the woman enquired, to which Aileen nodded and added with a slight puff of her cheeks at the heat after her struggle through the village with her case, "Yes, that's me, hello."

Telling her, "This way," the woman opened the outer dark wooden double doors and led her into a pebbled stone mosaic laid courtyard to reveal more doors to two apartments, one on each side of the courtyard. Inside the one to the left hand side the apartment had a quite reasonably sized lounge with a couch that had seen better days, a small table and a couple of chairs each side of it, a small coffee table, and a low two draw chest with an ancient looking television sat on top of it. The walls throughout were painted in an unimaginative very light magnolia, from appearance some considerable years previously.

As Aileen quickly glanced around surveying the room the Greek woman told her as she motioned towards an open door, "And this is the bedroom through here, with the kitchen and a shower room with the toilet, off of it."

The bedroom had a double bed and another chest of drawers, a couple of bedside tables, and a built in wardrobe in one corner, which the woman opened to show her. High up to one side of the room, fixed to the outer wall to the lane outside, was the air conditioning unit. The kitchen was the usual small, basic Greek apartment one, with actually only very basic facilities besides a fridge and a couple of plug-in electric heating rings for cooking. The shower room was equally as basic, with the water heater fixed high up on the wall, a small sink, the toilet, and a wall fixed shower that optimistically sprayed the water towards a drain in the centre of the room.

The apartment wasn't as good as the one she'd shared briefly with Sandra Weston in June in Lindos, not salubrious by any means. Functional was the best way to describe it. However, she decided it would do, saying a short, "Fine," as the woman pointed out each of the facilities, and then showed her where the switch for the water heater was located. She opened one of the bedside table drawers, removed the air conditioning remote control from it, and handed it to Aileen as she identified it to her. With that she said goodbye and left. Aileen immediately switched on the air conditioning, on to high speed fan. She slumped onto the bed to try it out. Finding that it was quite firm she muttered, "Hmm, needs a little bit of softening up I think." She quickly admonished herself. "But don't even think of inviting anyone to embark on any sort of sexual exertions on it for softening it up, girl. That's not what you're here for. Had enough of that last time."

With that she raised herself up off the bed, picked up her suitcase, put it on the bed and began unpacking.

5

Where to start?

Lindos in August, and even more generally, any Greek island in August, wouldn't have been her first place of choice to be holidaying. But technically this wasn't a holiday, and there wasn't really much choice, or any for that matter. This was where her mother had worked and lived for a couple of years in the seventies. So this was the only obvious place to start trying to discover the truth about her past, or at least her mother's, and maybe her birth father.

By the middle of the day the village was stifling. The maze of myriad picturesque white walled alleyways seemed only to amplify the searing August heat as it bounced off the walls and the temperatures reached the mid-forties. The air hung heavy and humid in the unrelenting sunshine. Most of the time any hint of a breeze was non-existent. Even when one did appear it felt like a hot oven fan had suddenly been switched on. The discomfort of the heat was exacerbated by the hordes of bustling daytime tourists on coach and boat trips to the village from Rhodes Town, filling the narrow alleyways to almost bursting point in places. Yet somehow, for some reason, all of that only seemed to add to the charm and appeal of the place, especially to the regular British Lindos tourist visitors staying in the village, as well as the Brit ex-pats who lived there all year round or for the whole summer season. Of course, the ex-pats would joke about the, "Bloody tourists" at times, but really they loved the bustle and the popularity of the place in which they resided. The bar and restaurant owners certainly did. It was their livelihood for six months of the year, by mid-September a pretty tiring relentless six months.

In the evening the character of the place changed as the tourists staying in the multitude of flats and apartments in the village made their way to the bars and many good restaurants for a pre-dinner drink and then a meal. The twinkling lights from the rooftop restaurants blanketed the village with a magical fairyland feel, and the illuminated ancient Acropolis above it rounded the picture off beautifully.

The first question for Aileen was where to start and who to talk to in trying to find out more about her mother's past and the two years she spent in the village in the mid-seventies. One decision was easy though. She would continue to call herself, and introduce herself, by the name Aileen Regan that she'd used when she had the holiday there almost two months earlier with Sandra Weston. That way at least she could try and get some conversations going about the past with some of the older Greek bar and restaurant owners she'd met before during that holiday, without any confusion over her name and having to explain that. Nevertheless, she was well aware that if she was asking around if anyone in the village recalled her mother, Mary O'Mara, the question of Aileen's different surname might come up. So, she would deal with any queries about that by simply explaining that Regan was her married name, and that she kept it after her divorce. Not strictly, or even remotely, true, of course, but no one would be likely to know that in Lindos. Whereas, she would explain, O'Mara was her mother's family name, her maiden name that she would have been known by when she worked in the village in the seventies.

The other easy, much more pleasant decision that she made immediately was that after all the travelling and stress of her final job for the Bhoys she deserved a couple of days initially just chilling out in the Lindos sunshine, enjoying the excellent beaches and the crystal clear blue sea. That would give her time and space to clear her head, work out where to go, who to talk to, and what to ask them first in the village.

So, that's precisely what she did. Enjoyed a couple of very hot, lazy days relaxing on Pallas beach, soaking up the sun and embarking on the occasional gentle swim to cool off. On the first evening she made sure she went towards the top of the village for a meal, to a restaurant she hadn't been in before on holiday with Sandra. She figured that way she was unlikely to bump into any of the Greek or Brit ex-pats working in the restaurants that she'd previously been in, and consequently wouldn't have to engage in weary conversations about how long she was staying or why she'd come back so soon.

That plan worked out fine for the first two days, and for the first night. On the second evening though she decided it was time to do some investigating on what she had come for. She would begin by asking some people - mainly the Greek bar and restaurant owners – who she had met on that previous holiday about possible contacts, people who may have known her mother when she worked in the village.

One such person was Jack Constantino, who owned the Courtyard Bar that she had been in a few times with Sandra. She remembered Jack telling some stories from the past about the village and his family to the two women in the bar late one night. So, Jack and his bar was as good a place as any to start.

However, she got side-tracked. The way to the Courtyard Bar from her apartment meant she had to pass Pal's Bar on the corner of the alley leading up to it. As she was passing one of the bar staff, Stelios, a dark curly haired Greek was outside collecting some empty glasses. He spotted her, saying hesitantly, "Aileen isn't it? You're back, that was quick. Your hair's shorter, but I thought I recognised you." He engaged her briefly in a conversation, telling her he remembered her from a month or so ago when she was in the bar with Martin Cleverley, whom he knew well as a regular Lindos visitor.

Pal's was packed as usual, although being only a small bar it didn't take many customers to fill it. Consequently, there was always a fair number of people standing outside drinking or seated on the cushions on the low stone wall to one side and the seats on the other side. The bar itself had a high ceiling with some traditional wooden beams. In the far corner, furthest away from the two sets of entrance double folding doors on each wall and next to the music console, was a very narrow, steep, spiral wrought iron staircase leading precariously up to the toilets. Pal's clientele was usually a mixture of middle-aged, or even slightly older, predominantly Brit tourists. Couples, many of whom returned to Lindos year after year, as well as its share of younger tourists. The always good music in the bar seemed to suit all their tastes and age groups. Many of the younger groups tended to stand outside in the alley drinking.

Aileen initially had no intention to stop for a drink there, and certainly didn't want to engage in any conversation regarding

Martin Cleverley. But not wishing to appear rude she replied, "A Gin and tonic thanks," when Stelios asked what he could get her to drink.

By the time Stelios returned with her drink from inside she had been engaged in conversation by a couple of guys from a group in their mid-twenties. At least, that is what she estimated their ages to be. There were five of them altogether, and they all looked of a similar age and were dressed in a similar way, of shorts, polo shirts – Lacoste and Ralph Lauren – and boat shoes or trainers. One of them asked initially if she was there on her own, followed by if she had just arrived. He appeared intent on what she immediately read as trying to chat her up. It seemed he was determined to just keep on talking without even waiting for her answers. She eventually managed to just reply a simple, "Yes, and yes," to his initial questions. He was ploughing on, telling her they'd been in Lindos a week and would be there for another one, while she reached into her small shoulder bag searching for some euros to pay Stelios for the drink. The Greek barman was now smiling at her and raising his eyebrows slightly at the guy's obvious attempt to chat her up. Before she could get her euros out, however, her new attentive would be friend produced a ten euro note and handed it to Stelios, saying, "I'll get this. Someone as lovely as you shouldn't have to buy her own drinks all the time." Then he added to Stelios, "Keep the change."

She should have been flattered by all of that, especially from someone she reckoned was probably twelve or thirteen years younger than her. However, she was determined she wasn't going to get involved with anyone in that way in Lindos this time, and certainly not someone like him, a lot younger than her. She was focused on what she had come to the village to do; find out about her mother and her past, and possibly her birth father. Besides that, the poor young guy obviously had no idea who he was dealing with. For almost twenty years she had been a trained assassin and wasn't some innocent middle-aged woman tourist on holiday alone, as he obviously thought. She could have 'eaten him for breakfast and then spat him out, was the thought that was going through her mind as he rambled on, accompanied by a self-satisfied slight smile.

She realised that he might take her smile as some sign of encouragement however, so she told him somewhat abruptly, "Thanks, I mean for the drink, not the compliment. If you'll excuse me I should go inside and say hello to the other barman, Lou, and Sarah, the owner's wife who's playing the good music."

A look of disappointment spread over the young guy's face, while a couple of the other guys in the group tried to stifle their amusement at what they saw as his rejection. The only brief dejected response he could muster was, "Oh, ok, well we'll be out here for a while anyway if you want a chat after you've done that."

She didn't, of course, but just nodded slightly indicating some agreement as she headed inside Pal's. She said her hello to Lou and Sarah, more of a wave and a smile of acknowledgement really over the loud music. Then she finished her Gin and tonic, spotted through the bar's large side window that her young admirer was now deep in conversation with a couple of women outside much nearer his age, and took the opportunity to surreptitiously slide out of Pal's side doors and up the alley towards the Courtyard Bar.

The Courtyard Bar was old style Lindian décor with its usual fair share of dark polished wood. The bar itself ran all along the length of the back wall, except for a few feet at the end where there was a doorway and narrow steps down to the toilets. At the opposite end was the music console, together with a larger and wider area with some tables and chairs and room for dancing, with stairs up to the open terrace.

By the time she got to Jack's bar it was gone eleven and it was still packed. It was busy, both inside and outside in the courtyard that gave the bar its name. The clientele tended to be slightly older than in Pal's, although still with a fair smattering of younger couples. The Courtyard had a good share of regular returning year on year holidaymakers, couples and families, many of whom sometimes came back two or even three times each summer. They liked the general atmosphere of the bar, as well as that of its friendly owner, Jack Constantino.

Jack was a stocky, dark-haired, quite tall man in his early fifties. Born and bred in Lindos, in entertaining his customers he could relate many stories from his youth in the village. He'd also spent some time in America a few years before he married back in Lindos. Besides his bar, or maybe as well as is a better way of putting it, his passion was his music. He was a great fan of Cat Stevens, or Yusuf Islam as he now called himself. Jack would regularly entertain his customers with renditions on his guitar or bouzouki of the songs of his favourite musician, particularly during the bar's regular Sunday 'Greek evening'.

The Courtyard Bar was also a popular late night watering hole for many of the Brit ex-pat workers and residents in the village, especially after the music stopped in all the Lindos bars at one a.m., as the local by-laws required. A late drink, sometimes a very late drink at three a.m. or later, could always be obtained in Jack's. Generally Jack Constantino was the epitome of the convivial Greek host. One of his best traits in that respect was his memory of faces and returning tourists.

Aileen managed to find a vacant stool at the far end of the bar and Jack's character was displayed immediately as he approached that end of the bar.

"Hi, you're back. I thought you would be. Very few people just come to Lindos the once. It's Aileen, isn't it? You were here with your friend and Martin, Martin Cleverley, about a month ago? They not with you this time?"

"Yes, that's right, Aileen, but no, just me this time. Can I get a Gin and tonic please, Jack?"

"Sure," and with that he set about getting her drink. As he placed it on the bar in front of her and she paid him she asked tentatively, "Martin hasn't been back then?"

"No, I haven't seen him. He left at about the same time you did, I think."

She knew full well he did, as she actually left with him to disappear back to London in order to avoid Sandra Weston and her crazy, obsessive husband. She wasn't minded to explain that entire bloody complicated story to Jack though.

Jack had heard rumours from his other customers and some Greeks in the village about the romantic and sexual entanglements between Sandra Weston, her husband and Aileen, and how Martin Cleverley had been dragged into them. However, he wasn't about to get into that by probing any deeper into it with more questions to her. So, he simply settled for adding, "Martin sometimes comes back late August, or early or mid-September for a week or two. I expect he'll be in then if he does this year."

With that Jack turned to go to the other end of the bar to serve some more customers, leaving Aileen to her G and T. As she sipped away at it and glanced around the bar she reckoned it was still far too busy for her to manage to get any sort of lengthy discussion with Jack about the past, and what she had come back to Lindos to find out. After an hour though, and after nursing another Gin and tonic, she managed to grab a quick word with him, telling him very briefly the real reason she had come back to the village and asking if he could help. She didn't go into great detail, thinking he was far too busy. She just settled for mentioning that she believed her mother had worked in Lindos in the nineteen-seventies. She never mentioned at that point that she was trying to find out who her birth father was and that she was trying to trace him, or even that she believed he was Greek and from Lindos. Instead, she suggested that perhaps they could meet in the bar when it was less busy? Then she could explain in more detail, and maybe he could help her with anything he knew?

"Yes, of course," Jack agreed, adding, "Why don't you come at around seven tomorrow night? We will have only just opened then and we shouldn't be very busy at all. I'm not sure how much I can tell you about those times, the nineteen-seventies, but you can tell me more about what you want to know. Maybe we can arrange for you to meet my mother. She'll definitely know more about those times than me.

"Great, thanks, Jack. I'll come in then," she agreed. Deciding that she'd had enough of Lindos nightlife for one night at that point she bid him, "Goodnight," adding another, "Thanks." Then she made her way out of the bar and through the village back to her flat.

As she strolled back through the village, maybe because of Jack and Stelios mentioning him, Martin Cleverley's name kept popping into her head. She knew he was a regular visitor, and that he'd more than likely appear back in Lindos at some point that summer, as Jack Constantino had suggested. She had not really given that much thought when she worked out her plan to come back. That was unusual for her, to miss something like that, she thought to herself. She usually planned everything down to the last detail, prepared for, and was aware of, every eventuality. That was what she'd been trained to do for the past twenty years. That was odd, missing that. Could she possibly subconsciously want to bump into him in the village, hoped she would?

She knew full well that would be awkward, to say the least. They'd had some pleasant sexual encounters in Lindos after they met on that flight to Rhodes. No, they were better than that, better than pleasant. They were good, bloody good, exciting. She knew that, admitted that to herself now, and at the time. But she had left him abruptly when they returned to the UK after they spent a few days together. And basically she did know deep down that she'd used Martin as cover to keep Richard at bay when he turned up there uninvited at the start of the second week of her holiday with Sandra. Now, as his name kept popping into her brain, she also had to admit that she'd grown somewhat attached and drawn to Martin during their time together.

She was going around in circles with it now though. So, she decided as she reached the door of the courtyard to her flat that she'd cross that bridge when she came to it if the situation arose and she did see him in Lindos. After all, Jack had only said that Martin, "Sometimes comes back late August or early or mid-September." Perhaps this would be a year that he wouldn't?

6

St. Paul's bay, sun, sea and more recollections of Martin

She spent the next day on the beach at picturesque St. Paul's bay at one end of the village, mostly alternating between intermittently getting into the cool, clear sea water and sheltering out of the sweltering August stifling heat on the sunbed in the shade beneath the rush covered parasol. She got down to the beach early, just after nine. It was just as well, as the limited number of sunbeds filled up quickly. By around ten-thirty the beach was completely full of sun worshipping tourists. Mid-August was the height of the holiday season, the peak of the Greek summer, with not just its airless and windless heat but also its clawing humidity. August was the start of the British school holidays, although, unlike other tourist spots on Rhodes and across Greece, Lindos did not experience as large an influx of families with children. Even those families with children who did make their holiday visit the village tended not to go to the beach at St. Paul's bay, preferring the larger and longer Main Beach or Pallas Beach. Increasingly in recent years they also tended to book at the all-inclusive complexes out of the village, up the hill in Krana, and stay around the swimming pools there rather than venture to the beaches.

The largest other group of tourists who descended on Lindos from around the start of the second week of August was the Italians, particularly younger ones, teenagers and slightly older. It was like an annual pilgrimage during the August Italian holidays. Many of them had Greek family links from the past.

That particular August day Aileen - as she consistently reminded herself she was known as in Lindos – was spared the company on the beach of any large group of young Italians. She only came across what appeared to be a group of four of them in the sea when she went in for a cooling off swim at one point during the day. Most of the rest of the people on the beach seemed to be British tourists, except for what she took as German being spoken when she overheard a conversation between a couple on the sunbeds beneath the parasol next to her. Of course, they could just as easily have been Austrian, she reminded herself. But she wasn't in the mood for engaging in any conversation, so wasn't about to enquire. She was enjoying the relative tranquillity and beauty of her St. Paul's bay surroundings far too much to want, or allow, anyone to intrude and interrupt it. The bright sun was beating overhead in the cloudless clear blue sky with its rays sparkling on the shimmering inviting sea gently lapping on the shore of the bay. Even the buzz and hum of the chatter of the tourists enjoying the beach and the cooling sea, supplemented sporadically by the Glass Bottom tourist boats entering and leaving the bay, didn't succeed in disturbing her overwhelming feeling of calm and tranquillity. That was something she had been searching for over a number of years.

As she dozed a little in the shade of her parasol after a light lunch at the small restaurant at one end of the beach she at last began to feel relaxed and able to put all the stress and drama of her past life behind her. She briefly tried to focus on how to play her meeting with Jack Constantino at seven that evening, trying to figure out what, and in what order, to explain to him what she was trying to discover about her family's past, or at least, her mother's. The warm air and the relaxing beautiful surroundings were too much however, and she soon drifted into another brief nap, convincing herself as she did that she could figure that out later after she'd left the beach. Before she actually drifted off though one thing she was clear about, and sure off, was that she'd made the correct decision to leave all of her past behind, and an excellent one about where to disappear to, the paradise of Lindos.

Just after five she decided that was enough sunning and relaxing for the day and made her way across the beach and up the slope to the top path with its wonderful panoramic view over the bay. Five minutes later she was pulling off her black bikini, replacing it with a thin light blue t-shirt as she slumped on the double bed, reached for the air-conditioning remote on the bedside table, pointed it at the unit high on the bedroom wall, and clicked it on to high fan. The cool air was an instant relief from the day's heat that had invaded every part of her body.

As she lay there relaxing on the bed though, the thought of someone leapt into her head once again. It wasn't someone she wanted to think about, or at least had tried to convince herself not to after his name was mentioned to her the previous evening by Jack Constantino. But for some reason she was still unable to completely remove Martin Cleverley from her head and her thoughts. It wasn't like her at all. When she set her mind to something or more specifically to block something or someone from her thoughts, she was always able to do that completely. Besides anything else that was what she had been trained to do over the past twenty years as an MI6 operative, and as an IRA infiltrator of that organisation – focus and not be distracted by personal attractions. All the personal associations she'd embarked upon during that time were for specific operational reasons, to get what she and those organisations sought.

"Bloody Martin Cleverley, why can't I get that bloody man out of my head?" she thought.

Deep down she was beginning to think that maybe she knew why, but for now she told herself it was because of Lindos. She knew he came there regularly throughout the summer and that at some point his name was bound to come up. She definitely couldn't get him out of her thoughts now though. He was well and truly in her head and he wasn't going to go away easily, not while she was on the bed in the position she was. She was lying on her back in the flimsy light blue t-shirt in the middle of the double bed, with the bottom half of her sun warmed body as naked as the day she was born. Now what was in her mind wasn't just his name, Martin Cleverly, but the man himself, and what they had done together more than once on another double bed in Lindos around six weeks before during the final week of that June. A small smile of satisfaction spread gently across her lips as her thoughts drifted to those moments they had together. She couldn't deny that she had enjoyed them, even though at the time she'd convinced herself that they were all part of her overall plan of revenge to destroy Sandra Weston, her career, her marriage, and ultimately take her life. She had enjoyed them a lot. She always did, of course, as part of any operation, with whoever the man was. But with Martin there was something different, some sort of emotional connection that she never usually let herself slip into. That was why she had to end it so abruptly; leave him and disappear because actually what was happening, what she was starting to feel inside, was worrying her. That wasn't supposed to happen. She was trained to make sure that didn't happen.

Maybe it was being completely relaxed and exposed to the Lindos heat all day, and the satisfying warmth of her body, but now her mind was truly fixated on the sex they had together in Lindos, her and Martin Cleverley, in his flat in the centre of the village. She had been the instigator on each occasion, deliberately determined to cement their attraction and connection in order to provide a screen between her and Sandra's husband, Richard. She used Martin as an effective barrier against Richard's insistent attentions and his refusal to accept that their affair was over. That was all there was to it, the brief relationship she had with Martin. At least, that's what she told herself at the time. She took full advantage of the situation that developed and, in effect, used Martin for her own ends. It was what she successfully contrived at the time in order to protect her overall plan against Sandra. At that point in the plan she no longer needed to cultivate Richard's attentions and infatuation. His usefulness in her undermining of Sandra in terms of the affair they'd had was complete, had run its course, or at least that part of it had. All that was necessary now was for it to be seemingly accidentally revealed to Sandra. So, that is what she'd manipulated through the text from Richard on Aileen's seemingly carelessly left phone on the Lindos Pallas beach while Aileen swam.

Of course, Richard then turning up in Lindos for the second week of the two women's holiday wasn't part of Aileen's plan at all, which is why she latched on to Martin as some sort of shield to fend off Richard's continuing obsession with her. Subsequently that is what she told herself, convinced herself. But undeniably she also quickly became aware at the time that her unforeseen and unplanned reaction to the sex her and Martin had together shocked her a little; shook her out of her cold, calculating, clinical, well trained comfort zone. It was good, bloody good. She reminded herself of it now as she lay there on the double bed with the cooling air from the air-conditioning unit wafting over her half-clothed body. Her reaction to those memories of the sex they'd had was almost instinctive. Focusing on what Martin and she had done together six weeks earlier she allowed her right hand to slide slowly down her still warm body in order to try and re-live some elements of those pleasures, only this time alone.

Part Three:
Some historical progress and a Lindos Friday night

7

Jack Constantino

Following her improvised pleasurable end to the afternoon Aileen drifted into a warm and comforting nap. She woke with a start as the alarm she'd set on her small bedside alarm clock beeped. It was six-fifteen. Just time to jump in the shower before going to meet Jack Constantino in the Courtyard bar at seven. Martin Cleverley was no longer in her head. Her self-administered therapy had dealt with that issue very nicely. After the shower she pulled on a pair of quite tight fitting white shorts and an off the shoulder plain black t-shirt, which she tied in a knot just above her waist to show off her already starting to get brown, quite flat stomach. A pair of smart flat black sandals with just a small amount of glittery decoration on the straps finished off the outfit. As she grabbed some euros from the bedside table, thrusting them into one of the pockets of her shorts, she caught a glimpse of her reflection in the mirror above the improvised dressing table. The image of herself, her already slightly tanned face, together with her white shorts, black t-shirt and exposed bare slightly tanned shoulder brought an approving, "Hmm … that'll do for a start," from her, followed by a slight grin. She picked up her little black leather Gucci shoulder bag from the dressing table and placed a small black notebook and pen inside, then headed for the door of the flat after one more glance in the mirror and a deliberate ruffle of her short dark hair on the top of her head.

Taking the few minutes' walk through the centre of the village to the Courtyard Bar she weaved her way through some of the early evening couples in the narrow alleyway; tourists on their way to an early evening pre-dinner drink outside Yannis bar or Giorgos. It was still a warm thirty degrees, humid, and with a distinct lack of any cooling breeze. The village was already beginning to fill up with the crowds of August tourist visitors. In an hour or so most of the restaurants, with their inviting rooftop views, would be full. For now though, a cold drink, alcoholic or otherwise, outside in the warm Lindos air was what many of the tourists sought.

She turned to the left at the corner by Pal's bar and headed up the alleyway to Jack's bar. As it was only early evening this time Pal's was empty and the two bar staff, Lou and Stelios, were too busy restocking the fridge and shelves with bottles to notice her passing.

As she entered the Courtyard bar Jack was also busy restocking one of the middle shelves behind the bar with bottles of the Greek beer, Mythos. He stopped, looked up, said, "Hi," and asked if she wanted a drink. Behind the other end of the bar Dimitris, one of the barmen, was also restocking some shelves with some bottles of another beer from a green crate on the floor. He stopped briefly to look up and say, "Hello," before continuing.

Aileen asked Jack for, "Just a coke, thanks." As he set about pouring it for her she sat down on one of the bar stools. He set the drink down on a beer mat in front of her and then walked around the end of the bar to join her on the next stool.

"Are you staying in the village?" he asked.

"Yes, an apartment just along the alley from Arches. It's okay, nothing special, but very convenient for everything," she informed him.

"Last night you said that your mother was working in Lindos in the seventies?"

"In 1976 until 1978, I found some papers after she died, and a notebook. She had written some notes in that with a date of 'summer 1976'. There was also what looked like a contract of employment as a Tour Representative with a company that specialised in holidays to the Greek islands, Olympic Holidays.

That was dated the twenty-fourth of May 1976. So, I assume that was when she came to work here, for two years, or at least from what I found, for two summer seasons."

"I was only young then, thirteen. There weren't many British Tour Reps around at that time. Tourism in Lindos had only just started to get going back then, but I can't say that I really remember many of them, if any. I was still at school so wouldn't really have come across them. What was her name, her first name? That might ring a bell."

"Mary," Aileen told him.

"Mary Regan, no that doesn't mean anything to me, I'm afraid, but-"

She interrupted to correct him before he could go on. "O'Mara, her name was Mary O'Mara, not Regan. Regan was my married name and I kept it after my divorce. Couldn't be bothered with all the bureaucracy of changing so many documents and things. O'Mara was my mother's family name, so that's the name she would have been known by when she worked here."

The bit about Regan being her married name wasn't true of course. However, she was adept at lying. She had decided that explanation as to why her mother's surname wasn't the same as the one Aileen was known as in Lindos, Regan, was the easiest way to deal with it. Regan was simply the name on the fake passport she'd been provided with by the Bhoys while she was on the operation to destroy Sandra Weston. It was the one she used when she was in Lindos six weeks previously with her, and she obviously wasn't going to tell Jack, or anyone else for that matter, that it was fake.

"Still doesn't mean anything to me, I'm afraid. As I said, I was quite young then in 1976, so I doubt if our paths would have crossed anyway. But what about the rest of your family, your father, or his side of the family? Did your mother not marry before you were born?" Jack asked.

She took a sip of her coke, and then a deep breath. "That's the real reason I'm here, Jack," she started to explain. "I was born in April 1978. My mother married an Irish guy, Niall, in April 1981, but I'm sure he wasn't my birth father. I knew him as my father ever since I was little, all the time I was growing up, but subsequently I guessed that he wasn't my birth father. I was registered on my birth certificate in my mother's family name, O'Mara, and it stated, 'Father unknown'. My mother would never talk to me about it, even when I was much older and kept asking. I know now that my mother was here for all of the summer seasons of 1976 and 1977. As I said, I was born in April 1978, and-"

"And the season usually finishes in October, maybe end of September back then." Now it was Jack's turn to interrupt as he simultaneously rubbed his chin with two fingers of his right hand. "So, that means you were probably conceived here sometime in the late summer of 1977?"

"Yes, that's what I figured. This is where my mother met my birth father. It must have been."

"Is that why you came here earlier this summer with your friend, Sandra?" Jack asked.

"No, that was pure coincidence. The holiday, and the choice of Lindos, was all Sandra's idea. I knew then about my mother being here, but I had other things going on then, plus I needed a holiday and I didn't want the whole of it taken up with this, which is why I came back."

Once again, she was being economical with the truth. The holiday was certainly part of "other things going on" for her, but no way was she going to reveal what they were.

Jack helped out though, or tried to, thought he was. "Like Martin?" he asked as she took another sip of her coke.

"What?" She was thrown a bit by his comment, and almost choked on her drink. She didn't realise that her relationship with Martin was so obvious, but rather than enquiring what he meant, or knew about that, she simply took a deep breath and decided to play along. "Yes, I suppose so, that was part of it."

As she was agreeing she was actually thinking there's that bloody name again. Why the hell does he keep cropping up?

"Anyway, I just want to try and see if I can find my birth father, and I thought he might still be here in Lindos." She tried to put Jack back on track on her main concern.

"But it could have been anyone, and it was forty years ago. How do you know where to start? It may not have even been a Greek. It could have been a tourist. I don't want to dispel any illusions about your mother, Aileen, but Tour Reps, here in the seventies ..."

He hesitated for a few seconds and rubbed the palm of his right hand across the back of his head and down to his neck, as if pondering on what was the most delicate way to put what he was about to say.

She stared at his seeming discomfort and waited. Eventually, he continued, "Well ... look, the whole village ... in fact the whole of Rhodes from what I've heard since, was, how can I put this-"

She didn't wait and let him finish, but instead helped him out of his obvious discomfort. "One big party, sex party, I'm guessing is what you're struggling to say, about to say?" She said it with wide eyes and a knowing smile on her face.

"Err .. yep, that would be one way of putting it, I guess. From what I've heard anyway. As I said, I was a bit young at the time."

She leaned forward, picked up her glass and took another sip of her coke, before telling him slowly and with a mixture of the sound of deliberation and determination in her voice. "That's okay, Jack. I'm a big girl and not stupid. I appreciate you trying to spare me any not so nice thoughts, or possibilities, about what my mother may or may not have got up to when she was working here, But, yes, I realise that, but I don't think it was a tourist, my real father, I mean. I believe he was Greek, from here in Lindos."

"Why? What makes you think that, seem so certain about that?" Jack asked with a quizzical, confused look on his face.

"As well as the Olympic Holidays contract of employment from 1976 and that notebook I told you about I also found three letters that were written in broken English to my mother from what I found. They were signed, 'Love, Dimitris'."

Jack leaned forward in silence towards her on his stool, listening intently, staring wide-eyed at her in surprise, and determined not to miss anything she told him as she once again picked up her nearly finished glass of coke, took another sip, and continued.

"In one of them he, this Dimitris, had written, 'I miss you very much, Mary. I wait you very long time in Lindos, to see you with our new arrival'. So, when I read that it started me thinking that perhaps my father was this Dimitris, a Greek. It seems a strong possibility given that I was born in April 1978 and that particular letter was dated March of that year, don't you think Jack?" Not pausing for him to answer she quickly added, "Plus, there is what he'd written about their 'new arrival'."

Jack sat back a little, and straightened up a bit on his stool as she finished. He looked bemused. For a long moment all he could manage to allow to emerge from his mouth was, "Phew."

"I know, that was pretty much my reaction too when I read that. You can imagine. At first I found myself reading it over and over, trying to analyse just what I thought he meant by 'our new arrival'. At one point I began to wonder if I was just misreading it completely, especially with his broken English. I tried to convince myself for a while that perhaps when he wrote 'with our new arrival' he really just meant my mother, Mary's, 'new arrival' back in Lindos in that summer of 1978. That perhaps his broken English had affected the meaning, and he was expecting her to return for a third summer working here. But I was already born then, in that April, so it is very unlikely surely that she would have been planning to do that in order to work, come back here. Maybe she'd told him about the baby, about me, and he was expecting her to come with me and live with him? If what he wrote, 'our new arrival' is taken at face value then it really does suggest that she had told him about me, and he was expecting just that, that we would all live together as a family-"

"In Lindos, here in Lindos?" Jack interrupted.

"No, I don't think that was what he, Dimitris, planned because in that letter where he wrote 'I wait you very long time in Lindos, to see you with our new arrival', he also wrote, 'But we cannot live here. It will be impossible. I have a cousin in Crete. We can go there'. But, of course, she never did come back after I was born, and I had never been here until just over six weeks ago. So, perhaps she never did tell him about me? Maybe she never even told him she was pregnant when she left at the end of that summer in 1977. After all, she would probably have been only two months or less pregnant. It's unlikely that it would have been obvious she was. So, maybe she did just string him along throughout that winter, not telling him she was pregnant, and he was actually simply expecting her to return for another summer in 1978 working for Olympic, as I said before. Perhaps his 'our new arrival' comment did actually mean her coming back, him seeing her again, and he was looking forward to their meeting? But that doesn't really explain why he wrote that they couldn't live in Lindos and 'It will be impossible' does it?"

She hesitated, sighed heavily, and rubbed her hand slowly up and down the side of her cheek before she added, "Who knows, Jack? After all is said and done I tend to think that what he wrote in the letter suggests he did know about the baby, me. I think it was me. I was 'our new arrival' that he wrote about. But I need to try and find out, want to find out, which is why I'm here. Find out if he, Dimitris, is actually my birth father."

Jack had sat in complete silence through all of that, except for a few deep breaths of surprise from time to time at what she was telling him. Once again there was a long silent moment between them as Jack attempted to process all he'd heard, while Aileen reached to finish off her coke.

Eventually, Jack told her, "You know Dimitris is a very common Greek name. It was even my father's name." He quickly realised what he was saying and added immediately, "Of course, I'm not suggesting it was him, definitely not. But it could have been any number of men in the village at that time. Was there no indication of his family name on any of the letters that you found, his surname I guess you'd call it in English?"

"No, none at all, on all three of them he just signed 'Love, Dimitris'. I knew it was a long shot, Jack, but I didn't know who to ask. I remember you telling us some stories about the village from when you were younger when I was here before with Sandra. I just thought anything you could tell me, even just about Lindos when you were growing up, might help. But obviously-"

He was scratching the top of his head with his left hand as he interrupted her, saying, "Not really, not me, but, as I told you last night, I'm sure my mother would be able to tell you more. Hopefully, help you, and her English is good, so that shouldn't be a problem. Anyway, I can help out with that if necessary. I'll ask her if she will see you, meet you. I'm sure she won't refuse. I should ask her first though. She loves talking about 'the old days', as she calls them. She would have been thirty-two in 1976, so she may well have known your mother. There wasn't a great number of non-Greeks living and working in the village then, so there is a good chance that she may at least have seen your mother around when she was working for Olympic. We had a different, smaller, bar in the village then. I remember that my mother helped out behind the bar there on some evenings. If your mother liked a drink she'd-"

"She was Irish, Jack, remember," Aileen interrupted.

"Yes, of course," he continued with a wry smile. "Well, I'm sure there couldn't have been many Irish people working in the village at that time, so there must be a fair chance my mother will have come across her and remember her. I'll ask her in the morning if she'll meet you. Maybe we can meet for lunch the day after next, the three of us, if you're free?"

"That would be great and lunch will be fine, thanks. Or if she can't make that, any time will be good for me."

"Okay, give me your phone number. I'll text you after I speak to her in the morning to let you know what's happening, and if it's okay with her. We can go to her house. It's in the village, towards the top, but we can meet outside the bar here at twelve and I'll take you there. I'll see if she would like to go out for lunch, but my guess is she'll prepare something for the three of us. She likes to cook and entertain. It's a Greek thing. And I suppose that would be more private for a conversation, lunch at her place."

He finished with a smile, then glanced over his shoulder along the bar seeing that he already had a few early evening pre-dinner customers that his head barman, another Dimitris, was looking after.

"Okay, if it's alright with you I need to serve a few people now. We are starting to get a bit busy," he told her.

She smiled and then replied, "Of course, and I need to go and get some dinner. Thanks again for all your help. See you later."

As she made her way out into the now even busier Lindos alleyways she felt that she'd possibly at least made some initial progress on what she was setting out to do. She decided she would head for a nice dinner to celebrate that at the Village House Restaurant just a few minutes from the Courtyard Bar. She'd had a very good dinner there with Sandra and Richard Weston the previous time she was in Lindos, even though Richard was a pain in the arse. The food was excellent, and the owner, Aris, was very welcoming and friendly.

8

An Antika and Porn Star Martinis' evening, then a pleasant Giorgos late breakfast

After her dinner at the Village House she went for a few cocktails in Antika, a bar in the centre of the village. She decided she wasn't going to have a late night, but it was only just after nine-thirty when she'd finished dinner, paid the bill, chatted to Aris about how the season had been for the restaurant, and left. Once again though, Martin Cleverley's name came up. In fact, as soon as she reached the top of the wrought iron steps leading to the restaurant's main dining area and Aris spotted her, he greeted her in much the same way as Jack Constantino had the previous evening.

"Welcome, you're back, and so soon, is Martin not with you?" he asked.

She ignored the reference to Martin, and nodded and smiled before replying, "Yes, I'm back." She tried to make light of it by adding, "I couldn't stay away from Lindos now."

Although she was determined after dinner not to have a long Lindos late night, she knew that if she went straight back to her flat at that early hour, just gone nine-thirty, she was very unlikely to be able to sleep. The music would be still playing quite loudly in the bars – until one a.m. – and even with the double-glazing of the bedroom windows of her flat it refused to be shut out. So, that's why she decided on a cocktail or two in Antika, just until it was a little nearer an hour when she would be able to get off to sleep.

Antika was a large, trendier bar in an old traditional stone building. It had various levels. There was a large area close to the entrance leading to five broad steps the width of the building up to the bar area, which in turn had a further stone staircase at the far end that lead to an area with tables and chairs outside at the back of the building. To the right of the bar was another stone staircase that led up to a roof terrace with more tables and chairs.

By the time of the evening that Aileen got there it was quite busy with after dinner drinkers. There were around thirty, mainly younger people, drinking in the bar area and what looked like a further dozen or so, mainly couples, outside at the back, sat at the tables. Because the whole bar area was quite large, and interspersed with high long wooden tables and stools, it didn't feel anywhere near crowded. As Aileen reached the bar and sat on one of the stools at it she quickly scanned the whole bar and concluded that the customers mostly looked like tourists. Behind the bar were what she estimated to be a late twenties barman and a slightly younger, very attractive barwoman with long dark hair, probably in her mid-twenties. To Aileen they both looked Greek. At the far end, behind the bar and obviously decorating it with her presence, was a tall, very slim, striking looking blonde woman, who certainly didn't look Greek. Aileen immediately reckoned she was Eastern European. All three of the bar staff sported black t-shirts with the word Antika written across the front in large white letters. The barman wore jeans, and the dark haired barwoman had a pair of denim shorts on beneath her black t-shirt. The blonde's decorative preference was for extremely tight, skimpy black leather shorts beneath her t-shirt.

She couldn't recall whether she had been in the bar before with Sandra and Martin, and this time she didn't get the "You're back," greeting, but just a smile from the barman before he asked what she would like to drink. She told him she wanted a cocktail, a nice one, but as he reached along the bar to hand her the cocktail menu she informed him that she, "Didn't have a clue what she wanted." She had no idea why, but she added straightaway, "Why don't you choose one for me."

He nodded, and smiled, as he replied, "Okay, leave it to me."

A few minutes later he placed the cocktail on a coaster on the bar in front of her saying, "Enjoy."

She lifted the glass and took a sip, then nodded slightly in approval, telling him, "Hmm ... that's nice. What is it?"

The smile returned to his face as he told her, "A Porn Star Martini," followed by an even bigger grin.

Now it was Aileen's turn to smile before she asked, "Really?"

"Really," he told her. "That's what it's called. You never had one before?"

"Never, it's my first" she confirmed, before taking another sip, and then adding, "But I'm sure now that it won't be my last."

He flashed another smile at her as he moved along the bar to serve some waiting customers. Around twenty minutes later she was draining the last drop of her cocktail from the glass. Before she could even place the empty glass back on the bar the barman asked her, "Another?"

"Why not," she told him, thinking that if nothing else a few of these would make her sleep, even with the music from the nearby bars penetrating her flat. This time though he passed the cocktail to the long dark haired barwoman to give to her while he continued to serve some more customers.

"What's your name?" Aileen asked as she placed the drink on the bar in front of her.

"Emma," she replied, followed by a brief small smile.

"And his?" Aileen asked pointing to the other end of the bar to the barman.

"Ledi," she told her.

"Well, he makes a very good cocktail," Aileen commented.

"Yes, he does," Emma confirmed, and then moved along the bar to serve some other customers.

By eleven-thirty the bar was filling up, and she was on her third Porn Star Martini, which she had now well and truly decided was the cocktail for her without doubt, even allowing for its name. She even intervened and recommended it to an English woman, with whom Aileen presumed was her husband, when they took a seat on the stools alongside her and the woman picked up the cocktail menu. By then though Aileen was almost finished with her third one and had decided enough was enough. She was sure that after three of those getting off to sleep would be no problem. So, she paid her bill, bid her new bar staff friends Ledi and Emma, "Goodnight," and made her way towards the door of the bar and out into the alley towards her flat.

Even though she slept well, thanks to the cocktails and the wine she'd had over dinner, she didn't wake the next morning until after nine. When she opened the shutters to her bedroom window the hot August Greek sun was already burning bright above in the clear blue sky. Hopefully she would hear from Jack Constantino sometime that morning about her meeting with his mother. But what to do with another free Lindos day? She really was on holiday now, starting her new life. Maybe it was the lingering effect of the cocktails from the night before, but she really was beginning to feel relaxed. All the stress and subterfuge of past twenty years of her secret double life was behind her. While in the shower she decided that in the spirit of that feeling she would go for a leisurely mid-morning breakfast before hitting the beach that afternoon. After all, there was absolutely no rush now for anything in her life, no deadlines any longer, no strict precise timetables and timings to adhere to. As she thought about a deep sigh of contentment welled up from inside her.

"Giorgos, a nice breakfast at Giorgos," she muttered to herself as she rubbed the towel over her short wet hair. She'd been there for breakfast on her final morning in Lindos on her previous visit, she reminded herself, with, "Err … Martin," before they fled back to London later that day. "Oh, bloody hell!" she exclaimed. "Get him out of my head."

Half-an-hour later she was sat at a small table outside Giorgos. The breakfast was too good to pass up, and she wasn't going to let thoughts that she was there last with Martin Cleverley keep her from it. Giorgos café bar was right in the centre of the village. In the daytime it always did a good trade, particularly around lunchtime when the customers were multinational. During that period the tourists came from Rhodes Town on the day trip boats or on the multitude of coaches, and the little café bar got more than its fair share of custom then for drinks, coffees and basic lunches. At that time it wasn't unusual to hear French, German, Italian and increasingly Russian, as well as English, being spoken amongst the customers usually sat at the tables outside the café bar as they tucked into their lunches while watching the hordes of fellow passing tourists.

Inside the café was bright and airy with a number of tables and chairs and white walls, and a long bar along the back wall. In the evenings Giorgos attracted mostly British couples and families, many of whom returned to Lindos year after year for their holidays, as well as to their favourite bar of Giorgos. The owner, Tsamis, was very popular with them. He was a hard worker, who always seemed to be there in the bar, but always had time for his customers with his Greek hospitality and friendly convivial character. Three televisions high up on walls throughout the bar showed endless repetitive British news and live sport, evidence of the origin of most of Giorgos' tourist and ex-pat clientele. As well as the younger Brits who came to work for the summer in the bars, cafes and restaurants there were a good number of older Brit ex-pats who lived in, or nearby, the village who frequented Giorgos from time to time, during the day and in the evenings. Most of them had come to Lindos regularly in the past when they were younger to work for the summer, had stayed, and now lived in the village or just outside all year round. Some of the female ones had actually stayed and married Greeks.

That morning Giorgos was busy as usual. All of the seats and tables outside, except for a lone small one with a single chair, were taken with customers either tucking in to their food and drinks or waiting for it. Aileen headed straight for it, and immediately tried to move the seat slightly to get some shade. The bright sun was casting its rays across half of the table and the seat causing her some discomfort, even with her quite expensive sunglasses. After some slight adjustment, however, she managed to ensure she was sat mostly in the shade.

A minute or so later Tsamis appeared to take her order. He was a man in his forties of medium height and build, with a dark complexion that matched his dark curly hair. The long hours on his feet working in the café bar obviously kept him fairly slim. Just like the other bar and restaurant owners he offered her a brief acknowledgement of her return, this time with a brief nod of the head and, "Welcome back."

Aileen removed her sunglasses, gave him a smile and a, "Thank you," before ordering some Greek yogurt, honey and fruit, plus some toast and a cappuccino. As Tsamis disappeared inside to get her order she replaced her sunglasses and settled back in her chair to relax and comfortably watch the world go by, or at least the tourist world. There was, indeed, a constant tide of the flow of busy tourist humanity making its way through the various Lindos alleyways and past Giorgos. Occasionally couples or groups would pause to check if there were any tables free before slowly moving on when it became apparent there weren't. It was approaching eleven o'clock and the first day-trippers from Rhodes Town were beginning to arrive on the coaches that parked at Krana up at the top of the hill outside the village. Soon, the boats from Rhodes Town also full of day-trippers, would be arriving down at the jetty at Pallas Beach.

She was enjoying her relaxing Lindos morning when her phone beeped. As she picked it up from the table she saw a notification of a message from Jack Constantino. After she tapped on it and opened it she read, "My mother says she will be happy to meet you and suggests tomorrow at 12. So, if that's ok for you let's meet outside my bar at 11.45 and I will take you to her villa."

Without hesitating she tapped out a reply of, "Great! Yep, that's fine for me. See you there. Thanks again, Jack." As she finished and sent the text she sat back in her chair once more feeling even more contented with the world and her new life. A few seconds later Tsamis appeared with a tray full of her order, including an appetising looking bowl of Greek yogurt, honey and various fresh fruit. Her new found contentment was reflected in her smile and comment to him of, "Mmm … that looks good, thanks." He returned her smile briefly and made his way back inside the café.

The enjoyment of her late breakfast and relaxed mood was interrupted just a few minutes later by a Greek voice saying yet again to her, "Hi, so you came back." She looked up from her bowl of yogurt, fruit and honey to see a young, good looking, dark haired Greek guy who had been walking by now approaching her table. Her slight frown must have indicated to him that she didn't really recognise him, so he helped her out.

"Angelos, from Lindos By Night. I met you a couple of times in June when you came to the bar, remember, with

Martin, Martin Cleverley, and then one night with your friend and her husband? At least, I assumed it was her husband. Not a very nice guy at all, as far as I could see."

What was going through her mind was that there was that name again, but nevertheless she managed to reply, "Oh, yes, Angelos, yes I remember now. You work up at the bar with the great views of the Acropolis, hi."

She didn't really want to engage in conversation, just wanted to enjoy her own company and the relaxed atmosphere. As it happened though, she needn't have worried. He made no attempt to find a seat to join her, and never even asked the question she anticipated about Martin that it seemed everyone else had asked her. Instead, he just added quickly, "Good to see you again. I've got to run. I'm working on my father's Glass Bottom Boat down on Pallas Beach this afternoon. You should come down sometime and take a trip. It's good, and only an hour, or maybe I'll see you up at LBN one night. Come up for a drink. See you later maybe?"

With that he turned and walked off down the alley, heading for the beach.

The rest of her late morning was thankfully uninterrupted, which allowed her to think a little about what she would ask Jack's mother when they met tomorrow. Even though she stayed for a second cappuccino she didn't really get it completely clear in her mind and decided she would play it by ear. Anyway, initially it would all depend on whether Jack's mother had any recollection of her mother.

Nearing one o'clock she decided to head back to her flat, cool off for a bit under the air-con and head for the beach around two for a swim and some more sun-worshipping. She decided on Pallas Beach this time, rather than St. Paul's, although she wouldn't be embarking on any Glass Bottom Boat trip for now, no matter how good Angelos had said it was.

She spent another very pleasant beach afternoon, although Pallas Beach felt even more crowded than St. Paul's had been the day before. She managed a few cooling swims though, and even started reading a crime paperback that she'd bought at Boston airport before her flight to Athens. She allowed herself a small smile of satisfaction as she pondered the fact that the only immediate decision looming on the horizon of her new life was which restaurant to choose to go for dinner that evening.

9

Symposio, Lindos By Night and new acquaintances

She settled on Symposio in the centre of the village for dinner, next to the Antika Bar she had experienced her Porn Star Martinis in the night before. As she'd passed it in the evening a couple of times she'd heard the English woman working 'on the door' of the restaurant, as it were - although there was no actual door, just a few traditional Lindos stone steps up to the restaurant entrance – giving a very persuasive run down of the place to some tourist couples who had stopped to check out the menu; describing to them the choices on the menu, as well as the excellent view of the illuminated Acropolis from the tables on the restaurant roof top dining area. So, that was where she headed for her evening meal after returning to her flat from the beach around seven, cooling off for a bit, showering and changing.

   She decided it was time to add to her feeling of Lindos wellbeing and new found calmness by dressing up a little. Consequently, she chose a short, quite low cut, plain black sleeveless dress and a plain thin gold necklace. However, she was sensible enough to already be aware that in Lindos, with its cobbles and in places uneven alleys, anything resembling high heel shoes amounted to dicing with death, or at the very least possible broken ankles. Consequently, she settled again for her flat, smart black sandals, with the small amount of glittery decoration.

   As she surveyed herself and her minimalist ensemble in the makeshift dressing-table mirror she nodded in satisfaction. Even though she had only been there a few days she already had developed a reasonable tan on her body and legs, as well as something of a healthy glow on her face. She had never been one for using a great deal of make-up. She believed that luckily she never really needed it. Now, apart from the slightest touch of pale pink lipstick and the briefest of eye make-up, the Greek sun had done her work for her. She felt good, bloody good, and now she also realised it was a perfect night on which to feel good, Friday night.

It was always easy in Lindos to forget what day it was. Days on the beach, and evenings and nights in the restaurants, bars and clubs drifted and fused into a blur of one and the same. But, it was Friday night, and Friday nights were traditionally always ones for relaxing and enjoying anywhere in the world. However, she was meeting Jack and his mother in the morning at eleven forty-five so she couldn't go too mad. Nevertheless, she was determined to enjoy her first Lindos Friday night of her new life. Maybe stay out a little later and go to one of the clubs.

This time the woman at the top of the steps of Symposio restaurant didn't have to persuade her. As soon as she said, "Hello," Aileen replied politely, "That's okay, no need to give me the spiel, I've come to try some of this lovely food I've heard you telling people about when I've been passing."

The woman showed her inside, asking as she did if she preferred a table up on the roof or one there. She was middle-aged and slim, with shoulder length dark black hair, and was impeccably dressed in a dark deep blue long dress. Even in her flat soled sandals she was tall.

Symposio was housed in another very imposing old Lindian style stone building. The entrance was through a raised terrace, which had three dining tables on it, at which customers could watch people pass by while they ate. Inside there were four more tables and a wrought iron staircase that led up to the roof terrace, where most of the restaurant's dining tables were located. High on the wall outside to the left of the terraced entrance was a digital display of the time, followed by the temperature. When Aileen arrived at eight-thirty it was showing a still humid thirty-one degrees. The warmth of the evening air was added to by the fact that there was no wind at all, or even the semblance of a breeze. Because of that Aileen decided on the roof terrace and the woman showed her to the wrought iron staircase in the corner that would take her up there. As she reached the top an older Greek guy greeted her, telling her he was the owner, Filip, and showed her to a table in the corner of the roof terrace with what he described as, "A very romantic view of the Acropolis."

She just smiled and never responded. Romance was the last thing on her mind at the moment, even in Lindos. She may not have had romantic company, but at least the food lived up to the build-up. She chose the Lemon Sole and accompanied it with a couple of glasses of pleasant Greek white wine.

After she had finished the main course Filip brought her a complimentary Greek desert. By close on ten she had paid the bill and was making her way downstairs to say, "Yes, it was very good, thanks, and bye," to the woman 'on the door', who had asked if she had enjoyed the food.

Where to go now for a few Friday night drinks? Maybe take up Angelos' suggestion and go to Lindos By Night to start. It was only a short walk up the alley past the Courtyard Bar and up a few steps. So, she'd start there, have one, and think about where to maybe move on to next, unless it was really busy.

The entrance to Lindos By Night was up an initial flight of around a dozen steps just thirty metres or so along the top alleyway. It had two bars. There was a long narrow bar to the left at the top of that first flight of steps, with an area full of tables and chairs outside to the right. Further up another flight of steps, there was another open seating area with tables and chairs and a small bar against the rock face. A key attraction of the top bar was its wonderful view of the Lindos Acropolis, especially when it was illuminated at night. As she entered the doorway to climb the first flight of steps Angelos was standing at the top of them with an attractive young blonde girl. They were chatting, but both ready to meet arriving customers.

"Good evening. You decided to take up my invitation then," he told her with an accompanying smile.

"I did, thought this would be as good a place as any to start for my first Friday night back in Lindos."

"This is Polly," He introduced the girl to Aileen. "Do you want her to find you a table upstairs?"

"No, that's okay I'll just have one drink at the bar. I'm sure I can find an empty stool there, if it's not too crowded."

"Not yet, but in an hour or so no doubt we'll be really busy," Polly told her, in an accent that revealed she was clearly English.

"Okay, good job I came now then," Aileen replied as she left the two of them and made her way up the second flight of stairs. There were, indeed, empty stools at the small bar at the top of the upper terrace area – all of them, in fact. So, she headed straight for one and as she sat down ordered a Gin and tonic. Looking around the terrace she counted only a dozen other customers seated at the various tables, mainly couples. Mike, the DJ, was pumping out his tunes from the raised platform and console in one corner of the terrace. As she surveyed it he offered her a nod of recognition. Perhaps he too remembered her from her previous visit?

By the time she was halfway through her G and T she was no longer the only occupant of the stools at the small bar. An English couple in their mid to late thirties arrived and sat on the two stools to her left. Aileen had engaged in a very brief conversation with one of the young Greek barmen when she ordered her drink as she sat down at the bar. It was the usual couple of questions from him, although for a change it appeared that unlike Angelos and the DJ, Mike, he didn't recognise her from her previous visit. He'd asked how long she was here for and had she been before. She gave him fairly short, straightforward answers of, "Not sure, a couple of months or so maybe," and, "Yes, once, earlier this summer."

His lack of any further response confirmed that he didn't remember her from before, although she didn't actually recall ever sitting at the bar on her previous visit. When she was there with Martin Cleverley the one time, and then Sandra and Richard Weston on another occasion, they had sat on the comfortable softer, lower seats – almost sofa-like – on the other side of the terrace, away from the bar. Angelos served them on those occasions, so there was no reason to think the barman would even have noticed her or the company she was keeping.

As the barman was preparing the drinks for the English couple he did though engage her in conversation once again, asking whether she was staying in the village.

"Yes, I've rented a flat in the centre of the village for two months. So-" she began to reply. But she was interrupted by the guy from the couple on the stools next to her who leaned forward towards the bar, turned the top half of his body in her direction, and asked across his female partner, "That's an Irish accent, isn't? What part?"

Aileen was a bit startled. She didn't really want to get embroiled in any conversations with strangers, even seemingly mundane and innocuous ones, preferring to keep a low profile for the start of her new life.

"Err ... southern Ireland." Her response was deliberately short, although the tone of her voice couldn't disguise her startled reaction.

The guy wasn't giving up though. "Yes, I thought I recognised that, but what part, what part of southern Ireland?"

The ingrained suspicion in her character kicked in. Why is he so keen on knowing the exact part of Ireland was what immediately leapt into her brain? The caution and scepticism of her past life had obviously not disappeared. She settled for an answer that was only partly true.

"Cork," she told him, and quickly tried to shift the focus of their fledgling conversation on to them, "Where are you guys from?"

"London," the guy told her.

Aileen had actually guessed that was the case from their accent when they ordered their drinks. In fact, that had fuelled her paranoia a little, stupidly she now told herself. Just because someone, or some couple, are from London doesn't make them automatically agents of the British Crown, MI6, looking for her. She needed to chill out and just relax, enjoy the surrounding of the wonderful place she was in. And anyway, they did just look like some regular English couple on holiday.

"It's our first time here, arrived yesterday," the guy told her while she was allowing the paranoia to wash out of her brain.

"It is a really beautiful place. We love it already." Now the woman was joining the conversation.

The woman was an attractive, what looked like natural, blonde with a tan that Aileen instantly thought must have been acquired before they arrived. Even though, as Aileen reckoned, she was in her mid to late thirties she had retained her good figure, which she was obviously not shy in showing off to its full. Her low cut vest like tight white t-shirt displayed the attributes of the top half of her body to the full and it was tucked into an almost micro black skirt with a wide leather red belt pulling in her trim waist to its best effect. The only spoilers to her outfit were her totally inappropriate for the Lindos uneven alleyways high-heeled sandals and the rather brassy type look that the clunky gold necklace she was wearing gave. The man was also good looking, in a much more sophisticated way. He was tall, around six foot, and wore a plain dark blue Ralph Lauren polo shirt and some white trousers, accompanied with a pair of dark blue suede boat shoes.

"Yes, yes, it is a beautiful place," Aileen agreed, before she picked up the glass and finished off her drink.

"You been before, or is it your first time too?" the woman asked?

Now the conversation between the three of them really was developing into much more than Aileen preferred. So, she simply answered, "Just the once, earlier this summer."

But the woman wasn't giving up. "And you came back so quickly. You must have liked it. That's what we've said already. We will definitely come back, but we're only here for a week this time."

Aileen was looking for a point in the conversation, a break, a short one at least, where she could get up from her stool, say, "Goodbye," and leave. It wasn't happening though. If anything her new acquaintances were determined to keep the conversation going. She cynically reckoned that the only conclusion must be that they were married, had been for some time, and were desperate for different company and conversation. She had no idea how long they had been married, of course, but a quick glance at the woman's left hand as she lifted her cocktail glass displayed conclusive confirmation of at least one part of Aileen's assumption – a wedding ring and an expensive looking diamond engagement ring. It didn't conclusively mean they were married to each other, however. It could just be-

Her meandering train of thought was interrupted though by the woman turning the top half of her body to face her, offering her hand towards Aileen, and saying, "I'm Elaine by the way, and this is Michael."

Aileen took the extended hand and somewhat awkwardly shook it slightly, telling them, "Aileen."

It was not something she intended to do very much at all during her stay in Lindos, give away her name, except where necessary for her investigation of her mother's past. She felt it was best not to give away too much information about herself, especially to complete strangers. It didn't feel secure. It was the way she had lived for the past twenty years. Even when she had given out information about herself during that time it had predominantly been false. Old habits die hard, and concerns and care over exposing herself by giving away too much, if any, information about herself and her life were very much part of her character. It was the way she had lived her life for over half of it.

However, she wasn't doing very well at extricating herself from her new found company. Perhaps she was out of practice, or maybe just very relaxed now, but before she could try to leave again Michael pointed out, "You've finished your drink. Let us get you another? And perhaps then you can tell us some good places to go in Lindos." He turned to Elaine and added, "We're having another, aren't we dear."

Elaine just nodded.

Aileen really was out of practice as all she could say, after a short hesitation, was, "Oh, ermm … okay, why not? Thank you. It's a Gin and tonic."

The three of them spent the next half-an-hour talking, mostly the couple asking Aileen about Lindos; the best beach, any restaurants she would recommend, or some good bars. By that time Lindos By Night had filled up considerably and she told them, "As you can see now this one is always popular later in the evening, but generally I've found that all of the bars are good, so are the restaurants."

"We found a good one last night," Elaine told her. "It was only our first night so we didn't venture far, didn't really explore the nightlife and bars. But the one we found near our apartment was good, and quite busy, the Lindian House. Have you been there?"

"No, not that one, I haven't, but I did overhear a couple on the beach talking about it today. They seemed to like it."

As they finished their second drink Michael asked Elaine, "Are we going to have another here or-"

Before she could answer Aileen interrupted, offering, "Let me."

Elaine's answer surprised her a little. "Thanks, but we were thinking of going back to that bar we were in last night, the Lindian House, weren't we darling?"

Michael nodded in agreement as Elaine added, "But why don't you come with us? You said you hadn't been there, so you can see what it's like?"

Maybe it was the effect of the alcohol, but Aileen was well and truly in the mood for a Friday night out in Lindos by now, so she readily agreed, "Yes, yes, why not? Thanks. Let's go and have a look there."

10

The Lindian House and Arches club; a surprising proposition and a questionable sighting – never a dull moment in Lindos

The Lindian House was towards the other end of the village, past Symposio restaurant and Antika Bar, through the small square with the tree in the centre surrounded by the low white wall, to the right of Bar404, and fifty metres or so up the slightly inclined part of the hill out of the village. Even though dodging their way through the busy evening drinkers hopping from bar to bar in the main alleyway it took them only three or four minutes to get to the Lindian House bar.

It had an inside bar, a garden outside, reached through that inner bar, with a number of high-backed wicker chairs and tables, and an upper roof terrace with more tables and chairs. The inner bar, which customers entered through, had an area for dancing, some stools at the bar that stretched all along one side, some short padded wall benches and a couple of tables. The DJ area and console was in one corner opposite the bar. It also had a magnificent wooden Lindian carved ceiling. By that time on that Friday night, gone eleven-thirty, the inner bar was packed, with some people trying to dance and other groups just standing and talking. The largest groups dancing and talking appeared to be part of a pre-wedding party, a mixture of members of the Bride's hen party and the Groom's stag party, predominantly in their thirties. The music blasting out was obviously carefully selected by the DJ for the age range of most of the bar's customers in the inside bar.

"Wow! It's certainly busy," Aileen exclaimed loudly above the music to Elaine and Michael as they squeezed their way through the gyrating bodies towards the bar.

"Even more so than last night," Elaine replied, equally as loudly.

They managed to find a corner at one end of the bar to squeeze into and Aileen attracted the attention of one of the young Greek barmen to order them some drinks. While they had a couple of more drinks they spent the rest of the evening watching the various stag and hen party members' antics and dancing until the music stopped at one a.m., as the local village by-law required.

Their viewing entertainment was only interrupted at one point around fifteen minutes before the music went off by one of the young guys in the stag group trying to entice Aileen to dance with him by attempting to grab her hand and persuade her away from the bar. Michael had gone off to the toilet, so perhaps the guy thought the two women were on their own. Anyway, Aileen gave him a friendly smile, but politely declined, withdrawing her hand from his grasp. The incident drew a comment from Elaine and she leaned forward to whisper it in Aileen's ear over the music.

"Looks like you've got an admirer, and a young one at that." A small smile emerged across her lips as she moved her head back away from Aileen's ear.

Although she refrained from voicing it to her two companions what was going through Aileen's brain was yep, I seem to attract them, or maybe it's just Lindos? But, no thanks, I don't need that at the moment. I can live without that, for now at least, got other things to concentrate on.

Michael was still in the toilet, which was just as well. Before Aileen could reply to Elaine's initial comment what she added just after she drew her face back surprised her. It was definitely not what she expected to hear at all.

"I can certainly understand that though. You do have a certain attraction. I think so anyway, and I know Michael does." As she told her that Elaine deliberately stared intensely and provocatively straight into Aileen's eyes.

Not exactly something you expect to hear from someone you had only met a few hours before. Aileen maintained a blank facial expression, determined to exhibit no element of shock or surprise at all. She was good at that. After all, she'd had plenty of training in it in her past. With as deadpan an expression as she could muster in the circumstances she merely responded with, "Oh, it's just young men I think. He's obviously had a few too many drinks." She was deliberately choosing not to address Elaine's comments about her and Michael's thoughts.

As Aileen picked up her drink, took a rather considerable sized swig for relief, and then placed it back on the bar in front of her it was now Elaine who tried to grab her hand. Not in as forceful manner as the young man had, but in a quite soft, obvious and meaningful way. This time Aileen found herself offering Elaine a small smile as she quickly withdrew her hand from the woman's grasp. She hoped it would convey just enough of an indication that she was declining what she assumed was some sort of invitation, although this time she was certain it wasn't one to dance.

It appeared that Elaine had taken the hint. Soon after Michael re-joined them from the toilet the conversation between the three of them returned to the more mundane topic of commenting on the gyrations of their various fellow Lindan House customers. However, Aileen did notice that immediately upon his return Elaine whispered something in Michael's ear. Her instincts suggested that Elaine was telling him that Aileen had declined their advances, and what would obviously have been some sort of offer to spend the night with the two of them.

Given the awkwardness of what had just transpired Aileen was relieved that there was now relatively little time before the music would stop, calculating that would be an appropriate point to make her exit and leave the company of her new found 'friends'. So, that is what she did, wishing them an awkward, "Goodnight," and "No doubt see you around the village over the next week." As she said that Elaine leaned into her to kiss her on the cheek, telling her, "Yes, I hope so," in a purposefully rather soft and seductive tone.

"Phew," Aileen mumbled as she emerged through the doorway of the Lindian House. Never a dull moment in this village, she thought. As she made her way down the slight slope of the alley outside the bar she could still feel the heat of embarrassment inside her from what had just happened. It wasn't exactly disappearing very quickly as despite the time of night it remained a warm, humid atmosphere in the narrow alley between the white high walls and shuttered shops. In her somewhat shocked and a little dazed state she thought there was no way she could go straight to bed after that. She definitely needed another drink.

From her previous visit she knew that the only places to get a drink at that time, gone one o'clock, and hear some music would be one of the clubs in the village. Arches was the nearest, just down the slope and up the alley opposite Yannis Bar. So, she headed there, not expecting it to be very crowded yet. For clubs in Lindos it was still early, even on a Friday night.

Appropriately the entrance to Arches was through an arched doorway into a courtyard. The interior of the club was through a door sound lock system. As it is in the centre of the village, and because of the ban on music after one o'clock at night, there were two doors with a compartment between them. As the customers came in the outer door was opened by one guy outside. Once they were all inside the compartment between the two doors and the outer door was closed the inner door was opened by another guy inside the club and the customers were let in. It prevented the noise from the music in the club from getting out and disturbing the residents in the village, breaking a local by-law. As a result no music could be heard outside in the courtyard and it was not really possible to gauge just how many people were inside,

Aileen had been there a couple of times with Martin Cleverley on her previous Lindos visit. She liked the place and its atmosphere. Inside there were two bars, one opposite the entrance and another at the far corner, diagonally opposite the entrance.

That particular evening Aileen was surprised just how crowded it was already, at a time still relatively early for Lindos clubbing. She decided that rather than fight her way through the crowds of clubbers – some of them attempting to find some space to dance – she would just get a Gin and tonic at the nearest bar, opposite the entrance. She'd had quite enough excitement for one evening from Elaine's evident proposition, so she would be quite happy now drinking her G and T alone at the bar, listening to the music, and people watching some of the clubbers. They were a mixture of young Brit and Greek bar and restaurant workers in the village, as well as some tourists. Although, because of the crowded nature of the club her view towards the far end of it, and the other bar, was somewhat obscured.

For twenty minutes she was more than happy with the relief of just her own company. So much so that having finished her first G and T she decided that she'd have another one. Just after she ordered it, and the young black barman placed it on the bar in front of her as she handed him the money for it, she realised she needed to go to the toilet. She knew from her previous visits with Martin that the toilets were outside in the courtyard, which meant she was faced with a dilemma of what to do with her fresh drink while she went. She certainly didn't want to trust to leaving it unattended on the bar, not just because someone might take it, but because she was always wary of the possibility of it being spiked with something. Not that she'd ever heard of that during her previous Lindos visit, and had no reason to believe that sort of thing happened here. But she wasn't taking any chance. She managed instead to get the attention of the black barman and asked his name. He looked a bit surprised, but told her, "Levi, is there a problem with your drink?"

From his accent she guessed he was English. She pushed her drink towards him across the bar, telling him, "No, no problem, but I need to go to the toilet and I don't want to leave it unattended. Can you put it behind the bar for me please till I come back?"

He just nodded, smiled and took the drink to place it on the low shelf behind him while Aileen made her way towards the inner sound lock door and waited for the guy to open it.

As she left the toilet a few minutes later and started to make her way across the courtyard back into the club she heard a shout from behind her.

"Hey! You're the woman from outside that bar from a couple of nights ago."

She turned around to see the owner of the voice was the young guy in his mid-twenties who had tried so hard to chat her up outside Pal's two nights before, and had paid for her drink.

"You never came back outside," he continued. His slurred speech revealed that he had obviously had a good night's drink. "You going back inside? We're all in there, my mates from the other night."

He was swaying a little as he spoke. Aileen thought the best thing to do was to humour him, thinking that as soon as she got back inside the crowded club it wouldn't be very difficult to slip away from him. So, she just responded with a, "Yes."

With that though he put his arm around her shoulders, swaying and almost leaning on her as he did so, and attempted to guide her with him towards the door. It wasn't very difficult for Aileen to stop walking and remove his arm from around her shoulders. He wasn't really in any fit state to put up much resistance. Besides, in her past she'd dealt with much stronger, bigger and tougher guys than him. She could easily swat him aside, especially in his obviously very inebriated state.

"Don't do that, please," she told him firmly as she removed his arm.

Unfortunately, his verbal mental advances weren't as feeble or as weak as his physical one and he replied, "Don't be like that. I told you outside the bar before that you were a very attractive woman. I'm sure you'd like a younger guy to enjoy yourself with tonight, wouldn't you?"

As he finished he attempted to place his arm around her shoulders again. In his drunken state he wasn't aware at all that his voice had been raised as he told Aileen that. Hers certainly was, deliberately so, as she told him firmly once again, "I said don't do that. Get off me, now!"

She was about to demonstrate forcibly to him that he really should do as she said, but that wasn't necessary as a large strong hand landed on his shoulder from behind him. The hand belonged to Chris, the large, well-built guy who worked as a 'meet and greet' person at the archway entrance to the Arches courtyard. He certainly wasn't someone you would want to mess with, and on the very rare occasions when there was any problem or incident with customers who had too much to drink and showed any aggression he dealt with them quickly, removing them from the club premises.

As he placed his hand on the guy's shoulder he simply told him, "Don't do that, sir. The lady told you not too."

The guy spun around, and for a fleeting moment it appeared that his first, somewhat unwise, thought was to confront whoever it was who's hand had been placed on his shoulder.

"Get off me! What's it got-"

His aggressive response petered out into the warm Lindos night air. As the size and stature of Chris loomed into his less than clear vision he clearly sensibly thought better of it.

At that point another man joined them from over by the courtyard entrance arch and told Aileen, "I'm the owner, Valasi. Is there a problem?" Before she could answer he added, "I met you before didn't I? You were here with Martin a few weeks ago."

The young guy looked startled, obviously thinking just what sort of hornet's nest had he stirred up here? Meanwhile, Aileen was briefly thinking Christ, there's that bloody name again, before she replied, "Yes, that's right, with Martin, but no, there's no problem thanks. I think the young man has had a little too much to drink."

"It seems like it," Valasi agreed, followed by a very slight nod to Chris, who now put his arm around the young guy's shoulders and told him, "I think it's best if you leave now, sir, don't you?"

The young guy looked nonplussed. It seemed his Lindos long Friday night had come to something of an abrupt, unscheduled end. Fully realising now that it would be very unwise to argue with the well-built Chris he basically could only mumble, "Err … err … but I just need to tell my friends inside that I'm-"

"No doubt you can call them after you've left. I presume you've got your phone?" Valasi told him.

He just nodded, and after another brief signal of a nod from Valasi, Chris guided the guy to the archway and out into the alley, bidding him a courteous, "Goodnight, sir," as he weaved his way down the alley towards the centre of the village.

"Thanks," Aileen told Valasi. "Now I need that drink that I left inside with your barman."

Valasi smiled and told her, "You're welcome, but if any of his friends inside cause you any problem just let one of my bar staff know and we'll sort it."

With that he headed back to stand with Chris by the archway and Aileen made her way through the sound vacuum and back inside to collect her drink. After all that she decided that would be her last drink for the night. Her glass was still quite full, so when she finished that one she'd be off to her bed. While she did that she found herself a spot at the corner of the bar and entertained herself by watching the various clubbers drinking and dancing.

Ten minutes or so into finishing her final drink for the evening, however, something more occurred on that eventful Lindos evening. Something she found difficult to cope with, or explain to herself. From where she was stood at the corner of the bar she exchanged a few brief words of mundane conversation with the barman, Levi. Just the usual questions like, "Is this your first season here? Do you like it?" Apart from that she spent her time watching other customers getting served at the bar and occasionally peering down the length of the club, looking at her fellow clubbers as best she could through the crowd. She had almost finished her drink when she looked behind her to check if there was a queue of people waiting to leave at the inner exit door to the sound vacuum area. If there was she might as well wait until that group had been let out and she would get herself at the front of the next one. However, as she looked over towards the door she got a surprise. There was, indeed, a group of seven or eight people waiting to leave. It was only the back of him that she could see, but the third person from the front looked familiar. She did a double-take to try and check, but she could only really see the back of his head. As the door opened just after she looked once more the man entered the sound vacuum compartment and the rest of those waiting piled in behind him.

She left the remainder of her drink and rushed as quickly as she could through the crowded club towards the inner exit door. However, she had to wait while those people coming in through the outer entrance door were enclosed in the sound vacuum compartment and then let in through the inner door. By the time she got out into the courtyard there was no sign of the man she thought she recognised. She walked quickly over to Valasi, who was still at the archway with Chris, and asked, "Was that Martin, Martin Cleverley who just left?"

"Sorry, we were talking to some Greek friends of mine who just arrived and were on their way in, so I didn't see the people leaving. I couldn't really say," he explained. "But I'm sure he would have said, 'Hello,' if he came in earlier, and I didn't see him so ... I've known him quite a few years."

"I see, I must have been mistaken. I thought I saw him leaving," Aileen replied. "It's not important though. I was leaving anyway. Goodnight, and thanks for the help earlier," she added.

"Goodnight, and if it was him, and I see him, I'll tell him you're here," Valasi replied.

As she made her way the twenty yards or so up the alley to her flat and bed, she shook her head slightly, mumbling quietly, "What the fuck was that? Why was I trying to catch up with someone I thought was Martin Cleverley when I'd decided there was no way he could be part of my life before? Stupid, bloody stupid."

What really troubled her was that almost subconsciously she set about trying to catch up with him, like some sort of reflex emotional reaction that she thought had been trained out of her years ago. Did that really mean that deep down, deep inside her, she was hoping their paths would cross again?

Part Four: 1976

11

Jack's mother – a history lesson and evasion?

Just before eleven forty-five the next morning Aileen was waiting outside the Courtyard Bar for Jack Constantino to arrive and take her to meet his mother. After her late Friday night she slept in, catching up on her sleep until ten-thirty. She'd taken a quick, deliberately luke warm shower, before grabbing a coffee and a croissant from the nearby Café Melia. She took advantage of more of the hot August sunshine while consuming those sat outside the cafe. Waiting for Jack she felt relaxed, pleased with her new life and its freedom in such pleasant surroundings, despite the approaching midday heat eroding most of the cooling benefit of her shower. She was starting to feel decidedly warm, starting to sweat a little. She had decided that the best way to combat the heat was by putting on her thinnest and lightest cotton, quite short, white dress, sensibly topped off with a wide brimmed straw hat displaying a broad white ribbon. She had removed it and was fanning herself in order to try to cool down when Jack appeared from down the small flight of steps from the alleyway above the bar.

"Good morning," he greeted her. Seeing her hat fanning actions he added, "Sorry have you been waiting long? We did say eleven forty-five."

"No, that's okay. Only got here a few minutes ago, just got a bit warm walking through the village."

"Yes, it can be hard work dodging the tourists at this time of day in the crowded alleyways. That's why I usually go along the back alleys at this time," he told her. "We can go that way, along the back alley to my mother's. It's not very far along there."

He pointed back up the steps as he told her that and Aileen placed her hat back on her head, saying, "Okay, let's go," as she did.

As they reached the top of the small flight of steps he told her, "I think I told you that my mother's English is quite good. She picked up quite a lot of it when she used to work in the small bar her and my father had here before the Courtyard, from the English tourists mainly when they first started to come to Lindos in larger and larger numbers in the seventies. Anyway, if there's anything she's not sure about I can always translate."

"Yes, you did tell me, but I'm sure it'll be fine, Jack. We'll manage."

Just as he thought, what he'd said wasn't new to her.

Trying as much as possible to make it sound like just a casual enquiry, changing the subject she asked, "I think you said a couple of nights ago that you've seen no sign of Martin recently, since he left at the end of June? So, he hasn't been in the bar since?"

Jack just shook his head once, telling her, "No, he hasn't. As I said, he usually comes back in late August or early to mid-September, so I haven't seen him recently."

"It's just that I thought I saw him last night leaving Arches. I only saw his back, or what I thought was his back, through the crowd. It was really busy. Perhaps not, but I did think it was him briefly," she explained.

"I don't think it could have been. He usually comes in the bar the first night he arrives, and he hasn't been in, so …"

"Hmm … I must have been mistaken then. Oh well, as I said, it was crowded. He was leaving and I didn't get a clear view of the guy."

She didn't anticipate or expect what he told her next. That was much more of a surprise, and a worrying one for her.

"There was a guy in the bar asking about you last night, though. Well, I assumed it was you he was asking about."

She tried to ensure that she displayed no element of surprise or concern on her face or in her reaction. So, she just said in as relatively matter of fact way as possible, "Really? Me? What makes you think that?"

"He asked if I'd seen an Irish woman on her own in the village, whether anyone like that had been in the bar over the last few nights. There are a few Irish people who come here on holiday regularly and use the bar. I know them quite well of course, as regulars. But they are either couples, or groups of two or three or more Irish girls. You're the only one who has been in the bar on your own recently. That's why I assumed it was you he was asking about, although he didn't actually ask about you by name. Maybe a friend of yours?"

Continuing to appear not overly concerned while they walked along the back alley, she informed Jack as nonchalantly as she could, "Shouldn't think so, no one knows I'm here. It was a bit of a spur of the moment thing, deciding to come. What was he like? Was he English, Irish?"

"No, not Irish, English, mid to late thirties I'd say, tall, and looked quite fit. When I asked he said it was his first time in Lindos. He only stayed for one drink. I told him that there was an Irish woman who'd been in, although I never named you. I told him that you hadn't been in the bar last night at all. It was quite late on, so I said that I didn't think you'd come in now. Then he asked if you were staying in the village and did I know where. I just told him I didn't know, which I don't anyway, so-"

"It wasn't my friend Sandra's husband was it, Richard? He was here with us at the end of June for part of our holiday," she interrupted, now sounding a little more concerned.

"No, I remember him. He was a bit of a prat. No, I would have recognised him straight away. He was unforgettable. As I said, a bit of a prat, in fact, a lot of one." Changing the subject, Jack added as he pointed to a flight of six more stone steps, "My mother's place is just at the top of these."

Aileen's mind was still dwelling on what he had told her. She surreptitiously bit her bottom lip slightly as she turned over in her head what he'd said. What was going through her brain, now in overdrive, was who the bloody hell could it have been that was asking about her? It obviously wasn't Martin. Jack knows him and would have said, and he'd just told her he hadn't been in the bar. If he was English it wouldn't be one of the Bhoys. It didn't take much deduction for her to swiftly come to the conclusion that it must be one of the bastards from

MI6, looking for her because of her disappearance from service in the agency. Who knows, perhaps they'd somehow figured out it was her who had done it and they were hunting her down for retribution for Sandra's assassination. It was odd though that they hadn't asked Jack about her by name. As far as MI6 was concerned she was Aileen Regan. That was the false name and passport the Bhoys had produced for her to infiltrate MI6. So, if the guy asking Jack about an Irish woman was an MI6 agent, why did he not ask him using her name? The only explanation that she could think of was that the agent assumed she would be using another false name. Still seemed odd though, and not very professional or efficient, even for MI6.

Her deliberations were abruptly interrupted as they reached the top of the steps and Jack rapped the iron door knocker on the large dark wood door, telling her, "This is it."

That prompted Aileen to put any thoughts out of her mind for now about just who the guy asking about her was, and instead concentrate on what she wanted to ask Jack's mother.

As the door swung open it revealed a woman who had retained her elegant and stylish good looks to very good effect. She was of average height, with well-groomed shoulder length grey hair that framed her high cheek bones perfectly, contributing to the overall immediate striking impact of her appearance and her face that was one full of the character of her years. Jack had told Aileen previously that she was now seventy-two years old, although her overall appearance definitely belied that. That was added to by the plain and simple, but smart and effective, calf-length black cotton dress she wore.

As she held the door open she said, "You must be Aileen. It's good to meet you. Do come in."

"Thank you for seeing me, Mrs " Aileen started to reply as she removed her hat and stepped inside to a short hallway. Before she could finish, however, Jack's mother interrupted with, "Please, call me Eleni."

"Then, thank you for seeing me, Eleni," Aileen repeated, accompanied by a slight warm smile.

At the end of the hall Eleni led them into a good-sized lounge, then through some large glass sliding doors on one side of it and onto a terrace with a wonderful panoramic view of Lindos bay. The terrace was surrounded on all sides by a low white wall. Being at the top of the village had the advantage of looking down on the whole of Lindos out towards the Acropolis and the bay, making even the climb up the slight hill and the steps very much worthwhile. In the centre of the terrace was a large painted white circular wrought iron table with four chairs covered in comfortable looking detachable dark green cushions. A large beige linen parasol shade emanated from a hole in the centre of the table, providing ample shade from the now scalding hot sun.

Even though Aileen had only walked along the short hall and through the lounge she could observe that many of the elements of what was obviously a traditional Lindian style villa had been preserved, despite some apparent modernisation, such as the large glass sliding doors. A lot of the dark wood fittings, so typical of Lindos interiors, had been carefully preserved.

"Wow! What a great view," Aileen remarked as the three of them emerged onto the terrace.

Eleni allowed a brief smile of satisfaction to spread across her lips as she looked over at Jack and replied, "Yes, I love it. Of course, Jack says I should move now. He says the steps and the hill are getting too much for me, and since his father died four years ago he has been constantly telling me I should leave here. He's tried to persuade me to move somewhere where it's flatter, or even in with him and his wife. But I love it here, and I love this view. I love being able to sit here and see it every day. I still feel fine, feel fit, so why should I move?"

Jack sat in a respectful silence while his mother explained. From his fidgeting body language he obviously disagreed, but wasn't about to air that view in front of a guest in his mother's house.

In any case Eleni never really gave him any opportunity to do so as she continued.

"Take a seat, Aileen. I've prepared us a small Greek lunch, just some pittas, humus, tzatziki, some olives and a Greek salad. I'll just go to the kitchen and bring it out. What would you like to drink, a small glass of cold white wine perhaps? I'm having one."

"That sounds very nice. It's very good of you. Thank you, yes, a small white wine will be lovely, and perhaps some water please? I must say, your English is very good."

"No wine for me, I'll just have a small bottle of Mythos please mother," Jack told her.

"Okay, well you can come and help me bring it all out here," Eleni told her son, adding to Aileen, "Thank you, I've picked up a lot of my English from English tourists over the years."

As the two of them disappeared inside Aileen placed her straw hat on the table, took her small notepad and pen from her bag, and then relaxed back on the cushioned chair enjoying the wonderful view of Lindos village and the bay shimmering in the heat below. This was definitely better than pushing a bastard under a London tube train, or spending her life shooting people. Her calm, relaxed mood was abruptly interrupted, however, by recalling what Jack had told her on their walk to his mother's place. Just who was the guy asking about her in the Courtyard Bar? If, as she'd convinced herself seemed most likely, he was an MI6 agent, what was she going to do about him? Kill him? Another assassination? Was she ever going to be able to be completely free of that and her previous life, ever going to be able to put it all behind her once and for all?

It seemed bizarre to be contemplating that in such beautiful surroundings, gazing out at such a lovely view. She was forced to put all those thoughts out of her head for now though, as Jack and his mother emerged out onto the terrace with trays full of food and drinks for lunch.

"This looks great. Thank you again, Eleni. I am getting to like your village of Lindos more and more every day," Aileen remarked.

"Jack said you are staying for a couple of months?" Eleni asked as she leaned across the table, picked up an empty plate and began to serve some of the Greek salad on it before handing it to Aileen.

"Yes, that right, maybe even a bit longer, depending on what I find out about my mother's stay here. She was here for a couple of summers from 1976."

"Jack told me that's what you wanted to talk to me about. There weren't many here then, but I do remember one Irish woman here around that time. Would that have been your mother?"

"Yes, I guess so. She was from West Cork, just like me."

"Well, as I said, there was an Irish woman working here then that I remember, but her name was O'Mara, Mary O'Mara, not Regan. Jack told me your name is Regan?"

Aileen thought briefly about interrupting her to explain, but decided it was best to just let her carry on and explain after.

"In fact, for the first couple of weeks after she came to Lindos that first summer she worked in our family bar, a small one we had in the village before we got the Courtyard Bar. It was up the alley next to what is now Socrates Bar, where the Crazy Moon Bar is now. I don't think she liked the long hours, and she managed to get a job as a Tour Rep with Olympic Holidays after those two weeks. They were starting to really take off here at that time as more and more British tourists started to come here. We stayed friends of sorts, more acquaintances I suppose you'd say, if that's the right word in English."

Aileen nodded, confirming it was.

"Anyway, we weren't what you'd describe as really good friends, but I used to see her around the village. And she used to come into the bar for a drink from time to time, sometimes with some of her Olympic clients, British tourists. She always seemed very popular with the tourists, especially the young men."

As she finished saying that last sentence Eleni allowed herself a small knowing smile.

Now Aileen was excited at what she'd just heard. In her excitement she was eager to interrupt, but she didn't want to stop Eleni's flow of recollections. Eventually though, after she finished Aileen told her, with a betrayal of clear excitement in her voice, "That was my mother. Mary, Mary O'Mara. That's my maiden name, O'Mara. Regan was my married name and I kept it after my divorce as I couldn't be bothered with all the bureaucracy of changing it."

Once again, Aileen wasn't being truthful about her surname being different from her mother's. It was easier to use the same explanation she'd given Jack in his bar two nights ago.

A look of amazement stretched across Eleni's face as she slowly lowered her fork onto her salad filled plate. She hesitated for a few seconds, looking as if she was searching for what to say next. There was a clear reticence, even incredulity, in her voice as she looked across at Aileen and said eventually, "So, that was your mother? Mary was your mother?"

It was as if she didn't want to believe it, or at the very least was now wondering just how to continue and answer any questions Aileen had about her mother and her time in Lindos. How much could she reveal? How much should she reveal? She knew there were other people, Greek families, who, like her, lived in the village today who would have been living there in those two summers when Aileen's mother lived and worked there. Lindos was a close-knit community back then, still was now to some extent, and Eleni wasn't a gossip. She didn't indulge in the everyday stories that some of the locals repeated in the various cafes and bars, some of them from the distant past. Not least because there was always doubt in her mind as to just how true they were, how much they had been coloured and embellished by often romanticised times past in the village. As far as Eleni was concerned those were black and white times, with sepia pictures, but now some of the stories she had overheard in the village cafes between some of the locals appeared to be technicolour portrayals of what had happened back then.

While those perplexing thoughts raced through Eleni's mind Aileen was confirming the answer to her question, and expanding, raising even more of a dilemma in Eleni's mind as to how far she should go in telling Aileen what she remembered about her mother.

"Yes, Mary was my mother. But finding out more about her stay here is only part of why I came, and I was hoping that someone, you now perhaps, could help me with the more important part of my reason for being here; to find out about my father, my birth father. You see-"

Eleni interrupted, fearing what was coming. "Your father, I don't see how I-"

Now, it was Aileen's turn to interrupt, saying bluntly, "I think he was Greek, from Lindos."

To Aileen's surprise Eleni's face and actions betrayed no emotion whatsoever. She merely reached for her wine glass and took a sip, then told Jack to go and fetch the bottle from the fridge as she wanted a top up and she was, "Sure Aileen would like another glass."

As he started to get up to fetch the botte of wine Aileen looked across at Jack and frowned a little in disbelief at Eleni's apparent lack of reaction and complete disregard of what she had just told her. "No more wine for me thanks, Jack," she told him.

"Just for me then," Eleni responded.

Realising that Eleni was not going to offer any response to her assertion that she believed her father was Greek and from Lindos, Aileen relayed more to her of what she knew in an attempt to explain why she had come to that conclusion. She put down her fork, took a deep breath, and sat back in her chair.

"I was born in April 1978 in West Cork in Ireland, Eleni. On my birth certificate it states, 'Father unknown'. My mother never disclosed the name of my birth father or included it when she registered my birth. She married the man I grew up knowing as my father in 1981, three years after I was born. But I know he wasn't my birth father. He couldn't have been. My mother was obviously here in Lindos when I was conceived, which must have been sometime in July in 1977. I asked my mother a number of times who my birth father was and she refused to tell me. She never even told me he might be Greek. I only started to think that when I found what I did after she died. While I was clearing her house I found some stuff in an old shoe box. That included what looked like an employment contract with Olympic Holidays dated May 1976. There was also a small notebook in which it appeared she made some notes about Lindos, with dates in the early summers of 1976 and 1977."

Eleni simply sat back passively in her chair, expressionless, with not the slightest hint of any kind of emotion across her face as Aileen continued.

"I didn't really see much of my mother at all over the ten or fifteen years or so before she died. I was too caught up in my work, my job, and that caused me to work all over the world, although I had a home in America. That was where I was based, I suppose still am. I remember a few bits from when I was a kid about my mother and my step-father, but I never had any brothers or sisters, never really had much of a family so to speak. So, that's partly why I wanted to come here and see if I could find out more about my birth father after I discovered the stuff in the shoebox. That, and what it stated on my birth certificate, 'father unknown'."

At that point Jack returned from the kitchen with the half empty bottle of wine and proceeded to refill his mother's glass.

"Interesting don't you think mother, especially the letters?" he asked.

That comment did at least prompt a more active instant reaction from Eleni. She sat forward and straightened up in her chair, asking, "What letters?"

"Oh, sorry, Aileen, you haven't got to those yet," Jack explained.

"No, was just about to."

"What letters?" Eleni asked again, now appearing a little agitated, moving forward a little more to the edge of her chair and beginning to fidget awkwardly.

"As well as the Olympic Holidays contract of employment and the notebook I also found three letters that were written in broken English to my mother. They were signed, 'Love, Dimitris'."

Initially Eleni returned to an appearance of displaying no reaction at all to what Aileen was telling her, continuing to sip her wine. That was until Aileen got to the signature part and the name, Dimitris. At that point she stopped sipping from her glass and held it slightly away from her lips in front of her looking stunned. It was obvious that what Aileen had just said about the way the letters were signed, and who by, the name, was something Eleni had no idea about. It was being revealed to her for the first time, and she was now struggling to hide her clearly shocked reaction.

   Aileen looked across at her face, glanced at Jack who was now sat back at the table, and then after a long moment of hesitation, as well as some bewilderment at Eleni's reaction, added, "There's more though. In one of them he, Dimitris, had written, 'I miss you very much, Mary. I wait you very long time in Lindos, to see you with our new arrival'. So, when I read that it started me thinking that perhaps my father was this Dimitris, a Greek. It seems a strong possibility given when I was born, April 1978, and that particular letter was dated March of that year, as well as what he'd written about their 'new arrival'. So, that's why I came back here, and why I asked Jack if he knew anyone I could talk to from that time. To try and find out who my birth father really was, and he suggested you might be able to help."

   After another long moment of silence, during which Eleni took another sip of her wine, still with a stunned look on her face she simply asked a little brusquely, "Do you have the letters here?"

   "In my bag."

   As she said that Aileen reached down for her handbag, took out the letters, and handed them across to Eleni.

   Jack's mother placed them on the table and then stood up, explaining that she was going to get her reading glasses. When she returned she removed her glasses from the case and put them on. She slowly picked up the letters, walked towards the edge of the terrace and the low wall, and read each of them studiously in silence, while Jack and Aileen exchanged puzzled glances. When she was part of the way through reading the final letter of the three she turned back to ask Aileen, "So, you think he meant you when he wrote, 'our new arrival'?"

   Aileen merely nodded and with that Eleni turned back towards the view of the village and continued reading. She stopped suddenly, looked up from the letter she held in her hand and stared in silence out towards the looming Acropolis. She stood there not uttering a word for what seemed like a very long half minute or so. Aileen and Jack exchanged bewildered glances in silence once more.

Eventually, this time without turning to face them, Eleni asked, "What does it mean do you think, this bit where he writes, 'But we cannot live here. It will be impossible. I have a cousin in Crete. We can go there'?"

Aileen looked across at Jack, frowned and shrugged her shoulders towards him. Not entirely sure why Eleni was asking that she just replied, "I assume by 'here' he means Lindos, but I don't really understand why."

"Yes, that's the way I read it, Lindos. They couldn't live in Lindos together, and with a baby, you."

While she said that Eleni remained standing with her back to them. She had removed her reading glasses and was once again gazing out over the sun-drenched beautiful white houses of the village and the Acropolis towering over it.

Another minute or so passed while she continued to stand there and gaze out at the village, all the while clasping the three letters tightly in her right hand which she had allowed to drop down by her side. It was as though she was desperately trying to figure out what to say, how to respond. Finally, she turned and walked back to sit once more at the table. As she lowered herself into her chair she handed the letters back across the table to Aileen. Then still without speaking she leaned forward to pick up her wine glass and finish the last of the wine within it.

She placed the glass back on the table and took a deep breath, as if she was deliberately composing herself, or at least trying to recompose herself.

"Well, Dimitris is a very common Greek name, Aileen," she eventually began, in an almost 'matter of fact' manner. "It was even Jack's father's name so-"

"Yes, he told me," Aileen interrupted.

Eleni cast a glance sideways at Jack before she continued, "Oh, he did, well, at that time, in 1976, there were quite a few youngish men called Dimitris in the village, so-"

Now it was Jack who interrupted. "Yes, there were. For instance, the husband of mother's best friend, Cristina, was called Dimitris, wasn't he mother, as well as quite a few of the guys who worked in the bars and the restaurants?"

"Err … yes, yes, that's right. Yes … err … there were quite a few guys in the village with that name." Eleni seemed a little flustered now, and was hesitating, but eventually continued, although avoiding as she did so expanding on any reference to her best friend and her husband."

She was rambling a little now, however, and Aileen was struggling to really follow or understand at that point the relevance of what Eleni was telling them. Nevertheless, she thought it best not to interrupt and ask, but just to let her continue.

Jack decided otherwise though. "What are you saying, mother? I'm not sure I follow, and I don't think Aileen does either judging by the look on her face."

Eleni leaned forward and poured herself some water into an empty glass while Jack and Aileen waited for her explanation. She took a drink from it and then continued. What she said surprised Aileen, and even Jack to some extent. It seemed like an almost brutal acute handbrake turn change of direction. It was a clear change of the subject in respect of the name Dimitris, as for some reason only known to her she completely ignored any reference to whoever the Dimitris in Aileen's mother's letters may have been.

"Tourism was just starting to really take-off and expand in the village at that time. Your mother was one of first Tour Reps, not just for Olympic, but in general. It was a time of, how can I put this delicately, a crazy time. A time when people really enjoyed themselves, especially young tourists and the Tour Reps. There were not always barriers, and even if there were they were often pushed to the limits by them. We saw it quite a bit in the bar in the evenings. So, I'm sorry to tell you, Aileen, but I think it honestly really could have easily been one of the young British tourists who is your father. From what I remember, your mother was in our bar with quite a few of them on a lot of nights over those two summers, and from what I heard back then around the village it wasn't just our bar. She often went off to the club, the disco down by the Main Beach, with them, especially during that second summer of 1977. I saw her there with groups of tourists quite a few times during that summer. She was there every time I went down there anyway, and always with groups of young British tourist men. She always said hello to me, but she was pretty drunk quite a few times, so it seemed to me. Although, one thing I will say about your mother, is that she could definitely drink. It did take quite a lot to get her drunk, and alcohol was really cheap here then for the tourists."

This wasn't exactly what Aileen was hoping or expecting to hear. Her early excitement had been overwhelmed and dampened by quite a large dose of scepticism over just why Eleni had suddenly changed tack and was now disparaging her mother's character, apparently gladly. However, Aileen was far from stupid. One of the things she'd learned during twenty years of training was to look behind what someone was actually telling her, and ask why they were telling her that. So, in her mind she was mulling over the question of quite why Eleni had suddenly changed the overall direction and emphasis of her recollections. Why was she now deliberately completely ignoring the question of who Dimitris was and relaying this other, somewhat strange, narrative? At that point she decided to challenge her on it, and try and bring her back to what was of most interest to her.

She looked across at Jack briefly, who was looking equally as confused by his mother's sudden change of focus, and then asked, "But what about Dimitris, Eleni? Do you really have no idea who he was, who he could be?" Her voice changed to an ever so slightly more aggressive tone as she quickly added two more questions. "But why are you telling me all this about my mother and young British tourists? Do you think she was lying when she wrote those letters to Dimitris?"

Eleni sat back in her chair, took a sip of her water, followed by another deep breath, before she answered, with her voice now betraying an element of forceful determination.

"Because, Aileen, no, I'm not saying she was lying. But you don't really know if she, your mother, knew for sure it was this man Dimitris who was the father, your father. You only know, only can see, what she wrote in that particular letter, perhaps after she had written previously, at another time, and told him he was? But how do you, we, know that she knew that for certain? How could she be so sure, and for what reason? And I certainly don't recall anyone saying that they knew she was pregnant when she left here in that October in 1977."

Eleni now appeared absolutely determined to put some seeds of doubt in Aileen's mind. Her latest comments appeared to completely contradict what seemed to Aileen a logical deduction from what was in Dimitris' letter about 'our new arrival', that it was his baby, her. What Eleni was trying to do didn't make sense. Aileen realised what she was trying to do, but was now totally bewildered, wondering just what possible motive Eleni could have to try and persuade her away from that assumption?

Eleni was set on that path, however, and never let up at all for one second in trying to plant those seeds of doubt in Aileen's mind. The Irish woman was still trying to read behind what she was now doing, and figure out why as Jack's mother continued; all the while he also looked equally bemused.

"As I said before, you have to realise and fully understand just what it was like here then, Aileen, in the village, with all those tourists arriving in greater and greater numbers, especially the young ones."

Aileen could see that Eleni wasn't going to be deterred in any way from saying what she obviously now intended to say, so she just let her ramble on without interruption. And Jack certainly wasn't going to interrupt his mother at that point, even if he also could not really be sure why she was saying what she did.

Eleni merely got increasingly off the subject of Dimitris.

"The tourists started to come at first in the nineteen-sixties, towards the end of those years, when some of the big tour operators from inside and outside Greece got involved and started to bring groups to Rhodes. It was the charter flights, you see. They made it cheaper and easier for the Germans, although initially it was mainly Scandinavians."

As she spoke Eleni had got up from the table and wandered over towards the low wall surrounding the edge of the terrace once more, continuing with her back turned on Aileen and Jack sat at the table. Aileen actually thought she saw Jack raise his eyebrows and shake his head slightly once again portraying his bemusement at what his mother was now telling them. The Irish woman exhibited no emotion whatsoever, even though she shared his bewilderment, thinking it was simply best to let Eleni go on until she had finished what she was obviously determined to tell them. Maybe there would be some point to it eventually that would in the end lead back to Dimitris.

"It was TUI you see. Well, that's what they're called today, of course. Back then it was called Touropa, and they brought the Germans."

She let out a little chuckle as she added, "Of course, the Germans had come before, in 1943, but that's another story, and these Germans were a lot friendlier."

That comment drew another exchange of glances between Aileen and Jack. A frown spread across his face as Eleni continued after a brief pause, turning around to face the two of them.

"Anyway, as I said before, by the middle of the nineteen-seventies the tourism business in Rhodes had really built up, including places like Lindos, and especially for the young Brits, young men and young women. It had a drastic affect, not just for the tourists and economically for the bar and restaurant owners, but also for the social life in Lindos and other tourist spots on the island. The Greek boys, as well as some of the older guys, had a great time. They were just what some of the much freer, liberated sexually, young, and not so young, women from places like Germany, Sweden and Britain came to Greece for and hoping to find. The reputation of the Greek young guys for their mythical good looks, at times over-stated of course, spread far and wide amongst some of the northern European females, and drew them to places like Rhodes and Lindos for a good-time holiday. It was like a whole exciting new world in the late nineteen-sixties and into the seventies for the young Greek guys, just as much as it was for the young northern European women who came here. It's hard to even try to describe it to someone who wasn't here. I was in my twenties and believe me it was all new to us here. And then in 1974, just as I reached thirty, the Military Junta dictatorship was overthrown, and suddenly we all believed we were free. It really did seem then that there would be a new world for us."

Now it was Eleni's turn to slowly shake her head slightly as she paused and made her way back to sit down at the table.

"But that doesn't mean-" Aileen started to say, taking advantage of the gap in what was becoming a bit of a Lindos historical tourism monologue. She never got to finish her sentence voicing her reservations though. Eleni interrupted and continued, with what seemed to be even more removed from what Aileen was seeking to find out.

She allowed herself another small chuckle as she told Aileen, "The funniest thing was that at the very same time as the country's military leaders in their various common important uniforms and sparkling rows of medals were being overthrown, kicked out from governing the country, the young Greek men in places like Lindos were increasingly adopting a common uniform of their own that they thought was necessary to attract the north European female tourists."

She paused briefly to allow herself another chuckle, and then leaned forward to pour another glass of water before continuing and explaining.

"Their common uniform usually consisted though of shirts that were often open down to their navels, revealing a gold chain hanging from their neck. Their equivalent of the overthrown military leaders' medals I suppose you could say. That was accompanied with bell-bottom trousers. I suppose they thought it was fashionable at the time, and attractive. And it did seem to be with the German and British women and girls, from what I saw."

Aileen had really no idea quite where Eleni was going with this revelation of Lindos social history, if anywhere. She resigned herself to just sitting and listening, as well as nodding occasionally, although she really didn't know why she felt it necessary to even do that. It was plainly all she could do at that point, all that Eleni appeared determined to allow her to do. It was a case of waiting for Eleni to finish, while politely humouring her obvious self-indulgent reminiscing. Eventually, it was Jack who interrupted and asked, seemingly deliberately, "Would you like a coffee now, Aileen?"

She looked relieved. It was etched across her face as she replied, "Yes, thanks Jack, that would be good. I could do with one now."

Eleni started to get up to go and make it, but Jack told her, "It's ok, mother, I'll do it."

As he left the terrace and headed inside to the kitchen Aileen tried once more to get Eleni back to the subject of the mysterious Dimitris. "So, was Dimitris one of the Greek young men dressed like-"

Eleni wasn't letting her do that though. It was plainly obvious to Aileen that she wasn't going to. She was increasingly beginning to realise that was the case, although she still wasn't at all sure why. But Eleni's obvious evasion of discussing anything that might relate to who Dimitris was merely raised her suspicions even more about what it was she was avoiding telling her. What was she so determined to hide?

Whatever it was, Eleni was definitely determined not to deal with it. She ploughed on with her Lindos reminiscences, completely ignoring Aileen's attempted intervention related to Dimitris. She stared into the distance and out over the view of the village once again.

"So, you see, Aileen, Lindos, and Rhodes in general, were a real hot spot in the 1970s. Life in Lindos was changing fast back then. Traditional ways were being challenged by the new social responses of a new generation. The older people's roots and ways of life, their cultural identity I suppose you'd say, were being questioned and confronted by the youngsters, and by tourism and the influx of tourists. A lot of the older men actually encouraged their sons to go after as many foreign tourist girls as they could. Maybe they thought they'd missed out on that themselves, the sexual revolution that had been happening elsewhere in parts of the world. Meanwhile, their wives were also Greek mothers who had learned to never criticise their sons. It wasn't part of their culture to do so. Instead, they simply blamed the breakdown in morals on the foreign girls. It was easier for them to do that. What you have to understand is that at that time it was extremely rare for Greek women to have any pre-marital sexual relations. Whereas for the Greek young men it became almost a daily occurrence for them to engage in holiday romances with foreign women tourists, mainly northern European women. Perhaps I should say it became a weekly or two-weekly occurrence as the women tourists came and went. One lot would leave and there would always be another lot arriving to take their place throughout those summers. Of course, some of the Greek men actually ended up marrying the women tourists, the ones that came back for a holiday here time after time, until they lived here and then married. To be fair to the men though, it wasn't only the sex that they embarked on with the women. They showed them around the island, took them to some of the tourist spots, took them to, and showed them some of the clubs around the island, particularly in Rhodes Town. So, overall at that time there were many sexual relationships, or rather sexual encounters. Some developed into love affairs."

At that point Jack returned with the coffee, but it didn't stop Eleni, who continued as Jack poured it for them all.

"It did have wider social implications for places like Lindos, because it meant that the young Rhodes men at that time now had an incentive not to leave to look for work on the Greek mainland or even abroad, but instead stay on the island. They also had an incentive to look elsewhere rather than the Greek girls. One effect of that was that traditions and customs changed slightly, and began to be challenged. It actually became increasingly more difficult for families on the island to marry off their daughters to the young Rhodes men as they focused their attentions more and more on the foreign female tourists. I remember one year there wasn't even a single wedding in the village."

"I see. That must have been-"

In an optimistic hope that what Eleni was now relaying to her about the young Greek men and foreign girls was going to lead her to getting back to talk about Dimitris and her mother Aileen tried once more to intervene after she'd taken a sip of her coffee and placed the cup back on its saucer on the table. Eleni wasn't finished though.

"Not only did they, the young Greek men, become exposed to more, I suppose you'd call them, cosmopolitan European ways that were basically unfamiliar to them, but, ironically, they actually became a key element in the promotion of the rapidly developing and expanding Greek tourist industry, particularly on the islands. They were a sort of tourist attraction. If you like, they were magnets attracting the northern European women to the islands in their thousands in the nineteen-seventies. And many of those women never came just the once. They would come back more and more, over and over again, and bring more and more of their female friends with them. They acted like some large group of unofficial female advertising and public relations executives for places like Lindos, telling their female friends how great it was. How friendly, and all the rest, that the Greek young men were."

Eleni's voice dropped a little in tone and volume as she finished saying that. It was as though remembering and recalling those times had finally made her weary. As though saying it had depressed her, depressed something inside her. She stopped, picked up her coffee and took a sip.

After a long moment of hesitation as the three of them sat in silence, with a strong hint of exasperation in her voice Eleni added, "So, that is what your mother did. She came on holiday with some friends one year, and then came back the following year, 1976, to work here. By that time many foreigners began to work on the island, and some of them settled here, especially the women as it was not uncommon for local men to eventually marry their foreign summer loves, as I said before."

In the hope once more of getting her back on to what she wanted to hear about most Aileen took advantage of the brief mention of her mother by Eleni to ask a somewhat rhetorical question, as she already knew the answer. "But my mother never did?"

Eleni looked across with confusion on her face as she knew Aileen was obviously aware of the answer to that question. Unfortunately, that merely prompted her to become more defensive once more. A hint of aggression returned to her voice.

"Obviously not. From the letters you have it seems she obviously met this Dimitris and maybe they were lovers. All I know is that she stayed here over the first winter at the end of the 1976 season, but then she left abruptly at the end of the following summer in 1977. That's all I know really, all I know about her and any Dimitris."

She was clamming up again. This was getting, no had been, torturous, excruciating, Aileen thought. She'd heard a nice Lindos tourism history lesson, but not much, if anything, about who was Dimitris. Who her father was if it was him. What is more, she was now convinced that a lot of that had been a deliberate diversion by Eleni. There was something more she knew about who Dimitris was, but was purposefully hiding it. From her past life Aileen could quite easily read between the lines and tell when someone was hiding something, or at the very least avoiding telling the truth, deliberately avoiding disclosing information. She was well aware that was what Eleni had been doing through her diversion into a Lindos history lesson.

Because of that, for a very fleeting few moments Aileen even began to wonder if, in fact, Dimitris was actually Eleni's husband, Jack's father, or maybe instead her friend Cristina's husband, Dimitris? Perhaps Eleni had some inkling, saw some signs of it, the affair, back then in those two summers of 1976 and 1977? What if she did and she had refused to admit it to herself or confront Jack's father over it all the time up until his death? But now she had seen it with her own eyes, there in black and white in the letters. Perhaps what shocked her was that she recognised her husband's handwriting. No, surely not. Aileen quickly dismissed that idea, and anyway Eleni was hardly going to admit her suspicions if she'd kept what she actually thought, or maybe even saw, to herself over the past forty years or so. Besides, all that would be way too weird. Jack would be what, her half-brother? She was going round and round in circles in her head. So, she decided that enough was enough. If she was going to get anywhere near the truth of what she wanted to know she would have to take the direct, blunt approach.

12

Jack's mother – finally, the truth perhaps, plus a surprising revelation

Aileen finished the last dregs of her coffee, placed the cup back on its saucer once more, and then leaned forward to look Eleni directly in her eyes as she asked bluntly, "So, Eleni, what was his family name, Dimitris?"

Eleni looked stunned, and even Jack had a bit of a frown of surprise on his face at the somewhat abrupt tone of Aileen's question.

"Err …" Eleni hesitated and stumbled over her words as she tried to respond. "Why do you possibly think I know that after all that I've just told you about what Lindos was like back then?" she eventually managed to say.

Aileen wasn't being deterred though. "Because I think you know. I think all that you have just told us was a complete smokescreen to get away from the subject of who Dimitris was, and I have no idea why you won't say. No, that's not true, maybe I have a suspicion, I think I do know why you won't say."

Now it was Jack who looked shocked at the forceful abrupt tone in Aileen's voice. "Hang on, Aileen, that's-"

He started to try to intervene, but he never got very far. Aileen wouldn't let him. She wanted to make her point and she'd decided that there was only one way to do that, by being forceful and direct. It was a questioning technique that she'd learned very well previously in her MI6 training. Be blunt, be direct and assertive, and don't let the person being questioned wriggle around with their answers. Above all, shock them with the forceful directness of your questions and the rapidity of them. That was precisely the technique she now adopted.

"Do you think that Dimitris was your friend Cristina's husband, the one you mentioned earlier? You see, I think you do, Eleni, maybe you even know it was."

Eleni merely sat motionless, stunned and staring into space out over the Lindos rooftops. Unlike Jack, who was at a loss for words, not knowing quite what to say, she did at least look as if she was trying to carefully consider her response as Aileen reeled off another awkward statement at her.

"I saw your face when I first mentioned his name. I saw it in your face when you were reading those letters. I saw your expression change, saw you hesitate when you read the signature. Perhaps you recognised his writing? To me it was as good as written all over your face that you knew, or at least thought you knew, exactly who Dimitris was."

When she eventually cleared her mind Eleni initially tried to respond. However, her voice was broken and she faltered as she replied, "You were mistaken. I don't ... I don't know where ... where you got-"

Aileen intervened forcibly once again when Eleni faltered once more, determined not to let her off the hook. "I think you do. And I think you know it was your friend, Cristina's husband. He is the Dimitris in the letters, isn't he? He is my father. I don't know how you know, but you do. I suppose I even understand that it could be difficult for you to reveal that, what with him being your friend's husband. But don't you think I have a right to know? Please, Eleni, tell me, tell me what you know."

Aileen was now practically pleading with her. Eleni got up from her chair and walked slowly back and forth once across the terrace. As she stopped to face them a few feet from the table she was biting the inside of one side of her lower lip slightly.

"Are you okay mother," Jack asked, looking concerned, and then glancing across at Aileen with a less than pleased look on his face. "Shall I get you some more water?"

"Yes, please," she answered quietly.

She remained standing there while Jack poured some water into her empty glass and then handed it to her.

She took a swig, allowed herself a small sigh, and then, much to Aileen and Jack's surprise, said, "I saw them. I saw them together that summer, the second summer Mary was here."

Aileen leaned forward to sit on the very edge of her chair, thinking that at last Eleni was going to tell her something that she wanted to know. Perhaps her old MI6 technique and training had come in handy after all, even though she had been determined to leave all that behind her.

"I saw them in the alley late one night, in June I think it was, that second summer in 1977. It could have been early July, but I know it was the evening of one of the festival celebrations in the village, maybe the Medieval Festival night. That is in June usually. Anyway, the village was busy. Most of the main alleys were packed, as well as the Main Square where the festival stalls were, even though it was late. Most of the village was there at the festival, locals and tourists."

She stopped to reach for her glass and take another swig of water, while Aileen and Jack sat in silence transfixed, wondering just what was coming next.

Eleni placed the glass back on the table and decided to sit back down in her chair before resuming.

"We'd been down in the Main Square, Jack's father and me and two other couples from the village who were our friends. There were some stalls in the square and food and drink. It was a good evening. Warm, of course, and most of the locals had turned out for the festival, as well as a lot of the tourists."

She let a slight smile invade her lips at the thought of what were obviously good times, while she once again stared out for a few seconds across the Lindos rooftops towards the Acropolis, figuring out quite how to tell what she was going to say next.

"Because we knew most of the locals and tourists would be at the festival we decided to close the bar at six. There was no point in keeping it open. Anyway, it must have been around ten o'clock I think when I decided I was tired and wanted to go home. Your father wanted to stay for a few more drinks with his male friends, Jack, so I set off to make my way home on my own. But the village was still busy, with crowds in the alleys and most of the shops and kiosks still open. So, I decided the quickest route would be up the slope by what is now the donkey station and along the top alleyway to our place, here. There was an almost full moon and a clear sky, but there were not many lights along there in those days, so it was pretty dark. But when I got about three-quarters away along the alley, just before the slight kink in it by the patch of rough ground now, that's when I saw them. It was dark, as I said, and I only glimpsed them up some steps off the alley going further up to the top of the village. They never saw me, or at least, I'm sure he didn't. He had his back to the opening where I passed by. Anyway, they were too busy locked in what looked like a passionate kiss. She was up against the wall and he was pressed up against her, with her leg raised and wrapped around the top of his leg from what I could see. Obviously I didn't stop."

"But if it was that dark, and you only saw them briefly, how do you know it was them?" Jack asked

"It was dark, but I'd seen Mary in the square at the festival. Not to say hello, but I just saw her across the square with some of her Olympic Rep friends. She had a bright yellow short dress on. It stood out when I saw them, even in the dim light. Part of it was pulled up on one side where she had her leg wrapped around him. He had an equally distinctive bright white shirt on. I saw him in it in the square earlier too. In fact, he was with some Greek guys, some of whom I knew. When I went over then to ask him if Cristina was with him he said she hadn't come because she had a bad headache. We were good friends the four of us, me and my Dimitris, Cristina and her Dimitris. So, I definitely recognised him in that alley, and not just from his white shirt, even from the back, and even though I only got a brief glance."

"And you never said anything, not even to Cristina, nor to him, Dimitris? Not to my mother either?" Aileen asked.

"No, no one, I never even told Jack's father. I suppose I just convinced myself that it was a one-off thing that they had on that night. Maybe they had too much to drink at the festival and got carried away. At one point I even tried to convince myself that perhaps it wasn't him, Cristina's Dimitris. And I'm sorry, Aileen, but as I said before, your mother had plenty of male admirers, and was, how can I put it, very friendly with a lot of them, young locals as well British tourists."

She looked a bit rueful as she added, "People made mistakes, especially in the holiday atmosphere of Lindos even back then, and the sometimes crazy nights here."

Aileen never commented, but she was thinking that she had, indeed, known that top alley, and an encounter quite close to that particular part of it herself when she was in Lindos at the end of June. That was with Richard Weston, and was another story for another time though. She decided she needed to concentrate on what Eleni had been telling them.

"And my mother never said anything to you about it, you seeing them?"

"No, I did think at one point that she must have seen me, or at least made out an image of someone passing by at the bottom of the steps into the alley where they were. But I didn't really know her that well, as I said before, and maybe she didn't see me or if she did, didn't recognise me. I saw her and spoke to her a few times over the rest of that summer when I bumped into her in the village, mostly just to say hello, but no, she never said anything to me about it. As I said, I merely thought that maybe it was a one off, and so I should forget it. I certainly never saw them together again at any time that summer, not even just talking to each other in the village during the day."

"So, you've really no idea then if that was part of an on-going affair, starting from the first summer my mother was here in 1976, or whether it was just a one-off?" Aileen asked, still perched forward on the edge of her seat.

"No, no idea at all. I'm sorry. I definitely didn't know they were having an affair, if they were. In fact, even to this day I never really even knew about any possibility of an affair between them until I read those letters earlier. And, as well as all the things I told you earlier about your mother, with the tourists and young Greek guys in the village, that is why I can't honestly say for certain that Cristina's Dimitris was your birth father," Eleni explained. "Although if he was, that is obviously why he wrote in one of those letters that him and Mary couldn't live in Lindos if they were to be together. If it was him, he was married and the scandal in the village would have been too much. I do know that Cristina's Dimitris had family, cousins, in Crete though, so maybe …"

Her voice tailed off. She hesitated for a moment before adding, as if still trying to persuade herself and Aileen that what she had just told her just couldn't be true or right. "But as I said, they were crazy times. Your mother was no Saint. She was a very, very good looking, attractive young woman. So, despite all this I've just told you, I still think your father could just as easily have been one of the young British tourists on holiday here in that second summer, Aileen."

Aileen wasn't buying that now though. She adopted her blunt, direct approach once again. "Is he still in Lindos, Dimitris, or do you have any idea where he is now? Still with Cristina? The only way to solve this mystery is to just ask him."

Eleni looked a bit shocked once again at the aggressive edge to her voice and the manner in which Aileen rapidly rattled off her questions. She looked across at Jack briefly, before telling Aileen equally bluntly, "He's dead. He died five years ago, a year before Jack's father."

A frown of disappointment immediately spread across Aileen's face. She slumped back in her chair and simply muttered, "That's a pity." She quickly remembered herself and added, "I'm sorry. I didn't mean to appear insensitive. I'm sorry to hear that, about both of them."

"Thank you, but we lost Jack's father four years ago, so I still miss him of course, but it gets easier. But it means we will, you will, never know the answer to your question about who your birth father was, or at least, whether it was Cristina's Dimitris. And I'm sure you understand when I say there is certainly no need for Cristina to know anything about any of this. I'm sure she doesn't know anything about it. If she did I'm certain she would have told me, confided in me I think is the way you say it in English."

"I see," Aileen started to reply. "Yes, that's the right word, and I do understand what you're saying."

"We were good friends, best friends back then, and still are, even closer friends since both our husbands died. That's why I'm sure she would have told me if she knew anything, particularly since her Dimitris died. There's really no point now in bringing all this up with her is there?"

"No, no, obviously, of course, you're right, there's no point." Aileen looked deflated at what she'd just heard. All her earlier optimism had drained out of her as she remained slumped back in her chair. She was left in limbo. Possibly having identified her birth father, but still with some doubt left in her mind, and with no way of resolving that mystery in her life, the mystery of her past and of her roots.

Eleni, on the other hand, looked relieved to have finally unburdened herself after all those years, and got what she had kept to herself off her chest. "Would you like some more coffee," she asked. Her voice was much lighter, betraying her relief,

"Err … yes, yes, I think I need it now," Aileen replied, followed by a heavy sigh.

"Jack will make some fresh," Eleni told her, leaning forward, picking up the almost empty cafetiere from the table and passing it to him.

"Thank you anyway, Eleni. Not just for the coffee, but for what you've told me. It can't have been easy, with it possibly being related to your best friend. I understand, and can see now, why you were so reluctant earlier. But, thank you. I was sorry to sound so aggressive before." Aileen was much calmer now. Any aggression had melted away.

The two women sat there exchanging pleasantries about the view and about Lindos in general, while they waited for Jack to return with the fresh coffee. When he finally emerged from inside the villa with the newly replenished cafetiere and began to pour the coffee, much to Aileen's surprise Eleni took the subject of their conversation back to her mother.

"I suppose you do know why your mother chose to come and live and work here? Why she chose Lindos?"

Aileen looked a little confused by that question as she replied, "No, I don't know. I assumed it wasn't for any special reason, just that she had been on holiday here the previous year."

Eleni took a sip of her coffee before telling her, "It was because your grandmother was here in 1943 when the Nazis were here and had occupied Rhodes. That was the reason your mother decided initially to come here on holiday and then come back here to work. That was what she told me during those two weeks after she first arrived and was working in our bar."

Once again Aileen looked surprised as she said, "I never knew. My mother never told me that, but-"

She went to reach in her handbag draped over the back of her chair, but while she did that and before she could finish Eleni interrupted. She hadn't finished her revelations.

"I told my mother, Jack's grandmother, at the time about why Mary had come here. She remembered her, your grandmother, Bernadette, from back then in 1943. She said everyone knew her as Bernie. Well, everyone in the Partisans, that is. That's what she called herself. They were good friends, my mother and Bernie, apparently. My mother wasn't much taken with Mary though."

Aileen stopped rooting around in her bag, looked up and across at Eleni saying only, "Partisans?"

"Yes, that's what my mother told me. I suppose you could refer to them as Greek Resistance, to the Nazi occupiers I mean. That's right, I mean that's the right words in English isn't it, Jack?" Eleni tried to explain.

"Yes, that's right," Jack confirmed. "The Nazis came on to Rhodes and took over the occupation here after the Italian occupiers surrendered, or rather, after Italy surrendered to the Allies in 1943. But the Greek Partisans, the Resistance, continued after the Nazis arrived, with some assistance from the British."

"Yes, I know what the Partisans were, know a bit about them," Aileen began, looking more confused than ever. "But my grandmother was Irish, like me a staunch Irish nationalist my mother told me. What was she doing here with the British and the Partisans?"

"I guess that's another long story, and I don't really know all of it," Eleni replied. "However, it would be-"

Aileen's excitable curiosity had re-emerged and had got the better of her once more as she interrupted with, "Is she still alive by any chance, your grandmother?"

Before his mother could reply Jack let out a small chuckle, accompanied by a slight knowing shake of his head. "Oh yes, definitely, very much so. She's ninety-one now, but you wouldn't think it. She still tells me off like I'm still a five year old. And she has all her faculties, and her memory is good, believe me, very good. She can tell you things about Lindos from years ago that I've forgotten myself."

"Do you think she would she see me? I would love to hear what she remembers about my grandmother," Aileen asks.

"That's what I was going to suggest just now," Eleni tells her. "I'm sure she will. She loves nothing better than talking about the 'old days', as she puts it. Of course, she doesn't speak English quite as good as me and Jack, or she doesn't think she does. But her English is good. She told me that she picked up quite a bit of it initially in the war, from people like your mother I guess, and the other English men she was here with, and since then from the tourists. She's-"

"So, my grandmother wasn't here alone then. There were others here with her who were English?" Aileen interrupted.

"That's what she said, two English men. She can explain it all to you, no doubt. She lives here with me, but she's sleeping now. She always takes an afternoon nap, well, actually increasingly around midday these days. I'll ask her later if she'll meet you, and I can let Jack know. We can arrange something here in a day or two probably. I'm sure she'd love to meet you and tell you what she knows about those times, although she's always telling they weren't exactly all good times."

"That would be great, thanks."

Aileen poked around in her handbag once more and this time she finally pulled out the folded in half foolscap sized brown padded envelope that she'd discovered in the top of her mother's wardrobe. She reached inside, pulled out the Greek medal with the dates of 1943 and 1946 inscribed on it, and asked Eleni if she had any idea why Aileen's mother had those?

Eleni reached over and took it from her, but merely shook her head slightly and told her, "No, no idea, but perhaps my mother will know, can help, if you show it to her when you meet. I'm sure she will."

"Okay, I'll bring it then, and a couple of others I found when I cleared my mother's house. There was some other stuff that I found too that have here with me, including what looks like a Greek identity card for my grandmother. I'll bring it all with me."

"Yes, I'm sure my grandmother will love to see it, and help you with it if she can."

With that Aileen was feeling a bit more positive once again. She might not have been, or will be, able to identify her birth father, but it looked as though she was about to discover a whole new chapter of her family history on her mother's side.

"Okay, I've taken up enough of your time now, Eleni." As she said that she got up from her chair and added, "Thank you again, and thank you for your hospitality and the lovely lunch."

"It was nice to meet you, and to try and get some things cleared up that had been bothering me for quite a few years," Eleni told her. "Well, maybe not cleared up, but certainly off my chest, is the way I think it is put in English," she added. "I will talk to Jack's grandmother about you meeting her soon and he can let you know a good time and day, hopefully suitable for you."

"Yes, thanks again, I'm free most days, only the lovely beaches here to occupy me most of the time," Aileen said with a smile.

Eleni and Jack showed Aileen to the door, and she told him, "Goodbye, and thanks Jack. I'll probably see you in the bar later."

With that she made her way down the steps outside the villa, and then on down through the baking hot white walled Lindos alleyway towards her flat, consoling herself as she went that she had at least uncovered one strong possible explanation of who was her birth father. After such an intense, but interesting, few hours though, she decided that she needed a short siesta under the cooling air-con in her flat. A cool shower, a nice dinner, and a few well deserved drinks in the Lindos bars later, were on her evening agenda. What Jack had told her earlier about the mysterious guy asking about an Irish woman in his bar had almost completely disappeared out of her mind.

Part Five:
A past life that lingers

13

The old Kathleen revisited

She plumped for Italian for dinner for a change, at Gatto Bianco restaurant just across the square from the Amphitheatre. Seafood pasta and a small mixed side salad with a cold glass of Italian white wine, all consumed on the restaurant's roof terrace, with yet another stunning view of the illuminated Acropolis. In the end she'd slept beneath the cooling air-con in the bedroom of her flat for almost four hours. She considered going to the beach rather than the siesta – or whatever the Greek equivalent was – but the cool of her bedroom was more inviting after the somewhat stressful, intense lunch she'd had with Eleni and Jack.

An equally cool shower, a pair of figure hugging clean white shorts that she felt she could 'carry off' even at her age, a red t-shirt tied at the waist, and some comfortable white trainers were her choice for that particular Lindos Saturday night. She stole a quick look in the mirror, then picked up her phone and placed it in her handbag, along with some more euros. Finally, she put a very small plastic perfume spray vial in the bag, which she always carried to use to try and keep her at least smelling fresh in the Lindos evening heat. As she made her way through the doors of the courtyard of her flat and into the alley towards the restaurant the heat hit her. Built up through the day, it lingered between the white walls of the narrow alleyways, sustained by the crowds of tourists making their way to the various restaurants and bars. It felt like there was no relief from the August warm evening air anywhere. She had rapidly become acclimatised to it, and knew to dress accordingly in the evenings, which is why she chose the outfit she did.

It was Saturday night, a Saturday night in approaching mid-August, and the village was at its busiest. It was a time of the annual traditional Italian holidays, and large numbers of them descended on Rhodes, including Lindos. She'd forgotten that when she plumped for Italian food that evening. The restaurant was almost full, although the owner, another Valasi, greeted her as she entered the ground floor courtyard of the restaurant. He found her a table for one on the roof terrace. It was the only one available.

As she surveyed her fellow diners, couples and groups of mostly Italian tourists interspersed with a few British ones, she contemplated how she had become easily accustomed to dining alone. In fact, she now realised that strangely she preferred it. No need or incentive to make inane conversation, or even debate with a possible dinner companion which restaurant to choose. Maybe the contentment she had sought in leaving her past life behind her had actually arrived, perhaps propelled somewhat by what Eleni had eventually told her over lunch. Even though that was by no means conclusive, certainly not as conclusive as she would have liked, it still felt as though it represented some sort of final closure of her previous life. She couldn't understand why exactly, but finding out who her father may have been, or at least possibly been, had acted like some sort of cleansing process, washing away all her past of the last twenty years. She still wondered what Eleni's mother, Jack's grandmother, was going to tell her about her own grandmother being in Lindos during the war, but that could wait for another time, until Eleni had arranged for them to meet. For now, this was a Lindos Saturday night, and her freshly cleansed self, inside and out, was determined to relax and enjoy it.

After dinner she decided to start with one drink at the Atmosphere Bar at the top of the village by Lindos Reception, where tourists staying in the village were dropped off and picked up by their airport coach transfers. It was only a couple of minutes' walk, but uphill most of the way. She had been there before, with Martin, on the first night that they ended up in bed together during her previous visit. As she made her way up to Atmosphere she was glad she had worn her trainers. The uphill path through the alley wasn't always even and was a little worn and shiny in places. By the time she made it up there she was certainly a little warm and definitely needed a drink. She decided to go inside the bar to benefit from the air-con, rather than join the many customers pleasantly seated outside chatting, listening to the music, and enjoying yet another view of the illuminated atmospheric Acropolis.

As she came though the wide opening into the bar the jovial Greek owner, Stavros, looked up from behind it and immediately told her, "Welcome, welcome back." It seemed that every Greek bar owner, or at least those in Lindos, always automatically remembered their past returning tourist customers, or made sure that they appeared to. Even though she reckoned she'd only been there the once, that time with Martin, Stavros was no exception. Like many of the Lindos bar and restaurant owners he was very convivial and friendly, well known to the many British couples, families, and groups of individuals who returned regularly year after year to his bar.

Aileen responded with a smile. As she took a seat on a bar stool she told him, "Thank you," followed by, "It's good to be back. Can I have a Gin and tonic please?"

Stavros began to ask, "How long-", but his question was interrupted by a woman in a couple sat at the other end of the bar who had escaped Aileen's notice.

"Aileen, I thought we would bump into you again on one night here."

"Elaine, and Michael, yes, it's a small village, so I suppose we would."

There wasn't a great deal of enthusiasm exhibited in Aileen's voice, although she did at least try to disguise her thudding disappointment at bumping into these two again. She tried to continue her brief conversation with Stavros, telling him, "How long here, not sure really, maybe a couple of months, maybe less."

As he placed her drink in front of her on the bar and Aileen paid him for it he commented, "Well, that's a good long time. September and October are nice months to be here, a lot cooler than this."

At least he didn't ask her about Martin, although she would have preferred to continue her conversation with him rather than her new found friends, Elaine and Michael, at the other end of the bar. She didn't get the chance.

"Come and join us," Michael said as she took a first sip of her drink.

What was actually going through her brain was, "Shit!" However, she knew there was actually no way of turning down the invitation. That would have proved to be a very awkward half-an-hour or so while she drank her Gin and tonic, and there was absolutely no one else at the bar that she could try to use as a diversion and run blocking interference by engaging in conversation with them. So, she eased herself off her bar stool and moved along to sit on the one nearest to her new friends, which just happened to be the one next to Michael.

Okay, she was thinking, just engage in some inane, mindless conversation about Lindos, the bars, and ask what restaurants they had tried? That would be harmless surely. Then finish her drink and make up some excuse about meeting some people in the village before eleven. That shouldn't be too difficult. It was already gone ten-fifteen.

So, that's what she did, listening to first Michael and then Elaine rambling on about what restaurants they'd been too, and even what dishes they'd had, in somewhat great inane detail. That was followed by her being treated to a long exposition about a day trip they had taken to Rhodes Town, and how fascinating it all was with, "All that history."

Even though Aileen had been there with Sandra Weston on her previous trip she couldn't be bothered to even try to interrupt and tell them. It wasn't worth it. In any case, she preferred them to go on about something like that rather than starting to ask anything about her, especially her past. She'd had quite enough of evasion and lies. So, she just nodded occasionally as if she was interested and let the both of them ramble on like some sort of mundane verbal relay team. In fact, inside she was chuckling to herself, realising that the old Aileen, or Kathleen O'Mara, would not have been anywhere near as tolerant. She would probably have just told them to go away and leave her alone, although most likely in nowhere near as polite terms. It was, or rather they were, undoubtedly excruciatingly tedious company, and the old Kathleen was just beginning to bubble below the surface inside her now.

Nevertheless, she was managing to survive the boredom reasonably well, or so she thought. She was just about managing to keep the old Kathleen under wraps, under control. At least, she was until Elaine realised after twenty interminable minutes that she had to stop talking as she was now desperate to go to the toilet. She had barely disappeared through the door to the toilet in the corner of the bar when Michael turned on his adjacent stool towards Aileen and asked, seemingly innocently, "So, what have you got planned for the rest of your Lindos Saturday evening? Anything exciting?"

"Just a club probably, Glow or Arches I guess, but I'm not sure how exciting it'll be whichever one I end up in."

No sooner had the words come out of her mouth than she realised it could have been a mistake telling him that. What if the two of them decided they wanted to join her? That was the last thing she wanted. It was bad enough being stuck with them for the best part of an hour now. She definitely didn't warm to the prospect of spending another couple of hours, or even more, clubbing with them. As it turned out though he had other ideas in mind, as she soon unexpectedly and surprisingly discovered.

"Well, there is another option if you're looking for excitement," he responded, fixing a look straight into her eyes as he did so. His fixed stare was accompanied by him placing his right hand high up on her bare suntanned left thigh, just below the bottom of her shorts. He added, "You could always come back to our place. It'll be fun, just the three of us. I know Elaine would enjoy it."

Aileen glared back at him intensely in silence, letting him finish. The menace of the old Kathleen was clearly exhibited in her eyes. Not that he noticed. Then she deliberately and slowly moved her eyes to briefly look down at his hand, which was now attempting to squeeze her upper thigh. What she then told him plainly had the desired effect as a mixture of shock and even an element of fear spread across his face. He was clearly only anticipating at the worst a polite, "No, thanks." He got more than he bargained for however, much more.

She moved her eyes back to hold a fixed stare directly into his face. Then very firmly, but purposely softly, and with a very clear meaning that was beyond misunderstanding, she told him, "Remove your fucking hand now you creep, or I'll remove it for you and break your bloody wrist." As she finished telling him that she allowed a deliberate broad, menacing, chilling smile to spread right across her lips.

He was so stunned that he didn't actually immediately remove his hand quickly enough for Aileen's liking. So, while he was still trying to process what she'd said she reached down with her left hand and quite gently lifted his hand off of her left thigh and placed it on his right one. All the while she maintained her fixed stare of obvious complete contempt directly into his face. However, she wasn't finished with him by any means. Almost smelling the fear she had instilled within him the old Kathleen was now resurfacing with a vengeance, and she was almost enjoying it. As she released his hand she added with an equally determined firmness evident in her still soft voice, "Don't even think about it, little man. You have no idea, you and that little wife of yours, just who you're dealing with. You just think I'm some sad, lonely woman on holiday here looking for some cheap, quick screw, like you two. You're wrong, very wrong. You couldn't be more wrong. And I'm sure you definitely wouldn't want to suffer the consequences of that."

That last sentence was said into his face with a slightly raised voice, and now accompanied by a look of cold, calculating anger. He just sat completely still, motionless, with his mouth half open, clearly totally shocked by what he was hearing. It was a veritable tsunami of forceful invective that utterly floored and overwhelmed him. Any actual fear he might have allowed to overcome him up to that point was about to be totally exacerbated by what she told him next in her continued low, soft, but demanding firm voice, while she maintained her menacing fixed glare closely into his face.

"If I ever bump into you two again while you're here on your holiday, and if you ever dare to try that again, ever dare to touch me, grope me, I'll cut your bloody balls off you prat and mush them into pulp to present them to that dim wife of yours.

Now, when she returns from whatever she's been doing in the toilet you're going to suggest the two of you leave while I sit here and finish my drink. And don't even think about suggesting we all leave together, because that's not going to happen, as, if you do, I might just be tempted then to do sooner rather than later what I've just told you. Anyway, I'm guessing you don't actually want that to happen now, me to leave with you two?"

As she finished Aileen tilted her head slightly to one side, signifying to him that she took his expected agreement for granted, then grinned and turned back towards the bar, picking up her glass for another sip of her drink. At that point Elaine returned from the toilet, just as Stavros was asking Aileen from along the bar, "Everything okay? More drinks?"

She smiled across at the Greek owner and told him, "Fine, thanks, but no, no more drinks. I'm still finishing this one, and these two are leaving."

Michael lifted himself off the bar stool, still feeling a little shaky over what he'd just been told as he did so.

"Oh, are we-" Elaine started to ask, looking confused over what Aileen had just told Stavros, and presumably assuming that the Irish woman was going to be in their company the rest of the evening, and possibly all that night.

"Yes, yes, dear … err … I thought we'd head into the village now. Maybe get an early night? Or a relatively early one, I suppose," Michael informed her.

"Yep, sounds like a good idea. Goodnight and take care the two of you going down the slope. It can be slippery in places," Aileen said with a deliberately false smile.

"Yes, goodnight, and see you again," Stavros added.

Elaine still looked confused as Michael ushered her out of the bar and into the warm late Lindos evening. Only once they had completely left the bar and the outside terrace area did Aileen allow herself a small voluble chuckle.

"Something amused you?" Stavros asked as he heard her.

"Only this place, Lindos I mean, not your bar of course, Stavros. But I will have another drink now, thanks."

She was feeling a mixture of excitement over a short recourse to her old self, as well as being a little concerned in case she'd exposed publicly too much of her past character, of her trait of focused single-minded, cold, calculating nastiness. She had to admit that she had enjoyed it though, even if she had been determined not to draw any attention to herself in Lindos in that, or any other, way. Anyway, they were just two complete strangers she'd come across, or to be more accurate, had tried to latch on to her. They shouldn't be a problem, especially given the look she had seen on Michael's face when she obviously put the fear of God in him.

She allowed herself another small chuckle at that thought as Stavros brought her new drink and said, "Well, something has obviously clearly really amused you on a Lindos Saturday night."

"Yes, yes, it has," she confirmed. "And I intend to make the best of it, my Lindos Saturday night."

14

More from her past

She finished her second Gin and tonic twenty minutes after she'd despatched Michael and Elaine out of her Lindos Saturday evening, said, "Goodnight," to Stavros, left the bar and started to make her way down the first part of the slope back into the centre of the village. It was just gone eleven. Too early to go to a club, so she headed for a couple of drinks in Pal's. It was usually busy at that time of night, and she liked the music the owner's wife, Sarah, played.

In fact, the whole village was still busy, with groups of tourists sitting outside some of the bars such as Yannis and Bar404 in the small square in the centre. Others were simply moving from one bar to the next through the narrow warm alleyways. There was a Saturday night buzz throughout the whole village, although it was actually like that on most nights in Lindos in August.

As she anticipated, Pal's was no exception, although being a relatively small bar it didn't take many customers inside to make it crowded. Others either stood outside in the alley or sat out there at the few tables. Aileen managed to squeeze through the first of the two open doorways of the bar, the nearest one as she approached the bar from the alleyway leading from the small square in the village centre. A couple - a middle-aged man and a woman - moved away from one corner of the bar slightly to allow her to reach it and try and attract the attention of Stelios behind the bar to order a drink. The two barmen, Stelios and Lou, were being kept busy by the customers needing serving, but eventually Stelios spotted her and she ordered another Gin and tonic. He had an unpleasant surprise for her, however, as he handed over her change.

He leaned forward over the bar so that she could hear him better over the music and told her, "There was a guy in here earlier asking about an Irish woman staying here in the village, asking if I knew of one." She once again tried to maintain a blank look even though inside she was concerned, as Stelios continued. "I assumed he meant you, but I just told him there were a few Irish tourists here at this time. I never told him anything more than that though. Unless I know the person asking I tend not to give out too much information, if any."

Other customers at the bar were waiting to be served, so Stelios moved away to serve them before she could comment. A couple of minutes later, however, he was back at her end of the short bar, by the corner, pouring some shots for a group of two couples who were standing nearby. As he did so, one of the guys from the couples looked over at her, said, Hi," and then asked if she'd like a shot with them.

She looked a little startled initially, but then told him, "Err … yes, thanks, why not?"

Stelios poured her a shot of Jägermeister. It wasn't exactly her favourite. However, after what Stelios had just told her she thought she needed something quite strong. Stelios poured himself and the other barman, Lou, one, and the two couples, the two barmen, and Aileen raised their glasses simultaneously as Stelios told them. "Yammas," before they all downed them in one.

Aileen's facial reaction as she swallowed it totally betrayed her lack of love of Jägermeister. Spotting it, the guy who had offered her the shot remarked, "Not your favourite then, Jägermeister?" He quickly added in a broad scouse accent, "I'm James, by the way." Pointing to his female partner he added, "And this is Katy. Your first time here?"

She held out her hand to both of them as she replied, "Aileen, but no, I've been here once before. I'm guessing you are regulars."

Before they could answer Stelios did it for them. "Here lots, they are regulars," and he added with a grin, "We can't get rid of them."

Aileen took advantage of Stelios being at their end of the bar to lean over it and ask, "What did he look like, the guy who was asking about an Irish woman? Was he English or Irish, very young?"

"English, very English, posh accent, I'd say in his thirties," Lou interjected, overhearing her question. He added to her earlier surprise though when he pointed across the crowded bar towards the large window on the far side and told her, "He's sat outside at one of the tables opposite the crepe place. There, that's him."

He was pointing at a man sitting at a low white table outside with his back to the window, wearing a black polo shirt and beige chinos. He had short dark black hair and from only a quick glance, from behind, he looked quite fit, although it wasn't easy to tell from that angle."

Trying to look as unconcerned as possible after her quick glance across at him through the window, she told the two barmen, "No, no idea who he is. Maybe one of those guys who were trying to chat me up outside here the other night. You remember, Stelios, he insisted on paying for my drink."

In reality, she knew it wasn't one of them, for the same reason as Stelios pointed out, "Could be, but I thought they were younger?"

"Most of them were, but a couple of them were older," she suggested, although knowing that wasn't true. "Anyway, I don't want that crew bothering me again, so do me a favour and don't let on I'm here if you have to go out there please."

In fact, she had a pretty good idea who the guy was; obviously the same one who was asking about her in Jack Constantino's Courtyard Bar the night before. She could pick them out a mile away; smell them, like a sixth sense. Black polo shirt and chinos, slicked back short hair, all that was standard, supposed undercover MI6 uniform. She was sure, had no doubt about it.

For over an hour she stayed inside the bar, chatting to her new friends James and Katy, but occasionally, as discreetly as possible, glancing across the bar and through the window to check he was still there. Despite being engaged in various conversations, mostly about Lindos, in her mind she was trying to think through just what to do about him.

Just after twelve-thirty she once more glanced across at the window and he'd gone. She never saw him leave, and had no idea in which direction he had gone. She had another drink and continued talking from time to time with Stelios, as well as Katy and James, until the music finished at one o'clock. As she finished the last drop of her final Gin and tonic she announced that she was off to Glow. When Katy said they would be in Arches later, Aileen told them she'd probably only have one drink in Glow and then maybe come into Arches for one after that before going to bed. So, she'd probably see them there.

Glow was less than a minute from Pal's, up the alley and a few steps, and to the right just past the Courtyard Bar. As she got to the few steps leading up to the Courtyard Bar she thought for a brief moment that she glimpsed someone - a figure in the darkness further up the steps towards the top alley – peering down at her from out of the shadows. She stopped for a second, but when she looked again there was clearly no one there. Maybe she was now just getting paranoid after hearing all these stories about someone asking about an Irish woman. That's what she convinced herself.

Glow was quite busy, mostly with young Greeks. Saturday night seemed to be the night when local young Greeks went out clubbing. She made her way to the bar and ordered yet another Gin and tonic. The accumulation of the drinks was beginning to take effect. She wasn't drunk by any means, but nicely relaxed was probably the best way to describe how she felt. That relaxed feeling was definitely removed though from her surroundings, or to be more accurate her fellow Glow clientele that evening. She felt decidedly old, almost ancient, compared to the overwhelming majority of young Greek men and women in the club. Probably young boys and girls would be a better way to describe them. She would definitely only have the one drink and then make her way to Arches, as she told Katy and James. Because of that she didn't exactly dwell over consuming her drink, although she knew not to drink it too quickly given that she was already beginning to feel a little light headed.

In effect, she was only in Glow for around twenty minutes. Approaching one-thirty she made her way to Arches, by what she had determined was the shortest and quickest route. That also had the advantage of avoiding the main alleyway through the village and its possible groups of drunken tourists, especially any groups of young British guys who might suddenly decide in their drunken state that they want to stop and try to chat her up. So, she chose to make her way up the few steps immediately opposite Glow towards the top alleyway that ran behind the Courtyard Bar. Then she would cut down one of the alleys running off it to the left that led down to the entrance to Arches.

The path was a little uneven, but she wasn't actually paying much attention to her earthly surroundings as she made her way along the alley, preferring to gaze up at the clear sky and its myriad of bright, sparkling stars. Not something you could ever observe in the cities these days with their large scale pollution.

Around twenty-five yards or so along the starlit alley from the rear of the Courtyard Bar, at one of its darkest parts, while she was still gazing up at the heavens a figure jumped out from one of the recesses in the wall behind her that led to some steps down to one of the alleys running into the centre of the village. A bare, strong, male arm grabbed her around the neck from behind while his other hand, the right one, immediately thrust a gun fitted with a silencer against her right temple. The man struggled to try to drag her back into the dark shadow of the recess. Even though she couldn't see his face she knew instantly that it would be the guy who had been sitting outside Pal's, the one who had been asking about an Irish woman in Pal's earlier and also in Jack's bar the night before. Even in the shadow she could make out the black short sleeve of his polo shirt. She was certain now that he was from MI6.

As he attempted to drag her back into the recess, obviously intent on killing her, he stumbled slightly on the rough, worn ground of that part of the alley. She had learned quite quickly from her two visits to the village that some of the paths could be treacherous, slippery, and shiny from the years of donkey hooves passing over them every day during the summer season. She had almost fallen foul of them in one place in the village during her previous visit in June. Now, however, she was more than grateful for them, and the donkeys. This was one such path, or at least this part of it was, leading as it did from the donkey station in the Main Square up to the top of the village by the Atmosphere Bar and Lindos Reception. As she felt him partially lose his footing, and with as much strength as she could muster, she immediately pushed all her weight back onto him with a heavy thrust, while he attempted to steady himself and retain his arm-lock around her neck. The two of them fell backwards to the floor of the pitch black recess. As he fell he initially struggled to retain his grip around her neck, but as she fell on top of him she intentionally smashed the back of her head full into his face with as much force as she could summon up. The crack of his nose was audible, and he let out a voluble yell of, "Argh." Simultaneously, the back of his head hit the hard flagstone ground and a piece of loose broken stone which lay on it, causing trickles of blood to begin to flow from an open wound. The pain from the force of the crack on his nose from the back of her head, as well as the wound to the back of his head, caused him to release his arm-lock around Aileen's neck and to drop the gun to the ground out of the grasp of his right hand. Aileen quickly leapt up from her position on top of him on the ground and picked up the gun.

"You bitch, you fucking Irish bitch," he tried to scream at her while he writhed in agony on the ground clutching his face, now streaming with blood. His hands over his face muffled his scream somewhat, however. It was very unlikely that there would be anyone out in that part of the village at that time, but she was relieved that his scream of anger and agony was muffled and was not likely to be heard anyway.

She pointed the gun at him telling him quietly, but firmly, "Yes, I fucking am. A bitch, that's what those shits you work for trained me to be for twenty years. Bloody MI6, don't bother to deny it. I know your sort. Can spot you a bloody mile away. I knew that as soon as I spotted you outside that bar earlier."

He now lay motionless on the ground. The full effect of her assault on him was beginning to kick-in and he was groggy from the blow to the back of his head, as well as the pain from his broken nose. Even if he had all his senses and could, he wasn't bothering to deny it, or for that matter, even confirm what she'd just told him. She knew from her own training that he wouldn't. He would have been trained not to. Even though she needed to ask, she guessed he wouldn't answer her next question either.

"You here alone, or are there more of you bastards here looking for me?"

She was right. He never answered. He just stared hazily up at her standing over him, his hands now covered in the blood from his nose, while that from the wound on the back of his head continued trickling down the back of his neck, soaking into the collar of his black polo shirt.

"I didn't think you'd tell me that. From working for those shits for years I knew you wouldn't. I guess you know that though. But I don't work for them anymore, so I don't have to pretend anymore. I decided I wanted my life back. In any case, in reality I never did actually bloody work for those sodding Brits with all their Secret Service games."

He started to think that if she was telling him all that then she wasn't actually going to kill him. He was wrong.

"Get up, get up!" she told him forcibly. "And put your hands on top of your head," she added as he staggered to his feet to face her in the darkness while she remained pointing the gun at his face in her right hand. As he managed to stand up straight immediately in front of her she lifted her left hand, stared coldly straight into his eyes, and then, much to his surprise, stroked his right cheek tenderly. His eyes widened, completely uncertain and bewildered as to what was likely to happen next. As she finished stroking his cheek and continued to stare intensely into his fear riven eyes he started to ask, "What, what are you going to-"

He never got to finish. She allowed a broad smile of mischievous contentment to emerge across her lips, and then placed the index finger of her left hand on his lips in order to indicate he should stop speaking. Finally, she planted a tender kiss on his right cheek as she moved the gun to press on his left temple. He started to force a slight smile, anticipating relief that she wasn't actually going to kill him. No sooner had the smile started to spread across his lips though, and as her smile returned, even broader, she brought her bare right knee up in a rapid action with great force into his balls. He groaned in pain and doubled over slightly. As he stumbled forward she followed up with a full bloodied kick to his groin area, landing her trainer covered foot with full force perfectly.

He let out another groan as she told him, "You're going to be my message to that 'old boys club' you work for. Don't bloody mess with me is what it'll tell them."

He was gasping for air having sunk to his knees and doubled over completely in front of her from the blows. His gasping for air and his groans of discomfort lasted only a second or so more, however, as she instantly reversed the gun in her right hand and smashed the handle of it into the rear of his skull with as much force as she could muster. She knew the precise fatal spot to aim for, close to the initial wound from his fall earlier when he cracked the back of his head on the flagstone and loose stone. Years of training by his 'old boys club' employers had taught her well.

He slumped further forward onto the ground in front of her with one final groan of pain and then lay there face down totally motionless. She quickly checked for any pulse and that he was dead. She knew instantly exactly what she was going to do next. The rough and shiny ground of the alleyway had not only provided her with the opportunity to escape his grasp, but now it was going to provide her with what she hoped would be believed as the cause of his death. She carefully lifted his body up from the ground, making sure none of the blood spread onto her clothes. Most of it had soaked into his polo shirt anyway. Then she manoeuvred it down the three small steps into the equally dark alleyway that led down into the centre of the village. She guessed it was one that wasn't used very often, by either locals or tourists. At the bottom of the steps she took his head and smashed it once more against the white wall shrouded in darkness and shadow. This time though it was the top of his forehead that split open, and as she allowed his body to fall to the floor at that spot she ensured that some of the blood from his forehead deposited itself on the wall above his body at head height. Her plan was that any possible police investigation would merely assume that he'd had too much to drink, lost his footing in the darkness and stumbled at the top of the steps, cracking the back of his head on the ground there, then tried to recover and get some help, but instead fell down the steps, cracking his nose and forehead against the wall. Through the window outside Pal's she'd noticed he was drinking what looked like at least three Gin and tonics or possibly Vodka and tonics. So, she knew he had alcohol in his system, and the police would no doubt discover that in any autopsy. Perhaps it wasn't going to be enough to suggest he was completely drunk, but it could, or should, be just enough to suggest that he lost his footing because he'd had a few drinks. In any case, she'd heard a few stories of tourists losing their footing in some places in the village because of the rough or shiny paths in the alleyways and suffering broken or sprained limbs, even during the day and not having had any alcohol. So, the scenario she had now contrived shouldn't be too hard for the local police to believe and come to that conclusion.

The one thing that remained for her to deal with was the gun. She wiped the blood off it as best she could with some tissues from a packet she always carried in her handbag. Now though, she had to dispose of the tissues, as well as having the question of what to actually do with the gun. She dismantled the silencer and carefully wrapped it and the gun in some more of her tissues, then placed them all in her handbag.

Finally, she checked the pockets of his chinos. There was nothing, except some Euros and a mobile, but no identification, not even any indication of where he was staying. Oddly there was no key of any sort or even a card from any nearby hotel or accommodation. She frowned, puzzled as to how that could be, but took the phone to check it later somewhere safe before disposing of it. It definitely wasn't an expensive one and from the look of it she guessed it was a 'burner' phone. She'd had plenty of them given to her when she worked for MI6; mobiles with prepaid minutes and definitely without any sort of mobile network supplier contract. She anticipated it would have very little information or contacts on it. Nevertheless, she hoped it might give some clue as to whether he was alone in Lindos or whether there were other MI6 operatives with him. It was turned off, obviously so there was no chance that it would make any sound while he was hiding in waiting to attack her. She knew better than to turn it on at this point, however, in case there was any chance it could be tracked later by his employers in the British Secret Service, even if it was a 'burner' phone. She just placed it in her handbag, pleased that it was a good job she had actually chosen to use her reasonably sized one to go out with that night. She certainly wouldn't have been able to fit the gun, the silencer, the blood stained tissues and the phone into her other smaller handbag.

That thought made her realise that she was actually now surprisingly calm, remarkably so considering the turmoil and her actions of the last few minutes. Obviously some of the attributes and characteristics of her past life hadn't left her completely. She hadn't lost it. She still had all her old skills. Nevertheless, she took a deep breath to compose herself even more, at the same time realising that she needed to get away from there as quickly as possible before there was any possible chance that someone would actually be using that particular alleyway on their way to their apartment at the top of the village. Her first instinct was to head straight back to her own apartment, if nothing else in order to clean up the gun and stash it somewhere there before figuring out how and where to dispose of it. The sea was the obvious choice, but not now at that time of night, although it would obviously have to be at night.

She checked her clothes and luckily found no traces of blood on them. She could feel, almost taste, the smell in her nostrils though. It was a familiar one to her. It was the smell of death. She had smelt it many times before. Others may not, but she could always smell it, on her, on her clothes, in her hair. It lingered. She searched for the small vial of perfume spray in her handbag, beneath the gun, the silencer, and the tissues. It wasn't a discernible odour to anyone else, the smell of death, but it was to her, merely in her mind probably. She squirted two short sprays of the perfume to either side of her neck. It was just a reassurance really, a bizarre sort of comfort blanket.

She dismissed the idea of heading straight for her apartment. From her past experience in these sorts of situations she knew that the best move now would be to be seen by a lot of people immediately; people who would certainly remember her at this specific time should any possible police investigation develop concerning the guy's death. She would set about now ensuring that people remembered her at this particular time. Even though from the way she had staged the scene of his death she was pretty certain the police would rule out any foul play fairly quickly, assume it was just a bad accident. Her past experience also told her that there was no way they would be able to pin down the exact time of death, only a broad period. Consequently, ensuring that she was seen by a number of people in a bar somewhere in the village during that period of time would give her some sort of alibi, should she ever by any chance need one.

Where she was heading for when she was attacked, Arches, would no doubt have people there who would remember seeing her. It wouldn't be difficult to ensure that Chris at the entrance did, as well as Levi, one of the barmen. But she decided Arches was not a good choice, for now at least, so she immediately ruled it out. There was no way she wanted to be seen coming down from the top alley at this time by people going into the club or possibly even by Chris working at the entrance into Arches' courtyard. That would place her much too close to the proximity of what she had just done.

Instead, she decided she would go back up to the top alley and walk further along there, once again fairly sure it was very unlikely that anyone would be coming along there at that time of night and see her. She would then go down the alley to the left after the one to Arches and into the Crazy Moon cocktail bar, which she was sure would still be open. She'd been there once before during her previous Lindos visit in June at around this time of night and there were some people still there having a late drink. Also she recalled that there was usually no one on the entrance there, which was also an archway into a courtyard from the alley. At that time of night she was sure that would still be the case. Consequently, as long as it was, there was no possibility that anyone would see which direction she came from, down from the top alley. So, that is what she did, after first checking closely once more that her clothes and the exposed parts of her body didn't have any signs whatsoever of any blood from the guy's wounds. There were none.

Crazy Moon was one of the relatively newer bars in Lindos, at least it was in its latest incarnation. It had been a few different bars previously. Through the Lindian stone arched entrance it had a pleasant garden courtyard outside the bar with a number of tables and chairs. Inside, the small bar was nicely decorated with some great photos of various music icons on the walls.

As Aileen made her way through the stone archway, crossed the courtyard, and approached the doorway to the inside bar a young blonde woman standing by the doorway, who she took to be a waitress, greeted her with, "Hi." Aileen responded with a, "Hi," of her own, followed by asking, "Is it too late for a drink, although I actually need to use your toilet first to be honest."

As far as Aileen could see as she stood at the doorway there were still eight people inside sat at the bar drinking, as well as the two couples she'd passed at the tables outside. So, the young woman, who was obviously English, told her, "No, it's fine, never too late in Lindos for a drink. What can I get you while you use the toilet?" She pointed and added, "It's over there in the corner of the courtyard."

Aileen told her, "A Gin and tonic, please, with ice and lemon." She definitely needed another one now.

When she got in the toilet she carefully firstly checked that there was no one else in there. When she'd made sure that was the case she quickly removed it from her handbag and washed the gun, removing any trace of any remaining bits of blood. She dried it with some toilet paper from the nearby cubicle. Then she flushed that and the tissues which she'd had the gun wrapped in, as well as the blood stained tissues she'd previously wiped it down with in the alley, down the toilet. She placed the gun back in her handbag and re-zipped it. Finally, she looked in the mirror to check once again that there were no traces of blood on her clothes at all.

As soon as she emerged from the toilet and went into the inside bar she set about quickly making sure that as many people as possible remembered her being in the bar at that specific time, just as she planned. Should the local police decide to investigate further rather than just accepting the guy's death was an accident and, by any chance, she came under suspicion, she would have a good alibi. She was well aware that if they did do any sort of investigation at all that involved trying to find out who the guy was, and what his movements in Lindos were that night, then it was likely they would interview some of the staff and the owners in the bars. That meant Stelios and Lou in Pal's were certainly likely to remember him and the fact that he was asking about her, or at least, "an Irish woman." Furthermore, Jack would no doubt remember him asking about her in the Courtyard Bar if they interviewed him. However, she was totally in control now of all eventualities, all circumstances. Once again she thought to herself that she obviously hadn't lost it, being completely cool and calm in tight and difficult situations under pressure.

So, she took a seat on one of the stools at the bar and as the blonde young woman delivered her drink she deliberately engaged her in conversation, asking, "Are you working here for the summer?"

"Well, yes and no really. I'm working here for the summer and every summer now, but I live here. My mother lives here, and my brother, and my partner over there is a co-owner of the bar." As she told Aileen that she pointed to a youngish Greek looking guy at the far end of the bar talking to a couple of customers.

Aileen took the opportunity to ensure that the young woman knew exactly who she was as she told her, "I'm Aileen by the way. Irish, as you can no doubt tell. Here for a couple of months, I think. Well, I've rented an apartment here for that long anyway. I'm trying to trace some of my past family who were here. My mother worked here in the nineteen-seventies."

"That's sounds interesting," the woman told her, followed by, "I'm Emily."

They chatted on and off for another thirty minutes while Aileen drank her Gin and tonic. In between time she also made a point of introducing herself to a couple of middle-aged English women who were sat on the stools next to her at the bar. In turn, they introduced themselves as Gill and Anthea. She made sure she engaged them in conversation. It was just standard stuff about Lindos and how many times they had been mainly. They were regular visitors over many years apparently, often a couple of times each summer. They seemed to be enjoying their cocktails, and appeared to have had quite a few by that time of night.

By just after two-thirty she was satisfied that she'd done enough of making sure people remembered she'd been there at that time. Having finished her drink and paid she wished, "Goodnight," to Emily and the two women, then made her way back to her apartment.

As soon as she got back there she removed the gun and silencer out of her handbag and placed them underneath some of her underwear in the small chest of drawers. She would dispose of them in the sea off the rocks in St. Paul's bay tomorrow evening, under the cover of darkness. Then she took the guy's phone and some Euros out of her bag, put them in the pocket of her shorts, and left her apartment. She headed the twenty yards down the alley to the entrance to Arches, where Chris greeted her with a smile and a, "Good evening."

She returned his smile, accompanied with a "Good evening," of her own. "Can't stop, need the toilet urgently," she explained as she then headed across the courtyard and into the women's toilet. As soon as she got into one of the toilet cubicles and locked the door she removed the phone from her pocket and turned it on to check the record of the guy's recent calls. As she anticipated, it displayed that his last call was to an unidentified number. She adjusted the volume on the phone to its lowest point and then pressed 'Recall'. What appeared to be a well-educated voice answered, asking in a very low monotone bureaucratic manner, "Is there a problem?"

She hung up straightaway and immediately turned off the phone. She figured that even if MI6 were able to trace the phone's location by any chance - which she seriously doubted if it was a 'burner' phone - then from that very brief time she'd switched it on there was at least a chance that they might assume someone had merely stolen it from their agent, gone to Arches, and tried to use it. A tourist, perhaps, and even when MI6 did eventually discover that he was dead maybe they would simply assume that the phone had been taken from his dead body by some opportunist tourist passer-by.

She didn't recognise the voice that answered of course, but she was very familiar with the procedure and that monotone phrase of response. It was definitely an agent's contact at MI6 – almost an MI6 'helpline' for agents in trouble, or at least facing what the Agency liked to refer to as, 'difficulties' or 'a 'problem'. She knew and recognised it because she had been familiarised with it herself when on missions, along with being issued a 'burner' phone. It was part of her training, and she'd even had recourse to use it a couple of times.

"Fuck, this was supposed to have ended," she muttered quietly as she put the phone back in her pocket. She would dispose of it with the gun and the silencer, although separately. She flushed the toilet, just in case any woman was waiting outside to use it and had any doubt about what she'd been doing in there. Then she took another deep breath, uttered another quiet, "Fuck it," to herself, followed by, "A drink, I need another bloody drink." She opened the cubicle door to be confronted by a young English woman who had, indeed, been waiting. "About bloody time," she told Aileen as she brushed past and into the cubicle.

Aileen glared at her, but never bothered to respond. She'd had enough confrontation for one night. She walked quickly across the courtyard, waited for the outer sound lock door to be opened, and then headed inside for a final Gin and tonic. As she made her way through the busy clubbing clientele towards the bar opposite the door she spotted James and Katy from Pal's earlier. They were being served by Levi, the barman she'd spoken to the night before in the club, and were chatting to him as he made their drinks. She went over to them to say hello and James insisted on buying her a drink. As she relaxed with them over the next hour - chatting, listening to the music and watching the clubbing dancers - she couldn't help thinking once again that at least there was one thing she was sure of from her evening's experiences. She definitely hadn't lost her nerve or her skills of the past twenty years.

The following afternoon she overheard what she took as verbal confirmation of that self-belief. She was relaxing on Pallas Beach after the stress of the night before, waiting to hear from Jack about a day and time to meet his grandmother. She was on the point of dozing off for a short nap after a swim when she was disturbed and couldn't help but overhear a middle-aged English woman, and what she presumed was her husband, seated on nearby sunbeds speaking quite loudly to a similar English couple on the beds in front of them. She didn't hear the first part of the conversation, but what she did hear reassured her.

"They think he was drunk. That's what the woman serving in the supermarket told me this morning. It's slippery on the path up there and uneven, and there's not much light there at night apparently. That's what she said. She said she heard the police think he had too much to drink, fell down a few steps up there in the dark and hit his head on the stone path. She said one of the local women from the village, a cleaner in one of the bars apparently who lives in that part of the village towards the top, she found him early this morning on her way to work. She told the woman in the supermarket that there was a lot of blood on the path and on a wall. So, it sounds like he must have stumbled and then hit his head on there as well. Drunk and dazed, I guess. Sad though, dying like that."

Aileen settled down once again, now more than contented to try and drift into a short nap, but her plan was interrupted once more by her phone beeping to signal she had a text message. It was from Jack, confirming that his mother and grandmother would meet her the next day, Monday, at four o'clock at his mother's villa again, and he would meet her there. She quickly sent him a brief reply that it was fine by her, thanked him again, and that she would see him there.

This time she was able to drift off into her short nap, perfectly contented in the hot Lindos sunshine.

15

Inspector Yiannis Papadoulis

Aileen decided to sleep in a little on Monday morning. Not that it made much difference to her life now in Lindos. There was no more rushing to meet deadlines about where to be to deal with her next target, or to liaise with her accomplices. Despite what had happened two nights ago she was feeling pretty calm. She'd spent a very relaxing Sunday on Pallas Beach, just like a holidaymaker. Later, in the darkness of that evening, she had disposed of the gun, the silencer, and the guy's phone by tossing them into the sea separately from the rocks near the opening to St. Paul's Bay.

Even when she did finally surface from her bed at just after ten she was not in any hurry to begin her day. She wasn't meeting Jack, his mother, and grandmother until four. In the meantime she would embrace the pleasant slow Lindos life; pull on a pair of denim shorts and a baggy blue t-shirt, and have breakfast of coffee, Greek yogurt and honey in the sunshine of the courtyard of her apartment. While she did so she'd tussle with the biggest decision of her day, which beach to go to before her meeting.

As she was contemplating whether or not to have another coffee in her courtyard or go to Giorgos for a leisurely cappuccino on her way to Pallas Beach the loud rap of the large iron knocker on the door to the courtyard abruptly disturbed the enjoyment of the solitude of her surroundings. She was puzzled. She obviously wasn't expecting any visitors, and if it was the woman who owned the flat she had a key, so wouldn't need to knock.

She slipped her flip flops back on and walked across to open the door. A tall, quite slim man, with thick dark black hair, in his mid-forties, and dressed in a short sleeve light blue shirt and dark trousers, asked in a thick throaty Greek voice after she opened the door, "Aileen Regan?"

From his appearance and general manner she knew instantly what was coming next. Before she could answer he held up a police officer's identification card towards her, and simultaneously informed her, "Inspector Yiannis Papadoulis, Rhodes police."

She stood holding the door open, in no hurry to invite him into the courtyard as she confirmed, "Yes, that's me. I'm Aileen. Is there a problem, Officer?"

He didn't provide a direct answer, merely asked, "Would you mind if I come inside. I have a few questions that you might be able to help us with. It shouldn't take long."

She held the door open a little further as she told him, "Yes, of course. Come in, have a seat, but what is this about, questions about what?"

He made his way in silence across the small courtyard and took a seat at the plastic table where she had been having her late breakfast. As Aileen joined him he took his small black police notebook and pen out of the top pocket on one side of his shirt.

She was trying to remain cool, something at which she was well practiced. But as he opened his notebook and scribbled something in it, presumably her name, the time and date, she tried to convey her relaxed mood by asking him, "Would you like a coffee? I was about to have another."

He, on the other hand, was determined to be focused and professional.

"No, no thanks. It's about the body of a man that was discovered in the village early on Sunday morning, in one of the alleys leading to the top alleyway."

"Yes, I overheard some people talking about it on the beach yesterday afternoon. It sounded terrible, and very sad, and in such a beautiful place as this. I think they were saying he was drunk and slipped on the path? The paths and alleys can be quite treacherous in places. I've almost slipped myself here a couple of times, and they must be even trickier if you're drunk."

He let her go on. While she did so he briefly scribbled something in his notebook once more. As he finished, looked up and across the table at her, with an attempted look of bewilderment on her face she added, "But what has it got to do with me, Officer? I don't follow."

"The man had no means of identification on him when he was found, not even anything that indicated where he was staying in the village, or even on Rhodes. So, we've no idea who he was and what he was doing here. We assume he was on holiday, but we are just trying to find out his identity. We deployed a squad of officers from here and Rhodes Town to go around the bars and restaurants in the village last night with a photo of him, not a very flattering one unfortunately because of his injuries. Anyway, we thought that might help us identify him and his movements on Saturday night if anyone remembered him. The preliminary pathologist examination suggests he died sometime between one and four or five on Sunday morning."

He deliberately stopped at that point, waiting for her response, to see what it would be.

"Why me though?" Aileen asked. "What makes you think I may have known him?"

He removed a photograph from inside the back cover of his notebook and slid it across the table to her, not answering her question, but simply telling her, "This is him."

She picked it up and looked at it for a few seconds, then shook her head slightly and simultaneously pulled a negative look across the bottom of her face. She could feel he was watching her reaction closely, but she was determined not to give anything away. Eventually, she shook her head once more, and told him, "No, no idea, Inspector, never seen him before. Sorry, I can't be of any help, but you didn't answer my question. Why did you think I'd know him? I'm just wondering what brought you here to me."

Once again the Inspector didn't answer her question and instead scribbled something briefly in his notebook. She was well aware that he was playing games with her, deliberately not answering her questions, and presumably hoping she would panic and give something away inadvertently. So, she took advantage of the pause in his questions to tell him, in as pleasant and relaxed manner as she could, "I'm going to have that other coffee now, if that's ok with you. Are you sure you don't want one."

"No, I'm fine, thanks," he replied.

She got up from the table and went inside to the small kitchen to make herself another coffee. While she waited for the kettle to boil she took a couple of calming deep breaths, telling herself to relax and not to get uptight about his obvious game playing. Then she peered out of the small kitchen window onto the courtyard to see the Inspector once more scribbling in his notebook. So far, so good, she thought as she made her way back into the courtyard.

As she sat back down in one of the plastic chairs and placed her mug of coffee on the table she tried once again. "So, Inspector, something must have sent you here to ask if I knew this guy?"

She'd been really careful so far, even told herself a few moments before to relax, but as soon as that last sentence came out of her mouth again she realised it could be a mistake. Did what she'd just asked again exhibit too much concern over what had brought him to her door? She tried not to highlight that any further by simply reaching for her mug of coffee and taking a sip.

He closed his notebook and looked across the table at her while he rubbed his chin, clearly considering how much to tell her and how to play it. After a long moment he told her, "Some of the staff that my officers interviewed in one of the bars last night remembered him, and the owner of another bar also did."

Now he scratched the back of his thick black hair slightly, signifying his attempt to qualify that. "Well, they remembered him but couldn't identify him as such, in that they never knew him or had any name for him. They just all thought he was English. It was just that they recalled him being in their bar on Saturday evening, the bar staff of Pal's Bar did, while the bar owner of the Courtyard Bar remembered him being in there having a drink the previous evening."

He stared straight across at her closely as he added, "And one of the barmen in Pal's, Lou, told us that he pointed the guy out to you on Saturday night because he was asking about you. He said the guy was sat outside the bar, but you just told me you'd never seen him before. The Courtyard Bar owner told us where you were staying, so I thought you may be able to help us."

She was coolness personified as she put down her mug of coffee and asked, "So, this was him, the same guy?"

She pointed to the photo that was still on the table, trying to look as surprised as possible. She deliberately didn't wait for the policeman to reply.

"Yes, that's right, Inspector, Lou did point him out to me, but all he and the other barman, Stelios, told me was that the guy was asking about an Irish woman, not specifically about me. Jack Constantino, the owner of the Courtyard Bar, also told me there was a guy in his bar asking about an Irish woman. But I'll tell you what I told all three of them, the guy could have been asking about anybody. There are plenty of Irish female tourists here, and even some Irish women who live and work here. So, I never assumed it was me that he was looking for. In fact, as I said, Lou did point him out to me, but I was inside Pal's, it was crowded, and the guy was sat outside at a table opposite the Crepe place in the alleyway. Lou just pointed him out to me through the large window on one side of the bar. I was stood at the bar and the guy had his back to the window. All I saw was the back of his head. That's why I never recognised him from that photo."

She pointed to the photo again before she continued.

"No one I know even knows I'm here, so why would I think he was looking for me, especially when I never recognised him at all, even if it was only from behind? So, I assumed it could have been anyone, any Irish woman he was looking for, not me. Why would I think otherwise?"

While Aileen was explaining all that to him he had opened his notebook once more and was scribbling down a few more notes.

Aileen waited, finishing the last drop of her coffee. Eventually, the Inspector never responded to her last question and merely asked, "But you never spoke to him?"

"No, not at all, not that night, not ever. For most of the time I was in there I was talking to a couple who are regular visitors to Lindos and Pal's, English tourists. I left around one when the music went off. He wasn't there then, outside. I presume he'd left, but I obviously didn't see him go."

"And you came back here then?" Papadoulis asked.

"No, I went to Glow."

"Did you stay there till late?"

"What? Hang on, Inspector, what is this?" She was deliberately feigning a mixture of outrage and confusion. This had gone on long enough as far as she was concerned.

"I thought you said it was an accident. Why are you so interested in my movements that night? Not that I've got anything to hide, of course, but do you have some suspicion it wasn't an accident?"

She thought that may have been a bit of an over-reaction, not the effect she was aiming for at all. So, she didn't wait for him to respond. Continuing to try to sound a little offended, with a lot less force in her voice she quickly added, "No, for your information and your records, Inspector, I didn't stay in Glow until late. I had one drink then went to the Crazy Moon cocktail bar around two, I think. I spoke to the partner of one of the guys who owns it, Emily, as well as a couple sat at the bar next to me. Emily served me. After that I went to Arches for one more drink. Also, for your records, I spoke to Chris who works on the door there on the way in and when I left, plus I had a drink in the club with the tourist couple who I met earlier in Pal's, James and Katy. I don't know their surnames. I only met them that night. Stelios and Lou in Pal's might do. They said they were regular tourists to Lindos and regulars in Pal's. There were too many Greek youngsters in Arches for my liking, and too crowded, so I only had one drink. Apparently, it's always like that on a Saturday night, so Chris told me as I left. Then I came back here to bed."

She finished her long detailed explanation of her movements on Saturday night by returning to a much softer tone. "Sad though, as I said before, especially to think that some poor guy on holiday lost his life in an accident not far from here. Unless, of course, you do have some reason to suspect it wasn't an accident, Inspector?"

The Inspector nodded occasionally while she told him all that, and intermittently once again scribbled in his notebook. He was a little surprised at the amount of detail she had just reeled off about her Saturday night movements.

As he finished writing the final time in his notebook he looked up and told her, "No, we've no reason at all to suspect that it was anything but an accident. Certainly nothing at all from the initial pathologist report suggests that. It seems he died from the injuries to his skull, and from what we found at the scene, the blood on a nearby wall and the stone slab path, it looks like he simply slipped and cracked his head on the path, and then on the wall as he obviously tried to get up after the first fall. There was some alcohol in his blood stream apparently, so he had been drinking. However, the pathologist's report said it wasn't really excessive. Although, as you said, the paths can be really slippery in places in the village, and it doesn't really take very much alcohol, if any, to make negotiating some of them a bit tricky at times, I suppose."

"Oh, so it was an accident then? I was just a bit confused as to why you were asking me about him, and about my movements on Saturday night," Aileen said, trying to sound much calmer.

"As I said before, it's about identification really, Miss Regan, we thought there might be some possibility that you could identify him, particularly as we thought he'd been asking about you in some of the bars. But, as you've explained, it obviously wasn't you he was asking about."

The Inspector hesitated for a few seconds at that point and looked her straight in the eyes intensely as he added, "Some other Irish woman presumably. It's just a case of trying to find out initially who he was."

He could stare across at her as intensely as he wanted, but she was far too experienced to be rattled in any way by that sort of approach. Although it did make her wonder if he had some inkling that, in fact, what had happened to the guy wasn't as clear cut an accident as she had made it appear.

After a few more seconds he picked up his notebook and pen, indicating he was ready to leave. As he stood up from his chair he asked her quite casually, "So, how long are you on holiday here for, in case we need to talk to you again? At the moment I can't see why there would be any need for that, but just in case."

"I'm not on holiday. I came here to try to trace one part of my family's history, my birth father to be exact."

"Oh, I see, I automatically assumed-"

He was standing looming over the table as she interrupted. "Yes, I suppose people would really. But I decided to come for a couple of months possibly, to see what I can find. Well, that's how long I've rented this place for."

He sat back down as he asked, "So, part of your family is Greek?"

"My birth father, I think, possibly. As sure as I can be. My mother was Irish. She was here in Lindos working as a Tour Rep for a couple of summers in the mid-seventies, and I was born in seventy-eight, April. On my birth certificate it states, 'Father unknown'. So, I put two and two together and thought perhaps she met my birth father here. But she left at the end of the summer in 1977, when she must have been pregnant with me, and she never married whoever it was, is my birth father. He could have been Greek, or from what I've learned so far here, he could have simply been a tourist. I gather the tourism industry was just beginning to take off here then."

She was throwing some background, seemingly mundane, information at him. She thought for a minute that when he got up from the table he was about to leave. However, she recognised that he'd dropped in what appeared to be an innocent enough question as he appeared about to do so. It was a technique she'd used herself on occasions in her past life. So, she knew exactly how to respond; with a raft of general information that was not directly related to the subject of the interview or interrogation.

However, he tried another probing question.

"That's a nice long time to be here. September and October are always the nicest months, I think. So, a holiday of sorts at least. It' good that you can get so much time of work. What is it you do in Ireland?"

He was probing for more background.

"I don't. I live in Boston in the U.S. I'm freelance, work for myself, which is why I can take time off when I want, and as much as I want. I've been living there a few years now, even got an American passport."

She thought immediately that was a mistake, telling him about her passport. She was slipping. Out of practice at lying, or at least at giving out as little information as was necessary.

"Freelance at what?" he probed a little more.

She sat back in the chair. As she did so she picked up her sunglasses from the table and put them on, commenting, "That sun is bright," and then adding, "Security, I'm a security adviser."

Technically that wasn't a lie, just a little economical with the truth. It was what she told people in general if they asked.

The Inspector simply responded with one word, "Interesting."

"It pays the bills, but I'm not sure it's that interesting, Inspector. People always want security advice though. There are plenty of opportunities and work out there, especially in cyber security these days, which is what I've been branching out into recently. It's still mainly property, homes, offices, factories, shops, malls, though, all sorts really, particularly in the U.S., which is why I moved there a few years ago."

He had got enough of her background in terms of what she did for a living by now, however. Or he thought he had. So, he attempted to take her back to what she'd told him a few minutes before. He couldn't really see or identify how it might be connected in any way to the death of the guy two nights before, but he wanted to dig a little more.

"Any luck?"

It threw her a bit, for the first time in their discussion.

"With what?"

"Your birth father, any luck here tracing him?"

"Some, maybe, I'm not sure really. Jack Constantino arranged for me to meet his mother. I met him when I was here previously in June and he seemed to know a lot about the village, and-"

"So, this is not your first time here then?" The Inspector interrupted.

"No, second time. Anyway, apparently Jack's family had another bar, smaller than the Courtyard, in the seventies and he said his mother would be able to tell me quite a lot about Lindos at that time, and about some of the people here. When I met her a few days ago it turned out she did know my mother, but not that well. She told me that my mother actually worked in their bar for a couple of weeks when she arrived at the start of the summer of 1976, before she then went and worked as a Tour Rep. That's how she knew her, and why she remembered her, because she said at that time there weren't actually that many Irish women working here. Not like now, I guess."

She dropped that last comment in deliberately in order to just reinforce her earlier explanation of why when the guy in the supposed accident had asked about an Irish woman in the village he could have been asking about anyone, but not her.

"So, did she help, what she told you?" Papadoulis asked.

"Sort of, one possibility, but it turns out he's dead now. So, it's difficult to find out for sure, not least because there are complications, Inspector. I'm sure you'll understand if I don't go into them. As I'm sure you'll know, it's a small village and it's sometimes best to leave the past …well, in the past really. If some people don't know what happened then it is probably best left like that after all this time. In any case all this about my family history and Lindos hasn't really got any bearing whatsoever on why you came to see me has it?"

Being a Detective Inspector, and knowing Lindos fairly well, Papadoulis was naturally intrigued by what she had just told him. However, he also recognised that she was right. It didn't have any bearing whatsoever on what he was presently investigating, at least as far as he could see.

Consequently, in answer to her question he simply told her, "No, not at all, obviously, but good luck with your family investigation."

With that he got up from his chair once again and told her, "Okay, well thanks for your help. I better let you get on with your day now."

"Yes, thanks, to the beach, I think, and good luck with your investigation too, Inspector," she responded, although she definitely didn't mean that. She couldn't resist one last comment though.

"It's sad, though, such a tragic accident in such a beautiful place."

After she let him out of the courtyard she returned to sit for another few minutes in the sun, convinced that she was in the clear as far as any Rhodes police investigation was concerned. As she sat there contented in that assumption however, something else was nagging away at the back of her mind. She knew for sure that her former MI6 employers wouldn't give up that easily in search of retribution. Not only for her suspected assassination of Sandra Weston, as well as their recent discovery of all of her undercover activities over the past twenty years for the Bhoys in infiltrating the agency, but now for her killing of the agent they sent to Lindos to eliminate her. Would she ever be free of all this?

Lindos was obviously now no longer the safe haven she'd anticipated it would be. She had no idea how, but somehow they'd found her. She would have to leave soon, perhaps to another Greek island, with yet another change of identity. She possessed a number of false passports supplied by the Bhoys, for a range of her false identities. Maybe she would use one of those? Maybe revert to her real name, Kathleen O'Mara, and use that one. She was pretty sure MI6 had no record of her under that name. All they knew her as was Aileen Regan.

First though, there was the meeting with Jack's grandmother later that day.

16

Inspector Yiannis Papadoulis - a 'duck' and a mysterious dead end

On his way to the small Lindos Police Station towards the top of the village Inspector Papadoulis decided it was time to pick up a mid-morning snack. In fact, a late breakfast to have with his anticipated coffee back at the station. From Aileen Regan's apartment, and then the little square with the tree surrounded by a low white wall, he took a small diversion. Instead of going straight up the alleyway to the station he cut down the one to the left of Bar404 to Café Melia in the square by the Amphitheatre. Although he'd been stationed in Rhodes a few years now he had partaken of Melia's delicious freshly cooked croissants a number of times in the past, as well as more recently on any necessary police Lindos visits. He was particularly partial to the chocolate ones, and he wasn't going to miss out on the opportunity to indulge himself with some of those once again. His current investigation appeared to be quite straightforward; an unfortunate accident. Nothing that he'd just heard from Aileen Regan had made him suspect otherwise, even though he still had no idea of the dead man's identity. Nevertheless, there certainly didn't seem to be any apparent urgency attached to the investigation. He'd only managed to grab a quick cup of coffee as a substitute for breakfast before he left home in Rhodes Town that morning. Consequently, why not take his time and get some of his favourite tasty fresh croissants for a proper late breakfast with another cup of coffee at the station.

Papadoulis had been promoted from Sergeant to Inspector at the very same time as his previous boss, Inspector Dimitris Karagoulis, was murdered by members of the Czech mafia six years previously. It happened during part of a murder investigation in Lindos they were both engaged on at the time which took them to the Czech Republic. As he was with him at the time Karagoulis was killed Papadoulis was lucky to escape the same fate.

The previous few years for Karagoulis had been traumatic, a bit of a Greek tragedy. His wife had left him, wanting to return to live in her home city of Athens. The Inspector had been posted to Rhodes from there some years earlier. In fact, he hadn't been given much choice over the posting. He'd messed up badly on a case in Athens. The price for that imposed on him by his superiors was the choice of a transfer to Rhodes or early retirement, neither of which he found very attractive.

Karagoulis was a good detective, if not always an orthodox one in terms of his methods of investigation. He loved the big city environment, as well as the day to day crime issues and events of a city like Athens. In comparison Rhodes was a bit of a sleepy backwater most of the time. Although, during the slightly more than ten years of his posting on the island Karagoulis had been engaged in three separate high profile murder case investigations, the last one of which resulted in his death in 2010. For the previous two years he had descended into bouts of alcoholism and melancholy, brought on by his disillusionment with his job and loneliness after his wife left him. The exception to that were the final few weeks of his life when he was lifted out of it by a recent relationship he had re-ignited with a woman police pathologist in Rhodes Town, Crisa Tsagroni. She was a clever, no nonsense woman in her mid-forties, who had retained the good looks and figure of her youth, complimented by her attractive shoulder length, typically Greek, jet black hair. They had known each other for a number of years through their work, and Karagoulis had never hidden how he felt about her, even while he was still married. In fact, after his wife left him to return to live in Athens they had a brief affair, which eventually led to his divorce. Karagoulis wasn't exactly a stunningly attractive man, especially as Greeks go. He was quite short, bald-headed, and had a small dark moustache etched across the top lip of his round face. However, Crisa Tsagroni and he had a certain rapport between them, which often spilled over into obvious flirting. Although she never responded or gave him any encouragement beyond that until after his wife left. Eventually, however, she couldn't cope with his drinking, and wasn't slow in telling him that. That was when she ended their first affair. It was only when he vowed to stop, shortly before he was killed, that she once again returned his advances. In his late fifties, Karagoulis was due to retire soon, and they had actually begun to plan a life together.

As his Sergeant, Papadoulis initially found it hard to relate to Karagoulis after he was posted to Rhodes, particularly over some of his idiosyncrasies in investigating and attempting to solve cases. Karagoulis was an avid, keen and enthusiastic proponent of Greek mythology, and was never reticent in attempting to apply some of the theories of it, and fables from it, to his investigations. Initially, Papadoulis found that irritating, obtuse, and odd. Over their years working together, however, he actually grew to like Karagoulis' often quirky approach, and in some cases appreciate their relevance. He even picked up some interest in parts of Greek mythology himself. He learned a lot from him. He was literally by his side when Karagoulis was killed, and still missed him and his unorthodox approach. Karagoulis sometimes gave off an impression of a bumbling and disorganised set of thoughts during an investigation, but behind that he hid a fine brain and a forensic mind. In contrast, Papadoulis gave off an impression of a much more organised and methodical approach, although he was no less a good detective than his former boss.

If nothing else, one thing Karagoulis and all the trials and tribulations of the final few years of his life had taught his Sergeant was that life was short, too short. You should enjoy it while you can and appreciate what you have. In Papadoulis' case that was a lovely wife and two children, as well as a good job that was not too stressful most of the time in the wonderful surroundings and weather of the island of Rhodes. The case of the unfortunate mysterious man that he was presently investigating certainly appeared to be not too stressful, at least from what he'd discovered so far; a straightforward accident it seemed, and a pretty usual run-of-the-mill Rhodes investigation.

Café Melia was quite busy at that time of day, mid-morning. It was a popular café for tourists on their way to the beaches at St. Paul's Bay. They would collect some freshly made baguettes, rolls, or Greek Cheese pies from Melia for their beach lunch. As the Inspector entered the café the enticing aroma of the freshly baked croissants filled his nostrils, becoming even more tempting as he waited in the queue behind two English tourist couples being served.

Lindos was a village. Word, or gossip, even exaggerated rumour, travelled fast, and far and wide, particularly amongst the tourists. So, it was no surprise to Papadoulis when he overheard the conversation which he did between the two middle-aged English tourist women in the couples ahead of him. He even allowed himself a little partly subdued smile and a very slight shake of the head.

"Yes, I heard about that. I heard a couple talking about it on the beach yesterday. The woman said that she heard he was drunk, really drunk, paralytic apparently."

"Oh, I didn't hear that he was that drunk," her friend commented, "Just that he slipped on the path up there and cracked his head open. It is quite slippery up there in some places. You have to be careful."

"Yes, it is, and not the best place to be walking if you have had a good drink, especially at night. It can be quite dark along that alleyway. We stayed up that part of the village last year and we were always careful."

"They say they don't know who he was, had no identification on him apparently," one of the women added as she rooted around in her beach bag searching for her purse to pay for the baguettes and bottles of water she had just bought for her and her husband.

"Oh, but I heard he was Russian, so they must have some idea who he was to know that presumably," her friend replied as she too paid for her baguettes and water.

As they left and Papadoulis ordered four croissants he smiled briefly once more, thinking, not very seriously, that perhaps he should have asked the two women what or who their sources were. Being fairly sure it was only unreliable beach gossip, however, he thought better of it.

A few minutes later he entered the small office at the rear of Lindos Police Station which he and his Sergeant from Rhodes, Antonis Georgiou, temporarily occupied while carrying out their investigation. It had recently been updated, which basically meant a new, much more up-to-date computer and a coat of magnolia paint on the mostly bare, decidedly unfriendly looking walls. The two metal desks had retained their status and position though, having not been replaced, despite each of them acquiring a considerably more comfortable looking new chair. The only things that broke up the monotony of the bare walls was a fair sized white Incident Board and a new air-conditioning unit high up on the wall which faced onto the outside alley. The Sergeant had stuck a photo of the dead man on the board and written a couple of question marks alongside it with one of the nearby markers. There was not even a small window through which the bright Lindos sunlight could intrude upon the monopoly of the artificial strip lighting, but at least the air-conditioning unit kept the office at a bearable temperature, even in high summer.

"Breakfast? I've got us a couple of croissants each, chocolate ones," Papadoulis said as he came through the office door and held up the brown paper bag of croissants in the direction of his Sergeant.

"Definitely, sir, I'm starving, didn't get time for anything before I left home this morning. I'll make some coffee," Georgiou replied as he headed over towards the small unit in the corner of the office and the kettle on it next to a couple of mugs and a jar of instant coffee.

While the Sergeant left the office to fill the kettle with water Papadoulis tucked into the first of his croissants. As the Sergeant returned he told him, "Hmm ... delicious, always are from Café Melia here."

While they waited for the kettle to boil, and as Georgiou started on the first of his croissants, the Inspector got up and walked over to the white, almost bare, Incident Board. He picked up one of the markers and wrote to one side of it, away from the photo, 'Aileen Regan' and a couple of more question marks.

"Did you get anything from her, sir," Georgiou asked.

"Not really, a bit of background on why she's here and for how long. She said a couple of months probably."

"That's a long holiday," the Sergeant commented.

"She's not here on holiday. Something to do with tracing part of her family that she thinks was from here apparently."

Papadoulis took his notebook out of his pocket and opened it while he remained standing in front of the Incident Board, and then scanned one of its pages briefly.

"So, Sergeant, she's here trying to trace some of her family history. She thinks her birth father was Greek, from Lindos. Something about her birth certificate stating 'Father unknown', and her mother being here working in Lindos in the mid-seventies for the two summers before she was born."

The Inspector wandered slowly away from the board and scratched the back of his head momentarily before he added, "There was something a bit odd though. When I showed her the photo of the dead man at first she said she never knew him."

He stopped and scanned his notebook once again. "Now, what was it she said exactly? Oh, yes, here it is. She said she'd never seen him before. But when I told her that one of the barmen in Pal's Bar told us he'd pointed out the dead man to her she backtracked a little. She claimed that he'd only pointed the man out to her through the window of the bar when he was sat outside, and that she'd only seen his back."

"That could be a reasonable explanation though, sir," the Sergeant suggested. "What about the 'Irish woman' stuff, though? What did she say to that?" As he finished asking Georgiou placed the Inspector's mug of coffee on his desk.

Before he answered Papadoulis turned around and walked back to the board, picked up the pen and wrote 'IRISH WOMAN?' in large capital letters beneath 'Aileen Regan'. He turned around, walked over to pick up his coffee and took a sip.

"She said that could have been anyone, and that there are plenty of Irish tourists in Lindos at any time, which I suppose is true."

"And all over Rhodes at this time of year, not just here," the Sergeant added.

"Yes, I suppose so, Sergeant," Papadoulis agreed, somewhat wearily.

He sat down at his desk and stared across in silence at the almost bare white Incident Board for a long minute. Georgiou knew his Inspector's methods well enough to know not to say anything, but simply join him in silent contemplation while he took a seat at his own desk. He took advantage of the silence to tuck into his remaining croissant.

Eventually Papadoulis broke the silence. "Maybe we are simply looking for something that isn't there, Sergeant. The Americans have a saying, supposedly attributed to a poet of theirs, James Whitcomb Riley, in the nineteenth century. I think it goes something like if it walks like a duck, swims like a duck, and quacks like a duck, then most likely it's a duck. It called abductive reasoning, a form of what's known as logical inference, which starts with an observation or set of observations and then seeks to find the simplest and most likely explanation for the observations. Unlike deductive reasoning, it provides a plausible conclusion, but doesn't positively verify it. So, abductive conclusions have a trace of uncertainty or doubt that remains, which is expressed in terms such as 'the best available' or 'the most likely' explanation. Abductive reasoning implies the best explanation."

Papadoulis looked across at Georgiou, who was displaying a totally confused look across his face. It was hardly his old boss Inspector Karagoulis' use and application of Greek Mythology analogies in attempting to solve cases, but in his own way Papadoulis thought what he'd just said had its unorthodox similarities and quirks. Karagoulis would have been proud of him.

With a small ironic grin on his face he added, "The things they teach you these days in Detective Inspector training courses, eh, Sergeant. Anyway, to cut through all that theory, what I'm saying is, maybe it's just a duck we have here."

"A ... a duck ... a duck, sir, yes, I see."

He wasn't sure he did completely, but Georgiou also knew his Inspector well enough through previous investigations to realise when something was still bothering him. Duck or no duck, this was one of those occasions.

Papadoulis put down his coffee mug and rubbed the fingers of his right hand backwards and forwards slowly across his chin. Eventually he said, "But ..."

He never completed what he was about to say. Instead, he reached over to pick up his notebook from on the desk, and peer into it and his notes for a few seconds once more.

"But what, sir," Georgiou asked.

The Inspector began to tell him, "It was just …"

He was searching through the pages of his small notebook, turning them over furiously.

Eventually he said, "Yes, here it is. Something I wrote down while she was answering one of my questions. It was just a feeling, an impression, I got from what she said and the way she said it. When I asked about her movements on Saturday night after she left Pal's Bar she got a bit agitated, asked me why I was so interested in her movements if the guy's death was an accident. She asked if we suspected it wasn't an accident. It wasn't like she was raving at me or anything, but she seemed a little disturbed by my question. It was almost as if she was determined that it was an accident, or at least that we should believe it was, accept that it was. Then she launched into a very detailed, extremely detailed it seemed to me, explanation of her movements that night after Pal's, including volunteering the names of people she said she spoke too in the Crazy Moon cocktail bar, as well as staff on the door in Arches Club. It just all felt a bit too rehearsed, almost too detailed, even down to the times she reeled off of when she was in those places. I wrote them down, here in my notebook."

He pointed to the open page in his notebook.

"If they are right, those times, and she is telling the truth, there is no way that she could have been involved in the man's death at the time when the pathologist estimated it happened. She had a perfect alibi, almost too perfect."

He shook his head slightly in bewilderment before he continued.

"Besides anything else, even if she was involved in the guy's death, she would surely have been covered in his blood at the time that she said she was in Crazy Moon. That's assuming that it actually wasn't an accident, of course."

"Or a duck, sir," Georgiou tried to inject the slight relief of a comical comment.

"What?" Papadoulis asked.

"Sorry, assuming it wasn't a duck, wasn't an accident, sir," the Sergeant tried to explain. Realising his Inspector wasn't now in any sort of mood to be amused he quickly suggested, "I could easily check that out with those people. Check with the people at Crazy Moon if what she told you was correct, that she was there at the times she said she was."

"You should do that, Georgiou, although with the amount of detail she went into, especially the times, I'd be amazed if she was lying. It just felt like she had a nicely constructed alibi though."

At that point the computer on Georgiou's desk pinged and he peered at the screen, scanning the message on it.

"It's an email from the police in London, sir. They have no match whatsoever for the fingerprints and DNA sample details of our dead man that the lab in Rhodes Town sent them."

Papadoulis scratched the top of his head once again and wandered over towards the Incident Board. He stood staring at the photo of the man and his injuries for a minute or so, once more in complete silence.

"So, who is he, our mystery man, and what was he doing here? Was he here as a tourist or for some other reason? And why was he asking about an Irish woman? Who was this Irish woman he was looking for, was so keen to find?"

As he finished speaking Papadoulis rubbed his right hand across the back of his stressed and tightening neck. Then he picked up a marker pen and wrote all those questions on the board beneath the man's photo. As he finished writing he stepped back a couple of paces from the board. Still staring at it he said, "Well, I suppose there is at least one thing we know now about our mystery man."

"What's that?" the Sergeant asked after a few seconds as Papadoulis stopped speaking without going on to explain.

"Well, if the U.K. police have no match for his fingerprints or DNA at least he can't have any criminal record."

"No, sir, I suppose not."

"Doesn't mean he wasn't a criminal, of course. Just means he'd never been caught, and maybe if it wasn't an accident it was some sort of revenge killing. Falling out amongst thieves, perhaps? Who knows? It's certainly a mystery."

It was clear that something about the case was nagging away at Papadoulis; that they had managed to turn up very little information about the mystery dead man. Irrespective of whether it was actually an accident or not he couldn't get past the fact that they had been unable to identify him or even where he was staying.

He walked back to his desk and this time perched awkwardly on the corner of it. Looking across at the Incident Board, still clutching the marker pen and clicking the top of it on and off in frustration as he spoke, he went over some of the unanswered questions, once again.

"So, no one knows this man, not even where he was staying. Why did he not even have any hotel or apartment key, or some sort of card from a hotel or complex, or anything from where he was staying on him? And no identification whatsoever. Why no mobile phone? All we know from the staff at Pal's Bar, and from Jack Constantino, is that they are all pretty sure he was English. But the U.K. police say they have nothing on him that matches the prints and DNA information."

"Not everyone here on holiday takes their phone out with them in the evening though. So that might explain that, sir. He may just have left it wherever he was staying," Georgiou suggested. "We still have officers going to apartments throughout the village with his photo, as well as up at Krana to the holiday complexes. Maybe they'll turn something up from the owners or the staff, or even the tourists?"

"Maybe, let's hope so," Papadoulis agreed.

He levered himself off of the corner of the desk and walked back across to the board to add underneath the man's photo and the other questions 'Where was he staying?'

"There is still this Irish woman thing that I can't get out of my head though," he started to say. "It's basically the only thing we know about him, except that it seems most likely he was English."

He used the end of the marker pen to tap her name written on the board as he continued, "But Aileen Regan says it couldn't have been her because she never knew him. She said she only saw him once from behind through a window when one of the barmen in Pal's pointed him out to her while he was sitting outside the bar. So who was it he was so desperate to find, and why? Who was the bloody Irish woman he was looking for?"

Papadoulis was going around in circles and getting increasingly frustrated over not even coming up with ways to try to find the answers to some of his questions.

"What about this woman, Regan, though, sir?"

Georgiou tried to help ease his Inspector's frustration.

"What do we know about her? Where does she live in Ireland? What does she do for a living? It must be pretty good if she can spend a couple of months here. Maybe we could do some investigating on her and contact the Irish police? We only have her word for the fact that she didn't know our dead man. Even if she didn't actually kill him, what if she's lying and could tell us more about him?"

"She doesn't, she doesn't live in Ireland," Papadoulis replied. "She said she lives in Boston, America, and has been there a few years. She said she is a security adviser, freelance, and works for herself. She moved to the U.S. because there is plenty of that type of work there apparently, and now she has an American passport."

He ended by saying to Georgiou, "Good point though, Sergeant." Papadoulis clicked the top of the marker pen once again and turned around to quickly write all those questions on the board beneath the name 'Aileen Regan', along with 'Boston', 'U.S. passport', and 'freelance security adviser'. At least now the board wasn't looking quite so bare.

As he finished writing Papadoulis turned to tell Georgiou, "Okay then, let's do some digging on Miss Regan. Do the usual social media search on her for a start. While you're doing that I'll get on to the American Embassy in Athens to check out that she does actually have an American passport and see if they can tell us any more information about her, such as confirming that she does live in Boston for a start. Not sure if they'll be able to do that, but they should be able to help on the passport."

After he explained who he was and that he was investigating a death in Lindos on Rhodes, the Inspector's call to the American Embassy in Athens didn't provide any further immediate information, however. Once he ended his call he informed Georgiou that he had been told by an embassy official, the Administrative Consul, that they didn't have full access to those records in Athens, so he would need to contact Washington and get them to check. He said he would get back to Papadoulis as soon as he could, but as Washington was seven hours behind Athens it was only very early there at present, barely six a.m. Consequently, it could be a few hours or so.

As Papadoulis finished telling his Sergeant all that there was another pinge on the computer. Georgiou looked at the screen and clicked to open up the email attachment.

"It's the full autopsy report, sir."

He scanned it, searching for and reading out the key relevant parts.

"Err … a broken nose caused by a blow to the face, possibly from a fall into the wall by the deceased … cause of death a head trauma, a fracture to the skull from a blow to the head by a blunt object … err … probably the relatively large stone that was found at the scene covered in blood, which had been detached from the path slab previously, presumably by wear and tear on the path … most likely scenario is that the large stone inflicted the initial, eventually fatal, injury from a fall by the male, who then attempted to get up dazed, stumbled down the steps and fell again hitting the front of the skull against wall … err … led to profuse bleeding, concussion, and substantial eventual blood loss while the deceased lost consciousness."

The Sergeant stopped speaking for a few seconds and continued scanning the report until finally adding, "Err … it doesn't say anything different from the pathologist's initial preliminary report in respect of alcohol, sir. It just states that there were some traces of alcohol in the blood stream, but not an excessive amount. I'll print a copy."

"So, as we thought before, he wasn't exactly paralytic in terms of the amount of drinks he'd had that night," Papadoulis pointed out, obviously indicating his lingering reservations about the possible accident.

"No, but the ground can be a bit rough and slippery up there in places, sir, and dark at night," the Sergeant added.

Georgiou went back to scanning a range of social media, searching for anything on Aileen Regan, while the Inspector returned to standing in front of the Incident Board contemplating the various questions that were now written on it. After a couple of minutes, however, he scratched his head with his right hand once more, then glanced at his watch, and seeing it was gone one o'clock simply said, "Lunch, I think," immediately suggesting, "Perhaps some more food will prompt our brain cells a little, Sergeant. While you carry on with that I'll go and get us a baguette each from Melia. Cheese, tuna, ham and salad, or?"

"One of their delicious homemade feta and spinach pies please, if it's all the same to you, sir. Thanks," Georgiou suggested.

"Good idea. I'll have one of those myself. Back in a few minutes." With that Papadoulis made his way out of the office and the Police Station into the bright blistering Lindos sunshine and the alleyway on his way to the café.

When the Inspector returned with their pies he was surprised to be told by Georgiou that he'd already received a call back from the American Embassy in Athens.

"They said they had no record at all of any United States' passport issued in the name of Aileen Regan."

"Really? How can that be? What about confirming her living in Boston?" Papadoulis asked, with incredulity clearly evident in his voice.

"They never said. I assumed that if they had no record of a passport in her name they wouldn't have any record of her living in Boston, sir."

"Not necessarily, Sergeant. The majority of Americans don't actually have passports. I saw somewhere that only around twenty per cent do. Just because someone doesn't have a passport it doesn't mean that where they live isn't registered somewhere."

The Inspector sounded a little angry at having to explain that to his Sergeant. However, Georgiou attempted to get himself out of that particular hole by pointing out, "But she must have a passport, sir, otherwise she wouldn't have been able to travel here would she?"

"That's true, Sergeant. Maybe it's not an American one though, despite what she told me. Miss Regan is rapidly becoming as mysterious a figure as our dead man."

"Well, at least the embassy came back quickly, sir. So, at least we know that much, a bit more, or that little about her now. I suppose that is the more accurate way of putting it. Maybe we should check with the Irish Embassy in Athens, sir? To see if they have any record of a passport in her name?"

"Yes, yes, do that, Sergeant. And we do, don't we … know a bit more about her … and they did, didn't they …" Papadoulis hesitated between phrases, and then stopped speaking altogether. What he was saying wasn't really making a lot of sense to the Sergeant, as he once again walked over to stare at the board, and in particular the name 'Aileen Regan'.

He turned around to face Georgiou sitting at his desk and starting on his feta and spinach pie and said, "Odd, that's very odd. What time is it exactly?"

The Sergeant looked a little bewildered as he thought Papadoulis would surely know that as it was only twenty minutes ago that he'd told Georgiou it was just gone one o'clock and he would go and get them some lunch. Nevertheless, he answered, "Almost one-thirty, sir."

"Exactly," the Inspector exclaimed, "And in Washington it would only be six-thirty, early morning."

"Yes, sir, it would."

"But that's very odd, very odd, isn't it? The U.S. Administrative Consul in Athens told me that it could be quite a few hours before he got back to me about the passport because of the time difference between here and Washington. But he came back within an hour, and it's only around six-thirty in the morning in Washington now."

"Maybe it's all digital, electronic, online though, sir. Perhaps, they didn't have to wait for the offices over there to open up to get in touch with Washington after all?"

"Perhaps, but why did he tell me they would? Surely, if anybody, he would know that, wouldn't he? His title suggests he's in charge of administration doesn't it? Surely he'd know if they could access the records electronically online."

"But it wasn't him who called back, sir."

"Oh, I see, obviously just some clerk or other then, who obviously knew far more about electronic access to those sorts of things, I suppose."

"I don't think so, sir, no, not just a clerk. It was a bit odd though. At first he wouldn't say who he was, his position in the embassy I mean. But I pushed him, and explained that I needed to know exactly what his position was for the record and the purposes of our investigation as he could be anybody. He was very reluctant and took a lot of persuading. Eventually he told me he was the Deputy Chief of Mission. When I asked him if he could expand on that a little for the records of our investigation, tell me exactly how that position related to information concerning possible American passport holders like Aileen Regan, he, still rather reluctantly, said that it included responsibilities for the embassy section of the U.S. Immigration and Customs Enforcement Agency."

Papadoulis stood in silence in the middle of the office slowly shaking his head from side to side in stunned disbelief, trying to process all the Sergeant had just told him. He turned around once again to stare at the Incident Board, remaining silent for another long minute. Then he added, 'no U.S. passport' to the board beneath 'Aileen Regan'.

Finally, he turned back to face Georgiou and said, "That is the number-two diplomat assigned to an American embassy, the Deputy Chief of Mission, obviously not some clerk or other. And that U.S Immigration Enforcement Agency is not just some bureaucratic department concerned with passports. In fact, it is a U.S. Federal Law enforcement agency within the U.S. Department of Homeland Security. Yes, Sergeant, it is principally responsible for immigration and customs enforcement, so maybe some involvement in relation to passports, but it has additional responsibilities in countering transnational crime. I went to a conference in Athens on that sort of thing, transnational crime, a couple of years ago. That's how I know all this."

Now it was the Sergeant's turn to have a look of disbelief spread across his face at what he'd just heard from his Inspector.

"But, but … and I gave the guy a hard time at first when he wouldn't say who he was. And why-"

He was probably about to say the same thing as the Inspector when Papadoulis interrupted him, but he never got the chance.

"Yes, Georgiou, yes, precisely, why is the number two U.S Embassy diplomat in Athens calling us back on what appeared to be a quite innocuous enquiry about a supposed American passport holder? Why did we get a call back from someone who holds a senior position connected to the U.S. Department of Homeland Security? Very odd that they came back so quickly, and even odder, and suspicious, that someone so senior should get involved."

Papadoulis turned back to stare at the board and the name Aileen Regan there once again. After a puff of his cheeks he said, "My guess is that there is more to Miss Regan than meets the eye, and that the Americans certainly know a lot more about her than we do. Although, I also suspect that there is no way they are going to tell us quite what."

"But how is all this connected to our dead man, and what may or may not have happened, sir?" the Sergeant asked, a clearly totally bemused tone in his voice.

Papadoulis turned away from the board once more and replied, "Well, perhaps it's not, not connected at all, Sergeant. Perhaps it will turn out not to be necessary, but if we can't come up with anything else, and if I'm still not fully convinced it was an accident, then I think we will need to go and have another word with the mysterious Aileen Regan. Ask her just why the Americans tell us that they have no record of her having one of their passports when she told me that she did. This case just gets stranger and stranger, yet it did appear at first to be one of a straightforward unfortunate accident. For now though, it will probably be best not to go stirring up any hornets' nest involving the American Secret Service agencies, of whatever form, at least not until we are certain that it has some connection to our enquiry into this man's death. The last thing we want to do is get involved, and start poking around, in something that doesn't concern us."

The Inspector couldn't resist one final comment though as he now headed over to pick up his feta and spinach pie. "Hmm ... the mysterious Miss Regan. Mysterious indeed," he mumbled before he proceeded to take a substantial bite out of the pie.

As he did so, and Georgiou finished his, the Sergeant asked, "Coffee, sir?" To which Papadoulis replied, "Yes, thanks," as he eased himself into his chair behind the desk with the remainder of his pie.

As the Sergeant brought over Papadoulis' coffee the Inspector was finishing the final mouthful of his lunch. "Very good aren't they, sir, the pies," he said.

"Excellent," Papadoulis agreed. "I should have bought us two each."

At that point the phone rang and the Inspector answered it.

A very refined English voice at the other end of the line asked, "Can I speak to Detective Inspector Yiannis Papadoulis please?"

"Speaking, who is this?" the Inspector asked.

"Sir Peter Stanhope, the British Ambassador to the Hellenic Republic, is my full title, more commonly, the British Ambassador to Greece."

Papadoulis was dumbstruck, wondering what a call from such a person could bring, as the Ambassador continued.

"I believe you have the body of a British citizen killed in an unfortunate accident in Lindos on Saturday evening, Inspector."

It wasn't a question, by his tone it was obviously a statement of fact.

"Yes, but we are not sure that-" the Inspector started to respond, intending to point out firstly that they had no evidence at all that the dead man was a British citizen. He never got the chance.

"Good. The Vice-Consulate in Rhodes Town will be in touch shortly, within the hour, Detective Inspector, to make the necessary arrangements to collect the body for return to the U.K.-"

"But-" Papadoulis tried to interrupt. However, the Ambassador wasn't going to let him.

"I presume it is in the mortuary in Rhodes Town?"

"Well, yes, but hang on, we-"

Once again the Inspector had no success in trying to interrupt as the Ambassador told him, with a clear forceful authoritative, abrupt tone in his voice, "No you hang on, Inspector. This is a British citizen and, as I just told you, our Vice-Consulate will be in touch soon to arrange for the body to be collected. That is the end of the matter. I trust you understand. Now you just get on and arrange it quickly."

The Ambassador didn't wait for Papadoulis to reply and the line went dead as he rang off. No sooner had Papadoulis put down the phone, accompanied by a puff of his cheeks in exasperation as he slumped back in his chair, than it rang again.

This time a female voice told him, "I have Police Lieutenant General, Nikolais Kouris, Chief of the Hellenic Police, calling from Athens for Detective Inspector Yiannis Papadoulis."

The Inspector thought he had obviously suddenly for some reason become a very popular person for so many important people to want to speak to him as he confirmed, "Yes, Inspector Papadoulis speaking."

"Okay, I'll put you through," the female voice told him.

"Hello Inspector Papadoulis," a man's very important sounding voice came down the line.

"Hello, sir." Now Papadoulis was wondering what exactly this call would bring.

"I understand you have the body of an English man who died in an accident in Lindos a few nights ago, Inspector."

"Yes, sir, that's correct, although we are not entirely sure it was an accident. We are still investigating as it-"

Once again Papadoulis never got to finish what he was saying. The Hellenic Police Chief was clearly not interested in hearing his reservations.

"I understand the body is in the Rhodes Town mortuary, Inspector?"

Papadoulis tried once more. "Yes, sir, but-"

However, yet again he never got to finish what he was saying.

"Good, it will be collected later today by the British Vice-Consul in Rhodes Town so it can be returned to England. They will be in touch with you within the hour to arrange that. Is that clear, Inspector?"

"Well, actually, sir, the British Embassy in Athens have just been in touch, telling me the same thing."

"Good, get it sorted immediately, Inspector, and then that's the case closed. That's an order. It was an accident. Now, I'm sure you'll want to get on and make the necessary arrangements. Goodbye." Before Papadoulis could say anything more the Chief of Police rang off.

The Inspector replaced the phone and then wearily slumped back in his chair once again. He shook his head slowly from side to side a couple of times in silent disbelief and then let out a huge sigh. After a few seconds more he informed Georgiou, "The Chief of Police in Athens has just ordered me to release the body to the British Vice-Consul in Rhodes Town to be returned to England, and that is the end of our investigation, case closed."

The Sergeant looked at him with a similar amount of disbelief across his face.

Papadoulis got up from his chair behind the desk and once more walked across to stare at the now much fuller Incident Board. After a few seconds standing in front of it he scratched the top of his head with his right hand and said, "Hang on, how do they all know for certain that our dead man was a British citizen? The Chief of Police in Athens, the British Ambassador, they are all so certain. But there was nothing, nothing on him at all, that could tell us he was. So, how do they know for sure?"

He shook his head once again in bewilderment, this time in a much more agitated manner. "They obviously know a lot more about all this than we do, Sergeant. But they certainly aren't going to tell us. There's obviously a lot more to this mysterious man's death than meets the eye."

"But that is the case closed though, sir?" Georgiou asked, adding, "And back to Rhodes Town for us now then?"

With a distinct resigned tone in his voice the Inspector replied, "Well, if it looks like an accident, it probably is an accident as far as we're concerned, as well as far as the Chief of Police is concerned, it seems. So, it seems it's obviously a duck after all, Sergeant. There's no more to it."

Georgiou smiled slightly once more at that last 'duck' comment by Papadoulis as he asked, "And Aileen Regan and her supposed American passport, sir? Will we still go and see her about the mystery of her non-existent American passport? Should I still get on to the Irish Embassy to check up on her?"

"Why? Not our problem, Sergeant. Life's too short. Let's just get out of here and back to Rhodes Town."

Part Six: 1943

17

Battle of Rhodes and invasion

Rhodes was formally annexed by Italy as part of the Dodecanese in the Treaty of Lausanne in 1923. In the 1930s, Mussolini aimed to make Rhodes a modern transportation centre through a program of Italianization that would be at the heart of the spread of Italian culture in Greece. His Fascist programme aimed at modernising the island did have some positive outcomes. It resulted in the construction of a power plant to provide Rhodes Town with electric lighting, as well as the building of hospitals and aqueducts. By 1940 around 40,000 Italian military personnel were stationed in the Dodecanese islands, and Italy used the islands as a naval staging area for its invasion of Crete in that year.

On the 28th October 1940 Mussolini gave the Greek government an ultimatum of surrender or be invaded. Greece rejected it and Italy invaded from already occupied Albania. A basically run-down Greek army defeated the Italian invaders, which constituted the first Allied victory of the Second World War. One key consequence was that Hitler was forced to delay his planned invasion of the Soviet Union and instead divert Nazi forces to the Balkans to help subdue the Greeks, eventually succeeding in forcing the Greeks to surrender in the spring of 1941.

Mainland Greece was then divided between Germany, Italy and Bulgaria, with Italy occupying the bulk of the country. German forces occupied the strategically more important areas of Athens, Thessaloniki, Central Macedonia and several Aegean islands, including most of Crete. The Bulgarians occupied territory between the Struma River and a line running through Alexandroupoli and Svilengrad west of the Evros River. Italian troops started occupying the Ionian and Aegean islands on 28th April 1941. In early June they occupied the Peloponnese, Thessaly, and most of Attica.

The Italians were therefore responsible for most of Greece, especially the countryside, where any armed resistance might take place. However, the Italians adopted a rather relaxed attitude towards their security duties. To some extent they were justified to do so. The Resistance movement was still forming, and until the summer of 1942 they faced little real opposition and considered the situation to have been normalized. The Germans limited themselves during the first period of the occupation to the strategically important areas, and their forces were minimal.

On Rhodes the Italians took control and the new Governor of the Italian Dodecanese established his headquarters in the Palace of the Grand Master of the Knights of Rhodes. Italian troops were allocated to, and stationed at, seven defence areas on the island. Some were on the coast and others inland. One of them was the Vati Area, which spread from the Lindos headland in the south-east to Alimia bay in the west. In total there were around 34,000 Italian troops on Rhodes by September 1943. In addition, the Italian Air Force had 3,000 personnel stationed there and about sixty-five aircraft. The Gadurra air base, near Kalathos, had no planes however, as its torpedo bombers had been moved back to Italy months earlier. The Kattavia airport had been abandoned early in 1943 and rendered unusable. The only active air base was in Maritsa.

The build-up of the German military presence on Rhodes began in January 1943. Prior to that they had tried several times to reach agreement with Mussolini to put the whole of the Aegean under German control. Eventually they reached an alternative agreement to place two Flak anti-aircraft batteries on Rhodes in order to strengthen the defence of the island, particularly the air base. The agreement included provision for German military to train Italians in the use of the Flak anti-aircraft batteries and then leave the island. However, their stay was prolonged on the pretext of the planned shipment of more batteries to Rhodes.

Towards the end of January 1943 four German officers who were experts in coastal fortifications arrived on the island, and in April a German Panzergrenadier battalion – motorised and mechanised infantry - landed on Rhodes. These were organized as combined arms formations, with six battalions of truck-mounted infantry organized into either two or three regiments, a battalion of tanks, and a complement of artillery, reconnaissance units, combat engineers, anti-tank and anti-aircraft artillery.

Disregarding Mussolini's views the German military began moving onto Rhodes in large numbers. At the end of June a German General was despatched to the island to form the Sturm-Division Rhodos, which proceeded to begin a military exercise near to the Italian defences eleven kilometres from Rhodes Town. German troops already stationed on the island were supplemented with various smaller units from nearby Aegean islands, culminating in around 8,000 troops being stationed on Rhodes at that time with one hundred and fifty armoured fighting vehicles. In addition, the German's set up, and operated, a communication network separate from the Italian system. Its command was based in the village of Eleousa in the foothills of Mount Profitis Elias. Ironically, the village was originally built by the Italians, including the Italian sanatorium and the aqueduct above the village. The village's original name was Campochiaro.

Italy surrendered on the 3rd of September 1943 when an armistice was signed between Italy and the Allies. The Armistice of Cassible was not made public and announced however, until the 8th. The announcement, and the armistice, came as complete surprise to the Italian military leadership on Rhodes. The memorandum from the Italian Supreme Command in Italy to the High Command of the Italian armed forces in the Aegean on Rhodes with the instructions of how to proceed was to be sent by air, but bad weather prevented that. Consequently, the courier with his memo message was stuck in Pescara in Italy when the public announcement was made.

So, with no orders, and lack of information about the general situation of the Italian armed forces, the High Command in Rhodes faced a dilemma; should it continue to fight alongside

German forces on the island or remain loyal to Italy and surrender. In the evening of 8th September the Governor of the Italian Dodecanese established contact with the German military commander on Rhodes urging him not to give any orders to his troops that could provoke reactions by Italian troops. The German commander agreed that he would cooperate with the request. By eight-thirty that evening there was still no direct information or orders available from the Italian Supreme Command in Italy.

In fact, at that time all the Italian Governor and his military leaders knew was very little basic information from what became known as the Badoglio Proclamation. That was a speech read out on Ente Italiano per le Audizioni Radiofoniche, the public service broadcaster in Fascist Italy, at 19:42 on 8th September by Marshal Pietro Badoglio, Italian head of government at that time, announcing that the Cassibile Armistice between Italy and the Allies, signed on 3 September, had come into force. The key part of the statement was that, "all acts of hostility against the Anglo-American force by Italian forces must cease everywhere. But they may react to eventual attacks from any other source".

The Italian Governor on Rhodes interpreted the words, "any other source," as meaning the Germans and that any aggressive action by German forces was to be opposed by armed force. Consequently, when at midnight that evening on the 8th the German military commander on Rhodes requested that he be allowed to freely move his forces in order to be able to quickly oppose any possible British troops landing on the island the Italian Governor refused. This lead to a heated argument between them over the disposition of German troops on the island.

In fact, there was no likelihood of British troops landing at that time. However, a British plane did drop thousands of leaflets over Rhodes ordering the Italians to take control of the German positions and to move their ships and aircraft to British bases away from the island. The Italian Governor refused to comply.

Tensions between the Germans and Italians were rising, however. At nine o'clock on the morning of the 9th a German officer and a group of soldiers turned up at Rhodes harbour, which the Italians had closed, and asked to occupy it. The port Italian military commander refused, resulting in a tense stand-off between the two military groups. A German steamer loaded with ammunition was moored in the harbour, and her captain requested permission to unload its cargo and leave the island. The Italian military commander of the port initially denied permission and instead posted sentries to guard the ship. After several tense minutes, however, the Italian commander relented and the Germans unloaded the crates of ammunition.

However, the uneasy truce didn't last long at all. At around noon on the 9th the first German attacks began. Swift German action against the Italian Regina Infantry Division led quickly to their surrender. Italian artillery fire destroyed the German tanks that had occupied the Maritsa air base, but it also hit Italian planes that were still there. The Italian position and coastal battery near the Lindos headland was encircled by German forces on the 9th and after a short battle the Italians were defeated and taken prisoner. For the next twenty-four hours or so various armed conflicts broke out.

During the night of 9th September two British Majors and a Sergeant with a portable radio parachuted onto Rhodes. They were taken by the Italians to the Palace of the Grand Master to meet the Italian Governor of the Dodecanese, who they asked how long the Italian forces on Rhodes could hold out. They explained that it would be at least a week before any British forces could arrive. When the Italian Governor suggested British air strikes and landings in the southern part of the island in order to divert the German forces from Rhodes Town he was told the British didn't have the military capacity in the region at that time for those.

In the evening of 10th September German troops captured the Greek positions on Mount Paradiso and Mount Fileremo, close to Rhodes Town, and later that evening more Greek positions were taken. The Italian position and resistance was further severely weakened during the night of the 10th of September when Italian forces in Greece and on Crete surrendered to the Germans.

As well as the two British Majors and a Sergeant who parachuted into Rhodes in the night of 9th September three other British agents from the Special Operations Executive (SOE) had landed by boat under cover of darkness on the south-eastern part of the island at the end of July. The SOE had been set up in July 1940 for the purpose of conducting espionage, sabotage and reconnaissance in Europe against the Axis German and Italian occupying forces. The aim was to sabotage and subvert the Axis war machine through indirect, as well as sometimes direct, military objectives, including undermining and damaging the morale of the Axis' forces. It was believed that as a result the Axis powers would be forced to expend manpower and resources to maintain their control of the subjugated populations in the occupied territories. One belief was that the SOE, and their agents' activities, was modelled on the operations of the IRA in the Irish War of Independence between 1919 and 1921, particularly those of Michael Collins, an Irish revolutionary, soldier, and politician who was a leading figure in the Irish struggle for independence.

The three SOE agents on Rhodes based themselves in Lindos and the surrounding area. They initially integrated with, and assisted, the Greek partisan resistance against the occupying Italians, and then later against the Germans. Being undercover with those groups, and based in the south of the island some distance away from Rhodes Town, they made no contact with the British Majors and the Sergeant who parachuted into Rhodes. Not least this was from fear of exposing their presence to the German or the Italian occupiers, besides the geographical logistics of any attempt to do so.

At seven o'clock on the morning of September 11th German air strikes damaged an Italian artillery battery on Mount Smith on the edge of Rhodes Town, as well as disabling the Italian Navy radio station. The Italian Governor of the Dodecanese once more requested British assistance, but none was forthcoming, basically due to logistics and lack of military resource capacity in the area.

At ten-thirty that morning two German officers arrived at the Palace of the Grand Master and informed the Italian Governor of the initial surrender demands of the German

Military High Command. They comprised the immediate cessation of hostilities throughout the island, the release of all German prisoners, and the unconditional surrender of the Italian forces. The eventual final details of the Italian surrender would then be arranged and agreed with the German military commander on Rhodes. They added that the Governor had thirty minutes to decide and agree. Failure to do so within that time would result in the city of Rhodes being bombed.

Knowing that the bombing of the city would certainly result in civilian casualties the Governor agreed to the initial demands and then agreed to negotiate the rest of the surrender details. At three-thirty later that afternoon the Italian Governor and the German military commander on the island met near the city of Rhodes. They agreed that the Italian would retain his position as Governor and that the Italian military units would not be disbanded, but would be disarmed, with the exception of the Italian officers, who would be allowed to keep their weapons. The German military commanders would remain outside the city of Rhodes and no German military units would enter it, except under specific agreed conditions at the time. Whilst the Italians agreed to those conditions, unbeknown to the Germans they maintained a secret radio station and destroyed their secret documents and code books.

Some Italian troops on the island reacted with anger to news of the surrender, especially in those areas on Rhodes where they had successfully contained the German attacks, forced them to surrender, and taken prisoners. They believed in general that the Germans were running out of ammunition and fuel. Many of those Italians were given civilian clothes by their officers to avoid capture and mixed with the local Greek population. Over fifteen hundred Italian soldiers managed to escape from the island after the surrender, while a smaller number switched over to support and follow the German cause or that of its puppet state, the new Italian Social Republic. Many of those Italians who did not manage to escape from the island, avoid capture by the Germans, or switch over to support them, eventually starved to death in German prison camps on Rhodes. Between 1944 and 1945 there was a famine that also severely affected the civilian population of the island.

Some of the Italians who managed to avoid capture in September 1943 and mix with the local Greek population actually eventually engaged with the Greek Resistance in acts of sabotage against the occupying German forces.

18

Rhodes Town, the third week of August, 1943

The shadows were lengthening and the sky was darkening at nine-thirty on a steamy August evening in the old medieval part of Rhodes Town. The air was still, silent and gloomy with the burden of war. Nikos Papatonis waited in the deepest shadow of one of the alleyways leading off from the Street of the Knights. Every time he anxiously checked his old wristwatch it appeared that the minutes ticked by more and more slowly. His nervousness was visibly displayed by the small interspersed beads of sweat that nestled on his forehead in trepidation of being discovered. He wiped them away with the forefinger of his right hand once again. Then he tugged the brim of his cap down further over his forehead to just above his deep dark eyes, covering even more of his swept back jet black hair and leaving only the lower part of his long angular face beneath his eyes exposed. He was in his early thirties. He wasn't a tall man, just of medium height, and that evening he was quite shabbily dressed, as was usual for him. He didn't have the luxury of an extensive or expensive wardrobe. A fact that was amply displayed by the well-worn outfit of cheap dark trousers and dark navy blue shirt which he wore that evening. It had obviously seen better days.

Just as he glanced down at his watch once more a voice, soft and low, and with a distinct German accent, emanated from out of the shadows, speaking a single word in English.

"Well?"

"Schmidt?" Papatonis asked.

Without confirming, a tall man with short fair hair, dressed in more expensive looking clothes of a black shirt and trousers emerged out of the darkness and asked in an abrupt whisper, "How many? And who?"

The Greek told him, also in a whisper, "Three, two English men, and an Irish woman."

"To do what?" the German asked, with an equally abrupt tone, adding, "How long, and where are they staying?"

"To help and liaise with the Resistance, disrupt and destroy what they can with sabotage and espionage. They are part of some Special Forces group of the British, Special Operations something or other. I wasn't told, couldn't get, the full name."

"Executive, Special Operations Executive," the German informed him. "Yes, we know all about that British organisation. They've been training people for it since 1940. Our information is that they have over ten thousand operatives trained now."

"Really, well, anyway, that's a lot and-" Papatonis started to comment, but the German wasn't interested in his opinion and interrupted with an opinion of his own.

"What? ... Oh, yes ... but if they've only sent three here they can't think Rhodes is very important. From what we've discovered about the Allies' invasion plans we thought they'd send more here. Perhaps, there are different groups of these British operatives that have landed on the island which we don't know about yet."

He rubbed his chin with two fingers of his left hand as he said that. Papatonis shrugged his shoulders, indicating that he had no answer to that as the German repeated part of his earlier question.

"So, how long, and where are they staying?"

"They are in the south, but they move around, mainly Lindos, Pefkos and Lardos. The Resistance moves them all the time, for safety. The Italians don't have a clue. The three of them have been here almost a month now."

"Bloody Italians are fucking useless. Do they suspect you?" the German asked.

"No, I don't think so. I've even managed to get quite close to the woman."

"Been in her pants have you?" The German allowed himself a slight mocking smile as he asked that, and then added before the Greek could reply, "Well, I suppose if it gets us what we want to know. Anyway, we'll be in control here soon, not the useless lazy Italians."

The Greek ignored his question in the first part of that. Instead, with some surprise in his voice he asked, "Really? When, how?"

Now it was the German's turn to ignore the question.

"Just do what we pay you to do. Do this well and I'll make sure those that will be in control here soon remember it. You just let our man in Lardos know if the bloody Greek resistance, together with these British agents, have any sabotage attacks planned. He'll pass it through to me here in Rhodes. And see what you can find out about any planned Allied invasion. You should be able to find out something on that while you're getting into the woman's pants, shouldn't you? Assuming she actually knows anything, of course. But, then why would they be sent here if the Allies weren't planning this as part of their southern Europe invasion?"

"You think that might be really why they're here then, and not only to help the resistance with sabotage?" Papatonis asked.

The German hesitated for a moment while he looked around behind him to ensure that there was no one around except the two men.

He turned back to face the Greek and then moved closer to grab hold of his shirt in his left hand and glare menacingly straight in his face.

"You don't tell this to anyone you understand? If it gets out I will know where it has come from and I will kill you myself, slowly and painfully, very painfully. You got that?"

Papatonis nodded slightly as he responded with a clear trace of fear in his voice. "Of ... of course, yes ... yes I see."

"Good, as long as you understand."

The German released the grip on the shirt as he continued. "We know from our intelligence that they, the Allies, are going to invade through Greece, not Sicily. The body of a British Royal Marine Major was washed up from the Atlantic near a place called Huelva off the south-west coast of Spain. According to one of our agents there it looks like he was a courier as he had a briefcase full of operational documents marked classified that were about the Allied invasion of southern Europe, as well as his identity card. The documents showed that the invasion would be staged in Greece and Sardinia, but not Sicily."

The German scratched the back of his head as he finished speaking, and then added thoughtfully, "So, perhaps that's why they have sent these Special operations agents here now. But why only three?"

"As I said, all I've heard from others in the group is that they are here to support the Resistance in their planning and operations of sabotage and espionage. I've heard nothing about Allied invasion preparations at all," the Greek told him.

"You've obviously got some more work and digging to do to find out anything you can from the Irish woman on that then, anything you can find out about the Allied invasion. She may not know anything, of course. It may not be within her operations or rank, but, if nothing else, at least you'll get to get into her knickers again, won't you. That'll be some reward and pleasure for you won't it."

As he finished the German allowed another small ironic smile to creep across his lips. Before **Papatonis** could answer he added firmly, "As soon as possible. Find out anything you can as soon as possible and pass it through Lardos to me."

With that he disappeared back into the shadows of the dark Rhodes night and was gone.

Part Seven: August 2016

19

Jack's grandmother and recollections of the war

Aileen arrived promptly at Jack's mother's villa at four o'clock on Monday afternoon for her meeting with his grandmother. Following her encounter earlier that day with the police Inspector she decided that the best way to cool down, physically and mentally, was to grab a few hours on a sunbed on the Main Beach, interspersed with some very enjoyable swims in the clear water of Lindos Bay.

Even though it was approaching late in the afternoon there was absolutely no possibility whatsoever of the August Lindos heat diminishing. The build-up of it in the narrow white walled alleys throughout the day from early morning meant it lingered long into the warm evenings and night. Anticipating that, after she returned from the beach and jumped into a quick shower she merely slipped on over her underwear a cool, sleeveless, short light blue cotton dress, as well as her flat sandals.

When she knocked Jack opened the door to the villa, showed her through the lounge, and out onto the terrace again, where Eleni and his grandmother were seated at the round table in the cooling shade from the parasol above it.

As they reached the table Jack told Aileen, "This is my grandmother," and then proceeded to introduce Aileen to her. She told Aileen, "Pleased to meet you," followed straightaway by, "Please, call me Maria."

Her English was surprisingly good. When Aileen complimented her on it to that effect and thanked her for seeing her she responded modestly, "It could be better, but I learned quite a lot during the war, as well as from the tourists here over the past thirty years. I've been looking forward to meeting you. Eleni has told me a little about you and why you are here."

Maria was a short, quite frail looking woman of ninety-one years old. Jack had told Aileen previously though that she was still very active and had all her faculties, even her memory was good, as Aileen was shortly to find out. Her hair was very grey, almost white. Despite having it tied back it could clearly be seen that it was expectedly thinning. Her lined faced displayed all the character of her ninety-one years. She appeared totally relaxed and comfortable, at ease with herself as she sat back in her chair. Before Jack could sit down with Aileen to join the two women at the table Maria told him to get them all some cold lemonade from the fridge. There was a jug of it that she had freshly made that morning. The way the old woman was instructing her grandson like he was still a young boy made Aileen smile.

As Jack disappeared into the kitchen to fetch the lemonade and some glasses Maria told Aileen, "You look a lot like your grandmother. Your hair is different, I suppose. Hers was naturally red she told me, although she said she died it black just before she came here in 1943, to make her look more Greek. It was short, like yours, though. It had to be really for her in those days. But you have very similar looks, and, oh how do you say it, the face?"

"Facial features, mother, "Eleni helped her.

"Yes, yes, of course, stupid of me, yes facial features, very similar," Maria scolded herself slightly for not having the right words.

"I don't remember her that much. She died when I was still a child. I've seen some photos of her since, photos my mother had. From those I suppose I could see that we do have some similar features," Aileen agreed.

"Your eyes are definitely hers, the same. I remember them well, sparkling and dark brown. Irish eyes we called them. Sometimes you could see the mischief in them. Beautiful, she was a beautiful woman, your grandmother, and a very brave one, a very, very brave young woman, only twenty-four when she came here."

Maria hesitated for a moment as she finished that last sentence and stared past Aileen and out across the terrace at the Acropolis and Lindos beneath them. There was a brief second of sadness that clouded her eyes. Then she explained her hesitation. "Sorry, memories … anyway, yes, she was a beautiful woman your grandmother, very attractive, and most of the time a warm personality. Although, when she needed to be she could be very determined, detached and cold, ruthless some people said. I guess that was what she had been trained to do."

That last comment struck a chord with Aileen. It was all too familiar. She realised that Maria could have been describing her rather than her grandmother.

The tone of Maria's voice tailed of slightly, with an element of sadness once again invading it as she remembered that last part of what she said. At that point Jack emerged from the kitchen with their lemonade. He poured them all a glass and sat down at the table to join them.

As he did so Aileen told him, "Your grandmother thinks I look like my grandmother, especially my eyes."

"Really? And do you think I have your eyes, grandmother?" Jack asked, with a smile.

"We are not here to talk about you, Jack. Aileen wants to hear all about Bernie," Maria scolded him gently.

He never responded, just picked up his glass and took a sip of the lemonade like some told off naughty schoolboy.

"I came to know her as Bernie, although her full name was Bernadette of course, her real name. But I only got to know that when she told me after she came back here in 1946. Anyway, that's what she preferred, Bernie," Maria said to Aileen. "But I expect you know that. Of course, when she came here in 1943, was here, she had forged identity papers, they all did, the three of them. There was your grandmother and two English men. In the Resistance we never knew their real names at that time. We never got told them, and anyway we didn't want to know. That was best. We only knew them by the Greek names on their forged Greek identity cards. Bernie's was Alexandra, Alexandra Callas, like the famous opera singer. It was fake, of course, a fake name, but in Greek it partly means beautiful or good, which is ironic because she was beautiful, but she wasn't always good, your grandmother."

Maria paused and smiled about that.

While Maria paused for a moment Aileen wondered briefly quite what she meant by, "wasn't always good." Then she reached down into her handbag on the floor and took out a folded foolscap envelope. She took out the Identity Card which she had discovered in her mother's house after she died and handed it across the table to Maria, asking as she did so, "Is this it?"

Maria took it and held it in silence for a moment while she gazed down at it and the photo on it of a very young looking Aileen's grandmother. Aileen thought she noticed a small tear in the corner of one of Maria's eyes as she told her, "Yes, that's her, that's Bernie, or as it says in Greek, Alexandra."

As she eventually handed it back across the table Maria added, "She shortened that as well with us in the Resistance, Alexandra to Alex. We never even knew where they came from, the three of them. Although, of course, there was a tinge of an Irish accent in Bernie's speech when she talked with us. She disguised it well, however, if she ever spoke to anyone outside the Resistance in the village or locally, and on the very few occasions she had to speak to the Italians or the Germans. She spoke good Greek you see. All three of them did. They were agents in what was called the British Special Operations Executive, the SOE they called it most of the time. Not that they mentioned it very often at all, very little in fact, deliberately. Bernie told me later that in their training before they came here they were told constantly to always remember who you're not, to live every minute of every day as who you are supposed to be and forget completely who you were in the past. They were told they should treat everyone that they met here on Rhodes with suspicion; the local shopkeeper, the local Greeks, even us, her colleagues in the Resistance. Luckily though, she grew to trust me, as a woman friend. She said she needed one person, someone, a woman preferably, that she could trust."

Aileen shook her head from side to side slightly as she said, "I'd no idea, and especially that she spoke Greek. I can't imagine where she learned that. It must have been part of her training for that SOE, I suppose."

"Yes, I think that was what it was," Maria agreed. "You said she died when you were a child? So, I don't suppose you heard any of this from her?"

"No, unfortunately she died quite some years ago now. Did you know her daughter, my mother, Mary O'Mara, when she was here in the seventies?"

The tone of Maria's response was not good, "Yes, I knew her, although I expect Eleni has already told you about her. It's quite a story, I think."

Eleni exchanged a concerned glance towards her mother, with a clear frown across her face, and said quickly, "Yes, I've already told Aileen all I know about her mother." She hesitated for a second or two and then added, "And Dimitris."

Jack's grandmother once more looked directly across at her daughter and slowly shook her head from side to side, in obvious disapproval. Aileen decided from Maria's curt response, and shake of the head, not to pursue that for now though, and instead come back to it later. For now she'd focus on asking about her grandmother and Maria. However, there was obviously something that disturbed Maria and she wasn't happy about concerning Aileen's mother and Dimitris.

"So, how did they get here, my grandmother and the two men, and when?" Aileen asked.

"They were smuggled onto the island by boat into St. Paul's bay, in the middle of the night towards the end of July 1943. At first they helped us, the Resistance, fight the Italian occupiers on Rhodes, but after September that turned into fighting the Nazi occupiers. We weren't told much about them or the SOE, only as little as we needed to know to carry out espionage and sabotage with them. Bernie stayed with me in Lindos most of the time she was here and the two men stayed separately in different parts of Lindos and Pefkos. But they moved around constantly between Lindos, Pefkos and Lardos for safety, staying with those of us who were in the Resistance. Of course, back then the places we lived in were quite primitive in the villages, with no running water and very little electric in most places. When she grew to trust me more, like me I suppose, and we became friends, Bernie told me that she had been told, and believed, that the British had modelled the SOE on the activities between 1919 and 1923 of the Irish Republican Army in the Irish War of Independence from the British and the subsequent civil war. Given her Irish roots she found that what she called ironic."

Yet more coincidence with her own circumstances Aileen thought as she asked, "From what you've said you were an active member of the Resistance?"

Jack and Eleni leaned forward in their chairs. Jack put down his glass of lemonade having finished taking a sip. The body language of both of them displayed that they were now listening much more attentively to the conversation, particularly Maria's recollections.

"Yes I was a partisan in the Resistance," Maria responded. A veil of sadness descended over her face once more as she continued.

"When the Italian occupiers were here, before the Nazis came, invaded, it was different. We didn't want them here, of course, but compared to the Nazis, well, it was much easier here before with the Italians. They were still fascists, of course, but they were much more, sort of laid back, I suppose you'd say today. They were mostly based in Rhodes Town and never really bothered the populations of the small villages like Lindos very much, if at all most of the time. They were reluctant to venture outside what they viewed as the much nicer surroundings of Rhodes Town. That was obviously much more comfortable for them. We, in the Resistance, carried out sporadic occasional acts of sabotage against them, but none of those really provoked any serious response from the Italians. It was almost like some uneasy truce, or even a game in some way. We would carry out acts of sabotage and they would stir themselves briefly, but then it would all go quiet again for a while. That's really how things were for the best part of three years until that September in 1943 when the Nazis invaded and took over."

She stopped speaking for a moment as she reached forward to lift up her glass from the table and take a sip of the lemonade before continuing.

"The Nazi occupation was completely different, a tough time. Difficult to understand, to grasp how bad it was if you weren't here, and not easy to describe the horror of it at all. It was a difficult, unimaginable time, Aileen. You could be ground down by the Nazis and capitulate, and some Greeks even decided to collaborate, or you could fight them. I chose to fight them of course, eventually alongside your grandmother. The Nazis weren't exactly kind to the people here on Rhodes, us Greeks, although they weren't exactly kind to anyone anywhere were they?"

It was a rhetorical question and she didn't wait for an answer, while Jack, Eleni and Aileen sat in silence, transfixed by what she was telling them, fully appreciating the evident sorrow in her voice.

"Crops and livestock were taken by them and starvation set in on the island in that first winter at the end of 1943 and the first few months of 1944. Some people survived on what was referred to as subsistence fishing, when it was allowed by the Nazis. Food generally was scarce though, and hard to come by for the Greek population."

"Then there were the collaborators. There were what was called 'round-ups', not just on Rhodes, but all over the Nazi occupied parts of Greece. Crowds of Greeks were herded into the street and enclosed by Nazi troops so that Greek informers with their faces hidden by masks could point out left wing supporters of the Resistance for execution to the Gestapo and the Security Battalions of the Greek fascist supporters, which had been established by the collaborationist government to assist the Nazis. In the Resistance we heard lots of stories of the treatment that those picked out suffered, including things like the stripping and violation of women as a common means to secure confessions."

The old lady paused once more, took a deep breath, reached for a tissue from the little box on the table, and wiped a small tear from one of her eyes. Eleni asked "Are you ok, mother? You can stop if you want."

Maria took another deep breath and then said, with her voice sounding a little broken, "No, no, it's ok." She wiped her eyes once more and then continued.

"It was common at that terrible time for Nazi style mass executions to take place in public all over Greece. They were aimed at intimidating the population, particularly the partisans and the Resistance. To reinforce the intimidation and the terror bodies were left hanging from trees, guarded by Security Battalion collaborators so as to prevent their removal. In response, the Resistance carried out counterattacks almost daily on the Nazis and their traitor collaborators. One key response by Greeks in terms of organisation was the Partisan movement, which I became part of, and which began in Athens. Soon, however, it spread to also be based in the villages, so that Greece was eventually progressively liberated from the countryside. Your grandmother, Bernie, and the two men who came here to Rhodes with her, as well as the organisation she was a member of, the SOE, played their part during that time in resisting the Nazis in operations and acts of sabotage with the Partisans all over Greece, including here on Rhodes. On the island there were also some Italians who joined us in the Resistance who had deserted after the Nazis invaded in September 1943 and the Italians were defeated."

She finished speaking and stared into space once more, beyond Aileen and out over the continuing shimmering white rooftops of Lindos. It was as though she was re-running those terrible times in her mind.

Even someone like Aileen, who could be cold, calculating and ruthless when she wanted, when it was required, was shocked by what she was hearing. "That … that does sound awful," she started to say. Meanwhile, Jack and Eleni merely exchanged a glance and remained silent.

"I know you say my Grandmother was a brave woman, but it sounds as though you were very brave yourself," Aileen added.

She looked back at Aileen across the table and told her, "Oh, I don't know about that. Sometimes you had to be. But, as I said before, they were difficult times. Even from those bad times there are still a few things that make me smile now when I think about them. We, Bernie and me, laughed about them later, but mostly those things and times were always mixed with dangerous occasions that were not so good, not so good at all. And there were a lot more dangerous, bad times, believe me."

Her voice tailed off once more for a moment before she continued.

"One day you could be facing a possible death and the next you could be living on your adrenalin and avoiding capture in the most unusual ways."

She paused once more while she picked up her glass and took another sip of the lemonade.

While she did so Jack said, "Do you mean the tunnel, grandmother? Tell Aileen about the tunnel."

"Tunnel?" Aileen asked.

"Yes, looking back on it that was a bit of a funny situation, although it didn't seem quite like that at the time and it could have turned out badly for us, Bernie and me. It really started the night before with the ambush. We ambushed a Nazi convoy on the road between Kalathos and Lindos one night early in October 1943. There was Bernie and me, and the two other SOE guys, plus ten Resistance fighters. We planted a couple of landmines beneath the road. One of the SOE guys got the information from London - passed to them from one of their informers in Rhodes Town - about a Nazi troop movement from Kalavarda barracks on the north-west coast to the south of the island on that night. Bernie and the two SOE guys had a radio that they used to transmit regular weekly reports of Nazi troop and naval movements on Rhodes to London. I presume the SOE informer in Rhodes Town communicated the information the same way. There were two truckloads of Nazi soldiers and four machine-gun armed sidecars, with eight further troops. The information we got was that there would be about thirty of them, Nazi troops, in all, which meant we were outnumbered by more than two to one. That was just one of the more dangerous situations out of many over those few months after the Nazis invaded. However, we had the advantage of the landmines, which we reckoned would take out quite a few of the soldiers if our timing in detonating them was right. It was, and the mines did their job. A few of the soldiers may have survived, but we obviously didn't wait to check as a fire-fight with the Nazis in the machine-gun armed sidecars broke out immediately. Having taken out most of the soldiers on the trucks we now outnumbered the eight guys in the sidecars, and in a few minutes we had wiped them out. One of our Resistance fighters was wounded, but we were able to quickly disappear into the night with him and head back to Lindos."

"That wasn't our only act of sabotage, of course, but by the time that happened in October the Nazis were already taking a hard line and were hell bent on reprisals, and they didn't really care or bother much about finding just where the Resistance fighters were based, They would simply swoop down on a random area or village and go through it house by house, searching for anyone who they thought, or suspected, might be part of the Resistance. It was all about intimidation of the population by terror, threatening them into submission. Sometimes they would pick out a few Greeks from a village and execute them just to make an example, even if they had no idea whether they were Resistance fighters or not. They were terrifying times."

Again she paused for a few seconds and stared into the distance, obviously reliving it fleetingly in her mind, while Aileen, Jack and Eleni continued to sit in silence, before she continued.

"So, the next afternoon I was in Lindos Main Square with Bernie trying to get some bread from the bakery there, when a Resistance fighter appeared and told us to disappear quickly. He said they had received word from our Rhodes Town contact that there were a large number of Nazi troops heading to Lindos from the Kalavarda barracks. They had been seen passing through Kalathos, only a few minutes away. He said he'd been told there was also another group heading to Lindos from the direction of Pefkos, from their barracks near Gennadi. They had been spotted on the road near what is now Lindos Memories hotel, also only a few minutes away. We were stuck in the village with no way out at either end, up the hill to Krana or through the village and out the other end by what is now Lindos Reception. So, the three of us, Bernie, me, and the guy who came to warn us, hid in the tunnel on the rough ground above the drinking fountain in the Main Square. It's open now, but back then the entrance was covered with a large wooden door and some overgrown bushes. If you didn't know it was there you wouldn't have seen it or found it, and obviously the Nazi soldiers had no idea it was there. It actually comes out near the top road, near what is now Lindos View, but we thought it would be too dangerous to get out there as we would still have had to pass either the Krana end of that road or the Lindos Reception end, and there were bound to be Nazi troop road blocks at either end. That was their tactic usually, to seal off the villages while they searched through them"

"That's precisely what they did that afternoon in Lindos apparently. They went through the village from each end house to house, door to door, and randomly rounded up some people, including three of our Resistance fighters. Then they left, presumably to go back to their barracks, although those Resistance fighters were never seen again. We stayed in the tunnel for hours until darkness. Then, when we thought it was safe, we got out and slipped back to my place in the village."

As Maria told that story Aileen couldn't help thinking that it was difficult to imagine that the little old lady sat in front of her across the table now could have ever been a killer, a Resistance fighter. But she was, just like Aileen's own grandmother it seems, as she had just discovered. War does strange things to people, changes them, as does the struggle for freedom, as Aileen knew only too well.

Maria repeated, "They were dangerous times. In the Resistance we were all very, very grateful for what your grandmother and the two SOE men with her did for us. You couldn't put it into words really, whether in English or in Greek. Even though, being Irish, it wasn't her country's fight, your grandmother hated the Nazis and was determined to do all she could to help us. Although I never really figured out who she hated more, the Nazis or the English. I suppose that was the Irish in her, as we say." Her voice lowered in tone once again as she added wistfully and with evident great feeling, "Very brave, a very brave young woman though. You should be very proud of her, Aileen."

"Yes, yes, obviously, from what you've just told me I am now. I never knew any of that," she replied. As she did so

Aileen couldn't help thinking that, indeed, she was particularly proud of the bit about hating the English.

A little to Aileen's surprise though, Maria hadn't finished telling her about her grandmother and killing.

"Of course, in the Resistance it wasn't always, or just, the Nazis we killed, had to kill. During the war there were Greeks who weren't on our side, collaborators and informers for the Nazis. We even had a Nazi informer from Lindos in our Resistance group, Nikos Papatonis. It was Bernie who really discovered that, however. In the second half of October, not long after the convoy ambush on the road between Kalathos and Lindos, and our tunnel experience, things started to not go quite to plan on a couple of missions we'd set up. I did get a little suspicious then, and started to wonder if we might have a spy, a Nazi informer, in our group. One night while she was staying at my place, and before I'd told her my suspicions, Bernie said the same thing to me, that she thought that we might have an informer in the group. Her suspicions were aroused though for a different reason. She said that Nikos Papatonis had been flirting with her, and it was very obvious. At first she just thought it was a few random flirtatious remarks, compliments about her smile, her hair, even some comments referring to her, "optimistic bravery". But over a few days he carried on and tried to take it a bit further a couple of times. He was certainly an attractive, handsome man, with a dark swarthy complexion, some would say typically Greek no doubt, and swept back jet black hair. She told me that what really aroused her suspicion, however, was when he twice tried to ask her about the SOE. Apparently, he asked whether she was told much by the SOE about the British plans on any possible invasion of Greece. Bernie wasn't stupid in that respect. She'd been trained not to trust anyone and be suspicious of everyone, as I said earlier. So, she told me that it was obvious to her that he clearly thought it would appear that he was asking in a casual, subtle way. When he asked the second time and she told him she had no idea, that she wasn't involved in, and didn't have access to that sort of information, he tried to make light of it. He claimed he was only asking because he thought it would be good for the Greeks if the invasion was to come through

Greece, that he, and they, would obviously be relieved. She was well aware that those of us in the Resistance knew better than to ask those sorts of questions. I must admit I was a bit worried about just how close she had got to him, how close they had become, when she told me all that. However, I assumed she wasn't so stupid as to take it any further with him and have any sort of relationship."

"But she didn't, did she?" Aileen asked.

Maria ignored her question, either by design or accident. Instead of answering she merely went on, "When I thought it through at the time it occurred to me that Nikos wasn't always around when we were carrying out acts of sabotage or ambushes. For instance, he never took part in that ambush in early October on the road between Kalathos and Lindos, but I never really knew why. So, we decided to set a trap for him, just Bernie and me, to test out our suspicions. If he wasn't an informer then there wouldn't be a problem, but if he was we'd know what to do. Bernie played up to him, and responded a little the next time he flirted with her. When she did so she deliberately let slip to him that a shipment of arms for the Resistance was going to be brought into Pefkos by a small fishing boat, at the jetty, in two night's time. She made it look like she'd made a mistake in telling him, let it slip out accidentally. Then she told him that she'd got the information from the SOE in London, so he had to keep it to himself or it would mean trouble for her with her controllers and the other two SOE guys. Of course, there was no shipment, but I tipped off one of our group in Pefkos about our suspicions. It was a guy I knew I could trust. He informed me the day after that a small squad of Nazi soldiers had been spotted hiding near the jetty on the night we'd told Nikos the shipment was supposed to arrive. We knew for sure then that he was an informer."

"When Bernie saw him in the village the next afternoon she told him she was flattered by his compliments and flirting, and maybe they could meet somewhere more private. She said he was keen and didn't take much persuading at all. She suggested they meet down at St. Paul's Bay near the jetty and the chapel the next night at ten, and he eagerly agreed straightaway. It could have been risky as it was after the curfew, but the Nazis never really bothered coming into villages like Lindos that far south on the island very often to check on the curfew."

Aileen leaned forward in her chair eager to hear what happened as Maria continued.

"Bernie and I got down there just after nine-thirty that night. She waited in the trees by the entrance to the chapel and I hid in the bushes behind them, just a little bit further in the rocks. It was very dark and there was no light at all down there in those days, just whatever came from the moonlight, but we both had small torches. Just before ten Bernie spotted him coming down the slope towards the chapel and whispered to warn me. As soon as he reached Bernie he grabbed her and started kissing her, quite forcibly, without even saying a word. He didn't seem to have any suspicion at all about what we had planned. His amorous intentions obviously blocked out everything around them. After a few minutes Bernie told him they should move back a bit more into the trees and towards the bushes, which was where I was hiding. I heard her tell him it would be safer there and that there was no chance then that any Nazi curfew patrol passing at the top of the bay would see them there. They were literally about two metres away from me. As they were kissing again Bernie had manoeuvred him so that he had his back to me, and ... and ..."

She hesitated for a moment, almost as though she was struggling to make herself say it. Aileen, Jack and Eleni waited in silence until she carried on.

"Sorry ... erm ... I waited for about half a minute, then as she drew back momentarily from kissing him I hit him hard on the back of his head with the butt of Bernie's gun which she'd given me."

This was all suddenly beginning to sound a bit too reminiscent to Aileen of her own recent experience.

"He lurched forward and as he began to fall Bernie caught him under his arms. He was very groggy and there was no way he could put up any resistance. I'd hit him too hard for that. She dragged him further back into the bushes and let him fall to the ground on his face. He was moaning, and groaning in obvious pain as she told me, 'Give me the gun and the silencer'. There was ... there was ..."

Maria hesitated momentarily once more.

"There was real hatred in her eyes. It was all over her face. Even in the poor light I could see that. She hated them, the Nazis and their informers and collaborators. Not on that night when we were killing Nikos, but another time later, that was when she told me that she hated them, the Nazis, as much as she did the English. That seemed odd to me, her hatred of the English, as she was here fighting for the British against the Nazis. When I said that to her she said that as far as she was concerned she was here fighting for us Greek Partisans against the Nazis. She said that the English Royal family were German anyway, or at least their family ancestors were. She said their family name wasn't Windsor at all. It was changed from Saxe-Coburg and Gotha to the English Windsor, from Windsor Castle, in 1917 because of anti-German sentiment in Britain during the First World War. That wasn't the main reason for her hatred of the English though. It was only when she explained the real reason why, her Irish nationalism, when she came back after the war ended that I understood."

Yet another similarity to her own life was the thought that was invading Aileen's mind as Maria continued.

"Anyway, Bernie took the gun, screwed on the silencer, told me to step back a pace so that none of his blood would get on to my clothes, and then quickly shot him twice in the head. Then she quite calmly put the gun inside her jacket. Thinking about it now, looking back on it, talking about it, it all seems quite cold bloodied, and I suppose it was really. But it was war, and in a strange way it all seemed so simple at the time. Bernie used to say all the time, 'We are at war. The Nazis and their collaborators are the enemy'. As far as she was concerned nothing was unthinkable towards the enemy in those circumstances. She would say, 'Anything could be true, even a lie'."

"What happened to his body," Aileen asked. "How did you dispose of it from down there in St. Paul's? I presume you couldn't just leave it there?"

"No, we couldn't risk that. In a way that was the worst part, the most dangerous. I had arranged with the guy in our group in Pefkos, the one who had spotted the Nazis that Nikos tipped off for our trap, I'd arranged for him to take the body out to sea from St. Paul's in a small boat and dump it. We'd agreed he'd turn up at ten-thirty, but he was late. At one point we thought he wasn't going to come, and we started talking about what we should do with the body. Then his little boat floated silently into the bay just before eleven. He had turned off the engine as he entered the bay, and the lights on the boat were already off to avoid being spotted. Apparently there had been a small group of Nazi soldiers down towards the jetty in Pefkos on curfew patrol and he had to wait for them to leave. It was unusual in Pefkos and Lindos, as I said before, but of course it had to happen that night. As I said, waiting with the dead body in the bushes for almost an hour was the worst part. Anyway, in the end we got Nikos' body into his boat and he gave him a burial at sea, you might say. Bernie said even that was too good for him."

"My throat is a bit dry now after all that talking," Maria added as she reached to pick up her glass and take another drink of her lemonade.

"That's an interesting, but obviously difficult story to tell, thank you," Aileen told her. Although from Maria and Eleni's exchanged glances, as well as their body language, she had the feeling that the old woman wasn't quite telling her everything. That the old woman and her daughter both knew something more, which she wasn't saying. It seemed she had deliberately avoided answering Aileen's earlier question about just how far Nikos Papatonis and her grandmother's relationship had gone. Also, of course, there was the obvious reaction between Maria and her daughter when Aileen's mother's name was mentioned, and then Dimitris' name.

She began to try to press Maria on that. "Is there something-"

But Jack's grandmother appeared intent on not letting her. Instead, she seemed determined to avoid saying anything more on that episode of Bernie killing Nikos or their relationship. She quickly changed the subject.

"As I said before though, there were some better times back then; not many, but some."

Maria smiled and reached over to squeeze Eleni's hand.

"In the autumn of that year was when I fell in love with Eleni's father. She was born in December the following year, just as the war was ending for us Greeks, with the Nazis at least."

Aileen decided to give up asking about her grandmother and Nikos Papatonis for now and, instead asked, "But did my grandmother know about the allied invasion? You said Nikos Papatonis had asked her about it, or probed is maybe a better way of describing it?"

"No, I'm sure Bernie didn't know anything about that. She was telling the truth when she told Nikos that. The Resistance picked up some things though. First we heard it was going to be Greece that would be that focus of the invasion, but that all changed. It wasn't very good news for us Greeks at the time, but later we were told that in fact it was a turning point in the war. As the Allies prepared to invade Sicily in 1943 they wanted to fool the Nazis into thinking that their attack would be aimed elsewhere, here in Greece. A plan was devised to deceive them. A body was dumped in the sea so that it would be discovered by the Germans and their allies and collaborators. It was dumped in the Atlantic off the coast of south-west Spain, near a place called Huelva apparently. Attached to the body was a waterproof briefcase containing fake secret documents that had been fabricated by the British Security Service and a fake identity card of a Royal Marine Major. The fake secret documents suggested that the invasion would be staged in Greece, rather than Sicily. The idea was to make German intelligence think that the Major had been a courier delivering the documents to a British General. Incredibly, the trick worked and the diversion of German troops to Greece played a major part in the success of the Sicily invasion, so we were told. Not that it helped us here very much. We had even more German troops to put up with. The story that came out after the war was that Hitler and his High Command became convinced Greece was the target. The invasion eventually led to the end of the war, of course. But then we were plunged into a civil war. That's another part of the story."

Maria sighed heavily at that point and reached for another drink of her lemonade.

20

Jack's grandmother and the civil war

Aileen hadn't forgotten her curiosity over the relationship between her grandmother and Nikos Papatonis, or the reaction between Maria and her daughter when Aileen's mother's name was mentioned and Dimitris. However, given Jack's grandmother's apparent reluctance to tell her more about those things she would wait, pick her moment, and come back to them later. While Maria took another sip of her lemonade after she finished telling them about the fake invasion story the three of them, Aileen, Eleni and Jack, sat in silence, taking in all she'd told them so far and allowing the old woman to take a short breather.

After a couple of minutes Aileen asked, "And the civil war? You mentioned it earlier. You were involved?"

"Yes, the civil war, I was" Maria started to say, but then hesitated for a few more seconds, considering where to begin.

"In many ways, although it was terrible, it still all appeared so simple back then, during the war. It was war and the Nazis were our enemy. Then, just when we thought the terrible times under the Nazis were coming to an end and the war finally ended, we were plunged into the nightmare of a civil war. It was horrific. Allies turned against one another, brothers against brothers, sons and daughters against fathers. A modern Greek tragedy unfolded. Many villages all over Greece were virtually depopulated by the civil war between 1944 and 1949. And, of course, during that time Churchill and the British sold us out."

"The first signs of the possibility of civil war actually came between 1942 and 1944, during the Nazi occupation. At that time resistance groups of different political affiliations emerged. The main ones were the National Liberation Front on the left, and its military branch, the Greek People's Liberation Army, which was basically controlled by the communists. There were some clashes between the resistance groups, but in the spring of 1944 an agreement was reached between them to form a national unity government which included National Liberation Front ministers."

"By the autumn of 1944 Greece had been devastated by occupation and famine though. Half a million people had died. However, the Greek People's Liberation Army had liberated dozens of villages and became a proto-government, administering parts of the country while the official state withered away. But after the Nazi withdrawal it kept its 50,000 armed Partisans outside the capital. In May 1944 it agreed to the arrival of British troops, and to place its men under the British commanding officer. Some of the English still say that they liberated Greece and saved it from communism. But that is the basic problem. They never liberated Greece. Greece had been liberated by the resistance groups on the 12th of October, 1944. The Nazis left Athens on the 4th of October."

"The British never arrived until the 18th of October. They installed a provisional government and prepared to restore the King. From the moment they came the people and the resistance greeted them as friends and allies. At that time we had no idea that we were already giving up our country and our rights. It was only a matter of time before the National Liberation Front walked out of the provisional government in frustration over demands that the Partisans demobilise and disarm."

"The negotiations in the provisional government broke down on the 2nd of December. What is commonly accepted as the lead up to the civil war took place on the morning of the next day in Athens in the central square of Greek political life. The National Liberation Front ministers resigned from the government and called for resistance after an order to disarm was issued to the Greek People's Liberation Army. A pro-National Liberation Front rally took place in Athens. Estimates were that the demonstration involved at least two hundred thousand people marching on Panepistimiou Street towards Syntagma Square. British tanks, along with para-military police units, were positioned around the area, blocking the way of the demonstrators. Eventually the Greek government para-military police, with British forces standing in the background, opened fire on the demonstrators, killing twenty-eight of them and injuring many others. The demonstration had been called against what was seen as immunity given to collaborators, as well as the general disarmament ultimatum, which had been signed by the British commander in Greece. Sadly, the crowd actually carried Greek, American, British and Soviet flags, and chanted 'Viva Churchill, Viva Roosevelt, Viva Stalin' in endorsement of the wartime alliance."

"The civil war actually broke out properly in 1946, when former Greek People's Liberation Army Partisans organized the Democratic Army of Greece. The communists supported it, deciding that there was no other way to act against the internationally recognized government formed after the 1946 elections, which the Communist Party had boycotted. At its height, there were around fifty thousand men and women in it, the Democratic Army of Greece. We, yes I was a member, started to form guerrilla groups named the Groups of Persecuted Fighters. Units of these groups had been established throughout Greece by the summer of 1946. The actual start of the armed struggle came with the attack on the Gendarmerie station, the para-military security police station, at Litochoro, near Mount Olympus on the mainland, by a small group of thirty-five partisan fighters on the 31st of March 1946. Twelve Gendarmes were killed. That attack is generally considered to be the start of the actual Civil War."

The communists formed an alternative provisional government in December 1947 and made the Democratic Army of Greece the military branch of that government. The neighboring communist states of Albania, Yugoslavia and Bulgaria offered logistical support to that provisional government, especially to the forces operating in northern Greece. However, Stalin had done a deal with Churchill and the British at the end of the war over the division of the Balkans and southern Europe, and so he, and the Soviets, offered no support to the Partisans."

"No surprise there, of course, in respect of those two," Aileen intervened. Clearly she was no great lover of Stalin either.

"No, I suppose not," Maria agreed. "Of course we found out much later when the correspondence was released publicly that as far back as August 1944 Churchill had written to the American President, Roosevelt, that he was very concerned about what would happen in Athens, and Greece in general, when the Nazis were defeated and tried to evacuate Greece. He was worried that if there was a long period before any organised government could be set up after they left then the National Liberation Front and the communists would attempt to seize Athens."

Aileen was amazed, and not a little impressed, at the grasp of information and detail, and in English, that this woman of ninety-one was exhibiting and relaying. It wasn't all exactly focused on her grandmother, Bernie, but nevertheless it was turning out to be quite a remarkable history lesson. She looked over at Jack and raised her eyebrows in appreciation, accompanied by a smile in order to try and demonstrate her admiration further. Jack reciprocated with a knowing smile of his own and a slight nod of the head in appreciation.

The woman of ninety-one wasn't finished yet though.

"There was no plot to take over Athens as Churchill believed. If we communists had wanted to do that we could have done it before the British arrived. During November, the British set about building the new National Guard to police Greece and disarm the wartime militias. In reality, disarmament applied to the Greek People's Liberation Army only though, not to those who had collaborated with the Nazis. In the middle of November the British started releasing Security Battalion officers. Before long some of them were walking freely in the streets of Athens wearing new uniforms, including some from collaborationist units which had been integrated into the Nazi SS during the occupation. The British army continued to provide protection to assist the gradual rehabilitation of the former collaborator units in the Greek army and police forces. When Bernie came back to see me in 1946 and we talked about all this she told me that she'd seen a British SOE memo urging that, 'the British government must not appear to be connected with this scheme'. So, Churchill and senior British military officers knew exactly what they were doing, despite the fact that the ordinary soldiers of the former Security Battalions were the Nazi collaborationist scum of Greece. Basically, Churchill switched allegiances to back those who supported Hitler in the war against his own former allies, the Greek resistance fighters."

"It was also revealed subsequently, long after the end of the war and the civil war, that at a conference in Moscow on the 9th of October that year, 1944, southeast Europe was divided into areas of influence, as I mentioned just now. Stalin and the Soviets took Romania and Bulgaria, while Britain, in order to keep Russia out of the Mediterranean, took Greece. That's why the communists got no help from Stalin during the civil war. Churchill wanted a confrontation, a showdown, with the communists, so as to be able to restore the King, who would be more supportive of British interests in our part of the Mediterranean. Churchill wanted, and sought, conflict. He was determined to show that in Greece the old order was back. Your grandmother suspected and understood that perfectly when she came back here in 1946, Aileen. She said to me once at that time that the British upper class, or the English as she always referred to them, believed they had some sort of inherent entitlement to rule the world as they wanted, in their own best interests, even if that meant suppressing and killing people. That was the way of the British Empire, as she put it."

Now Aileen felt she was also getting a lesson in international relations. Besides being a very brave one, this was a very clever, astute, old woman.

"However, there was something else in particular that drove Bernie on to want to stay and fight with us in 1946. Churchill set up what was called the British Police Mission to Greece. In 1945 he appointed someone called Sir Charles Wickham as its head. The Mission was to oversee the new Greek security forces. In effect, that meant recruiting the former Nazi collaborators. Bernie knew of him well or at least his reputation. She described him to me here in 1946 as, 'one of those people who travelled around the British Empire establishing the infrastructure needed for its survival and for British repression of people'. She had a phrase for it. Let me think, what was it now? Let me get it right."

For the first time the ninety-one year old woman was exhibiting signs of struggling with her, what up until then, had been an excellent memory and her English vocabulary. But that lasted only for a brief moment.

"Yes, yes, I remember now, Bernie called it, 'the story ... no, no ... the narrative ... yes that's the word ... the narrative of empire, the British Empire. She said that they, Churchill and his upper class English thugs and manipulators, as she called them, applied it to Greece. For her that was how colonialism worked. A similar process throughout the world of putting together three things, concentration camps, putting the murder gangs in uniform, and then labelling them the police. The British, or the English as she preferred to refer to them, particularly Churchill, used whatever means were necessary, one of which was terror and collusion with terrorists. It worked, and Wickham was one of the finest practitioners of it. In Greece he established one of the most vicious camps in which communist prisoners were tortured and murdered, at Giaros, an unpopulated island in the northern Cyclades. We knew it. It was terrible, an island that even the Roman Emperor Tiberius declared unfit for prisoners."

She hesitated for a moment once more, tutted slightly, and slowly shook her head demonstrating her disgust before continuing.

"Our communist sources at the time told us that British police serving under Wickham were regularly present in the camps. Bernie did some research, digging, on him through her various sources when she came back here in 1946. She found that he'd served in the Boer War, during which, as she put it, 'Concentration camps in the modern sense were invented by the British'. She wouldn't tell me what those sources were though. All she said was that it wasn't the SOE or contacts she had in the British Secret Service. I suspected it was some of her Irish Nationalist connections and sources. Anyway, I kept a close watch on Wickham's career. After Greece, he moved on to Palestine in 1948. What really drove Bernie on most to want to stay and fight with us against him and the English in 1946 though was that he was the first Inspector General of the Royal Ulster Constabulary, from 1922 to 1945. By infiltrating MI6 and the SOE she'd managed to see an MI5 report on him from 1940 that praised his personality and experience in doing in

Ireland after 1922 precisely what he was doing in Greece over twenty years later. That stuff on what he did in Ireland is partly why I suspected some of the other stuff she got on him came from her Irish Nationalist connections. She wasn't slow at displaying her anger over that, and his involvement then in doing Churchill's dirty work here, believe me."

Aileen thought that was the first time Maria had actually explicitly said her grandmother had infiltrated MI6. She'd mentioned her Irish Nationalist sympathies and support a couple of times, which automatically led Aileen to the conclusion that she was an undercover agent for the Bhoys. Now, however, with what she had just told her, Maria was confirming that there were an awful lot of similarities between Aileen's grandmother's life and her own inside the IRA. She sat forward onto the edge of her chair, placed her elbows on the table in front of her and her cheeks into her hands, eager to hear what more Maria would tell her.

"The British, and that means Wickham and Churchill, knew who those people were, the ones they put in uniform, and labelled them police to do their dirty work. They were former Nazi collaborators and thugs. They were the people who had operated in the Nazi torture chambers during the occupation, pulling out the fingernails and applying thumbscrews to the Greek Resistance prisoners."

Maria stopped speaking, got up from her chair and said, "Just a moment." She went inside to the lounge and a small bookcase in one corner of it. When she returned to the terrace and sat back down at the table she placed a book on it in front of her.

"Some of it is in here," she began to say as she opened the book. "It's a scrapbook that I've kept of various articles over the years, and it'll be more accurate than my memory." She turned some of the pages of the scrapbook and then added, "Yes, here it is, here they are, some of the articles."

She placed two of the long spindly fingers of her right hand on a page containing some Greek newspaper cuttings.

"This is an article published following the removal of the Military Colonels' Regime in 1974. It says that, 'It was revealed from documents recently released that by September

1947, the year the Communist Party was outlawed in Greece, nearly twenty thousand leftist Partisans were held in Greek camps and prisons.' Erm ... err ..."

She scanned further down that particular cutting and then continued reading from it.

"Twelve thousand of those were held in Makronissos, an island political prison from the 1940s to the 1970s. Almost forty thousand others were exiled internally or in British camps across the Middle East. A so-called process of repentance was carried out in the camps. Confessions were extracted through violent persistent degradation. Women prisoners had their children removed from them until they confessed to being things like Bulgarians and whores. Unbelievably, the processes and system of repentance eventually saw Makronissos looked upon by some people as some sort of school. People, the nationalists, described it as almost a national university for those inmates to be persuaded that their life belonged to Mother Greece. Those prisoners that went along with that, that were convinced of it, were visited by the King and Queen, and by Ministers and foreign officials. It was total indoctrination, designed to reform the inmates, and create patriots to serve the homeland."

Maria turned the page, pointed to another newspaper cutting from the scrapbook, and then continued.

"What you have to understand, Aileen, is that, as it says here in this article, 'Following the liberation of Greece from the Nazis at the end of the war by the following year, March 1946 1,289 suspected communists had been killed across Greece, 6,671 had been wounded, 84,931 had been arrested, 165 been raped, and the property of 18,767 was looted. More than 30,000 suspected communists had been imprisoned'."

She finished reading from the cuttings and looked across the table at Aileen, telling her with anger clearly evident in her voice and across her face, "Those responsible for the murders were collaborationist groups, national guards, rural police, as well as members of the British armed forces. Believe me, it was a dark, very dark, period in Greece's history, Aileen, to which, unfortunately, the English contributed and supported."

Aileen now detected some more small tears once again in the corner of the old woman's eyes as she took a deep breath, gulped and tried to continue.

"It's difficult to talk about some of these things, you understand. There were lots and lots of horrible stories about the camps, some of which we heard about at the time, but some only came out years later, in articles like these."

"Yes, of course, I understand, but if it is too difficult you don't have to-"

Aileen never got to finish what she was saying. Maria interrupted, telling her as she reached for a tissue from a small box on the table and wiped her eyes, "No, no it's okay. I'll be okay in a moment. I need to tell you. People need to know."

She took another deep breath and then continued.

"There were stories of children in the Kifissa prison in Athens being beaten with wires and socks filled with concrete. On the boys' chests they sewed name tags with Slavic endings added to the names."

She hesitated for a moment once more, gulped visibly and then added, "Many boys were raped. A female prisoner was forced, after a severe beating, to stand in the square of Kastoria in Western Macedonia in Northern Greece holding the severed heads of her uncle and brother-in-law. It's all in here in these articles. Those stories came out publicly in articles like these years later. In the Partisan Resistance they were passed on by word of mouth and through our communication network, but they were so horrible in many cases, like these I just read out to you, that they were difficult to believe."

Now it was Aileen who was shaking her head slowly from side to side in horror. She turned towards Jack and his mother and told them, "I'm sorry, I suppose you've heard all this before. It must be difficult to listen to it all again."

Jack and Eleni looked blank faced, white with shock at what they were hearing, as Jack replied, "No … err … no, not at all. We haven't heard this before actually."

"Shocking, it's horrible what people do to each other sometimes," Eleni added.

"I've never told them before today. We've never spoken about it, although I was never sure if they had read about it or not," Maria said, as she reached across and tenderly squeezed her daughter's hand.

Maria looked Aileen straight in the eye and told her with gritty determination echoing in her voice, "You know, Aileen, nowhere else in newly liberated Europe at that time were Nazi sympathisers able to, helped to, infiltrate the positions of the state so effectively, the army, the security forces, the judges. The civil war left Greece with a strong right-wing nationalist, anti-communist, security establishment, which eventually led to the establishment of the ruling Greek military dictatorship between 1967 and 1974, and a legacy of political splits that continue to this day. Polarisation, political polarisation, is that how you say it?" she asked.

"That's right, grandmother," Jack told her.

"So, yes, political polarisation," Maria continued. "I really do believe that the recent re-emergence of neo-fascism in Greece - some people prefer to just call it fascism - in the form of the present-day far-right party Golden Dawn has direct links to the failure to purge the state of right-wing extremists back then in the years immediately after the end of the war, the years of the civil war. Many of Golden Dawn's supporters are descendants of what were called Battalionists, the former Nazi collaborators I mentioned earlier that were used by the British and Wickham, who recruited them to the post-war para-military police. Many of the Colonels in the military dictatorship who seized power in 1967 were too."

"And that rise of fascism, or its resurfacing, is happening all over Europe these days," Aileen commented. "In France support for the National Front has been on the rise for a few years. Hungary has a government with ultra-right wing views. In some of the Baltic states memorial services commemorating local Nazis who joined the SS are held frequently, and are often attended by democratically elected government ministers. Paramilitary groups and political parties with allegiances to the memory of the Nazis' wartime collaborators are influential in the Ukraine, in Serbia, Croatia and Albania."

"Although it's only really in Greece that an unashamedly Nazi party, Golden Dawn, registered such impressive election results, and now we have Nazis back in our parliament," Maria told her. "The Spanish, the Irish, the Portuguese and the Italians have all felt the impact of the Eurozone crisis, but the impact of fascist parties has been nowhere near as great in those countries as here in Greece."

Aileen thought they were getting side-tracked from what she was much more interested in hearing about, her grandmother's time in Rhodes, and in particular any possible relationship she had with Nikos Papatonis. However, she couldn't resist indulging her keen interest in the international political economy and her knowledge of it, just as she had in the conversation she'd had on the plane to Rhodes a few days before with the English guy.

She leaned forward in her chair once again and explained.

"I think the main reason for that, Maria, is that the economic collapse in Greece was far more serious than in those countries, and throughout the Eurozone as a whole. And because it was the first collapse in the Eurozone after the global financial crash of 2008 it became a sort of testing ground, a laboratory I suppose you could say, for the so-called Troika's prescribed attempted remedy; the imposed policy of the Troika, the European Commission, the European Central Bank, and the International Monetary Fund. So, their ridiculous policy to tackle the most unsustainable public debt in the Eurozone, Greece's, was to force that government to impose the harshest austerity measures, accompanied by facilitating the largest bailout loans, all of which was bound to stifle growth in the Greek economy and ultimately make things worse not better. When it failed I saw figures that said almost a third of all incomes of Greeks, and a third of jobs, were lost, while the Greek debt actually increased. It seemed obvious to me at the time the bailout and austerity policy was imposed, as well as to any sane person let alone an economist, that if you cut incomes, benefits and jobs people are going to have less money to spend and the economy will not grow, but instead will go into deeper recession, which, of course, is what happened. Actually, the only thing that grows in those circumstances is not the economy, but people's fear and loathing of governments, and of whoever is imposing the policies, particularly the Troika, the European Union and the Greek establishment. That is prime fertile soil for resentment to grow around fascism. That's what happened in Germany after the First World War as a result of the terms the British, Americans, the French, and the other allies imposed on them in the Treaty of Versailles, which eventually led to the rise of Hitler in the nineteen-thirties. So, as you all know, that's what happened here in Greece recently after the economic collapse and the Troika bailout. By the time the Troika came to have to deal with the later debt problems in Spain, Ireland, Portugal, and Italy it had at least learned some lessons from what happened in Greece. So, it imposed lighter versions of austerity. The result was shallower recessions than in Greece and less room for fascism to flourish. You, here in Greece, were unfortunately the test case, and they got it badly wrong. That's what I think, anyway."

Now it was Aileen's turn to need another drink of her lemonade as she sat back in her chair. Jack gave her a nod of acknowledgement, seemingly impressed at her explanation. She put down her glass and said, "Sorry, I get a bit wound up about all that. I shouldn't have gone on like that about it. Sorry, Maria, we got side-tracked. Can we get back to the civil war?"

"Of course," the old lady told her with a smile, "But I must say first that you are obviously just as smart as your grandmother."

"Thank you, but you are being too kind, I think." Aileen was slightly embarrassed, which wasn't like her at all.

Maria continued, "Yes, well, the civil war. As far as we were concerned the British crime was to support people whose actions and record under the occupation by the Nazis put them beyond that, and who should have been prosecuted not supported. As I said before, it all happened because Churchill believed he had to bring back the King, wanted to bring him back to preserve British interests. But the last thing the Greek people wanted or needed was the return of a discredited monarchy backed by Nazi collaborators. That is what the British imposed. That has caused problems here in Greece ever since in my opinion, because all those collaborators went into the system, into the government mechanism, during and after the civil war, and their sons went into the military, as I think I also said earlier. Although we liberated Greece, the Nazi collaborators won the war, thanks to the British."

The bitterness in Maria's voice, and in her heart, came through fully in that last remark. She shook her head slightly from side to side once again, before she qualified slightly what she'd said.

"Don't misunderstand me though, it needs to be said that not all the communists were saints, Aileen. We knew that. The leftist Democratic Army of Greece weren't exactly completely innocent unfortunate victims. We heard that they took around fifteen thousand prisoners with them on their retreat from Athens in the civil war. As I told you before, we did some killing too, not just of Nazis. Some people acted out of revenge. Your grandmother, Bernie, and I know that. We did it in 1943, killing Nazis and collaborators, informers like Nikos Papatonis. In the civil war though, there were things we wouldn't do, a line we wouldn't cross. I think that's what you say in English, and that line for us was not to kill civilians, unless they were proven collaborators."

Aileen nodded her head in silent agreement at Maria's, "a line we wouldn't cross," question as she continued.

"In 1949 that whole Greek tragedy came to a close. In the summer of 1948, the Democratic Army of Greece suffered a catastrophic defeat, with nearly twenty thousand killed. And in July 1949 President Tito closed the Yugoslav border, denying them shelter. Finally a ceasefire was signed on the 16th of October 1949."

"The civil war was a cruel and bloody episode in British as well as Greek history, which every Greek knows in their soul, although differently, depending on which side they were on. It is mainly an untold story, an untold episode in Britain. Perhaps that's out of shame, or maybe through the arrogance of a lack of interest. It's a story that most of the millions of British tourists who come to experience the glories of Greek relics and monuments, or to disco-dance around the islands Mamma Mia-style, like they do here, are unaware of."

"The legacy of that betrayal has haunted Greece ever since. It has created a wide and deep, intense difference between people, between people on the left and the right. So, you have to understand that even in Greece today the events of December 1944, as well as the civil war period between 1946 and 1949, affect and influence the present because there has never been reconciliation here. In France and Italy you were respected in society after the war if you fought the Nazis, regardless of ideology. In Greece, you found yourself fighting, or imprisoned and tortured on British orders, by the very people who had collaborated with the Nazis in many cases. There has never been any payback, any reckoning here for that crime. Much of what is occurring in Greece even now is the result of not coming to terms with the past of what happened in the war here and subsequently in the civil war. They were sad times, very sad times."

The sadness of those difficult times was fully reflected now in the old woman's cracking voice. She wiped a small tear away from the corner of one of her eyes with a tissue once more before she added, "I suppose we should have known not to trust Churchill, given his past. Not long after Bernie arrived on her mission in 1943 she told me that she was informed during part of her SOE briefing before she left for here that it had been observed by the British that elements of the Greek right wing military, politicians, and the monarchists were much slower, and much more reluctant, in deciding to resist the Nazi occupation than their leftist opponents, and were therefore of little use. And yet Churchill ..."

At that point Maria's voice tailed off, and she stared past Aileen, across the terrace, and out over the panorama of the village for a moment.

Eleni broke the silence by asking her, "Are you tired, mother? Reliving all that has been tiring."

Aileen was torn between agreeing with Eleni, and asking Maria if she wanted to stop now, but still being anxious to find out what had happened between her grandmother and Nikos Papatonis.

In fact, she needn't have worried over that dilemma as Maria's response didn't betray any wish to stop at all as she told her daughter, "No, no, I'm fine, Eleni, don't fuss."

Then somewhat brusquely she told Jack, "Go and make us all some coffee. There are some small cakes in the bread bin that I made earlier for our guest."

21

Jack's grandmother and 1946; finally the secrets, the lies, and the truth

While Jack went to get the coffee and cakes Aileen couldn't help thinking that he and Eleni were dead right when they told her that Maria had retained all her faculties. The elderly woman in her nineties had, indeed, clearly retained all of them, including a good recall of events and facts, as well as her English language ability. However, it was clear that she was getting tired. Time was getting on. It was approaching six o'clock and Aileen wasn't sure just how much more time Jack's grandmother would give her, or possibly how much more time Jack and Eleni would allow her to give her. Eleni, in particular, seemed keen not to let her go on much longer, especially if it meant talking more, and disclosing more, about the possible relationship between Bernie and Nikos Papatonis, as well as that between Aileen's mother and Dimitris. So, Aileen was desperate now to get Maria back to talking about those if possible.

As Jack returned with the coffee and cakes he told them all that he had to leave now to open up the bar. "But I'm sure my mother and grandmother will look after you, and no doubt my grandmother has plenty more to tell you," he added to Aileen.

"Yes, of course, no problem. I'll come to the bar later after dinner for a drink. See you later, and thanks again, Jack," Aileen replied.

He said goodbye to his mother and grandmother, giving them each a kiss on the cheek.

While Eleni poured the coffees and placed a couple of the small cakes on a plate for each of them Aileen took her opportunity to ask Maria, "You mentioned a few times that my grandmother came back here in 1946?"

"Yes, that's right; they were all recalled to London early in 1944, your grandmother and the two men. In the Resistance we were never told why, and Bernie never said. I could see she was sad to leave, but she couldn't tell me why they had to go. She wasn't allowed to, she said. She came back in 1946, the year after the war ended. As I said before, she wanted to stay and fight with us, the Partisans then. That's when she explained and told me about her Irish Nationalist allegiances. I knew she must really have trusted me as a friend then when she said how she had infiltrated the British Secret Service, and the SOE, as a spy for them, the Irish Nationalists, the IRA. Of course, she explained that she hated the Nazis just as much as the English, as I said earlier. That is why she volunteered to come to Rhodes in 1943."

"So, the reason she came back in 1946 was because she wanted to fight with the Partisans against the British backed new Greek government?" Aileen asked. "That must have been difficult if she was still operating as an agent inside the British SOE."

"No, that wasn't a problem, because that wasn't the reason she came back," Maria started to explain. Frustratingly for Aileen she stopped speaking, picked up one of the cakes from her plate and took a bite. As Maria reached for her coffee on the table Eleni told Aileen, "Try one of the cakes, they're very good. Mother always makes good cakes."

"Oh, yes, thank you," Aileen said as she reached to pick up and take a small bite out of one of the cakes on her plate. After she finished chewing it and swallowing she asked, "Why then? Why did she come back then, in 1946?"

Maria finished her first cake, took a sip of her coffee, and as she placed her cup back on the sparkling white saucer on the table explained.

"For the medal, she came back for the medal. Well, actually she went to Athens first for that, and then she decided to get on the ferry and come here to see me. Anyway, that's what she told me."

Aileen reached down into her handbag on the floor once again and produced the folded foolscap envelope. "This medal?" she asked, as she pulled it out of the envelope and handed it to Maria.

She took it and held it in the palm of her hand, staring at it in silence for what seemed a long minute. Initially, Aileen thought she was trying to decide if it was the medal she had just mentioned, but, in fact, it quickly became clear to her that Maria was merely overcome with the memory of it, and of those times. A few real tears rolled slowly down her cheeks.

Eleni reached for a tissue from the box on the table and handed it to her, asking, "Are you okay, Mother?"

Aileen waited patiently for Maria to regain her composure.

"Yes, yes ... I'm okay, just give me a moment," she replied as she wiped the tears from her eyes and her cheeks. Attempting to choke back any more tears she eventually said, "I ... I ... it just ... it just ... err ... it just." She wiped her eyes again. "It just ... erm ... brought back a lot more of the bad memories of those times, but also, I suppose, the good memories of me and Bernie in those difficult times. Sorry."

"That's okay, I can understand it's difficult," Aileen sympathised.

Maria put down the tissue and tried again. "Sorry ... err ... yes, yes, that's the medal she was awarded in Athens, along with the two SOE men who were here with her. She showed it to me when she came here after Athens. The first date on it, 1943, is obviously the date Bernie was here, and 1946 is when she was awarded it in Athens. It's called the War Cross. It's a military decoration of Greece, awarded for heroism in wartime to Greeks and foreign allies. Bernie told me that it was awarded to her for bravery in helping our fight, the fight of the Greek Resistance against the Nazis. But it was difficult for both of us at the time. The Nationalist government had just been elected and the medal was awarded by them at that time to Bernie and the other two, in the middle of 1946. The possibility of the civil war against the nationalists and their British backers was growing. So I was not very enthusiastic about it, the medal. Bernie had also not been very keen on accepting it. She told me that when she got here after Athens. She knew the situation that was developing here, and she had no time at all for the Greek nationalists, their Nazi collaborator supporters, or of course, Churchill and the British supporting them. I suppose that's what got me upset just now. It brought it all back. It was an impossible situation for her, a very brave woman. As a member of the British SOE, and then a member of British MI6, she knew she couldn't refuse it, the medal. She wouldn't have been able to explain why she did that. It would have completely blown her cover in infiltrating those organisations for the IRA, or for the Bhoys, as she always used to call them."

As Maria stopped speaking, and reached to take another sip of her coffee, Aileen allowed herself a small discrete smile at that label, Bhoys, and the fact that her grandmother used it. She thought once again that it must run in the family, and that she'd definitely replicated her grandmother. It must be in the genes.

"As I said, Bernie was well aware what the situation was here," Maria continued. "She understood that a civil war was likely. She told me as much, and of course, I told her I knew that. That's why she wanted to stay, to fight alongside us again. She'd got leave from MI6 to come to get her medal awarded in Athens. So, she was supposed to go back to her post with them after a week, but she agonised about just staying here and fighting alongside us. That would probably have blown her cover as well, I suppose. In the end her IRA superiors ordered her back to London, to continue her work as a spy for them inside the British Secret Service. That's the reason she eventually told me about her IRA connection; to explain why she had to go back to London, instead of staying here. She obviously really trusted me. When she told me that I knew that she did, completely. And of course, she knew that I didn't have any time at all for Churchill."

The old lady reached for her coffee cup for another sip.

"I never knew, about her working for the IRA inside MI6 I mean; had no idea," Aileen told her. "My mother never mentioned it, although she never really told me much at all about my grandmother. As I said before, she died when I was very young, so I never really knew her or remember much about her. My mother showed me some family photographs she was in when I was a little older and that's how I recognised her photo on the identity card. Her dyed black hair in that photo threw me at first, because in every photo I'd seen of her she had lighter hair, reddish. Of course, it didn't show up as that colour in those old black and white photos my mother showed me. However, you could see it wasn't black, as black as it was in the Greek identity card photo. Anyway, so that's why she came back here in 1946, and that's when she told you about her and the IRA. Like you said, I suppose she had to, otherwise you may have thought she was deserting you, her good friend, just as the civil war was looming. It was good that she was honest with you, don't you think? About that, I mean."

Aileen was fishing, hoping that her last comment would prompt Maria into telling her more about what she really wanted to know; about her grandmother and Nikos Papatonis. She succeeded at last.

"Yes, good that Bernie was honest with me about that. Although, there was something else that she told me when she came back, that she was eventually honest about. That ..."

Maria stopped speaking and hesitated as she looked across at Eleni, who now had a very anxious look across her face and was shaking her head slightly at her mother. She was obviously trying to indicate to her that she shouldn't tell Aileen what she was about to. But it was to no avail. Maria visibly took a deep breath and then continued.

"When Bernie came back in 1946 she also told me she did have an affair with Nikos Papatonis in 1943. Obviously, it was before we found out he was an informer. She'd slept with him, had sex with him, quite a few times she said, over the three or four weeks before we trapped him towards the end of October and she killed him. In fact, she said it was still going on when Bernie and I spoke to each other about our suspicions just before we trapped him. That was obviously why it was so easy for her to get him to meet her down at St. Paul's Bay that night."

Aileen managed to look surprised as she said, "So, they were having an affair."

However, she wasn't completely surprised at all. She had guessed that it was something like that which Maria had been was trying to avoid telling her earlier. What she was hiding, what Eleni didn't want her to say. Aileen couldn't help briefly also thinking though, that her grandmother must have been a pretty cold-hearted person to be able to do what she did, kill Nikos Papatonis, having had an affair with him, while she was still having an affair with him. She was desperately hoping that she wasn't going to be haunted by all her grandmother's traits, like that one, all the rest of her life. Coming to Lindos was supposed to take her away from all that and put it all behind her, all the killing, even if she had been forced back into it out of necessity only a few nights ago.

"That must have been a really difficult thing for her to do, kill him like that while she was-" Aileen began to add.

However, Maria interrupted her. She hadn't finished her revelations about back then in 1943. If Aileen thought that what she had heard so far must have been difficult for her grandmother, it was nothing in comparison to what Maria was about to tell her. It certainly didn't require Aileen to feign any element of surprise at all. She was genuinely shocked. It explained completely why Eleni was so desperate for her mother not to tell Aileen everything, and was doing her best to prevent that in fact.

"Yes, it was difficult for her, of course it was. That's precisely what she told me when she revealed it all to me when she came back in 1946, about their affair and what had gone on between the two of them over those few weeks before she killed him. I was shocked about their affair and Bernie's involvement with him when she told me. I was even more shocked because I knew that he was married at the time and had a young three year old son. Bernie swore to me that she never knew that at the time of their affair. She said that she only found that out when I told her, after she'd told me about their affair.

"But how did he manage to hide that he was married from my grandmother in such a small village?" Aileen asked. "Surely his wife and son were in the village, and my grandmother would have known?"

"She wasn't. He sent his wife and son, Dimitris, to Crete before the Nazis invaded Rhodes. She had some family there. With Nikos involved in the Resistance, for some reason they thought it would be safer there for his wife and their son. Also, Bernie and the two SOE men made sure they didn't have much public contact, if any, with most of the people in the village in general. They were told to do that before they came. Remember, I said that Bernie told me that they were briefed before they came not to trust anyone, or at least only the very few people that they needed to, like me I suppose in Bernie's case. They kept a very low profile and we, a very few of us, looked after their day to day needs, like food and drink. So, Bernie wouldn't have learned in the village about him being married. Of course, as I said, I knew he was, but I didn't know they were having an affair, so there was no reason for me to tell or mention it to Bernie. They managed to keep that secret in the village too. Family bonds are very important to us Greeks. Something like that going on wouldn't have gone down very well in the village at all."

Aileen puffed out her cheeks and then said, "She was quite a woman, my grandmother."

She hesitated for a moment trying to gather her thoughts and decide quite what to ask next from a whole myriad of possibilities. Eventually she settled upon, "But didn't they, his wife and son, come back here when they heard he was dead?"

Maria shook her head. "No, not until after the war. His wife never even knew he was dead, even then when she came back. How could she have at that time? Communications between the islands was virtually impossible for ordinary Greeks, so she wouldn't have heard anything, not even that he'd disappeared. She probably wouldn't even have expected to hear from him given the situation at that time here and on Crete, with the Nazi occupation. We disposed of his body out at sea, remember, or rather one of our Resistance colleagues did. It was never found. Not that anyone looked for it. Very few people in the Resistance even got to know that he was an informer and had been killed. Basically, we kept it to Bernie and me, and the guy from Pefkos who disposed of the body, who I knew we could trust and who wouldn't tell anyone. It wasn't common knowledge, and it definitely wasn't the sort of thing that you talked about or spread around at that time. As far as most people in the Resistance, and generally in the village knew he had just disappeared, left the village. Some people assumed that somehow he'd gone to Crete to be with his wife and son. So, no one was that bothered about where he was. People had other things to worry about at that time with their own families. And the Nazis never came looking for him. In the Resistance, if you knew an informer had been killed you knew better than to ask questions, like by who. You didn't want to know. That way you couldn't tell the Nazis anything if you were unlucky enough to get interrogated. In the Resistance we all knew that. It was just one of the unwritten rules that we all followed. The Nazis obviously didn't know we had discovered he was an informer of theirs. If they came looking for him that would have exposed him as one anyway. I presume that's why they never bothered. To them he was just another Greek, not one of them, so why would they bother? They just used people like Nikos and then disposed of them. They had other things to deal with at the time as well, like a possible invasion by the British. When Bernie and the other two SOE men left here early in 1944 Nikos' wife wouldn't even have known he had disappeared, let alone that he was dead. So, there was no reason for her to return from Crete, even if it had been possible for her to do so, which it wasn't. So, that's why Bernie never knew about his wife and son until I told her in 1946."

Aileen was perched on the very edge of her seat and once again leaning onto the table with her elbows, her hands cupping her cheeks, while she listened intently to Maria. Eleni was also listening closely, but for a very different reason. Her facial expression revealed she was clearly growing increasingly anxious.

Eleni's anxiety went up a few notches, if that was possible, as Aileen asked, "Where is his wife now, still in Lindos?"

"No, as I said, she came back after the war, but she's dead now too, so is their-"

Much to Aileen's surprise Eleni interrupted her mother. "Mother, are you sure you're going to do this? Now, now after all these years? Are you really sure?"

Maria stared across at her for a few seconds and then told her firmly. "Aileen has a right to know, Eleni. The truth has to come out after all these years. Some people have a right to know if it affects their family. It's the only way to finally finish things like this, close it."

Eleni sat back in her chair, resigned to what her mother was about to tell Aileen.

Maria sat up straight and pulled herself closer to the table, then continued.

"Nikos' wife is dead now, as I said, and so is their son, Dimitris. He died five years ago."

She hesitated for a few seconds once again, and then added, "He was married to Eleni's best friend, Crisa, wasn't he, Eleni."

Eleni was obviously uncomfortable with what was being revealed. Now she hesitated for a moment and then simply said in a very low soft, resigned tone, "Yes, mother." It was as if she knew exactly what was coming next.

Aileen turned towards Eleni and said, "Crisa? The woman you told me on Sunday was your best friend, Cristina. So-"

Maria didn't let Aileen finish, or let Eleni respond.

"Yes, Crisa, Cristina, yes it is, Aileen, the same person."

Now it was Aileen who slumped back in her chair as she exclaimed in shock, "My god, really?"

She remained slumped back, silent, and open mouthed, for a seemingly endless moment in time, tussling with the implications of what she'd just finally been told; rapidly turning it over and over in her mind. Eleni merely stared across at her mother in silence, who was also now silent, closely watching Aileen digest what she'd just told her.

Looking shell-shocked and in a bit of a daze, although she knew the answer, Aileen couldn't help seeking confirmation of what she had clearly worked out in her mind. In reality, however, she wasn't looking for a reply. She already knew the answer.

"That was the same Dimitris who was probably my birth father; the same Dimitris who was most likely to have been the one who got my mother pregnant with me here in 1977?"

She stopped speaking briefly. She was still trying to digest all she had heard, while the three of them sat in an awkward silence.

"So, his father, Nikos, was married when he had an affair with my grandmother in 1943, and he, Dimitris, was married when he had an affair with my mother here in 1977 and got her pregnant with me."

She stopped speaking briefly once again, took a deep breath, and then said softly, with a trace of exasperation in her voice, "Phew, that's quite a couple of families. I suppose, as you said, my grandmother had no idea Nikos was married, but I'd be surprised if in 1977 my mother never knew Dimitris was."

She shook her head slightly as she finished that sentence.

For a very brief fleeting, confused, moment in the midst of her obvious shock, Aileen desperately tried to be clear in her now somewhat muddled mind that Dimitris, her probable birth father, had not been in any way related to her mother, Mary, when he got her pregnant. She quickly realised, however, that through the cloud of all the information she'd just been told she wasn't thinking straight at all. Although she now knew that her grandmother, Bernie, had an affair with Dimitris' father, Nikos, she also knew that she never got pregnant from that. She knew her mother, Mary O'Mara, wasn't born until 1950, and that Mary's father was an Irishman, also an IRA member, who Bernie married back in Ireland, in Bantry Bay. Aileen reassured herself that at least there was no hint of incest involved in the tangled web of all that she had just heard, simply intertwined lives and circumstances.

She sat in silence, still slumped back in her chair, while she ran all that through her mind, trying to unravel it. She didn't usually have any difficulty sifting through information and detail. She'd been trained that way for twenty years. This was different though. It was personal, about her family. Sure, it was what she'd set out to discover by coming back to Lindos, although she had no idea, and never expected all this; never expected so much of a tangled web of families and their history. To say she was stunned was an understatement.

While Eleni and Maria also stayed silent, exchanging occasional awkward glances and not knowing what more to say, Aileen was going over and over it, getting it straight in her mind, and trying to come to terms with it all. The father, Nikos Papatonis, of her own birth-father, Dimitris, had an affair with her grandmother on her mother's side of the family, Bernadette, who subsequently assassinated him. Over thirty years later Dimitris then had an affair with her mother, Mary, which resulted in her being born. But would Dimitris have ever really known what happened to his father, and that it was Mary's mother who killed him? That was just one of the many questions running through Aileen's head now. She quickly dismissed that as not very likely at all though. As Maria told her, Dimitris was only three years old and on Crete with his mother when it all happened. Even if his mother no doubt tried desperately to find out what happened to her husband, the people in the village wouldn't have known anyway, as Maria had also just told her. Only Bernie, Maria and her accomplice from Pefkos, who had the small boat and dumped the body in the sea, knew. For most of the people in Lindos Nikos Papatonis just disappeared, and presumably that is what Dimitris believed.

Aileen sat in silence - all three women did - while she ran all that through her mind, trying desperately to process all she'd just been told. The atmosphere had turned tense, especially between Eleni and her mother. Aileen rubbed the back of her neck with her right hand, as though it had been seized by a stiffness from what she'd heard and she was trying to relieve it.

After a couple of minutes all she could say, in a soft, low voice heavily laced with astonishment, was, "Well, turns out that I've got quite a family history."

While Aileen had been running all that through her mind Eleni sat staring awkwardly in silence over at her, with a dark, uncomfortable, fixed glaze that had rapidly invaded her eyes, exposing that she was now fully aware of what Aileen had just realised. Eventually she managed a hesitant, stuttering, "Err … err … yes, to answer your question, it was … it was the same Dimitris, and … err … yes, he could have been, could have been your birth father, but as I told you on Saturday, it's not certain that-"

Aileen didn't let her finish. Her confusion and shock had now turned to anger.

"You knew this all along didn't you, Eleni? You knew, but you let me continue to wonder."

"But … but … it's not certain that Dimitris was your-"

Eleni tried once more to explain, but Aileen wasn't in the mood to let her, and interrupted again.

"You must have known it was likely to all come out if I met your mother, Eleni; the truth, instead of the secrets and the lies. But is that what you wanted all along for some reason, for someone else to tell me, although I can't think why?"

"No, no, I … I just didn't think it all needed digging up again. I didn't think it was necessary, Aileen. Didn't think it was important any longer. It was all a long time ago, in the past. I didn't actually think either that it would all necessarily come out. I thought that even my mother wouldn't tell you."

Aileen's response was no longer soft and low. It was louder, considerably louder, displaying her anger. "What? You didn't think it was important that I should know that my birth father was the son of a Greek who had an affair with my grandmother; the son of a Greek traitor, a collaborator, an informer, who my grandmother killed."

Eleni sighed heavily, and then told Aileen, "Yes, I'm sorry. I can see why you're angry. I know I should have told you. But you know now, know everything, although it's still not certain that Dimitris was your birth father is it?"

"What about children? Did Dimitris and Cristina have any children?" Aileen asked, having calmed down a little and now thinking more rationally. "Maybe it will be possible to do some sort of DNA test and see if there is any match between us, them and me?"

"No, they didn't have any children. They have no family here at all now. They had some family, relatives on Crete, as my mother said earlier, but I have no idea if they are still there."

"I suppose I could try there, although it's a big island. I presume the family name, the name of his family relatives on Crete, is Papatonis, like Nikos'?" Aileen asked.

Eleni exchanged a quick glance with her mother and then answered, "I presume so, but we couldn't say for sure could we, mother? I think they were cousins, so it could be a different family name."

Maria shook her head slightly, a little wearily. Which gave Eleni the opportunity to tell Aileen, "Enough, I think that's enough now. My mother is looking tired. I think we should stop now, mother. I can see it in your eyes. They are looking heavy, and you've told Aileen a lot, gone over a lot of memories that are not all good. It's been a long afternoon."

Now it was Aileen's turn to take a deep breath and slump back in her chair again. Whether the old woman was tired or not, Aileen certainly was after all she'd been told. She was a pretty fit woman, but she was drained now completely, physically and emotionally.

She had calmed down and all her initial anger had almost subsided as she agreed, "Oh, okay, of course. Thank you, Maria, for all that, all that you've told me."

She finished speaking and gathered up her things to place them back in her bag. As she got up from her chair to say goodbye to the two women Maria asked, "Jack said you are here for a few months, I think?"

"Yes, I think so," Aileen confirmed, although actually she knew that was probably not going to be the case after what happened on Saturday night with the MI6 guy. She wasn't about to tell anyone that though.

"Well, if you think of anything more you want to know about those times in the war here, and the civil war, and about Bernie, do come back and see me," Maria told her. "Just let Jack know and he can arrange it."

"Of course, and thank you again, Maria. Goodbye, and don't get up. I'm sure Eleni can show me out."

Aileen said goodbye to Eleni at the front door to the villa. She was as pleasant as she could be in the circumstances. There was no real point in being anything other than that, even though deep inside she was still bloody angry at Eleni over her secrets.

She made her way down the few steps and the slope once again towards the centre of the village and her apartment. It was seven-thirty and the beautiful calm evening twilight was descending on the village. At least that helped her mood.

As she strolled down the alleyway the twilight prompted her to reflect on what she'd heard over the past three hours or so. What she had now discovered about her family past. Did her mother, Mary, find out about any of it when she was in Lindos over those two summers from 1976? So much of what she had just heard about her grandmother reminded her of, and reflected, her own life; the killing, and a relationship with a married man, just like Aileen's with Richard Weston, even if that was for her undercover role for the Bhoys. Most of all, there was the similarity of her grandmother's infiltration of the British Secret Service. At least now though she really did know many of the secrets, the lies, and the truth of her own family past; more about who she was, and where she was in her own life. Maybe all that will finally set her free to get on and live the rest of it.

Part Eight: Reflection, but lies, secrets or hope?

22

A chance encounter, a second chance?

Aileen's past life as an undercover IRA agent and an assassin was full of passionate ideals and beliefs, no matter what the risk. She had now discovered that it was much like her grandmother's. But she was tired of all that at this point in her life. That's why she came to Lindos. To get away from all that and find who she really was. However, what happened on Saturday night taught her that her past life couldn't be shaken off that easily. With the attempt by the MI6 agent to kill her it had followed her. She desperately wanted that life over and done with now though, more than ever, finished. She knew that after what had happened on Saturday night Lindos wouldn't be the safe haven for her that she'd hoped it would be. In the misty depths of her soul there slumbered those certainties that she had nurtured, and often relied upon for many years, her instincts. Those certainties and her instinct were now telling her that she would have to move on, and soon.

By the time she made it back to her apartment on that Monday evening she had settled on the fact that this would definitely be her last night in Lindos. She would move on tomorrow. Over dinner in one of the restaurants she would to think through her options of just where to disappear to next before another MI6 agent turns up looking for her. Perhaps to Crete, as she knew now that was where one part of her extended family appeared to originate from, not that there was much chance of finding them after all this time. Not that she was really that concerned to do so now. She'd found out quite enough about her family's past, or at least one side of it. In reality, knowing what she did about MI6 from her almost twenty years as an IRA infiltrator of that organisation, she could never be sure of being completely safe anywhere in the world. She knew they never gave up. Nevertheless, Crete might be a good enough starting point and she could always move on if necessary.

As she placed the key in the door to her apartment it was nearly quarter to eight. Even though it wasn't the most comfortable double bed in the world, the one in her apartment looked very appealing as she slipped off her sleeveless, short light blue cotton dress and her flat sandals. She was tired, drained from all that she had been listening to from Jack's grandmother for over three hours. She resisted the temptation of the bed, however, and instead headed for a quick, hopefully revitalising, luke warm shower.

The shower did the trick. A brief spray of deodorant and her favourite Armani perfume, a brush through her hair, just a little make up, and she was staring through the open doors of the built in wardrobe trying to decide what to put on for her last night in the village. It was still the middle of August. The evenings were full of the lingering daytime heat and humidity. It would be like that for at least another two weeks, not that it would affect her. She'd be gone.

She decided on a short white skirt and a loose bright green baggy t-shirt, which she adjusted to wear off one shoulder and tied in a knot above her bare slim waist and stomach. The white skirt, together with the exposed parts of her shoulder, stomach and legs showed off her good tan nicely. She slipped her flat sandals back on, grabbed her small shoulder handbag, and then stuffed some Euros and her phone inside it, which she transferred from the larger bag she'd taken to Jack's grandmothers. She took a quick look in the mirror, or at least she intended to. Even allowing for the relatively small amount of make-up what she saw stopped her in her tracks momentarily - a woman with a tired look of a dead weight in her eyes, a woman worn down by all the deceit and the killing. Perhaps, if she was kind, she could convince herself that it was simply the look of a woman who had mellowed. However, in reality she had to admit that probably it was merely that she was exhausted now by all the turmoil of her past secret life, all the deceit, all the lies.

She'd been on a journey to find herself, who she really was inside after all her various false identities and lives over the past twenty years, as well as to find out the truth about her family past. She hadn't managed to identify for certain who her birth father had been, but at least she'd heard some things that had given her a pretty good idea. In addition, she'd learned a lot that she never knew about her mother and her grandmother, and that there were a lot of similarities with them in her character and in the circumstances of all their lives.

The one thing she was sure about was that she would leave Lindos tomorrow. The more immediate decision she faced, however, as she closed and locked the door to the courtyard of her apartment was which restaurant to choose to go to for dinner on her final evening. She decided on Kalypso, just up the alley past Pal's Bar, between that bar and the Courtyard Bar. She hadn't been there before, so she thought she'd try something new on her last night. The restaurant had a good reputation.

Once again the alleys through the village were crowded with tourists, browsing the small shops or on their way to the restaurants or the bars for pre or post-dinner drinks. The swarms of bodies contributed to perpetuating the lingering evening August heat. The narrow alleys denied any breeze that might alleviate the heat and the climbing humidity.

It was only a short walk through the crowds from her apartment to Kalypso. However, she now found herself spending a substantial part of it constantly looking around, behind her and ahead, checking for the possibility that one of the tourists might not actually be what they seemed, but in fact be another MI6 agent sent to eliminate her. She suspected every person walking alone towards her as she dodged through the tourists. Thankfully, mostly they were couples or groups of four or more.

Kalypso was busy, but the woman who greeted her when she entered found her a nice table on the top terrace. She turned out to be one of the owners. Aileen settled on very traditional

Moussaka, with a small side salad and just a small bottle of water. She wanted to keep a clear head for tomorrow, and try and leave as early as possible for the ferry port in Rhodes Town. What she'd heard about Kalypso was spot on. The Moussaka was delicious, and there was plenty of it, too much for her in fact. The waiter and the owner, who visited her table to check everything was okay, were the very epitome of Greek hospitality, just like every other restaurant she had visited in Lindos and their owners and staff.

Suitably fed, she decided it would only be right to go to the Courtyard Bar just up the alley for a drink on her final night, although she would be very careful not to tell Jack or anyone that she was leaving tomorrow. She would just slip away without telling anyone in Lindos, so that if someone did come looking for her – an MI6 agent - no one would be able to help them about exactly when she left, let alone where she'd gone.

As she climbed the few steps to one of the entrances at one end of the Courtyard Bar it was approaching ten o'clock. She could hear the music from inside as she negotiated the steps, but the general noise emanating from voices inside suggested the bar was busy. It was, and quite crowded, so much so that there were no free stools at the bar to be seen. She managed to attract the attention of Dimitris behind the bar and lean between a couple on two of the stools to ask for a Gin and tonic. While she watched him pour it Jack spotted her and made his way towards her from the far end of the bar. What he told her filled her with a mixture of surprise and concern.

"Hi, there's a friend of yours at the far end of the bar. I told him earlier you were back in the village. He wants to know if you want to say hello."

Was it another MI6 agent, she instantly wondered. She turned away from the bar slightly, attempting to peer through the crowd, but there was no familiar face that she recognised, which only increased her concern. She couldn't see everybody at that end of the bar however, especially those seated on stools at the very far end. It was too crowded. In any case, just what familiar face was she expecting to see? No one knew she was in Lindos, except the possibility of MI6, of course. Jack did say, "Back in the village," so perhaps it was someone she'd met from Lindos on her previous visit in June. But who? There was no one who lived in the village that she could recall being that friendly with back then."

She turned back towards the bar to ask Jack who it was, but his attention had been attracted by a couple further along the bar wanting another drink. As she waited for Dimitris to deliver her drink she went over it quickly in her mind. Should she go and seek out this friend of hers that Jack had referred to, or just disappear back into the crowd of customers at her end of the bar and then leave? In the end she decided on the former. Better to deal with it here in the bar, in public, rather than be confronted again in one of the dark alleys later. In any case, she'd dealt with, and disposed of, one MI6 agent already, so she could certainly deal with another. She steeled herself, summoning up the old Kathleen once again.

As she weaved her way with her drink towards the far end of the bar, and through the groups of customers standing behind those on bars stools, the person she eventually saw sitting on one of the stools gave her more of a surprise than a concern. Well, to be accurate, it did cause her something of a concern, but it wasn't one relating to the possible loss of her life.

"Hello, Aileen, or should I say, Kathleen?" the man asked.

"It's Aileen here please, Martin." There was a mixture of surprise and not a little pleasure clearly evident in her voice. At least there was no hint of anger in his, much to her liking, merely a small trace of sarcasm.

"Look, I can explain," she added quickly, "but not here, not now. I can explain, tell you, and explain what happened, but not in public, at least not here where we can be overheard, please?" A pleading small smile was on her lips, which quickly turned into her slightly biting the bottom one.

"Fine, I look forward to hearing it, Aileen."

He was abrupt, but not visibly annoyed, as the slight smile he now returned at her confirmed. He deliberately put an emphasis on the pronunciation of her name, but it came across as quite light-hearted. He appeared remarkably calm about it all, about what had happened between them.

Martin Cleverley was a Professor of Greek Mythology at King's College London, or at least he had been when he first met Aileen that June on a flight to Lindos. Subsequently, he was offered, and accepted, a redundancy pay-off deal by the college at the end of July. They had been seated next to each other on the flight. She struck up a conversation with him as she noticed he appeared to be writing a novel on his laptop in front of him. Their relationship developed from there once they established they were both staying in Lindos; him alone, but her with her friend, Sandra Weston. They slept together a couple of times in the first week, but Sandra's husband, Richard, turning up unexpectedly at the start of the second week complicated things and events spiralled out of Aileen's control. Not least because of Aileen's deliberate planned - although she made it appear accidental - exposure to Sandra of her recent, by then ended, affair with Richard. Out of spite and retribution Sandra told Martin about it and pretty soon the trust between him and Aileen evaporated, fuelled by Richard's constant baiting of him.

Martin was tall, six foot one, with short light brown hair, and an angular clean shaven face with wide cheekbones that produced a pronounced jawline. He'd managed to avoid developing any obvious unattractive bulges around his waist as he turned forty, despite his fondness for the occasional beer, sometimes more. He'd been married for six years and been divorced for ten. Despite his supposed academic intelligence Martin Cleverley was a man prone to insecurities and doubts where women and relationships with them were concerned. In his profession in the lecture theatre, as well as in his writing, things came relatively easy to him, unlike his relationships with women. His brief relationship, if that was what it was, with Aileen in Lindos, and briefly after they were back in the U.K., was evidence of that and his insecurity. In particular, it had been easily played upon relentlessly by Richard Weston.

Aileen had persuaded Martin to leave Lindos with her impulsively on the spur of the moment back in June, a week after they first met, and go back to London. She said it was to get away from Richard Weston and his scheming. Once they got back to London they went to Brighton for a few days. She seemed determined that she didn't want to stay in London for some reason, and he readily agreed. However, the spectre of her relationship with Richard hung over them, especially his taunting of Martin. Trust broke down between the two of them, and Martin found it increasingly difficult to deal with her past with Richard, as well as what Richard had deliberately told him about his present relationship with Aileen, embellishing it as much as he could when Martin foolishly went to see him and confronted him one afternoon in his office back in London. Martin hadn't told Aileen he was going to do that. As a result they had a huge argument early that same evening over what Richard had taunted him with and while Martin was in the shower she left, disappeared without trace. He agonised, searching Brighton and London for her for three days, but with no luck. When he finally went to the offices where she worked in London, or he thought she did, he discovered that she wasn't who she said she was, or who he thought she was. Purely by chance, from a photo of them both in Lindos on his phone which he showed to a Human Resources Manager at the company, he discovered that they knew her there as Kathleen O'Mara, not Aileen Regan. But Kathleen O'Mara had left the company three weeks previously, they informed him.

Martin Cleverley was a man who looked for logic in everything. He needed that. It was ingrained in him from his academic pursuits, and beyond. What Aileen had done when she just disappeared without trace, without telling him, defied the logic that structured his world. He couldn't comprehend that at all. Now, it seemed, he was possibly about to retrieve and revive his logical world. Now, he was going to hear reasons from her for what she'd done, or at least, that is what she said she would tell him, but later.

"Let's have a drink here first, before we find somewhere less public where you can explain," he suggested. "I certainly need another one now. What about you?"

"I'm okay, thanks. I've only just got this one," she declined.

At that point the couple occupying the two stools to his left got up to leave and Aileen sat on the vacated stool next to him.

Greek mythology had been Martin Cleverley's only tangible love interest, some would say obsession, for most of the years since his divorce, rather than women. Or maybe that was simply a substitute for them, a poor one? Now there was a distraction from his Greek mythology, Aileen. He could feel it straightaway. He'd felt it in exactly the same way when they first met on the plane in June. There wasn't so much a spark between them as a constant continuous electric current. And sex with her was good, bloody good. One time when Richard Weston was trying to wind him up he told Martin that she loved sex. Lived for it. Couldn't get enough of it, of course with him, Richard. Then he told Martin that she'd said to him that it wasn't very good at all with Martin. But he knew that was a lie. That was just all part of one of Richard Weston's crude psychological games. Martin had seen how she enjoyed it with him. Seen how much she loved it with him.

Now, in the busy Courtyard Bar on an August Monday night the electricity was clearly a two way current. She wouldn't admit it to herself, but subconsciously she had been wondering, hoping maybe, that she would bump into him in Lindos again. She knew he was a regular visitor. Everyone had told her as much, the locals anyway. Maybe it wasn't so subconsciously. She had even imagined that she'd seen him a couple of times in the evenings. Mistaken, of course, perhaps?" She checked.

"When did you arrive?"

"Just this afternoon, really didn't expect to see you here again though, or to be honest, ever again unfortunately. When you disappeared like that I presumed it had ended between us forever."

Unfortunately is an interesting word for him to use, she thought. She told him, "There are no endings, only beginnings, Martin. A famous man, Thomas Cromwell, once said that. I believe it's true."

"Infamous," he commented.

"What?"

"Infamous, some people would say he was infamous. Not a very good man, in fact not a nice man at all, Aileen."

She permitted a smile to creep across her pink lips as she fixed a look into his eyes. "Clever though, Martin. He was very clever, managing Henry the Eighth and all those women, his wives."

"Yes, there is that," he agreed.

They were clearly sparring.

Changing the subject he asked, "Where are you staying? Here for a week, or is it two?"

"I rented an apartment just up the alleyway from Arches. It's ok, right in the centre of the village. The usual Greek and Lindos holiday apartment, I guess. What about you?"

"Same apartment I stayed at in June, my usual one. It's pretty functional and in the centre of the village too. Well, you know that of course. The bed is still bloody hard though, as you know too."

Yes, she did know, from their sexual exploits in June, which brought a wry grin to her face this time.

"So, how long?" he asked again.

She was about to answer him, but before she could Jack came along the bar to talk to them.

Clutching a drink of his own, he told Martin, "Nice surprise for you. Aileen has been talking to my mother and grandmother about her own mother and grandmother. Her mother was here in Lindos in the seventies working, and her grandmother was here during the war. And she's here for a couple of months too, like you."

"So, you're here for two months then," Aileen commented as she placed her empty glass back on the bar, indicating with a nod to Jack that she'd have another.

"Yes, two months, till the end of the summer. My university offered me a decent redundancy deal eventually, after a bit of haggling. So, I took it and decided to come back here for the rest of the summer to try and do some more writing. You've been talking to Jack's mother and grandmother then?"

"I've been trying to trace my birth father here. It's a long story. I didn't know until Jack arranged for me to meet them, but they knew my mother when she worked here for two summers from 1976, which is when she got pregnant with me, towards the end of the second summer. Jack's grandmother knew mine when she was here as an agent for an arm of the British Secret Service in 1943, the Special Operations Executive it was called apparently."

"Any luck, with your birth father I mean?" Martin asked.

"Some, pretty strong possibility I know who he was now."

"Was?"

"Yeah, if it is the Greek who I think it is. It appears he and my mother had some sort of affair here in that second summer. He's dead now though. So, there's no way of being sure unfortunately, and there's no relatives of his around in Lindos anymore, but I tried."

He reached onto the bar and squeezed her hand as he told her, "Well, that's something at least."

There was a considerable amount of obvious touching going on between them throughout their conversation.

Jack reappeared at their end of the bar with her new Gin and tonic. As he placed it on the bar in front of her he asked if what his grandmother had told Aileen was useful.

"Definitely, I never knew any of that about my grandmother. Didn't even know she was here during the war to be honest, Jack, let alone what she did." As she finished telling Jack that Martin asked for another drink of his own.

The drinks flowed for both of them over the next few hours. There was plenty of small talk, about the state of the world, including Brexit. There was more touching, plus a lot of laughing the more the drinks flowed, including about Richard Weston and his anger management issues. A couple of more times Jack joined them at their end of the bar, and more than once raised his eyebrows encouragingly in Martin's direction at how well the two of them appeared to be getting on.

Within an hour of their meeting Aileen was a transformed woman, visibly noticeably relaxed, and not just as a result of the drinks. She was laughing and smiling constantly with him. She hadn't felt like this for quite a while; relaxed and clearly flirting with a man, a man who she wasn't merely working on for her professional pursuits for MI6 or the Bhoys. Just as it had been previously in June, it was a consequence of her obvious clear attraction to him. The difference was that in June she was preoccupied with her mission, her assignment for the Bhoys, plus the annoying intervention of Richard Weston turning up in Lindos.

For Martin, she was becoming more and more attractive, exhibiting a confidence that was only adding to her now growing radiant personality. Once again she was having a devastating effect on him, similar to the one she'd had instantly when they first met on the plane in June.

They were getting on so well that any questions, or thoughts, about what had gone before between them when she suddenly disappeared had disappeared completely from his mind, for this evening at least. So much so that when it approached one o'clock and the music in the bar was about to stop, rather than go somewhere more private so that she could explain to him what had happened back then, and why, he suggested they go to Arches for more drinks. She readily agreed.

As they made their way arm in arm up the alley towards the club Chris on the door grinned, followed by a short booming laugh. Then he told Aileen, "You found him then."

"Eventually," Aileen replied. She explained to Martin, "I thought I saw you leaving here a few nights ago. Well, what I thought was you from the back, so I asked Chris and Valasi if it was you. Of course, they said it wasn't."

"I see. Busy inside, Chris?" Martin asked.

"Fairly, bit early yet though, as you know."

They made their way across Arches' courtyard and through the sound lock doors into the club. One of the English barmen Martin knew well, Pete, spotted him through the crowd from behind the bar directly opposite the entrance and immediately pulled up and opened a bottle of Alfa Greek beer for him. As the two of them made their way through the groups standing near the bar, and towards the less crowded end, Martin told Pete above the loud music, "And a Gin and tonic please mate."

"So, you assume you know what I'm drinking now do you? That's a bit presumptuous," Aileen told him with a smile and a wink, accompanied with another gentle squeeze of his arm.

He never bothered with a verbal response, instead preferring to return her smile and lean down to kiss her on the cheek. At that point he felt a tap on his shoulder. He turned around to see Valasi immediately behind him.

Like Chris, the owner also said to Aileen, "You did find him eventually then."

Aileen smiled and nodded. Before she could say anything, however, Valasi told them, "That calls for a celebration drink then I think, and for Martin's arrival, or should I say return."

He called Pete over and a minute or so later the barman appeared with shots for them all, including one for him.

With the noise of the music in the club there wasn't much opportunity for Aileen and Martin to have that conversation, her explanation of what happened before. They stuck to drinking. A couple of beers for him and two more Gin and tonics for her, and a lot more touching and squeezing, mostly with his arm around her waist.

23

More lies or merely economical with the truth?

After a few more shots, an hour or so later they were kissing passionately as they crashed onto the double bed in her apartment. The flirting and the drinking had proved to be an intoxicating combination; a pleasant prelude to what they both knew in the back of their minds was going to happen. It was, after all, what they both wanted to happen. It had been the same in June. The only difference this time was where they ended up, her apartment instead of his. The firmness of the mattress was remarkably uncomfortably similar, however.

After the third shot in Arches, of Tequila, she reached up and placed her left hand behind his neck to pull him into her and plant a passionate kiss on his lips. It was the first one between them since she walked out on him and disappeared in Brighton in June. It tasted just as sweet. She was just as forceful. The passion and the intensity of it left him in no doubt that she knew exactly what she wanted. She was certainly a woman who knew that. He learned that from experience not long after they met. He clearly remembered that the first time they had slept together in June it was after she had bluntly told him in another Lindos club, Glow, late one night, "I want us to go to bed now." So, it was hardly difficult for her to persuade him shortly after the kiss in Arches this time that they should leave and go to her flat. The obvious desire had overwhelmed them both.

They made their way through the sound proof doors into the courtyard. After Chris at the arched entrance bid them a, "Goodnight," with a wide grin on his face, they stumbled up the few metres of the alley to the door to the courtyard of her apartment. Once inside the courtyard though she grabbed a handful of his polo shirt and pulled him into another passionate kiss. As she finished and drew back she gripped his hand and eagerly pulled him towards the door of the apartment.

Eventually, having made it inside and fallen together onto the bed in an embrace and another kiss, she stood up in front of him lying on the bed, flicked the switch on the small bedside lamp, and rapidly yanked her t-shirt over her head to expose the top half of her by now quite nicely tanned body. She was very proud of her body for a woman of her age, vain almost. However, he was not about to mention that to her. This was hardly the time, if ever.

She stood motionless in front of him for a long half-minute while he lay there on the bed beneath her gaze. The stunning dark brown do-eyes of hers appeared to be penetrating every part of him. She was merely teasing him. Without allowing her eyes to shift from now being fixed on his she slowly unfastened her skirt and allowed it to drop to the floor. Instantly, in one seamless movement, she removed her black bra and pushed her skimpy black thong to the floor to stand naked in front of him.

Her forthright actions were those of a very confident woman. She did have every right to be proud of her very finely toned body. Maybe on the final limits of being described as lithe, but nevertheless still eligible for such a description. Her breasts were firm, nicely protruding, and perfectly proportioned. There was no sign whatsoever of any growing stomach. In fact, it was completely flat. Overall her whole figure suggested that she was a regular gym visitor, or at least cared about her fitness. Something she had obviously needed to pay attention to regularly in her past profession. Even without heels and shoes her legs were nicely shaped and equally toned, also enhanced by her tan.

While he was enjoying the view of her naked body she leaned down to unfasten his shorts and pull them off as he lay on the bed, revealing, just as she did in June, that he never wore boxer shorts, or indeed any underwear. As she let the shorts drop to the floor he pulled his polo shirt over his head and flung it off the bed. She paused, standing over him and staring at him intensely, once again in silence. She was making him wait. He stretched out a hand to try to grab the back of her thigh and pull her on to him, but she brushed away his hand and told him firmly, "Wait, don't be in such a rush."

He slid back onto the full width of the bed with its one thin white sheet and finally she climbed on top of him. He remembered this from before. She liked it. Loved it. To be in control was what obviously turned her on and he wasn't going to fight that, or disappoint her. Before though she had made him wait and satisfy her, meet her needs, before she let him anywhere near being inside her. This time was different. She was still in control, but this time she wanted him inside her straightaway, demanded it. And that is what she did, manipulated what she wanted, desired, in a matter of seconds.

Richard Weston had taunted him, saying how much she loved sex, craved it, couldn't get enough of it. With him, of course. Richard had taunted Martin that she had told him that sex with Martin hadn't fulfilled her. But that was not Martin's experience with her at all. Just like now, it was always great. She always gave an impression that was far from it not being fulfilling. Now she was astride his body, straddling him with him deep inside her. Thrusting inside her, although it was actually her controlling the thrusting, manoeuvring that part of his body which she wanted most. He lay there enjoying the sight and sounds of her writhing firm body and her moans of contentment above him.

At one point he attempted to reach up to caress one of her breasts and sit up slightly while still inside her. However, she brushed his hand away strongly once more, and then reached down to put the palm of her hand firmly on his chest to push him back down on the bed. All the while she carried on slowly rocking back and forth, up and down on him inside her. There was just the slightest grin of pleasure etched across her face throughout, which widened into a broad smile as the palm of her hand pushed him back down. He had found that somewhat disconcerting when they first had sex in June, but had now grown to like it a lot, along with her smile and her obvious enjoyment

Her face contorted spasmodically as she swayed back and forth, using him, getting the best from him. It was almost as if she was in some small waves of pain, but it was the pain of anticipation, although not wanting it to end, not wanting it to stop. Somehow though she could sense that he was reaching his climax. She told him loudly in a firm voice as she continued to rock back and forth on him, "Don't, not till I tell you when!

Don't you ... wait ... you just wait .... Just wait until I tell you!"

The image she gave off of an ice-cool, calculating woman, completely in control of her emotions was at once disintegrating before his eyes, and yet paradoxically demanding to be in control, and in one respect managing to be.

Gradually her rocking movement got faster. Her moans got longer and increased in volume. The rocking got even more frantic. Her hand pushed down even more firmly on his chest and her facial contortions became more frequent, until finally she proclaimed, virtually ordered him, "Yes, yes, yes, now, now!"

Her thighs tightened around his lower body as she threw her head back in obvious ecstasy. The sensual organs of their bodies exploded in a perfect unison of indescribable ultimate enjoyment, gratification, and fulfilment. After a wave of convulsions screaming through her whole body she slumped forward on top of him. She lay motionless, only the glistening perspiration of their bodies between them. After a couple of minutes she rolled off him. She turned her head towards him on the pillow, then brushed a lone strand of her damp dark hair off her face while simultaneously offering him a smile of obvious complete satisfaction and contentment, followed by a tender, soft, lingering kiss. As their lips met he could feel the warmth from the whole of her body. She drew back from the kiss and with another small smile rested her head once again facing him on the pillow while lying flat on her back alongside him.

She lay there in perfect silence scanning every part of his face, scrutinising every aspect of it, as they exchanged more smiles and soft, gentle kisses. She was naked and trembling, but not from any chill in the temperature in the bedroom. She hadn't even paused to turn on the air-conditioning as they satisfied their obvious mutual desires. He placed one of his hands gently on her flat, tanned, glistening stomach. He could feel the tiny tremors in the muscles of her flat stomach as he stroked her skin. The raging desire that had overwhelmed them, taken control of their bodies only a few moments before had cooled, been satisfied. Her sparkling, piercing, dark brown doe-eyes were fixed on him, searching into his, lost. He carefully took hold of her left hand and lifted it to his mouth. His eyes closed as he tenderly kissed the end of each one of her fingers slowly, and then her warm palm. As he released it she placed it gently on his cheek. A combination of weariness from the effect of their exertions, from the Tequila shots, and from an overwhelming warm feeling of contentment, was gradually creeping over them both. The last thing each of them saw was the satisfied relaxed face of the other as they drifted off into a deep sleep.

Just over six hours later she blinked twice trying to remove the traces of sleep from her eyes. The bright sunlight was struggling to force its way through the shutters of her bedroom. Through its very limited partial success the first clear image that emerged into her vision was Martin, sleeping soundly inches away from her. She spent a long minute gazing at his resting body beneath the solitary white sheet.

Perhaps last night will not be her final night in Lindos after all now. Although, deep inside she knew she had to leave. That was the only logical thing to do. It would be far too dangerous to stay and risk another MI6 agent turning up determined to eliminate her. Now however, there was the added complication of Martin and how she felt about him. He was an extra, unforeseen, factor in the equation that was the rest of her life. She didn't want to run out on him yet again. She was torn. Could she really tell him, tell him everything, everything from her past? And if she did, could she then manage to persuade him to leave Lindos with her?

She looked back at him sleeping, unable to decide there and then. She would see what the rest of the day brought, and hopefully then decide. Meanwhile, she gently slid out from beneath the thin bed sheet and pulled on the green t-shirt which she had taken off last night. In the small kitchen off the bedroom she made coffee for them both, and then woke him with a gentle, soft kiss on his cheek. As he opened his bleary eyes and smiled the smile of sleepy contentment she fixed another gaze into his face with her enticing, inviting dark brown eyes and told him, "Good morning. Coffee?" She placed it on the small bedside chest of drawers. As she turned back to face him he returned her gaze, then kissed her, before adding, "Good morning, thanks."

She walked around to the other side of the bed with her coffee, placed it on the bedside table, and then joined him under the sheet after she removed her t-shirt. She wasn't really that interested in paying much attention to her coffee for now. She had something else in mind. He'd managed only one sip of his before she took it out of his hand and placed it alongside hers on the bedside table.

"I intended leaving here today. That was my plan. But that was before last night," she told him suggestively as she pulled him on top of her and kissed him once again. He had no trouble figuring out what she wanted. He never bothered asking for now why she had intended to leave. That wasn't exactly the first thing in his mind at that moment, or anywhere else on his body. She placed her hands on his shoulders and gently pushed him down her body under the sheet, clearly directing him to precisely where she wanted him to go. The part of her body that she most urgently wanted him to pay some attention to, all his attention at that particular time.

He planted soft kisses across and down her tight, flat, tanned stomach as he made his way to the area of her body that most craved his attention. The area desperately desiring him. As he reached it and was about to do what she obviously desired she whispered, "I love it at this time. I love this in the morning. Waking up to it is best."

He set about eagerly giving her the pleasure she sought. Gently at first, with slow circular motions, but as her body convulsions grew in intensity, matched by her increasingly frequent and voluble moans of pleasure, his actions got quicker. She was a woman who clearly knew exactly what she wanted and how to get it, in every aspect of life and enjoyment. However, she was also clearly not always a woman in a hurry to achieve that. She reached down to grab his hair in her right hand and slow down his efforts. Still pressing his face firmly into her she told him softly between deep breaths and sighs, "Slowly ... slowly ... make it last ... I want it to last ..."

He'd never met a woman like her before. A woman who definitely liked to be, obviously needed to be, in complete control. It wasn't that he didn't enjoy it in some way. It was just different, a different experience for him. Of course, he had experienced it before with her back in June. However, that didn't make it any more unexpected, or different.

It seemed like a long time, but in reality it was only just over fifteen minutes, during which he did exactly as she asked, precisely what she desired. The volume of her expression of enjoyment remained at a constant high level throughout. Then suddenly the convulsions of her body hit a new level of force. She wrapped her thighs firmly each side of his head, squeezing in ecstatic concentration and pleasure as she screamed, "Oh, yes, yes, yes," followed by a low moan of blissful release and satisfaction. She lay there contented, with his face resting on her lower stomach for twenty seconds or so.

"Hmmm … I really do love waking up with that in the morning," she told him softly as she grabbed his hair once again, this time much more gently, and guided his face up towards hers from under the sheet. As he reached her glazed eyes she released her grip on his hair and moved her hand to behind his neck, drawing him into her once more for a passionate, lingering, warm kiss. As he rolled off of her to lie beside her again she asked, "But what about you? Don't you-"

She never got to finish. He was distracted, actually now strangely distracted to dwell on what she'd told him about intending to leave Lindos today. He surprised himself that he was more bothered about getting to the bottom of that than satisfying himself with her now. He interrupted to tell her, "Later, it's okay, I can wait until later."

She told him with a cheeky grin, "So, there's going to be a later is there?"

"Well, I just thought-" he started to say, but she didn't let him finish as she kissed him again.

He never got back to finish asking about what she'd said about leaving Lindos. Instead, there was something more important to him now on his mind. He moved the conversation onto something a little more seriously intense.

"You know I actually really don't know that much about you. I do know more about your family background now, well one side of it, from what you said was the reason you came back here. But your character, what makes you tick, like what makes you smile, what makes you cry? I don't know you well enough at all to know that do I?"

She turned her head to look him in the eyes. It was like she was exploring every aspect of his face again, every last bit of it, scanning it. She didn't really answer him though, other than a tantalising, "Wow! That's a bit deep, almost philosophical, Martin. Maybe you'll find out those things too, if there's going to be a later?"

She deliberately put more emphasis on the last word, teasing him over his use of it minutes before. Then she left him lingering, pondering over it, as she turned and reached for her coffee.

He was bewildered about how to interpret that, which was precisely the reaction she intended. Was she saying that he'd find out those things over time? That they would be spending more time together? Or maybe she wasn't? She did say, "Maybe."

She knew that at that time she wasn't really ready to tell him too much about herself, be too honest with him about it. She hadn't figured out completely what to tell him, how much of the truth. So, instead she turned his question around, turned it back on him as she returned her coffee to the bedside table.

"But I can say the same about you, can't I? I know you're a Professor of Greek Mythology, or were. I know you've been married. And you know I've been married. Neither of us have kids. We did all that on the plane in June, remember?"

"Yes, I suppose we did," he agreed. "But I meant what you're really like."

This was straying into dangerous territory now as far as she was concerned. So, she ignored his question and turned it back on him yet again. She was practiced at this, interrogation, twenty years practiced.

"Okay, you tell me, Martin, tell me about you."

Now he was reaching for his coffee as what immediately came into his mind was that despite being someone who confidently searched for logic in everything, largely as a result of his academic background, he knew only too well that he was totally prone to insecurities and a lack of confidence where

237

relationships with women were concerned. There was no way he was going to tell her that in answer to her question, however. Instead, he plumped for changing the subject.

She looked a little surprised by him going off at a tangent as he put his coffee back down and asked bluntly, "So, what actually happened?"

His change of direction confused her, or at least she decided to give the impression it did.

"About what, what happened about what, about you, Martin, about me, something to do with our characters?"

She was playing games, playing for time. She had a good idea what he was asking about. She knew it was bound to come up at some point after she put off talking to him about it in the Courtyard Bar the night before. She wanted time to think then though, although she was being genuine when she told him she didn't want to talk about it in public where they could be overheard. She needed time to think about, and decide, just how much she could tell him, should tell him. She knew that she couldn't tell him the whole truth. She reckoned that would be far too shocking for him. She was sure he would simply walk away from her if she did that.

It came as something as a surprise to her that she felt she definitely didn't want that to happen. That wasn't the cold, calculating, manipulative Aileen Regan or Kathleen O'Mara of the past twenty years. She was confused. She was accustomed to everything being clear and precise. She liked it that way; precision, certainty, and everything being planned down to the minutest detail. That had been the shape and rhythm of her life for the past twenty years. It had needed to be in what she did, kill people. Something had happened. Something had changed in her, changed her. Maybe it was him. Ever since she came back to Lindos she'd mistakenly imagined she'd seen him a few times. Was that really because she wanted to meet him again? She must have known deep down inside that at some point it was likely that their paths would cross in the village. She knew he came back regularly during the summer, sometimes three times.

He sat up and propped his head against a raised pillow, then turned it to look her straight in the eyes as he explained and tried again.

"What happened when you disappeared back in Brighton, left me without saying a word? I came out of the shower and you'd gone, disappeared, and your bag and all your clothes. I was frantic, distraught. I searched up and down the street outside that flat, the streets off of it, and even in the pubs at each end of the road, thinking you might have just gone there for a drink to cool down after our argument. But nowhere, you were nowhere to be seen. I lost track of how many times I called your mobile that night and over the next couple of days, but all I got was a voice message telling me the number was unobtainable. On the Monday morning I even went to where I thought I knew you worked, but they told me no one called Aileen Regan had ever worked there, had never worked for them."

He stopped for a few seconds and took a deep breath, desperate to not sound as angry as he had at that time after she disappeared. Meanwhile, she just stared ahead at the magnolia painted wall at the far end of the bed. A blank expression covered her face. She was still working out just how much she could tell him as he continued.

"It was only when by chance, as a desperate last resort, I showed them a photo on my phone of you with me here that they recognised you. That's when they told me your name was Kathleen O'Mara, not Aileen Regan, and that she, you as Kathleen, had worked there, but left a few weeks before. Then I was really confused, still am. Who was this mysterious woman with two identities that I liked, liked very much? The woman I had a great time with here, but who then just disappeared."

She turned to face him in response to his comment about how much he liked her. It pleased her. Before she could tell him that though, he went on.

"Look, I know we argued that night you left over bloody Richard Weston. I know I was a prat. It sounded as though I didn't trust you, and I guess there was a part of me that was insecure about that because of your past with him. But I should have accepted just that. That it was all in the past. You kept saying that I didn't trust you, but that I had nothing to worry about. I should have listened to you and ignored all his taunting, all his lies. I was an idiot."

She reached up to place her hand behind his neck to kiss him tenderly once again.

As she drew her face away his eyes were pleading for an explanation, one that he anxiously, painfully, wanted to like, wanted to accept.

"You told me last night in Jack's that you'd explain what happened, but somewhere more private," he said, maintaining his fixed pleading stare into her eyes. "Well, this is about as private as it gets, Ms Regan, or should I say, Ms O'Mara? You said you'd explain that for a start, your two names."

He wasn't actually coming across to her as angry, because he wasn't, deliberately so. What they'd done last night and this morning had erased any possible trace of anger in him. He even tried to make it more light-hearted as he added, "Just tell me what happened and I'll buy you a nice breakfast at Giorgos. That's got to be a good deal, don't you think?"

She placed her hand on his cheek yet again and kissed him, then turned back to sit with her back resting partly against the small headboard of the bed and the wall behind it.

"Okay, yes, that is a good deal, Martin. I'm starving anyway after all that exertion you put me through last night and this morning." She half-turned her head towards him again and allowed another broad grin to creep across her face. She wasn't mocking him. She was displaying her complete pleasure at what they'd done.

"But let me tell you it all, Martin, everything, before you say anything. Just let me finish, before you judge me please?" she asked.

He nodded in agreement. Although what was now racing through his brain was what the hell did she mean by, "before you judge me"? He decided that finding out what she actually meant could wait, until he'd actually heard her out, heard it all. Hopefully, what she was referring to, what he was supposed to be going to judge her on, would then be clear.

"More than anything else, what I'm about to tell you will explain what happened between me and that prat Richard

Weston, why it happened," she began, as she looked away from him and turned to stare straight ahead in front of her once more at the bare wall at the far end of the bed.

"I liked you, Martin, but I didn't plan to drag you into my messy life at that time. There was a lot going on with me then. So, when we met by chance on the plane I had no intention of getting into some sort of relationship. I was sure I didn't want that, but with you it just happened. I couldn't help it. I found myself liking you more and more here. We seemed to have some sort of connection, and I don't mean just the sex. It just developed from there, and that meant things became a lot more complicated. I thought I could try and fix it, make it easier, by suggesting that we left here unexpectedly. Get away from sodding Richard and Sandra Weston and all their nasty games and go back to London. Then I suggested that we go to Brighton together because I knew things, problems, might follow me back to London. When you agreed I thought that would give me more time, more space to sort things out."

She hesitated and briefly turned her head to glance sideways at him, trying to detect any glimmer of reaction on his face. There was none. Just a blank look as he listened closely. She turned her head back to gaze again at the far wall as she continued.

"Perhaps that's what I do, run away."

"I hope not, not this time. I-" he started to tell her, but she lifted her hand to his mouth to gently indicate to him to let her continue, even though she was pleased to hear that from him.

"Of course, it didn't, did it, didn't really give me more time? Bloody Richard Weston had planted the seed of doubt in your mind, especially when you went to see him that day in London and confront him. I wish you hadn't. I wish you had told me you were going to see him. I would have told you, begged you, not to. Not because I had anything to hide, but because I knew what a devious bastard he was. I wasn't really surprised when you came back repeating the lies he'd told you, or at least the doubt he'd planted in your mind from them. But I know I reacted stupidly when you asked me about them, about him. I made it about trust, you and me and trust. My head was all over the place at the time. But I panicked. I knew I couldn't tell you all of it at that time, everything, including all of it about him and me and what that was really about. So, as I said, I tried to get you to drop it, forget it, what he'd told you, said that it was all lies, and made it all about trust between you and me. I couldn't get you to do that, couldn't get that insidious bastard out of my life, our lives, or out of your head. Yet again all I wanted to do was run away. So, that's what I did. It seemed the easiest thing to do. No, actually, it was the only choice, the only thing I could do at the time."

She reached over and took a drink of her now barely warm coffee before she continued.

"So, I wanted to tell you everything at the time, about me and him, Richard, about my two names, but I couldn't. It was far too complicated then."

"But not now, it's not too complicated now?" he asked.

She shook her head slightly as she replied tentatively, "No, no, well I hope not, not now, not as complicated as it was then, I guess."

"So?" he said softly and shrugged his shoulders slightly. He was anxious for her to continue, but not to sound too much like he was.

"Well, yes, Kathleen is my real name, Kathleen O'Mara and …"

She stopped, hesitated for a few seconds, and then turned her head to look into his face once more. She was biting her bottom lip slightly, trying to decide just how much of the whole truth she could tell him, how much it would be wise to tell him. First she had to warn him though.

After a few more seconds she told him firmly, "Look, Martin, you can never repeat this, never repeat what I'm going to tell you. Never repeat it to anyone. If you do, we will both be in deep, deep trouble. More than you can imagine."

Now he was thinking back to her, "before you judge me," comment earlier and wondering just what it was that she was about to tell him that was so terrible. So terrible that he could never repeat it.

She got up from her side of the bed, walked around to his side and sat on the edge of it as close to him as she could to again look straight into his eyes. She bit the inside of her bottom lip in anguish slightly once again, released it, and then told him. She was just going to come out with it, at least the part that she had decided she could tell him.

"I was an agent in MI6 for almost twenty years."

A look of shock spread instantly across his face. That wasn't the "before you judge me" explanation he was anticipating at all. He shook his head once slowly ever so slightly and then sat in blank faced bewilderment as she continued.

"They gave me a false identity, MI6, as Aileen Regan."

That wasn't really a very good start in terms of the truth. It wasn't MI6 that gave her the false identity. It was the IRA. Of course she knew that, but she was sure that if she told him the whole truth she wouldn't get very much further with her explanation. She would end up having to go into great detail about her IRA connection, and as much as she liked him, she definitely wasn't prepared to do that. That would be far too dangerous, for both of them, even more so than revealing her MI6 connection. Anyway, she was certain that there was no way that he would know, or have any way of discovering, that it was the IRA and not MI6 that gave her the false identity as Aileen.

"They call it a legend," she continued. "It means it's not just a false name, but a whole past invented personal history and documentation; passport and the whole works, including a false birth certificate. Sandra Weston was my boss in MI6, well, one of them. She was quite high up in the organisation, although not when she recruited me to the agency at university twenty years ago."

The colour had drained from his face. Stunned, all he could manage was a muttered incredulous, "Sandra, the Sandra Weston who was here with you in June?"

She nodded slightly and replied. "Yes, that Sandra."

As she did so she looked straight at his face, only a few inches away from her as she sat close to him on the edge of the bed and continued.

"Anyway, the agency, MI6, had a lead from an informer inside the Russian Secret Service, the FSB, what used to be the KGB, that her husband Richard was spying for them. They were told that was why he'd married her years ago, to get close to her, and had been feeding sensitive stuff back to Moscow for years that he'd picked up from her. What MI6 weren't sure about, however, was whether he'd actually turned her, persuaded her to work for them, or whether it was all just him spying on her, somehow gathering sensitive information that she had access to without her knowledge and feeding it back to Moscow. She wasn't even supposed to tell him that she worked for MI6. So, as far as she was concerned he never knew anything about that. In the agency we weren't supposed to tell our partners in case it compromised us. Plus, it would actually have contravened the Official Secrets Act that we all had to sign. When I was married my husband never knew I worked for MI6. The agency gave me a meaningless bureaucratic title for my supposed work in the Ministry of Defence. That was all part of the legend. In Sandra's case she had her freelance fashion photography business which operated as perfect cover for her. It gave her access undercover to loads of fashion shows in perfect locations, lots of cities across the world, for MI6 missions."

He shook his head slightly from side to side once again in astonishment at what he was hearing. Not least because in June in drunken anger, and attempted revenge on Aileen for her affair with her husband, Sandra had tried to get him to have sex with her. Thankfully he refused. Aileen could see the amazement in his wide eyes, however, and stopped talking to briefly kiss him tenderly as she once again placed the palm of her hand on one of his cheeks. She moved back slightly towards the edge of the bed again before continuing.

"There's more, Martin. Anyway, as I said, MI6 had this information from one of their Russian informers that quite a bit of sensitive stuff that could only have gone across Sandra's desk, as we'd put it, through her department, was ending up with the FSB in Moscow, and the word was that it was coming from Richard. So, I was re-assigned to another section in the agency for what Sandra was told was a small promotion, so she wouldn't get suspicious. It wasn't of course, and I was presented with a job, a mission, and told I had to accept it, that I didn't have any choice. The Section Head even tried to dress it up as my chance to prove my best friend innocent. If only they knew."

Now it was Aileen who was shaking her head slightly, accompanied by a distant look on her face, as if she was distracted by that thought and that it was why she had stopped speaking for a moment.

"Knew what?" Martin asked.

"What? Oh, sorry, no, no, it was nothing. I just got sidetracked with something else that I remembered."

It was her final comment of, "if only they knew" that distracted her. As far as she was concerned Sandra Weston wasn't her best friend at all, but was the person she believed was responsible for the killing of her stepfather. She had been waiting for years to enact retribution for that. Now she had recently done so. However, she wasn't going to go into that with Martin, or explain it, so she continued.

"The job, the plan, was for me to get close to Richard, seduce him and have an affair with him. To try and find out anything that would confirm him and Sandra were working for the Russians, that she'd been turned, as they say. To find out whether she was passing the information on to him, or whether he was acting alone and somehow gathering information which she had access to. The Section Head told me I'd actually been selected for the mission, the job, because I was best placed as Sandra's best friend to get really close to them both. So, it was hardly very difficult to seduce him, get in his boxers; so bloody easy actually, no fun at all. According to the briefing the agency section provided me with he had a bit of a reputation for it anyway. I knew he'd been caught out by Sandra one time having an affair with his secretary. Plus, even if I say so myself, I did look rather stunning that night, all dressed up especially for it, the first night that I seduced him."

She allowed herself a slight mischievous grin at that last remark. She couldn't resist making it. That was her all over. Martin told her, "I bet you did," which provoked her to kiss him tenderly on the cheek once more.

"The agency, MI6, placed me in another department of the company that he worked for, in a different part of London. Where I told you I worked, which I did for a while, and where you went looking for me. He was a Senior Global Project Executive, but I was a P.A to the company's International Legal Director. So, our paths were never going to cross unless I made them. Which was just as well because I reverted to my real name, Kathleen O'Mara there, so that there was no chance he'd come across the name Aileen Regan on any company records or in internal company documents and information. The plan was to seduce him at the Christmas Party for all the departments in a hotel in Central London last Christmas. It nearly went tits up, literally, when a drunken buffoon from my department tried to muscle in on the conversation I was having with Richard at the bar in the hotel that night. I thought for a moment he might call me Kathleen, which would have blown my cover. But I managed to move him on, and then suggested to Richard that we adjourn to another, quieter, bar in the hotel. From there it was easy. He was staying the night and had a room in the hotel. He said he knew he'd have a few drinks and didn't want to piss around trying to get a taxi in Central London. His words, not mine. He was pissed though. So, that's when it started. That was the easy part. I knew he couldn't resist me that night. We met up a few more times after that, just for the sex really, as well as to try and find out as much as I could what, if anything, him and Sandra had been up to for the Russians. But I wasn't getting anywhere in terms of that. He wouldn't even talk about it most of the time, him and Sandra I mean, their relationship. All he said once or twice was that they'd had their problems at times. He knew that I was aware of that anyway. It was pretty much what Sandra had told me, although not in such a matter of fact way. She was a lot angrier about 'their problems', So, after a few months I wasn't getting anywhere and there was no progress on my investigation, not even the slightest indication of me discovering even if he was working for the Russians, let alone Sandra. Soon after that I came to the conclusion he wasn't and that most probably meant she wasn't."

"When I reported that to the agency the Section Head pulled the operation, told me to end it and my relationship with him. I tried, but the problem was he wouldn't, didn't want to. Richard Weston is a man who is used to getting his own way, being in control. You saw that for yourself. So, when I told him I wanted to stop he was angry. That didn't happen to him, the woman stopping their affair. I knew from the Section briefing info that he'd had plenty of affairs, but he was always the one to end them and go back to Sandra. A woman ending it wasn't in his playbook at all. But I did, and refused to see him again. He kept sending me endless bloody text messages, but I ignored them. Then at one point I replied and threatened to tell Sandra everything. He stopped for a while then. I was tired of it all, the deceit, the lies, the half-truths. So, that's when I quit the agency, MI6. You are never really free of them though. That's what Sandra reminded me of when I told her I was quitting, although I never told her about me and Richard, of course. I just told her I was tired of it all; the secret life, the double lives, and wanted a new life of my own. That was actually true."

It wasn't, not completely though. At best that was another half-truth. She had resigned from MI6 some time before she started the affair with Richard Weston. That affair was part of the IRA operation for the purpose of undermining Sandra, destroying her personally and then her professional reputation inside MI6, and ultimately killing her. However, that hardly fitted the narrative of the story Aileen was presently relaying to Martin.

"Then a few months later, after Richard had backed off completely it seemed and things had gone quiet from him for a while, Sandra came up with the bloody idea of us going on holiday together here in June. She actually tried to persuade me to come here with her because she said she needed some time away with a woman friend, away from Richard. As you can imagine I was very reluctant. She must have informed her Section boss at MI6 about the holiday. She would have been required to log it, including who she was going with, or even intended to go with, me. That's when my old Section Head called me and told me in no uncertain terms that I should go, that I had no option as far as they were concerned. As I said, you're never really free of them. For them, once you work for them you're theirs for life. They believe that they own you. They wanted me to give it one last try on the holiday with her, just the two of us. See what I could find out, if anything, about her, Richard, and the Russian leak. They simply didn't believe

Richard, and maybe her, were innocent. They couldn't accept it was the case. From the information they were getting back from their Russian mole it just didn't add up the Section Head told me, firmly. So, I came, which did have its benefits because luckily I met you."

He smiled in response to that last remark, which she reciprocated. Her last remark about luckily meeting him may have been true. However, most of what she had just told him immediately prior to that about the holiday with Sandra, as well as her old Section Head at MI6 getting back in contact with her and ordering her to go, wasn't. She had put the idea of the holiday into Sandra's head initially. She merely managed to make it eventually seem like Sandra's own idea a short time after, although Lindos was actually Sandra's idea. She knew someone who'd been and they recommended it. Overall though, the holiday was all part of the IRA plan, and Aileen's role in it, designed to destroy Sandra Weston.

She leaned over to kiss him briefly, determined to reinforce through her actions her last comment about luckily meeting him, before continuing.

"When Sandra told Richard about the holiday, and that I was going with her, he was spooked, as you can imagine. I think he thought that with the two of us away for two weeks together I might let something slip out, make a mistake, especially after a few drinks relaxing on holiday."

Not that she was going to tell Martin, but that was exactly what she intended to do of course. It was also part of the plan.

"That's when he got back in touch with me. He was angry, very angry. He wanted to come with us, but Sandra wouldn't let him, thankfully. That didn't put him off though, and he started bombarding me with texts again. I ignored them. But then that first week when we were here Sandra saw a text from him on my phone while I was swimming off Pallas Beach."

She omitted to tell Martin that particular text was provoked by Aileen herself, deliberately provoked by one she sent Richard Weston only a few minutes before she went for her swim, intentionally leaving her phone on the small table next to Sandra on her sunbed for her to see Richard's reply when it came through as the phone beeped.

"Sandra never said anything to me at first, but she realised then that we'd had an affair. Even if she had said anything, confronted me over it, I couldn't have explained to her why, of course. That would have blown the operation if he had turned her and she was also working for the Russians. Then, as you know, he turned up here at the start of our second week. That's when she got really nasty. They were a good pair the two of them, perfect for each other in that way. Perfect together if they were working for the Russians. I've known Sandra for twenty years, so believe me when I say she could be one nasty bitch if she wanted to be, Martin. That's why you got dragged into it all. That's why she tried to sleep with you here when she was pissed that night. Because she'd found out about me and Richard, and that from the text she'd seen he wanted to start up our affair again. That's what it said."

"Well, it was pretty obvious she was pissed that night. She even tried it on with the young barman in Crazy Moon," Martin interjected.

Aileen smirked at that as she commented, "I can easily believe that. That's her all over when she's pissed. Don't forget she was flirting heavily with some young guys outside Pal's one night in that first week."

"Oh yep, I remember that."

"When Richard turned up he got even angrier because I wouldn't go back to him. He didn't have a clue of course that in actual fact I wasn't interested in him in that way at all, and never had been, that for me it was all just a job, a mission. But then he got even more angry when he realised we were together, you and me, had been sleeping together. So, that's when and why he started to play his mind games. That's when I'd had enough of it all and why I wanted us to leave straightaway. I'd had enough of him and Sandra, as well as MI6 and their games. I thought we'd got away from him, the two of them, once and for all. But then you went to see him in London while we were in Brighton without telling me. That was stupid, exactly what he would have wanted, loved. He just played with your mind again. That's what he does. He loves it, lives for it almost. But you couldn't let it go, could you?"

Martin shook his head slightly, acknowledging she was right. It was stupid, but he said nothing.

"He really tried to fuck you up about me, about him and me. That's what he does, plays with people's emotions, with their minds. That's actually one of the reasons the agency was suspicious about him being a spy for the Russians. The way he plays with people's minds. The way he played with your mind. It's like he's been trained. With you he definitely succeeded. When you got back from seeing him you didn't believe me. When I said he was lying about us, me and him, having sex here in the alley along from Lindos By Night it was clear you didn't believe me. It was all over your face. That's when I knew, I knew you didn't believe me, that you didn't trust me. You just couldn't accept it when I told you he was lying. You just kept asking the same questions over and over. I could see it was nagging away at you inside as we argued. He was playing his games and he succeeded. He won. I couldn't see any way of convincing you that he was lying, and there was no way I could tell you all this back then with MI6 involved. I couldn't see any way out, any way to resolve it and get what I wanted, to be with you. I was just sorry I'd dragged you into all that shit. So, I decided the only way out was to just leave, disappear. It seemed the only thing to do, the only option."

She stopped talking briefly, looked him straight in the eyes once again, and took hold of his hand. Her eyes and every part of her were pleading with him to believe her as she told him softly with a slight hesitation, "So ... so that's why I'm Aileen Regan and Kathleen O'Mara, the same person. I used the name Aileen here as that was the one I used here in June, the one on the passport I travelled here on then. There was obviously no way I was going to explain my dual identity, all that I've just told you, to people here. So, it was easier to just stick to Aileen. After all that shit with Sandra and Richard, and twenty years of lies, deceit and half-truths I just wanted to get away from it all now, once and for all. That's why I decided to come here to try and find out about my mother and my birth father. I knew from some things I found in her place after she died that she was here in the mid-seventies, but as I told you before, it turns out my grandmother was also here during the war, which I didn't know."

As she finished speaking she leaned into him and gave him another passionate kiss. For a moment after he merely looked straight into her face inches away from his. He looked totally overwhelmed by all that he had just heard and simply remained silent. She gazed deep into his eyes once more, desperately trying to see behind them and figure out just what was going through his mind now. He said nothing for a couple of minutes, just continuing to look straight into her eyes. A small seed of doubt was starting to invade her mind.

She eventually tried to reassure him with another kiss and then told him in a soft, low voice, "But I liked you, Martin. All through those games and crap with Richard bloody Weston and Sandra here in June I knew that I liked you, grew to more than like you. It was just the wrong time and the wrong place back then."

"Well, I can certainly see now why you couldn't tell me all that before. I guess it was just a case of unforeseen events and circumstances; wrong time, wrong place, for both of us." He broke his silence with a blank, bemused look on his face as he half-turned away to stare across at the wall at the end of the bed again, shaking his head slightly.

She let him process it all, think it through. Something else she had learned in her past.

"The events and circumstances of us meeting on that plane, of what you had to do for MI6 with Richard and Sandra, and then him turning up here and causing all that crap," he eventually started to explain while he continued to stare across at the bare wall. "And then, of course, me going to see him in his London office without telling you and him winding me up. They all built up, contributed to a certain outcome you see, you and me arguing and you disappearing."

He was speaking, but in effect was simply verbalising all he was working through in his mind. It was the academic in him.

He turned back towards her. His smile told her now it was all okay. In his head the logical Martin Cleverley had found his explanation, even if somewhat detached and academic.

He had no idea, however, that what she had told him, in seemingly great emotionally charged detail, wasn't exactly the whole truth. Kathleen O'Mara was very good at being economical with the truth. It had been part of her training with the Bhoys. Just like her grandmother in the SOE when she was in Rhodes she had learned, been trained, to totally forget who she actually was, and live as who she was pretending to be, Aileen Regan.

It was a good explanation, and it appeared that Martin believed her completely. He seemed perfectly content with what she'd told him, the half-truth she'd told him. She was more than satisfied with that. And anyway, sometimes it's okay for people not to know everything, she convinced herself.

He opened his arms slightly and she slid between them to rest her back against his body as he wrapped them around her upper body. He stroked her hair. Her more relaxed comfort was only slightly knocked off-kilter when he asked, "And Sandra?"

"What about her, Martin?"

"Was she, was she and Richard working for the Russians after all? Did anyone find out?"

"Don't know, I never found out, never found out anything at all. But even if I did I couldn't tell you, Martin. Or at least I shouldn't. If I was still working for MI6 I'd have to kill you if I did, and we wouldn't want that now would we?"

She looked up at him above her out of the top of her eyes and smiled mischievously as she finished telling him that. Although he realised she was joking, and loved her smile, his curiosity wasn't satisfied. He wasn't finished enquiring.

"Is she still at MI6?"

"She was, I think, but another agent, a real friend who I've kept in touch with from time to time, told me that she'd heard Sandra had been killed. Terminated she called it, in their cold jargon. I've no idea about Richard though, and quite frankly, I don't want to, couldn't care less. Whether Sandra had been terminated because they actually found something on her and the Russians or not I don't know."

"Really? How was she killed? Do you know that?"

"No, don't know, my friend never said, and I didn't ask. In my experience it's best not to. She wouldn't have told me anyway, and I don't want to be dragged back into all that shit."

That was a less than half-truth. It was true that Sandra was dead of course, but she knew precisely how she died, and even who killed her. It was the woman now nestled in Martin's arms on that firm Lindos bed.

However, it appeared that he was finally satisfied with all he'd heard, and now had enough of her past. He turned her around in his arms and leaned down for another lingering, passionate kiss.

As their lips parted he told her, "I think I promised you a breakfast, and all that has made me hungry too now. Well, all that, and all that exercise last night with you." He winked and then gave her a contented smile, followed by a soft, sincere, "I'm glad you finally told me everything, explained everything."

She hadn't of course, but again he seemed satisfied with what he'd heard as he suggested, "Let's go to the beach for the rest of the day after breakfast."

She had clearly dismissed all immediate thoughts of leaving Lindos today as she readily agreed.

"Okay but not Pallas. It's too crowded. Let's go to that one you took me to in June at that hotel, Lindos Memories."

What she was actually thinking was that Pallas was a little too public for her now, just in case another MI6 agent might be snooping about looking for her. Memories' beach was out of the village and much more private.

"Good idea," he agreed. "But I need a shower and to change, get my beach stuff from my apartment. I'll meet you at Giorgos in forty-five minutes. Don't disappear, don't run off this time," he teased her with a broad smile across his lips as he pulled his polo shirt on over his head.

She climbed off the bed, grabbed a handful of his polo shirt in her right hand, and then kissed him once more, pressing her tender, soft, full lips firmly against his and entwining her body into his as much as was physically possible. He could feel her eager warm breath invading his left ear after she slowly removed her lips from his and tilted her head towards it to whisper mischievously, "Why would I do that and give up that breakfast you promised me?"

Her broad enticing smile and her piercing dark eyes that confronted him only inches away as she moved her head back from the side of his cheek had the instant mesmerising effect on him, driving him to want to take her straight back to bed. As soon as his reaction gave her the slight hint that was what was in his mind, however, and before he could act upon it, she put the index finger of her right hand to his lips and told him, "I want that breakfast now. We can continue this later, tonight. Go and get that shower and your beach stuff."

24

The hope and the fear

It was just after eleven o'clock when Aileen weaved her way along the alleyways from her apartment through the crowds of day visitor tourists from Rhodes Town perusing the multitude of little Lindos shops stacked with their souvenirs. The Rhodes sun was already high in the clear blue sky, beating down brightly on the flagstones of the alleyways. As she finally turned the corner opposite Pal's Bar to walk the few metres towards Giorgos she saw Martin sitting at one of the tables with a cappuccino outside the café waiting for her. He stood up to kiss her on the cheek as she reached the table.

As soon as she came into view when she turned the corner he was mesmerised. It was hot, bloody hot, but everything about her exuded coolness personified. She never lacked confidence in that respect, certainly not in terms of her appearance. Now that confidence, her vanity, was blooming, blossoming in all its glory. All the angst and stress of the past few days, even the past twenty years, seemed to have completely drained out of her. The idyllic paradise of Lindos had certainly contributed to that, even allowing for the episode on her traumatic Saturday night, which already seemed a distant memory. She felt good, relaxed, bloody good. She had put on a striking bright red bikini and covered it with a t-shirt of a similar shade of crimson, as well as another pair of tight white shorts. The red and white perfectly complimented her dark black hair and her exposed tanned arms and legs, equally emphasised by her bright white trainers.

To Martin she appeared a tanned, confident, relaxed woman; a vision. Just the effect she was aiming for. After his shower he'd simply settled for a pair of light blue swim shorts, also under a pair of white shorts, although nowhere near as pristine white or as crisp and new looking as hers. His choice of t-shirt had been a quite boring plain black.

Giorgos was starting to get busy. It usually did at that time of day. It was on the main route from the jetty at Pallas Beach where the day tripper boats from Rhodes Town docked for their passengers to go off and explore the village. It was a quite steep walk up the path from the beach, unless you took one of the Lindos taxis, the donkeys waiting with their owners at the edge of the beach at the bottom of the hill. The hill could be a challenge in the heat of the day. Consequently, some of the day trippers would stop off for a refreshing cold drink at the first café bar they encountered on reaching the village, Giorgos. That morning was no exception. While he waited the few minutes for Aileen to turn up Martin amused himself by trying to decipher and identify the various languages of the other customers seated at the tables around him. He'd identified German and French, some Italian, what he took to be Russian, and English, of course, although he was fairly sure that the couple speaking it were probably Scottish.

"You look great," he told her as Aileen took a seat opposite him.

"Thank you, I feel great, feels like I'm really on holiday at last. It must be you. You obviously have a very good effect on me."

She smiled at him and then rattled off rapidly, "Now, what about that breakfast you promised me? I'm starving. They don't do a 'full Irish' breakfast here unfortunately I guess, so it'll have to be you're plain English one. And I need fresh orange juice and coffee. Have you ordered yours?"

Before he could answer, the owner, Tsamis, appeared and answered for him.

"No, he hasn't. He was waiting for you, weren't you, Martin."

Tsamis gave him a quick wink and a slight smile, not even giving the Englishman a chance to reply before he took their order and disappeared back inside the café.

"Last night was good, bloody great," he told her with another smile of satisfaction while they waited for their breakfasts.

"It was, wasn't it," she agreed with a small satisfied smile of her own. "It was good before too though, with you here in June. I always thought that."

She reached over to grasp his hand as she continued, looking intensely directly into his eyes once again. "I don't think you realised, or maybe never really accepted is a better way of putting it, but I found myself liking you more and more here then. As I told you this morning, that wasn't something I'd expected or anticipated happening. It wasn't in my plans at all. But it just did, it just happened."

She continued to hold her fixed gaze into his eyes as she added, "I am really, really sorry I left, disappeared, when I did. Now though I hope you can see that I had other things I needed to do, had to do, loose ends to tidy up and finish. I couldn't just leave them. I had no choice because of what I did in the past, who I was then. After all that I told you this morning surely you understand now that is why I left you so suddenly?"

He squeezed her hand gently, and then lifted it to his lips to kiss it softly before he replied.

"I do, I do understand. Believe me I do. I was sorry too that I pushed you, wouldn't let it drop and simply believe you, trust you, over what Richard told me, what he tried to convince me about him having sex with you here in June. It was just that I was insecure, felt insecure with you after all that crap and games with Sandra and him here. But that's all in the past now, and you're completely free of all that. Let's put all that crap behind us. All I care about is the here and now, and the future."

She nodded and smiled at him; a soft smile that he took to be one of agreement. In fact, it was more one of hope. She was not really sure that was exactly completely true; that she was completely free of all that was in her past. She knew, of course, that she was definitely free of Sandra Weston, and hopefully of Richard. She was obviously not completely sure about being free from MI6 however, free from the possibility or the likelihood of them sending another agent to track her down and kill her. That was hardly something she could point out to him though, not having told him the whole truth earlier that morning, particularly about her having killed one of their agents only a couple of nights ago.

She merely settled instead for telling him, accompanied by reaching across the table and taking hold of and squeezing one of his hands, "I don't play those stupid, crooked games anymore; those games of truth and lies."

Once again that was also only partly true. She definitely didn't want to play the games of her past, with all its lies, deceit and false identities, as well as the killings. But she was only telling him barely half the truth, convincing herself that she wasn't actually lying to him. That thought was quickly pushed out of her head though by Tsamis appearing with their breakfasts.

After their breakfasts they made their way through the crowds of tourists to the Main Square to get a taxi to Lindos Memories Hotel and its quiet beach. She couldn't help trying as discreetly as possible to still look around at any individuals who they passed on their way through the alleys, wondering if one of them could possibly be another agent sent by MI6.

She tried to be as casual and relaxed about it as possible. However, as they reached the opening to the square Martin had obviously noticed and asked, "Are you okay? You seem to be looking for someone."

"I just like to look at people, watch them, that's all," she told him, trying to shrug it off and sound as nonchalant as possible. "It must be something to do with my past working for, you know, the agency. They used to tell me that my greatest strength was observing all those around me. Old habits die hard, I guess."

Just over five minutes later he paid the taxi driver and they walked hand in hand into the hotel. It was a light sandstone block complex of just two storeys, with an impressive view out over the swimming pool area to Navarone bay. The bay was known as that having been used for a scene in the 1961 movie 'The Guns of Navarone', starring Gregory Peck, David Niven and Anthony Quinn. The setting was very quiet and picturesque. It exuded a very relaxing, calm atmosphere. They strolled through the open central plaza of the hotel with its intermittent steps and guest rooms on each side. As they arrived at the end of it the small taverna covered area came into view on the right hand side of the swimming pool, as well as just beyond it the steps down to the beach with its shimmering white sunbeds and parasols.,

"I remember that as we were leaving when we came here in June you told me, promised me, 'Another time, we can do this again another time', didn't you. We had such a lovely day then. And here we are again. It's so beautiful here. Calming, relaxing, so, so pleasant," she told him.

It was just what she needed. Now she was glad she didn't leave Lindos today as she'd planned. Although, nagging away in the back of her mind she knew she would have to resolve that dilemma soon. That she would have to leave.

"Well, I do always try to keep my promises if possible," he responded with a small grin.

Still hand in hand, they went down to the beach and found a couple of the very comfortable sunbeds and a parasol that were free.

"Come on, I need a swim to cool down now," she told him as she pulled off her t-shirt.

The swimming at Memories beach wasn't quite as good as on Pallas Beach or the Main Beach. He reminded her from before that it could be a bit rocky and full of coral covered rocks before you got a bit further out. The sea was crystal clear once they were out there though.

Martin took her hand and they carefully navigated the worst of the coral covered rocks into the clearer sea. As they walked down to the sea she curled her hair up and fastened it on the top of her head, exposing more of her bronzed shoulders above her striking red bikini. The sun was sparkling on the clearer water further out. Everything about her was matching it as she plunged head first beneath the cooling sea, the soft ripples of the water she created mirroring the ripples of the effect she was having on him. He joined her immediately, plunging in head first beside her. As they surfaced she placed her arms around his waist and kissed him with just a hint of salt from the sea on her moist lips. During their swim the popular Lindos Glass Bottom Boat arrived in the bay and anchored further out while its customers leapt off the boat for a swim.

After their swim, and an hour or so of soaking up the hot Rhodes sun, they went up to the taverna for a pleasant light lunch whilst enjoying the great view out over the bay.

As they lay on the sunbeds in silence in mid-afternoon, almost dozing while soaking up more sun after lunch and another swim, she turned her head to look across at him and tell him softly, "I'm really glad we came back here, came back here together."

He reached over to take her hand and squeeze it as he met her eyes with his, displaying simultaneously a contented smile of agreement.

While she continued to gaze into his eyes there was a serious look across her face as she told him, "It feels like I've been on a long journey to get here in my life, Martin. But now that part of it is over, discovering part of my roots, one part of my family's tangled past. Now, at last, I feel that I can finally get on with my life."

He smiled at her once again. "Well, given where we are, it sounds to me like you've been on an odyssey. Putting on my Professor hat I'd say that for this part of your life at least, a Greek odyssey."

She grinned. A response to what she saw as his almost endearing characteristic need to analyse everything. The warmth and effect of her grin was transferred to her voice as she asked, "Oh, please do explain, Professor. I really could do with a Greek mythology lesson in these wonderful surroundings."

He realised she was teasing him, but he couldn't resist. For the moment the professional part of him outweighed the romantic, pushed it aside.

"Well, in Homer's famous poem, The Odyssey, it means a journey."

She did know that, but humoured him by continuing to grin attentively and not interrupt.

"There are three major themes: hospitality, loyalty, and vengeance. Of course, I'm not entirely sure that all or even any of those relate to what you came here to do, but you have obviously been on a journey and maybe some of those have been in it."

He had absolutely no idea just how accurate he was, although she daren't point that out to him. What was running through her mind was that there had definitely been vengeance in her journey, her odyssey. Vengeance against Sandra Weston and MI6 for what they did in setting up and killing her Irish stepfather.

As for loyalty, there was her loyalty to the Irish Nationalist cause, of course. That had never wavered. That particular essence of her hadn't changed. What was inside her, her soul, her beliefs were still the same. She couldn't, wouldn't, renounce her Irish Nationalism; couldn't renounce the cause and all that it stood for. That was a central part of who she was, and had been for over twenty-five years. Now, what she had discovered over the past few days from her family past was another part of who she was. That was also entwined with, and linked with, her Irish Nationalist beliefs through the Irish Nationalism of her grandmother, Bernadette.

She settled again for telling him at best another half-truth, or maybe a third of the truth to be accurate. Intentionally ignoring Homer's vengeance and loyalty themes, she focused on referring to his theme of hospitality.

"Well, it's definitely true that Greek hospitality is always a key thing here amongst all the bar and restaurant owners and staff. They are famous for it, and they are good at it. They have been good to me. In that part of my journey, my odyssey if you like, Jack and his mother and grandmother have been very hospitable and helpful."

His comments about her Greek odyssey, her journey, revived the thought that pretty soon she would have to take another journey and leave Lindos and Rhodes. To stay much longer wouldn't be safe. She waited another half-an-hour and then suggested they go up to the taverna for a cold beer. She would put to him about leaving over a beer.

After the waiter brought their beers she began to try and tell Martin in a quite calm and relaxed manner. "It is beautiful here isn't it. But I can't help-"

He was still in his Professor mode though, dwelling on Greek mythology, and interrupted her.

"Yes, it is. It's beautiful. In Greek mythology Helios, the God of the Sun, chose Rhodes to be his home. You can see why when you look at this view."

As he finished telling her that he picked up his beer and took a sip.

"Err ... I didn't know that." She was trying to sound as serious as possible now, but she wasn't sure she was really getting through to him. Consequently, she decided to be much more direct, forceful, blunt. She leaned forward in her chair and placed both her arms on the table.

"Look, Martin, yes it is beautiful here, of course it is. Lindos is a lovely place. Idyllic some people say. The problem for me here though is that it has too many memories, not very pleasant ones."

He put down his beer as a bemused look spread across his face, wondering just what she was going to say next. He was worried. Was she about to burst his pleasant bubble, their pleasant bubble?

She could see his expression had changed, but she knew that this had to be done now, dealt with now, and couldn't be put off any longer, no matter how lovely their day had been. She was desperately searching through her mind for a good way to do it, the best way to do it; a way that would persuade him.

"Of your family past, memories of your family past?" he asked.

"No, not those, mine, bad memories for me of what happened here in June."

She wasn't explaining it very well. She wasn't someone who was usually so tongue-tied. She was scratching around for a right way to put it to him to get what she wanted, wanted most of all.

"When bad things happen they don't really go away," she began to try and explain again. "I just don't think all that shit here with Richard and Sandra Weston can really go away, be put behind us, me and you, here, if we stay here. I know I'm finding it hard to, can't completely put it behind me. I know it will always be there while we are in this place, always just under the surface between us, waiting to resurface I'm sure if we stay here."

She knew she wasn't explaining it very well, or being completely coherent. That was the way she wanted to sound though, with just enough of a hint of desperation and exasperation in her voice. Now she knew exactly what she was doing.

Martin simply sat in silence. She was having precisely the effect she was aiming for. But she wasn't finished.

"Look, Martin, I know you said you're alright now with all that happened here in June, and then me disappearing like I did back in Brighton. But somehow, lovely as it is here in Lindos, I just think it would be better for us, easier to put all that completely behind us, if we went somewhere else."

Yet again she wasn't being completely honest with him. She'd concocted something that would hopefully persuade him, rather than the truth that she was worried an agent from MI6 would turn up looking to kill her because of her past IRA connection.

He had a blank, confused expression on his face, unsure of what to say, how to respond, but also not entirely clear what she was suggesting. He loved it in Lindos, and knew a lot of the people who lived there as friends. Where would they go?

She stared across at him intensely. Her eyes were pleading with his senses. She waited a few seconds, reached over to take one of his hands in hers, and then added just a few more sentences to try and clinch persuading him.

"It would be a clean break from my past life, but also a clean break with our past, what happened here and in London with Richard bloody Weston. We have too many bad memories here. Please, Martin, please let's just go."

He shook his head slowly slightly. It wasn't a good sign. He obviously still wasn't completely convinced as he voiced his reservations.

"But you can't just keep running away, Aileen. It feels a bit like déjà vu, feels like what you did to me before."

"No, it's not like that at all," she pleaded with him. "It's different this time. This time you can see that I'm not running away from you at all. This time I want you to go with me. I want us to go to Crete together. From what I've found out here it's where the man who I think was my birth father, Dimitris Papatonis, wanted my mother to go with him if she came back to Lindos in 1978 after I was born. He had some family there, cousins, Jack's mother told me. Perhaps, just possibly, there will still be some part of his family there. Of course, I have no idea where on Crete, and it's quite a big island, but I can try and see, do some searching starting with the family name, Papatonis. We can try and see, Martin, can't we?"

He sat and stared at her as she rambled on rapidly with all that, pleading. To him it was clear in her voice what she felt, what she wanted. After a few moments more silence he began to respond. It was obvious from the way he was speaking that he was thinking aloud. Although he was saying it to her, he was actually trying to persuade himself.

"Well, I have got a nice redundancy deal from the university. So, I suppose I've nothing really to go back to the U.K. for, nothing that I need to go back for. There's nothing forcing me to go back."

He hesitated again as she said, "So … so, why not? Let's go, please, Martin?"

She reached over, took his hand in hers once again, and squeezed it gently as she finished speaking. She was staring straight into his eyes, appealing to every part of him in order to get him to agree.

It was clear to her that he was obviously very tempted. She assumed that it was only what had happened before, when she disappeared, that was stopping him agreeing straightaway. She didn't have to wait long though.

He hesitated for another half a minute as he stared past her and out to the calm, clear blue sea in Navarone Bay. Then he looked back across at her and smiled in obvious agreement. She knew she could persuade him. She could most men.

"Okay, okay, why not, why not go with you, go to Crete with you, and maybe live there? I can write anywhere, and I'm sure it'll be better with you, writing. Anyway, do you know that the Minoans on Crete thousands of years ago were the oldest European civilisation?"

He smiled as he said that last thing. He was teasing her as he couldn't completely abandon his academic background, which amused her.

She returned his smile as she got up to walk around to his side of the table. She placed the palms of both of her hands on his cheeks, leaned down slightly, and kissed him with a deep, lingering passion that felt like it came from every part of her body. As she finished she whispered a very soft, low, "Thank you."

"I think you had better go back and sit down," he told her with a contented grin. "People are watching, and you seem to be giving the waiter and waitresses a nice show."

As she sat back in her seat he simply said, "When?"

Once again he was a surprised by her reply. She appeared to have it all planned out, as of course, she did. Like most of what she planned, it was all going to plan.

"Tomorrow, first thing tomorrow," she told him, almost nonchalantly. That was the way she was. She liked to have everything planned well in advance. That was the way of her life for over twenty years.

While he sat silently, bewildered once more, trying to take in the apparent urgency of that she added, "Of course, you should be aware that it won't always be easy, Martin, not for the both of us now. I'll never be sure that my past won't suddenly pop up to haunt me, or rather someone from my past."

Now she had got him to agree she was feeling confident enough to at least touch on some of the possible drawbacks of what she wanted them to do. Set out some of the small print, the 'terms and conditions', if you like. Her past training had taught her precisely how to do that, the approach to take to getting a deal. Get some sort of general agreement and then after that's achieved briefly mention, and throw into the conversation, any possible snags that might appear later. This wasn't some sort of negotiation on behalf of MI6, or even the Bhoys, though. This was about what she believed she wanted for her future – to be with him somewhere safe and free from all that was in her past. She just couldn't throw off all the traits of her training over twenty years though, even in this more emotional situation with him. She couldn't completely wipe away the old Kathleen or the old Aileen.

He looked a bit confused by that last remark about never being sure that her past wouldn't suddenly pop-up. He wasn't really certain at all what she meant by it. Maybe she was simply referring to what she had told him Sandra Weston had said to her about never being free of MI6? Before he could ask, however, he was thrown off balance once again by her next comment. Should he be completely happy at what she told him next or not? Things were happening, developing fast. That wasn't something that happened in the academic world he'd inhabited for most of his life.

She stared intensely straight across the table at him once more and again reached to take one of his hands in hers. Her piercing eyes were penetrating deep into his soul as she waited for ten seconds or more, all the while clasping his hand, and then told him softly, "But I love you, Martin. So, even though I'll never be sure that my past won't suddenly pop up to haunt me, I do want to be with you. I just wanted you to know that now about my past, but if I'm with you I know everything will be okay in our future together."

His face was completely focused on hers, with no movement except for the slightest of warm smiles starting to spread across it as she continued.

"I know that for sure now. I felt that was happening, something good between us, when we were together here in Lindos before, in June. And even for that brief time back in the U.K., in Brighton. I couldn't do anything about it then, couldn't drag you into all that mess of my past twenty years. But the past is not the present, Martin, and so now we have a chance to-"

This time it was his index finger that was being placed on her lips, indicating that she should stop talking. Her deep brown eyes were unavoidably drawing him into her, engulfing him as he told her softly, "I love you too."

She leaned across and kissed him once more. As she drew back he told her, now with clear enthusiasm in his voice "Okay, yes, so let's go tomorrow. Why not? Let's go to rete. I'll check out flights for tomorrow online on my phone."

There was one more final element to her plan for now, however.

She told him, "No, not a flight, Martin. Instead, let's go on the ferry from Rhodes Town. That'll be more romantic, and anyway after that we can go who knows where, and until who knows when."

His mind was caught in too much of a whirlwind to disagree, or even question her sudden preference towards romance and the ferry. He simply agreed.

"Okay, the ferry then. I'll check for one going early tomorrow morning. So this will be our last night here in Lindos then?"

She smiled the broadest one he had ever seen her smile.

"Yes, it will be our last. I suppose you'll miss it. So, are you sure, really sure, Martin?"

"Yes, yes, very, and as I said before, I've really nothing to go back to the UK for now I've finished at the uni, plus with Brexit coming I have a horrible feeling that England isn't exactly going to be a very nice place to live over the next few years."

Her preference for the ferry, and its romantic undertones, was another case of being economical with the truth. Although, once again she wasn't about to explain to him the real reason she preferred the ferry. A flight and the airport would be too exposed in case there was another MI6 killer searching for her. The ferry would be better. She would be less conspicuous there, less likely to be spotted, rather than at the airports, at Rhodes and landing on Crete. She knew that the agency, MI6, had their agents and paid informers dotted around everywhere. Who knows if they had some informers at Rhodes or Crete airports, but she wasn't going to take that chance. She thought that they would be much less likely to have any at the internal Greek ferry ports.

She had got what she wanted. One more night in Lindos and they could leave, together. She could feel all her anxiety subsiding inside her, dissipating, as if it was melting way in the hot late afternoon Rhodes sun. At long last a tangible new expectancy, optimism about the future was washing over her. Some elements of her old fears still lingered about another MI6 agent turning up in Lindos, but they would be gone soon. With every minute of planning to go to Crete, with every minute of being with Martin, they were diminishing.

25

The last night

That evening she put on her favourite dress for them to go out to dinner together. It was a stunning short, black, low cut, off the shoulder dress, which she complemented with a thin silver chain around her neck and black high heeled sandals for a change. She got exactly the reaction she wanted from him when she opened the door to her apartment as he arrived at spot-on eight-thirty.

"Wow! You look great," was all he could say before he kissed her lips, covered with the merest touch of pink lipstick.

He felt decidedly underdressed in his white shorts, royal blue polo shirt, and dark blue deck shoes, although it was actually the perfect clothes for the usual warm, humid Lindos August evening. The rest of his clothes were in his suitcase which he'd brought with him, along with his laptop and bag. As they'd left the beach at Memories Hotel earlier Aileen had suggested that he brought all his stuff to her apartment so they could leave early from there for the ferry in the morning. He didn't even bother to challenge her assumption that meant he would be staying with her tonight. He assumed that also.

As they left the flat and made their way to Symposio restaurant in the centre of the village Martin informed her, "I've booked the ferry to Crete for eight-thirty tomorrow morning, as well as a taxi from the Main Square at six-thirty. We have to change ferries in Athens, but we'll get to Heraklion on Crete in the late afternoon, and I've booked us a room at a nice hotel in Heraklion for the one night. We can look for an apartment to rent the next day either in Heraklion, or another place if you have anywhere in mind? Have you been to Crete before?"

"No, never," she told him. "You have been busy, but thanks, that sounds fine. You been there before?"

"No, first time for me too."

"A new adventure for both of us then," she told him.

Some of his confusion returned, however, when she added, "Look, this may sound a bit strange, Martin, but I don't think we should tell anyone we are leaving tomorrow. Besides anything else I haven't told my landlady as I don't want her kicking up and demanding that I pay her for the whole two months that I booked the apartment for. I expect you're in the same boat?"

Again, she was being economical with the truth. For obvious reasons known only to her, she definitely didn't want anyone knowing they were leaving, let alone where they were going.

"Err … err … but … but, not even Jack?" he stuttered, fully displaying his confusion.

"No, not even Jack. This is a small village. People talk to each other all the time here, gossip, and I would rather just not take the chance of it getting back to my landlady. You know what happens. We tell Jack, he tells some of his customers, one or two of whom happen to know my landlady, and before I know it she'll be banging on my door before we leave in the morning, or even later tonight, demanding the rest of her rent for the two months. And we certainly don't want that do we, her disturbing us tonight at an inopportune moment."

As she said that last sentence she lowered the tone of her voice deliberately and looked up at him with those intoxicating eyes of her, knowing that would persuade him. She was right.

"Okay, okay, I understand, but it will be difficult not to at least tell Jack, after all he's done for you won't it?"

"I know, but it's for the best, not even Jack, unless you do want my landlady banging on my door and interrupting us tonight?"

She was teasing him, with an enticing mischievous smile across her lips as she did so. She knew that, together with the tone of her voice now, as well as the way she was dressed, would clinch it.

"No, certainly not, of course not, of course I don't," he agreed. "Okay, we'll keep it to ourselves."

As usual Symposio was busy. It was a very popular restaurant, right in the centre of the village, with excellent food, good service, and a great view of the illuminated Acropolis from its rooftop dining area. As the two of them reached the top of the wrought iron staircase onto the roof the owner, Filip, greeted them.

"Welcome again," he told Aileen. "I see you've brought Martin with you this time." He gave Martin a handshake and a hug before telling her, "We're old friends. He's been here many times, haven't you, Martin?"

"Yes, Filip here has had a lot of my money over the years, Aileen," Martin said with a small smile at the Greek.

"So, a romantic nice table, and for two this time," the owner reminded her.

"Yes, for two this time. I was here on my own last time, Martin. So, the romantic table was a bit wasted," she added with an ironic grin.

As they anticipated, the meal was excellent, washed down with a decent bottle of red wine, chosen by Martin. By ten-thirty they were walking hand-in-hand up the steps to the entrance to the Courtyard Bar. The bar was busy at that time of night, with a mixture of couples sat outside in the courtyard braving the August evening humidity and those inside preferring the benefit of the air-conditioning and the music.

They managed to find a couple of vacant stalls at the far end of the bar and Jack came along behind it to say hello and take their drinks' order. Before Jack appeared she whispered in Martin's ear that as it was their last night she was going to have something different to drink, a Daiquiri.

Martin grinned and then told her, "Hemingway's favourite, or one of them. In Cuba they tell a story that Hemingway once drank sixteen of those in a day, but that he said you couldn't taste the alcohol in them."

"You've been there?" she asked.

"Yes, a couple of times. We'll go, together," he told her. She kissed him on the cheek, replying, "Of course."

Out of Aileen's vision Jack gave Martin a brief wink and a knowing smile at that. Martin was beginning to feel guilty. He'd known Jack many years and wasn't entirely happy about leaving Lindos without telling him and saying goodbye. It was almost as though Aileen sensed his uneasiness. The movement of her hand was designed to remind and reassure him. While Jack served their drinks and then chatted for a few minutes she made a point of reaching for Martin's thigh with her left hand, leaving it there and squeezing it from time to time. At one point while Jack was engaged in conversation with them she removed her hand from his thigh and placed her arm on Martin's shoulder, tilting her head to almost rest it against his. Now she was reminding him with all her body language of what they had agreed. All of that only made Jack smile a little more as he walked away towards the other end of the bar.

"So, Hemingway then, I guess you would know about him, you being a writer," she said.

"Well, I'm no Hemingway, believe me. For a start he had four wives, and I can't match that, or his drinking, and definitely not his writing, his writing style. He compared his style of writing to an iceberg. In fact, it became known as the Iceberg style, based on what was called the theory of omission. He believed the deeper meaning of a story shouldn't be obvious on the surface. It should shine through implicitly, hence like an iceberg."

He fiddled with his drink on the bar as he told her that, only very briefly turning his head to glance into her face alongside him the one time. All the while he was speaking he sensed her staring at him. He thought he could feel the warmth of her glare. He didn't really need to check.

She was fixing a long lingering stare onto the side of his face. But, in fact, she was trying to read in his facial expression just what he was actually thinking. Wondering if there might just be more, something deeper, behind what he was saying. Was he trying to hint in a subtle way that he thought there might be more, a deeper meaning below the surface to the story she had told him that morning about Sandra and Richard Weston and MI6, as well as the explanation for her two names? That would, indeed, be her iceberg; her IRA past.

As he reached to pick up his drink from the bar he realised that perhaps he'd been rambling on a bit about Hemingway and the technicalities of his writing style. What he told her next reassured her that she was obviously being paranoid and over-analysing his Hemingway comment. This time he turned his head to face her as he said apologetically, "Sorry, I can be a bit of a bore where writers and literature are concerned. What about you? Are you a bookworm? Something else I need to find out about you."

She gave his arm a slight squeeze, accompanied by a broad grin as she half-turned to face him again. He was totally surprised at her response, although not unpleasantly so.

"Without books history is silent, Martin, literature is dumb, science is crippled, and thought and speculation are at a standstill."

Her grin expanded into a broad smile as she continued, sensing his surprise. She enjoyed immensely surprising people who underestimated her, who never anticipated and expected what was within her. She was a clever woman, and she always knew it.

"Without books the development of civilisation would have been impossible. Books are engines of change, windows on the world. As a poet once said, they are lighthouses erected in the sea of time. So, books are companions, teachers, magicians, bankers of the treasures of the mind. Basically, and bluntly, Martin, they are humanity in print."

His eyes were darting rapidly over every element of her face, every part of it. They were captured by her smile and the glowing self-confidence that was portrayed right across it as he told her, "That's impressive."

She gave out a small chuckle as she stared back at him straight into his eyes. "It is, isn't it? Unfortunately, it's not mine though. I wish it was. It's from Barbara Tuchman, an American author who won the Pulitzer Prize twice. Bloody good though, don't you think?" As she finished she let out another slight chuckle of self-satisfaction.

She knew he did, knew he thought it was, "Bloody good." And she knew he would be impressed. That was what she intended, and she usually achieved her intended effect. She wanted to ensure that he knew she was one smart woman. Another smile was only removed from her face when she moved her head slightly to tenderly kiss him on the cheek once again.

For the next hour she deliberately whispered in his ear from time to time, placing her lips as close to his head as possible as she spoke, and at one point kissed him on the cheek again. Martin didn't exactly dis-like it at all. There was no indication whatsoever that he did. However, he was more than a little surprised as they finished their second drink, when she once again leaned in to whisper softly, sensuously, and provocatively in his ear, "Let's go now. I can think of a lot of better things we can be doing together on our last night in Lindos, can't you?"

"Well, the taxi is at six-thirty, so yes I suppose we should go off to bed now, although it's a bit early. My body clock is not really used to trying to get off to sleep this early here," he replied.

She grinned, stared directly into his face and raised her eyebrows, accompanied by mischief clearly dancing in her intoxicating eyes once more.

"Who said anything about sleeping straightaway? I'm sure I can find plenty of ways to eventually help you to sleep."

Jack initially looked surprised as Martin asked for their bill and told him they were off for an early night, or at least, a relatively early one. Although when Aileen this time leaned her head firmly on Martin's shoulder and then wrapped her arm around his waist the bar owner gave Martin a knowing smile of approval for their early night.

A little more than ten minutes later she was standing before him undressing as he sat on the edge of the bed still fully clothed. He loved watching her slowly undress. She knew he did, just as she knew most men she'd been with did. She enjoyed doing it. Eventually, once she was completely naked and her sensual exhibition was complete, she joined him on the edge of the bed. He ran his hand along her thigh and then over her lower body as she moved to lie back on the bed. He could feel the small tremors rippling within her in expectation. She reached up with her left hand and pulled him into her and a deep, lasting, longing kiss. She was now at last really delighting in the moment, perfectly relaxed and content, almost happy.

"It's later now, Martin," she whispered softly as their lips parted. "Later now, for you, for your turn, remember? What you told me this morning?"

A small smile emerged across his lips as he gazed into her eyes and told her, "Of course I do."

So, he had his turn.

But it wasn't sex they had that night. It was different, not like anything they'd done all those times before. This time they made love.

After, she wrapped herself around him, every part of him, as she lay with her head nestling on his chest. With the evident beckoning pull of sleep lingering wearily in her voice she tried to tell him that.

"That was different. This time it was different."

"Yes, it was," he agreed as he tenderly kissed the top of her head.

"It was. There are always two ways of looking at everything, Martin," she started to say while a satisfied glow coloured her cheeks. "And that was definitely another way, definitely a much better way, of …"

She never finished what she was saying. Instead, her soft voice tailed off as she drifted away into a warm, contented sleep.

26

The future – the nightmare or the dream?

She could see clearly the first flickering bright piercing rays of the rising sun that were just starting to penetrate the rear side window of the taxi as it sped along the empty road towards the Rhodes ferry port. It was as though she was being drawn towards them. She could already feel their warmth on her cheek, matching the reassuring warmth of Martin's grip of her left hand. Everything was blindingly bright and good in that world, her world. They were smiling at each other, squeezing each other's hand from time to time. She could feel him lean over occasionally to place a gentle kiss on her cheek. They were happy; setting off in the growing warm Rhodes sunshine for a new life together.

There was a dullness to the car sounds though. The sound of its movement across the road surface, across all the bumps and small potholes, the hum from the diesel engine, were all muffled. It was as if something was blocking her hearing, something blocking the clear transmission of the usual everyday sounds of the taxi journey. And then even that and all other sound vanished. She couldn't hear anything. It felt as though something, or someone, had turned off the volume. Next to her Martin was speaking. She knew he was because she could see his lips moving as she turned her head away from the car window and towards him. But she couldn't hear a sound, nothing of what he was saying, and nothing of any background noise. Just silence. A strangely warm yet disconcerting, unsettling silence. All the while there was the dazzling bright light from the rays of the rising sun that penetrated the taxi which blurred her vision, creating a strange hazy aura around his head and filling the whole of the taxi interior.

Then in her vision was a shaky blurred picture. They were walking hand-in-hand with their bags in the bright, clear, morning Rhodes sunshine up the ramp to the ferry. But they were alone. There was no one else around them, no one else boarding the ferry. Still there was complete silence. Not a sound. Nothing of the sea lapping in the harbour, not even the noise of the ferry's engines preparing to leave. No vehicles boarding the ferry. No noise from vehicles waiting to board. No sign of, or noise from, any passengers in the vehicles waiting to board. Everywhere was clear, bright, but empty. There were not even ferry crew members waiting to board passengers and vehicles. All around them was peaceful, satisfyingly bright, warm and comforting, deserted except for her and Martin hand-in-hand.

Suddenly, dramatically, her peace was destroyed. Her warm comforting vision was blown apart as the blinding flash of more brilliant lights crashed into her mind. A blinding flash of reds and light pinks, as well as a messy mixture of grey and white matter and splintering bone as her skull exploded and some of the mess of parts of her brain spewed over him walking next to her. She never heard it coming, whistling almost silently, beyond human hearing, through the warm Rhodes morning air. She felt it. Why could she feel it? Does anyone feel it, feel the pain as it smashes into their skull at great velocity? So, why, why could she feel it?

"No, no … ah… ah … no, no … not now."

She screamed loudly as she tossed around under the sheet, thrashing around like the waves crashing into Lindos Bay at the height of a winter storm. Despite the whirring air-conditioning her body was glistening with sweat, patches of which had penetrated the sheet covering them, or at least her part of it.

"Aileen, Aileen, wake up, wake up." He shook her with his hands firmly on each of her shoulders.

"What, what … what? What was …" She blinked to try to focus as he leaned over to turn on the bedside light.

"You were dreaming and shouting," he told her as he wiped some small beads of sweat from her forehead with his fingers. "What was it? What were you dreaming about? It obviously upset you."

She knew that it wasn't a dream. It was a nightmare. A nightmare based on the lies that were buried deep inside her, lies that she couldn't remove, try as she might. The bad things don't go away.

"I ... I ... not sure ... it was nothing really, just some crazy bad dream, I guess. We all get them from time to time don't we?"

She tried to brush it off. She certainly wasn't going to tell him that she'd had a nightmare of being the recipient of an MI6 bullet as they boarded the ferry tomorrow morning.

"I suppose so," he told her, accepting her explanation and stroking her forehead.

He got up and brought her a towel to wipe herself down. Then he got back into the bed alongside her, wrapped his arms around her and kissed her softly on the top of her head. "No more bad dreams, I'm here now," he told her softly as they began to drift off to sleep once more.

However, every time she closed her eyes now to try to sleep her brain wouldn't shut down. Her mind was running off in all sorts of crazy directions. What would tomorrow bring? What would the rest of her life be like? Would she always be running? Would there even be a rest of her life after tomorrow?

Craziest of all, what if Martin is the guy, another MI6 agent? What if he was all along, right from the time they first met on that flight to Rhodes in June? What if his mission was to get close to her and have an affair with her, just as her mission had been to get close to Richard Weston and have an affair with him? Then when the time is right, like tomorrow, eliminate her? What if the nightmare was her subconscious, her instincts hidden deep inside her surfacing, warning her? Why did he agree to go to Crete with her so easily?

After a few more minutes as she lay not being able to get back to sleep she told herself no, no, that really was completely crazy. Why would she think that about him? Her mind was in overdrive and playing games with her. But could she trust anyone now, or ever in the future, if she has one? The options and the possibilities that haunted her were swirling around in her mind.

Finally, at last the questions in her brain shut down and she drifted off once more.

Now she could see them on the ferry together, leaning on the handrail, kissing passionately and then watching the large burning sun climbing in the clear blue sky over Rhodes Town as the ferry slowly left the harbour.

She stirred once again though, this time not screaming out, but silently. This time it was a dream, a good, lovely one. He was sleeping soundly beside her with his arm across her, safely holding her to him.

She turned her head and stared at him sleeping, contented, happy. She wondered if tomorrow would bring the start of her wonderful new life, with all the trauma of the past twenty years behind her, or whether her nightmare would become a reality. Could she ever finally be free of the lies of her past and the memories that haunt her? Could she ever be free of them as long as it would never be possible to tell the truth which would finally really set her free?

As she lay there looking at him she recalled that someone once said, "That there are always words to live by." Was it Christine Keeler, or perhaps Stephen Ward? She was sure she'd read it somewhere, and she'd recently read Keeler's autobiography on one of her many transatlantic flights. So, maybe it was her. Anyway, for Aileen, or Kathleen, or whoever's name happened to be on her passport at various times, the words she'd lived by for twenty years had been lies, deceit, make believe, assassination, murder and killing. Now she wanted all that to end. She was convinced that she wanted different real words to live by, with Martin.

She thought of what she had told him earlier, that there are always two ways of looking at everything. She drifted off back into the void between sleep and waking, wondering which way to look at their future, her future from tomorrow. Would it be the nightmare or the lovely dream of happiness with him?

Che - links two sentences
(kay) always whether which or who

But
about who or con cui
with whom   cui
of whom   di cui
to whom (about whom) a cui
with which - con cui

Always avoid using 'with' at end sentence.
She is the girl I study with
She is the girl with whom I study

Printed in Great Britain
by Amazon